REACHING BEYOND
VERGE OF EMPIRE

JAMES AUSTEN WILLIAMS

Bloomington, IN Milton Keynes, UK

AuthorHouse™
1663 Liberty Drive, Suite 200
Bloomington, IN 47403
www.authorhouse.com
Phone: 1-800-839-8640

AuthorHouse™ UK Ltd.
500 Avebury Boulevard
Central Milton Keynes, MK9 2BE
www.authorhouse.co.uk
Phone: 08001974150

This book is a work of fiction. People, places, events, and situations are the product of the author's imagination. Any resemblance to actual persons, living or dead, or historical events, is purely coincidental.

© 2006 James Austen Williams. All rights reserved.

No part of this book may be reproduced, stored in a retrieval system, or transmitted by any means without the written permission of the author.

First published by AuthorHouse 9/7/2006

ISBN: 1-4259-2802-1 (sc)

Printed in the United States of America
Bloomington, Indiana

This book is printed on acid-free paper.

I wish to dedicate this book to my beloved wife

Vivienne

I would like to express my gratitude to all those who made the production of this book possible. May I also give a special thanks to my dear sister, Patsy, for all her efforts, help and guidance that she provided.

REACHING BEYOND
BOOK 1:
VERGE OF EMPIRE

PROLOGUE

The tiny G9 probe sped with incredible velocity into the new star system. Tau Ceti was still just a bright orangey dot at this distance. Nevertheless, the small craft had set a new record. At nearly 12 light years from Earth, it had successfully transmitted from further away than any man made object in space history.

The bulkiest machinery on board was its anti-grav generator that had been on line and active for weeks steadily reducing the craft's speed as it made its approach to the first of the planets, Hahl. The rest of the little ship consisted of an array of dishes, cables and lenses; a concentrated mass of detection and transmission equipment that looked untidy in its design. It was as if some imaginative child had begun constructing a toy and then had left it incomplete.

Hahl and its two globular shaped moons were all ice worlds. In spite of this, it was suspected by some scientists that Hahl may possess some sort of atmosphere. Ironically, it was the only planet in the system that had been officially designated a name.

Silently, G9 stirred as the onboard mini hyper-computer (HC) powered up for the approach. It noted a third object on the edge of the small frozen world's magnetic field; an elongated slab of rock no more than 5 kilometers long that took the shape of a split baguette. The discovery of a new body still conjured up excitement amongst some space buffs on Earth, but for most of the media, it would hardly be deserving of a footnote in some obscure scientific journal.

The proximity of the planet triggered all remaining surveillance systems to come on line. Automatically, a full sensor sweep commenced that began gathering quads of information. The HC collated whatever data it could, then dispatched it in pulsed digital streams back towards Earth's solar system.

Three huge cigar shaped objects emerged from the opposite side of Hahl and set up on intercept courses.

G9 scanned them, and transmitted a pre-programmed greetings message. They closed the gap and soon dwarfed the tiny probe with their massive size. G9 continued broadcasting as the objects matched course and velocity. They turned and assumed a triangular formation around the probe.

Suddenly, one by one, each of the gargantuan cruisers began erupting with explosions and fire. Their structures buckled and folded inwards. Shards of material broke off and spattered wildly into space. Two of the mighty vessels collided, adding to the tumult and chaos that ensued.

Two smaller cigar shaped vessels emerged from the hulls of one of the cruisers and somehow escaped from the destruction. Then in turn, one after the other, each of the huge vessels suffered catastrophic hull failures. Dramatic blasts split them wide open. Flames were quenched rapidly by the vacuum of space, but the tremendous heat glowed long after all had been destroyed or had died.

G9 continued its pass of Hahl. Studiously and efficiently it kept at its work, indifferent to the destruction it had left in its wake. Long after Hahl was receding behind, the two small craft pursued, struggling to make ground.

Hurtling relentlessly on, deeper into the system, G9's mission had originally been for a grand tour of the Tau Ceti family. Even using the gravitational effects of the inner systems' forces, it would take months to reach its next planetary target. It refocused its attention to the next approaching object and recommenced its sequence of analysis and transmissions to Earth.

Thin beams of light flashed and reached out to the little probe from the two chasing ships. G9 broadcast its greetings message again. The ships faltered in their pursuit and then blew apart.

Shortly afterwards, all G9's transmissions towards Earth ceased, and nothing more was ever heard from it again.

Roy Chivers hauled himself out of his hybo-cot. He straightened and stretched, rubbed his face, and scurried to the cockpit. Joey Bartlett, Raymond Hunter and Gillian Mosely were already there, sipping their coffees. Each wore a broad, excited grin.

"What the hell did we wake up for?" he yawned.

"Proximity alarm went off," replied Joey smugly.

Chivers looked out, but could see nothing but space.

"Nothing but vacuum," he said. "What're you all so chirpy about?"

Joey pointed in another direction.

"There!"

Chivers craned his head to peer out of the tiny cockpit and gazed at what the finger was pointing towards. His jaw dropped.

"Fucking mother of God!" he exclaimed. "Is it ..?"

"Dead as a dodo!" beamed Ray. "Docking in 15 minutes."

The massive alien vessel drifted, dark and lifeless like a hunk of carved rock. In size, the comparison between the two ships was like the difference between an elephant and a mouse. The alien's shape and colour revealed by sensors and searchlights formed a massive dark brown ovoid shape, but its features were far from smooth. Numerous longitudinals ran its length and every few metres clusters of convex bumps were set along the hull. Altogether it vaguely resembled a badly constructed airship.

"You sure it's dead?" said Chivers.

"Gull checked it out with a scan."

Gillian Mosely, nicknamed "Gull", nodded.

"It's as accurate a scan as we've got," she said. "Couldn't find nothin'."

"D'ya think the universal port will work?" said Chivers.

"No prob," said Joey. "You guys better suit up if you want a piece o' the action."

"You not cummin'?"

"Listen, I paid for this junk," replied Joey. "My credit, my ship, your risk."

Chivers grunted a reluctant acceptance.

"Besides, I'm missin' valuable time out 'cos o' this. You guys go do the burglin'!"

"Couldn't we just tow it?"

"We have to price up what we've got first," answered Joey. "Might be hollow."

Joey remained in the cockpit whilst the others suited up. He sat back, feet up and chilled out then slipped out a thin plastic tube from his sleeve pocket. He played with it between his fingers; caressing its smoothness and studying the light blue liquid trapped inside.

He gave the huge alien ship a good and covetous look over and then nestled into comfort, blissful of knowing he was made for life. The salvage meant they'd all be set up for ever. They wouldn't need to stake a claim on the new colony. They could go anywhere and live like kings.

Joey held the little tube and rolled it between forefinger and thumb.

"I deserve you for what I've found," he grinned, bit the end off the tube and drank the contents.

He checked the internal monitor and chuckled at seeing the others beavering away to try to breach the alien's hull, then he lay back as the narcotic effect took a hold of his consciousness. The music bathed him with sensual sounds and he mused over the prospects of being decorated in affluence.

Chivers, Hunter and Mosely hauled on the chain blocks together to force open the alien's outer hatch. Chivers cursed at Joey's idleness.

Eventually though, their efforts were rewarded. The hatch seal broke and the twin doors parted, albeit reluctantly. They paused for a moment's respite before continuing their assault on the inner port.

"Joey!" panted Chivers. "Joey we could use a hand!"

But Joey was too far gone with his music and drugs to hear anything. He had provided 90% of the finance for this expedition. He felt entitled to his moments of privilege.

"Joey!" called Chivers again. "The fuckers not paying heed. Could be a pile of shit in here and he wouldn't know."

They checked their suit readings and then forced the inner port ajar, just wide enough to squeeze through.

Inside, the three were greeted with long, dark round tunnels lined every few metres by what looked like ribs that they assumed were structural supports. The alleyways seemed to stretch for miles in different directions.

"Looks like the inside of a cat's gullet," complained Chivers.

"How d'you know?" replied Hunter. "Ever bin inside a cat's gullet?"

"You'd be surprised where I've been," he chuckled.

Something flitted across the alleyway about 10 metres further along.

"What was that?" called Hunter.

"What?" said Gull.

"Oh don't go all spooky!" retorted Chivers. He shone his beam gun ahead as far as he could. "Looks like a cross alley ahead."

"I don't like this," said Hunter. "It gives me the creeps."

"Having Joey on board does that," grumbled Chivers.

Joey's head was full of fuzzy erotic dreams. He moaned with the drug induced sexual fantasies permeating his mind. The music pumping in his ears made him feel heavenly. For a moment he decided to peep on the others to see how their little enterprise was fairing.

When he switched over to audio, all he heard was Roy Chivers' scream of agony.

"What the fuck?" he said sitting forward and trying desperately to clear the fuzziness.

He switched over to Hunters' suit display. It was still and looked as if it was pointing upwards. He blinked hard as something, that for a moment looked like teeth, closed on the view, and then all went black.

In his drugged up state he felt an emotion that was as close to fear as he could get.

He flicked over to Gull's view. She was running, but not just running, fleeing in stark panic. She was screaming in terror. She reached the partly open inner port and in her frantic state got stuck as she tried to get through.

"What the fuck's happening, man?" said Joey.

Gull was crying openly.

"What the fuck's happening?" he repeated.

"Joey!" she begged as she fought to free herself. "Oh God! Please! Oh please!"

The camera turned. Something was there for an instant. Gull's shriek froze his heart. The transmission cut.

Joey forced his mind to think; to overcome the effects. He pulled himself to his feet and turned. But, there was no time to scream. Blood splattered the cockpit and it was all over in an instant.

PART ONE:

MERCURY 4

CHAPTER ONE

The extreme cold and remoteness of deep space can promote the ultimate in loneliness even when you are not a solitary traveller. If the mind is allowed to wander, it can easily be drawn into the blackness of eternity and one may quickly find the consciousness slipping towards the full-blown terrors of agoraphobia.

The crewmembers of the deep space exploration vessel, Mercury 4, were to become the first humans to visit the Tau Ceti system. It had taken years of preparation, construction work and many resources to get a manned craft to reach that far into space.

Mercury 4 had shed its wormhole-forming ring eight months ago and, since then, had been gliding across the interstellar divide on sheer momentum. It was hoped that the crew would be the forerunners of a new civilization and an enlargement of the family of humanity across the galaxy.

Long and slim, Mercury 4 consisted of four decks running lengthways. Each deck was honeycombed with compartments that could be automatically sealed off in the event of damage.

Amidships, the pencil-like profile was interrupted by a bulge where two small shuttle craft were housed; their hulls protected by bay doors. When the doors opened it was like watching a beetle unfold its wings. Moving aft, the hull of Mercury 4 narrowed again then flared outwards towards its stern where the cargo bay, engine control room and main thruster compartments were located.

Mercury 4 had not been designed solely for surveillance work. On this mission, she had been elongated and packed with construction materials and equipment. It would be the first phase in full-scale colonization of the system.

There was some urgency being placed on the Earth Space Organization to find new resources and homes for the beleaguered peoples of Earth who had endured decades of privations, dwindling resources and environmental catastrophes.

For all its ample living space, a crew of only seven occupied Mercury 4. During deep space flights there would at most be only 2 people up and on duty at any one time. Low temperature levels and darkened conditions were maintained for unoccupied areas of the ship in order to conserve energy.

The off duty crew were kept in controlled hibernation during deep space. Unlike suspended animation, where some form of frozen state is used to preserve bodies, they would be kept in deep sleep. Each person's bodily functions were catered for by independent life support systems (LSSs) operating with at least half a dozen backups.

The ship's Hyper Computer (HC) was only there to monitor LSSs, but not interfere with any of the systems. In the event of a problem, the duty crewmembers would be alerted.

If they failed to respond, then other sleeping crew would be aroused. The chance was a billion to one, but it was designed that way in case the HC suffered a catastrophic failure and in so doing inadvertently killed off the sleeping crew.

Commander Dan Morris nestled his large frame into his command chair and gazed up at the void above him. It was a blackness blemished only by millions of tiny pinpricks of light that passed for stars.

Being captain of the ship did not excuse him from his duty to take a turn at watch keeping on the Bridge. Lieutenant Glenda Shaolin was his present company, but after handing over to him, would not be for much longer.

The only other human awake was Robbie Taylor, 1st Technician, who spent most of his duty time stationed in the Engine Control Room. The fully automated ECR ran without the need for a human presence. Although there was very little noise generated during interstellar flight, he seemed to have a compulsion to be wherever any hum of machinery might exist.

Mathew Kemel, Jenny Gold, Alan Young and Ami Wilson all slumbered blissfully in hibernation.

Dan felt a twinge of headache and pressed his forefinger against the side of his nose. He gazed thoughtfully for a moment at Glenda as she avidly studied her console as though there were hundreds of things happening at once.

He could not help but like her. British by birth with an Indian subcontinent bloodline, it was her infectious sunny disposition that made her attractive to him. She was not very tall, but was blessed with a pretty face and cute symmetrical features. She was also a very talented young woman in many ways, an excellent mathematician and fluent in 6 languages as well as a tough cookie on the chessboard.

Glenda sat in silence twirling a hair lock round and around. He had been there nearly five minutes, but she had hardly said a word and he was beginning to wonder if she had noticed him at all.

In the end, she broke her concentration and nodded acknowledgement, before continuing her fixated gaze on her panel.

"Quiet?" he said just to break the ice.

She just nodded and 'hmmd'.

"Alan safely tucked in?" she croaked after a while.

"Well, I didn't kiss him good night," Dan replied. "But, yes he *is* away to the land of nod."

"There's not much to hand over to you," she continued. "All systems are operating within normal parameters. Number 3 generator had one minor fluctuation in power when it ran a self diagnostic 3 hours ago."

"The way you're glued to that console, you'd think there was a war on," muttered Dan.

"I only want to make sure that everything is 'A' okay before I hand over to you," she retorted half apologetically for having kept him waiting.

"Ok!" he sighed. "No green aliens then?"

Glenda huffed with amusement. "You expecting any?"

"One never knows," he answered. "How about you?"

"I'm keeping an open mind about it," she responded. "We've had plenty of hoaxes before to learn not to get too excited."

"You're the only thing that gets me excited around here," said Dan.

Glenda chuckled.

"You're not still trying to get to bed with me?"

"Why the hell not? I am a man after all. It wouldn't be normal if I wasn't interested."

"Mat and Alan don't seem that interested," she remarked with a cheeky smile.

"Yeh well, they're gay! They wouldn't be, would they?"

"Mat's not gay," she corrected. "He's bisexual."

"He still sleeps with guys."

"That is an unfounded rumour."

"A rumour is good enough where he's concerned."

"You don't like him then?"

"To be honest," Dan snorted. "I can't stand the guy. He's here by default and as far as my opinion goes, he's spare luggage."

There was a pregnant silence.

"Anyway, when are you going to let me have my wicked way with you?"

"You are the Captain!" Glenda pointed out. "You are not supposed to cavort with junior officers."

"Well, there is no one else and you're not just a junior officer. You are a beautiful young woman and I fancy you."

"Did you miss out on taking your sex suppression pills?" she asked.

"They take a while to kick in," he replied. "I have to take double where you're concerned."

Glenda smiled, got up from her console and stretched.

"Want some coffee before I crash?" she said.

"Don't change the subject," said Dan with mocking rebuke in his voice.

"Are you harassing me?"

The question made Commander Morris defensive.

"I was just expressing myself. It wasn't intended to put pressure on you."

Glenda beamed and straightened her tunic.

"I did the course on men and their testosterone you know. Every six minutes is it? Anyway, I've been revising what we know about Hahl and it's moons."

"Albert and Victoria, they got called."

"Do you know which is larger?"

"Albert is heavier, but Victoria is slightly larger."

"Very good Commander. Why?"

"God Glenda. Do you have to interrogate me so soon after coming out of hibo?"

"Not if you don't want to."

She could see that Dan Morris was suitably embarrassed.

"Albert is believed to have a greater amount of heavy metals," she said. "That is why we ought to prioritize Albert for exploration."

"Of course I knew that."

"Then why didn't you say it?"

"Go to bed!" was all Dan could say.

Dan watched her stretch and yawn again. He spent a moment to savour the symmetry of her round face.

"You're staring at me again," she reminded him.

He got up to block her exit.

"How d'you find the time to learn 6 languages?" he said softly, leering at her.

He was powerfully built and not someone she could push past easily. A hint of consternation passed over her face.

"Well it helps if you have connections with the languages you're learning," she explained trying to edge past him. "My Mum was Bangladeshi; my Dad was Danish; I was brought up in Llandudno which is where I picked up Welsh and I learned Spanish and Russian at school."

"That's only 5 languages," said Dan moving up close to her.

"Doesn't English count as a language?" she said trying to squeeze by. "Do you mind?"

He gave way a little, but she still had to slide past. For a moment he felt a sexual surge of desire for her, but resisted and let her move to the hatch without further hindrance.

"Now, do you want a coffee before I go?" she smiled.

"No thanks," he replied morosely raising his mug. "I've already got one. You go get your Z time."

Dan sighed, took his brew, and moved over to the navigation console. His headache made him wince. He rubbed his forehead but dismissed the pain as probably an adverse reaction to deep sleep.

"Would you like a game of backgammon?" said the HC in a seductive female voice.

"No thanks, Sharon," he replied. "Why do you ask?"

"You look like you could do with some pastime activity and I know how you like backgammon."

"That's very perceptive of you, but I'd rather run through a few scenario exercises for when we arrive at Hahl."

"Very well Dan," said Sharon. "Which scenario would you like to start with?"

He rubbed his head again.

"Can I just have a review of the mission objectives first?"

"I'll retrieve the data," replied Sharon.

"Thank you."

Dan tapped at his keyboard pad and a list was displayed on the inset monitor. He pondered over the readout:

MERCURY 4, MISSION TC003
MISSION OBJECTIVES:
1. REACH TAU CETI SYSTEM
2. ERECT & ACTIVATE DATA & NAV GUIDANCE BEACON
3. OVERSEE THE CONSTRUCTION OF TEMPORARY SPACE CONDUIT & PREPARE FOR ARRIVAL OF CONSTRUCTION CRAFT
4. EXPLORE NEIGHBOURING SPACE OBJECTS
5. ASCERTAIN THE FATE OF PROBE G9 - TC001
6. SCAN FOR THE PRESENCE OF ALIEN LIFE WITHIN THE SYSTEM

No.1 was a typical objective for any mission. Reaching Tau Ceti should be no problem. It would mean the mission would be declared a success regardless of the outcome of any other objectives.

"Sharon, how far behind us is the construction vessel Taj Mahal?"

"It is estimated from the latest data, that the Taj Mahal is 15 days behind Mercury 4."

Earth Space Organization seemed to be in one hell of a hurry to push for colonization. There would normally be a gap of months or even years after a surveillance visit before they sent in the builders.

"Okay Sharon, I'm ready for your scenario drill. Can we start with arriving in the Tau Ceti system?"

"Please continue!" said Sharon.

Dan took up his position in the command chair.

"Commence scenario!" he ordered.

"You have not selected which program you wish to run," Sharon pointed out.

Dan huffed in frustration.

"Select at random!" he retorted.

"Scenario 11 loading," answered Sharon. There was a moments pause.

"Program running," she said.

The large view screen then showed a bright orange star in the centre, but nothing else happened.

"What's going on?" queried Dan. "Why is nothing changing?"

"Program running at normal speed," advised Sharon.

"God damn it, Sharon!" Dan cursed. "It's gonna take a week to run this one. Can you speed things up a hundred times and start with Mercury 4 being two AU s from Hahl?"

"Distance 2 Astronomical Units. Program speed one hundred times normal. Awaiting your command for activation."

Dan settled down again and took a deep breath.

"Activate program!" he said.

The view screen reset with Tau Ceti still a bright spot, but this time there was a much duller object, about half the size of a ping pong ball in visual range.

"Approach speed 282.5 mega-metres per minute," Sharon advised. "Impact in twelve seconds. Ten, nine, eight ……"

"Oh shit!" exclaimed Dan. "Reduce program speed to normal!"

Sharon had reached five seconds then cut in to confirm that normal program speed had been re-established.

"Initiate breaking trajectory! Calculate orbit requirements for Hahl!"

"Overshoot inevitable due to late initiation!" said Sharon.

"Ok! Ok!" huffed Dan. "I've obviously ballsed this thing up. Let's take the scenario back to twenty times normal speed and run program at 3 AUs from Hahl. Oh, and Sharon, this scenario is one player only."

Without warning, ship's maneuvering thrusters came on line and powered up. The ship lurched as the grav stabilizers failed to counteract the thrust in time.

"What the hell are you doing?" Dan screamed.

"Taking evasive action," Sharon replied calmly.

"To do what?"

"Unidentified object on collision course in immediate path. Brace for impact in ten, nine…"

"What the fuck is going on?" cried Dan in panic, frantically searching the scopes.

"…four, three…"

"I can see nothing," he looked up and out at the space directly ahead. The ship lurched again as the thrusters came on full.

"…two, one."

It was less than the blink of an eye and then was gone. Dan wasn't sure if he had seen anything at all.

"What the fuck was it?"

"Unidentified object," was all Sharon would say.

"Was it alien or a piece of rock?"

"Identification uncertain."

His head throbbed. He pressed his skull hard, got up and then collapsed to the deck.

Glenda checked the readouts on her cot and satisfied herself that all systems were functioning properly. It took several minutes for her to decide on her mental program selection. She had been procrastinating for the whole week before, but now was forced to choose from the shortlist she had made up. She typed in her chosen entries, some educational, some entertainment, then pressed the activate button.

"You have chosen only seven for a selection," said a soothingly soft feminine voice. "The recommended minimum number is ten."

Glenda huffed in frustration then tapped in another three selections. A green light came on to indicate that the cot computer was happy now.

At last, she was ready and climbed in. She sat for a while giving the life support monitoring sensors and cables a final check over. She brushed a few strands of hair from her face, even though most of it was tied up and in a net; then lay back and nestled into a comfortable position.

"Are you ready for hibernation, Glenda?" said the voice.

Cots always made her feel a touch anxious. In the back of her mind was the worry that it would be the last time she would ever be conscious and that something dreadful would happen during her long slumber. She took a few slow, deep breaths before answering.

"Ready for hibernation!" she said quietly.

"Starting hibernation sequence," said the computer.

The cot lid whirred shut. Panel lights illuminated. There was a gentle hiss as a misty gas filtered in. Being in a hibernation cot was not dissimilar to being in a womb. The gas was laden with nutrients that the body absorbed during the sleep process. Glenda gave a little gasp as the sweet, thick vapours entered her lungs and enveloped her body.

She felt the ship shudder and lurch. Something was wrong. She tried to lift an arm to abort the hibo sequence, but the arm was too heavy and already she was drifting off and slipping into her own world of sleep and dreams. Reality was gone and all that remained was peaceful bliss.

CHAPTER TWO

How long he lay there for, Dan had no idea. His vision and hearing returned through haze and white noise. He got up, straightened his tunic and flopped back in the command chair. He rubbed his hands over his face, but had no memory of what had happened. Confused, he fumbled to open the personnel files on his screen then scrolled down the crew list and selected Mat Kemel.

Mat Kemel was the only crewmember who was not a full member of ESO staff. He scan read through his educational background and qualifications and selected the psyche report.

Suffers mild claustrophobia. Marginal pass for space walking. "Dreamy with a tendency to drift off into his own world," said one comment. Stress test was passed, but with the lowest mark amongst the crew. He had claimed that he had been unable to find the test room and that it had affected his score.

He grunted and frowned. If it were left to him, Kemel would not have been allowed on board. He could see why he was not a full member of ESO with an assessment like that. He closed the file and got himself another coffee.

His headache had worsened slightly.

"Probably due to too much coffee," he thought. "Sharon, let me have a visual display of the sleeping crew!"

The screen showed a row of closed sarcophaguses, but no one specifically.

"Let me see Glenda Shaolin!"

The view switched to the bust of Glenda. Her sleeping face was a picture of tranquility. Dan stared lustfully at her. It made him anxious and he rubbed his chin briskly before suddenly snapping out of the hypnosis.

"Off view!" he shouted.

He struggled to remember how he had got to the Bridge. It felt and seemed that he had lost chunks of recent memory. It bothered him, but he was a proud man and dismissed the need for a medical diagnostic. Instead, he decided to go on rounds of the ship to freshen himself up and get some exercise. Maybe that would ease his concerns.

According to the personnel location indicator Robbie Taylor was in Science Lab 1 adjacent to engineering. He would pay him a visit; challenge him to a game of Zero G Squash.

"Sharon, I'm goin' on a tour of the ship and will probably end up visiting young Robbie in SL1. Let me know if I'm needed for anything!"

"That is what I am programmed to do Captain," came the response.

All was silent as he roamed the ship. It was eerie, with alleyway after alleyway lighting up as he approached and dimming once he had passed. The low temperature steamed his breath and he fastened his over-jacket.

It felt so incredibly lonely. He recognized the phobia of silence that was beginning to affect him. A scampering sound came from somewhere in the darkness where he had just passed. Did he imagine it? He coughed just to make noise and comfort himself and then began humming.

The scampering noise came again. He stopped and looked back. Whatever it was remained, unseen in the shadow beyond his vision. It lurked there, stalking him.

"Sharon, is there anything else in this corridor besides me?"

Sharon did not respond. More scampering, but closer now and this time he was convinced that whatever it was, it was not on its own.

He felt fear grow from the pit of his stomach.

"Sharon?"

More scampering, it sounded like a host of invisible animals. Small creatures were there, in the darkness and gathering, unseen and following him. What did they want? What could they be?

"Sharon?" he shouted, the first vestiges of panic now etching into his voice.

He swallowed and calmed himself and then resumed his path, walking slightly faster this time. Behind him the invisible host hurried after him.

He ran. They ran. Matching him for pace.

"For God's sake Sharon! What the hell is it?"

Sharon still did not reply.

He was fleeing now; rushing to get away from his pursuers, but they kept with him, matching his speed. He reached the central stairs. The things were close on his heels. He tripped and fell headlong. The grav safeties activated. He floated down at half grav descent, twisted in mid-air and flung an arm up to shield his face.

In spite of the softened landing he sprawled ungainly across the deck and screamed.

"You alright?" said Robbie.

He lowered his arm and stared bewilderingly at the stairs. There was nothing there.

"You alright?" repeated Robbie and offering him a hand. "You look like you've seen a ghost."

"Err, I'm fine," Dan swallowed getting himself up and trying to compose himself. "Just tripped, that's all. I'm fine now."

He rubbed his head. The head pain had not subsided. Perhaps he should get it checked out after all.

Robbie looked at him warily, but he could not conceal his embarrassment.

"I was, I was just doing rounds," he stammered. "Thought I'd pay you a visit. I guess I must have spooked myself."

"I heard you calling Sharon."

"Yes, she didn't respond."

"She doesn't respond in alleyways in conserved power conditions. You have to use a station to communicate with her."

"Of course, I should have realized."

In the lab, Robbie disappeared behind a facemask, a mass of tubes and power packs.

"What are you up to?"

"Oh, I was having a look at one of our laser systems," Robbie replied burying his head behind his contraptions.

"I hope that's not dangerous."

"Shouldn't be. The power supplies are all isolated."

"What's wrong with it?"

"Nothing. I just wanted to check it over."

Robbie strained as he reached to adjust a bolt. "You never know. I might be able to make it more efficient. Thought I could maybe increase the yield by another 20%."

"Unlikely," snorted Dan. "The best technicians in ESO put that together."

Robbie was annoyed by the comment.

"Well you never know," he retorted. "They don't know everything. Anyway, what was all that movement with the ship earlier on? I nearly crapped myself."

Dan stared blankly.

"You okay?" said Robbie. "You don't look too good."

"Huh? Oh, I'm just fine."

"The sudden movement earlier? What happened?"

Dan didn't know what he was talking about. He had no memory of any movement.

"Err, just some tests," was all he would say and turned to leave. "I'll give you a thrashing at squash?"

"See you in thirty minutes," Robbie grinned.

He waited a few seconds, took off his goggles then checked outside in the alleyway to make sure Dan had gone.

In a cabinet marked 'Personal Equipment' he peered in through the door and smiled.

"I'm going to enjoy you tonight," he murmured.

Dan strolled back towards the accommodation and stopped outside Glenda's cabin. A small red light shone to one side of the door.

"Captain's inspection!" he announced. "Unlock cabin door."

There was a faint hiss followed by a dull thud. The light changed from red to green. Dan pressed the entrance button and the door slid open.

Inside was spacious and tidy as it was supposed to be when a person left it to go into hibo. At one end a door led to the en suite bathroom. Dan opened it and sniffed the air. He was sure he could smell Glenda's fragrance from her last shower. Tell tale drops of water had pooled on the deck and had not yet evaporated.

He opened the cabinet. Empty, as he had expected it to be. All personal items had to be stowed in sterilization units. The cabins themselves were meant to be self-cleaning. Sharon would dispatch a cleaning droid to vacuum and disinfect all surfaces. Any scuffs or dirt spots on the sides of furniture would be identified and removed whilst the human occupant was quietly incubating.

"Sharon!" said Dan.

"Yes, Commander?" came the reply.

"There are still water spots on the bathroom deck."

"I will instruct a cleaning droid to correct the anomaly right away."

Dan moved for the exit, but then noticed something jutting out from behind Glenda's desk. He slid it out and held it in both hands. Glenda's painting.

It was a portrait of a coastline. Luscious greens and browns of fields, trees and fences on one side; and an azure sea on the other side. Most of the sky was a featureless blue except for a few fluffy white clouds here and there. Over the sea in the distance an ominous dark cloud seemed to be forming.

Well, he hadn't known that Glenda did painting as a pastime. He smiled, replaced the painting and left.

Outside Hibernation he paused, took a few steps passed and then returned and went in.

He linked his fingers and cracked them with a stretch and gazed lustfully down at Glenda's passive form. He felt his body stirring at her pleasing features, then leaned over, and kissed the glass above her face.

Dan had 10 minutes warm up in the zero grav squash court before Robbie arrived.

The arena was a rectangular six-sided space. There was no ceiling, but 2 opposing 'floor' playing surfaces instead; 2 sidewalls, a back wall and a strike wall. The strike area on the wall consisted of a square with 2 circles, one inside the other. A line was drawn through the middle of the circles. The outer ring served as the base line and the inner one the service line.

"Who serves?" said Robbie.

"Don't you want to warm up first?"

"I'm warm enough," replied Robbie. "I'd rather get on with it."

Dan pressed his forehead and squeezed the bridge of his nose.

"You okay?

"I'm fine," Dan replied. "Just a hibernation headache."

"Do you want me to serve?"

"We'll play for it! Ready?"

Robbie gave a nod. Dan struck the ball with a tap. Robbie darted across the floor to meet the return ball. Dan came back with a shot just inside the outer ring and Robbie failed to reach it."

"Okay, you serve," Robbie conceded. He moved to a covered control panel by the entrance, opened the flap and flicked a switch. "Gravity off!"

Dan waited whilst Robbie plodded in his mag trainers to his start position, then clouted the small ball into the service area. Robbie belatedly leapt to meet the return ball and missed.

"One nil!" Dan announced. The next serve and Robbie faired no better.

"Two nil!"

Third ball, and Robbie managed to get a shot in. Cat like, Dan was there to meet it, and the ball rebounded passed Robbie for another point.

Point after point and game after game went Dan's way and at the end Robbie was disillusioned and forced to concede to the onslaught. The match was over well within the hour.

"I think I need more practice," he admitted floating limply near to a wall. "I fancy a drink."

"We don't have alcohol on board."

"I meant fruit juice," retorted Robbie. He swam to the entrance and quickly packed away his racket. Without further comment he grabbed a towel and smartly left the court.

Dan cursed and plodded over to the control panel to restore gravity, but as he tapped out the command he froze.

The scampering sound was there, somewhere in the court. Slowly, he turned to the direction the noise was coming from and scanned the court. There was nothing visible, but then he realized it was coming from a ventilation grill in the deckhead. This time it did not stop with him staring at it. The scampering increased in volume.

The hairs on the back of his neck bristled as whatever it was, came right up to the covering and stopped.

Transfixed, he studied the vent and, without thinking, his hand switched off the gravity and he found himself propelled toward it.

Slowly he closed, his fear increasing with every centimetre. He had to see. He had to know. He reached the vent and tensely held position right next to it. His eyes focused on the covering. His head pounded.

Cautiously, he peered into the holes in the grill, but could see nothing. His face closed all the way up to it. He thought he saw movement. What was in there?

Suddenly, a long, thin silvery insect leg stabbed out from inside and at his face. He screamed in sheer panic and pushed away, crashing headfirst against the deck and passed out.

He had no recollection of how he had gotten there, but later, in the semi-circular holo-cinema, Dan found himself sitting almost opposite to Robbie. The movie was set in medieval times and both men watched without saying a single word to each other. Dan did not feel like conversation and, for some reason, Robbie was reluctant to talk anyway and left as soon as the movie had finished.

Dan felt depressed and snubbed, and made his way to the small mess room. He ordered a hot snack from the auto-chef and sat alone to mull things over. The meal was enjoyable; nicely balanced with melted cheese and various sauces on top of potato and bacon.

A cleaning scutter entered when he was nearly finished. It patrolled up and down the deck vacuuming dust from the already impeccably clean deck. Dan watched the little machine go through its routine, before it turned for the door to continue its labour somewhere else on the ship.

He rubbed his forehead again. The headache had eased earlier on, but had now grown again in intensity.

"Sharon," said Dan loudly. He wanted to hear his own voice as much as to say anything important.

"Yes, Dan?" the female computer voice replied smoothly.

"Where's Robbie?"

"First Technician Robbie Taylor is in his cabin," she answered.

"What's he doing?"

"That information is restricted," she advised. "Knowledge of personal activities in cabins requires security clearance."

"Of course," Dan acknowledged. "Is he asleep?"

"Negative."

"Is he reading?"

"That information is restricted."

"Ask him if he would like to play chess with me?"

Nearly a minute passed, then Sharon replied. "He does not want to play chess. He says he is busy."

"Could you replay his statement?"

"One moment, please!"

Robbie's voice came over the intercom.

"I don't want to play bloody chess. 'am having my own fun. Tell him I don't want to play chess. I'm busy."

Dan thought for a few seconds, then got up and went to Sick Bay. He registered himself for a full bio-scan with the Hypo 180 Auto Doctor.

The procedure lasted barely ten minutes and diagnosed that he had a non-specific illness, but instructed him that he should return to hibernation where a full assessment would be made and treatment could commence. An odd piece of advice he thought.

He made his way back to his own cabin and stripped off to shower. When he was finished, he browsed for a book from the Star Library, selected one that he wanted and typed in the required code. There were a few clicks and whirrs and then the reading pad flashed "Ready".

He blinked and held his head in his hands. Amazingly, the headache was gone. He felt great. There was no need to go back to hibo as a sickie.

He settled into his comfi-chair and pressed the control pad and the "on" switch to begin his read - "Great Expectations by Charles Dickens".

CHAPTER THREE

By the time Mercury 4 had gotten within ten days of Hahl, all crewmembers were up and about. Commander Morris insisted that the team run through all the preset drill scenarios to make sure they were up to speed with everything.

They would have to complete at least four scenarios each day. It was monotonous work, but it had to be done in order to maximize the chances of the mission achieving maximum success.

At the end of the first day's events everyone except Science Officer Mathew Kemel stood down. It was his turn to be on duty watch.

During deep space flight there had been no strict requirement for someone to man the Bridge all the time, but with the Tau Ceti system only days away, Commander Morris had ordered that twenty four hour duties to be maintained.

Not being a full member of ESO, Mat's rank on board was more of an honorary title for this mission only. He was not a tall man, but what he lacked in stature he more than made up for in intellectual ability. He prided himself on his freelance civilian status within the organization. Nevertheless, although he joined in willingly with any shipboard activities, he preferred to keep his own company. Mat often felt that others brought him grief either by highlighting their own success or failure, or by some other egotistical put down of him. "People = Pain" was one of his mottoes.

He leaned over a console and focussed on his sensor readouts.

Dan Morris was just at the door entrance on his way out when he noticed Mat's attentiveness. That was another petty hate he had of Mat Kemel: his apparent odd behaviour. Commander Morris had never had time for non-ESO staff and he made no secret of his dislike of having such people on board his ship. To him, Kemel demonstrated a lack of commitment to the cause. The irritation the man caused him made it difficult to suppress his feelings. He felt he was like a rash that wouldn't go away.

"Why did he not sit down like other people?" he thought.

"Problem?" he asked abruptly. Mat did not answer. Commander Morris was noticeably exasperated by the lack of response. It was yet another annoying feature in Kemel's character.

"Got something?" he said a good deal louder. It was enough to break Mat's concentration.

"Err, I'm not sure," he responded. "It's probably nothing."

He came over to him. Kemel was the only one amongst the crew to keep his hair anything other than cropped short.

Dan Morris saw it as a display of both defiance and vanity. It was one more item on the list of dislikes he had on him, but he tried hard to contain his exasperation.

Mat straightened himself and took his gaze from the readouts to look at the big man. Dan Morris pushed out his bodybuilder chest. He emitted a sense of presence that made Mat a little uneasy.

"Well?" Dan said, with as much self control as he could muster.

"I'm not sure," replied Mat. "Two or three times we seemed to have picked up trace elements."

"Look Mr. Kemel, why don't you just state your meaning?" he said with half concealed venom. "Trace elements? Of what?"

"Well I'm running a match comparison, but it is possible that it could be evidence that G9 was here."

"G9?" said Commander Morris skeptically. "We are still in deep space. Even if G9 was not atomized and scattered as far apart as possible, which it probably is, we are extremely unlikely to have anything on it."

"I know," Mat replied. "That is why I can't be sure and need to carry out a full diagnostic as well as a spectral analysis comparison."

Dan raised an eyebrow and turned to leave.

"You do that," he said, "and let me know if you come up with anything! How long will it take?"

"For ever if you keep bugging me," Mat said quietly and almost out of earshot.

Dan's nostrils flared, but he held back his anger somehow and let the comment pass for now.

"Like I said, let me know if you come up with anything!"

Mat ignored him, having returned to leaning over the console and his study.

In the mess, Dan sat down to a coffee with Jenny Gold, Alan Young and Ami Wilson. He frowned and rubbed his forehead again. The damned head pain had returned. He'd had a full week of being free from it, but it had returned almost as soon as everyone had awakened. Now, having to endure it once more was wearing at him.

The auto-doc had said he was no longer ill. It had found nothing wrong, so maybe it was psychosomatic.

"Problem?" Jenny inquired seeing his expression.

"Not really," he replied.

"So there is a little something?"

"Oh, it's just Kemel," he sighed.

"You don't much care for him do you?" she continued. "What's he done now?"

"Well, it's mainly his mannerisms I suppose. I just find him irritating."

There was a pause as the others gazed at him waiting for an elaboration of his statement.

"He thinks he may have found a couple of particles belonging to G9."

"G9?" Alan chirped in a high toned staccato voice. "Very unlikely I'd have thought."

"Exactly!" said Dan. "But he's so vague and comes over as indecisive."

"And you find him irritating?" added Jenny.

"Am I that transparent?" he frowned.

"It was clear from training that you weren't keen on him being on this mission at all," she went on. "I remember you saying that you didn't like part time astronauts on long term space flights."

"Well, I don't see why all ship's staff shouldn't be full members of ESO. It's not as if we're short of talent. I think he shows a lack of commitment. Basically, I think he's disingenuous."

"So, you don't like him because he has different views?" said Jenny.

"Have you got a sweet spot for him?" Dan said with unconcealed irony.

"N-no," she stammered and looked away. "Just, that everyone has *some* redeeming features."

The mess door opened. Mat entered and the conversation died. He moved over to the drinks' dispenser.

"Any results?" asked Dan.

"Uh, inconclusive," Mat replied fumbling to extract his cup from the dispenser. "Uh, there was a possibility that a grain or a few atoms from G9 may have strayed across our path. However, the sample was too small to be certain. You can't tell with just molecules."

"Why would particles decide to detach themselves from out here?" asked Alan.

"Well, it may have been that at some point near to us, in a relative sense of course, that some equipment on board was activated and that it was sufficient to dislodge a few molecules."

There was silence.

Dan was incredulous. "Oh, come now! In all the vastness of space we happened to stumble across a few molecules from a long lost probe we are looking for? Do these molecules have G9 embossed on them?"

"Log data indicated that we may have past an object of unknown origin a few days back," replied Mat.

"May have past?"

Mat huffed and turned to face them, coffee in hand.

"The data on the object has for some reason been lost or erroneously archived."

"This, this object is G9?" said Alan.

"No, I don't think so," said Mat sipping his drink and stretching out the attention.

"It may have had something to do with why the alleged G9 molecules were here in this sector of space."

No one said anything.

"Has anyone seen the latest news?" said Ami in an obvious attempt to change the subject.

"I'd hardly call any news we carry news," responded Alan. "It's all months old."

"Yes I know but we haven't seen it yet that's why it's still news to us."

"D'you want it on?" said Jenny getting up to press the remote control.

A wide bulkhead screen burst into life with a well-groomed female newscaster featuring. Dan surveyed his crew mates. Only Jenny bothered to look back at him.

"I'm going to my cabin. See you later!" he said and then got up and left, deliberately avoiding any eye contact with Mat.

CHAPTER FOUR

Jenny flung the frisbee hard and low to Mat's right. With the gravity deactivated, Mat thrust away from the bulkhead and whirled across the gym to intercept. It was the sort of game that could be played with or without gravity, but Jenny thought it more fun without.

After collecting, he twisted and, steadied himself using a combination of gravity trainers and his umbilical line. Then, in one movement sent the disk spinning diagonally passed Jenny. She reached desperately, but missed only to see it clatter into the bulkhead and come back into the middle of the room.

"9 to 3, I think that makes it!" declared Mat.

"3 to 9," she panted. "Mind you, I'm sure that shot was out of court."

"Not from where I was watching," he answered. "Sharon, was that shot from me in or out?"

"The projectile struck the bulkhead boundary two centimetres outside," said the computer. "I confirm 2-10. Jenny Gold is the winner of the first game."

"Well, it *is* only the first game." said Jenny and quickly scooped up the disk and, with a slick twist of the torso launched a concealed spinning shot. Mat reacted like a cat, but could not stop her scoring.

"Not very sporting," he smiled. "You think you'd give me a chance seeing that I've never played before."

"Who said anything about being sporting?" she retorted. "It's all about winning."

After a short rally he actually won the next point. Jenny then tried another quick serve, but this time, Mat had the move covered and elegantly returned a shot that caught her out of position. The scoring was much closer in the second game, but progressed with Jenny maintaining dominance and eventually winning 10 to 7.

Into the third game, Mat started well and went 5-1 up, when the sound of the door opening distracted him to allow Jenny to score.

Commander Morris appeared in the entrance and stood watching without saying anything.

His presence seemed to affect Mat's play and Jenny quickly levelled the game. Mat was needled.

"Commander Morris do you mind?"

Morris did not reply, but just continued to stand and stare.

"Are you okay?" said Jenny.

"When you've finished, I want to see Mr. Kemel's deep space dust analysis report."

"Did you have to visit here to ask me that?"

"Don't question me, Mr. Kemel!" He barked angrily. "As captain I am allowed to go where and when I choose. You should remember that! I want to see your report within the hour!"

He left.

"Wow! Has he a problem or what?" Jenny said, noting Mat's vexed expression. "Shall we call it a day?"

"No, let's at least finish the set."

The game swung more and more in Jenny's favour and at three games to nil, Jenny suggested they concluded in view of the time.

Mat pressed the caller on Dan Morris's door. A "Please Enter" light came on and Mat stepped into the lion's den.

Commander Morris was sat behind his office desk reading through some messages on his desk screen.

"Your report!" said Mat, firmly placing a data pad on the desk.

Commander Morris seemed preoccupied at first and said nothing.

"Will that be all?" prompted Mat.

"Not quite," came the reply.

Dan Morris stood up from his office chair and held a fixed stare as he moved around the desk to face Mat. He was several centimetres taller and about twenty years older with tinges of grey etching his side burns. His close-cropped fair hair and chiseled features contrasted with Mat's brown, collar-length hair and broad face.

"You probably realize that you are not my favourite person on board," he began. Mat opened his mouth to speak, but a raised finger silenced him.

"The other members of this crew had to go through intensive training and pass some pretty tough selection criteria to be here. They automatically have my respect because I have confidence in them. You, on the other hand, have short circuited the system and have gotten here by other means."

"I have had to work no less hard than …….."

"Don't interrupt me! You will have to earn respect from me because you have not proven yourself up to it!"

He shifted feet and began to pace in front of Mat.

"We are soon due to enter the delivery part of our mission," he went on. "There may come times when prompt and efficient replies and reports are essential. There will be no place for ums and ahhs and maybes. I cannot make correct decisions based on reckonsoes. You need to considerably sharpen up your act, Mr. Kemel."

"Will that be all?

"Not quite. There is one more thing."

He paused and it seemed for a moment as though his eyes glowed green. Mat focused on them, not sure whether he had seen anything at all.

"When on the Bridge the captain is addressed as "Sir!"."

His breath smelled of acetone as he leaned toward Mat, before hissing: "Dismissed!"

Mat left without a word, but he felt uncomfortable about working under a captain that seemed to have such an irrational dislike of him.

Glenda was sat in the pilot seat when Mat entered the Bridge. She could see that Mat was perturbed about something.

"What's up?"

Mat grunted an inaudible response.

"He's had a go at you, hasn't he? What did he say?"

"Oh it's nothing," he replied glumly. "I guess Commander Morris isn't too keen on me that's all. I don't know what I've got to do to change his mind."

"Try not to worry about him. Just concentrate on what you have to do and be yourself."

"I intend to, but I could do without someone like him dribbling all over my shoulder."

The Bridge hatch slid open. Dan Morris entered followed by Jenny Gold. He sat himself in the command chair and surveyed the Bridge, then rubbed his forehead in his habitual manner. Mat shifted to the science console and focussed on his data readings.

"Any evidence of G9 today?" said Commander Morris with obvious sarcasm.

"As a matter of fact there may well be," Mat answered nonchalantly. A third particle was detected about 300,000 kilometres back and sensors briefly indicated there may also be a piece of debris in orbit around Hahl."

"Sensors surely can't be sensitive enough for that?" Morris scoffed.

"They can be extremely sensitive if they have been calibrated to look for such things," said Mat. "I did that 2 days ago."

Silence fell on the Bridge though Commander Morris noted a touch of triumphal point scoring in the way Mat spoke.

"There is something else," Mat blurted suddenly.

"What?"

"Nothing is certain," answered Mat, " but, there are trace elements of other fabricated particle materials."

"What the hell's that supposed to mean?"

"It means that there is some evidence of a ship or ships that were in this sector, but not of human manufacture."

"Is this taken from your lost archives?"

"No, that information seems to have been mysteriously dumped. It is from the same sensors that I've used to scan for G9."

"Aliens?" said Glenda.

"Possibly."

"Is nothing certain with you, Mr. Kemel?" retorted Commander Morris.

"Space science is not an exact science. We're dealing with microscopic particles in a vast vacuum. It isn't …"

Dan Morris shifted impatiently in his seat and slapped the arm of his chair.

"I'm not interested in lectures! Miss Gold, check internal comms and systems!"

Jenny went through the routine of checking comms and internal energy outputs.

"Engine Room, Bridge comms check."

Alan Young's toned voice came back a little loudly causing Jenny to reduce the volume.

"Lighting systems checked and okay. Power supply, excellent condition. Damage detection systems working. All minor systems and back ups operating at normal capacity, Captain."

"Glenda! Report on navigational status and hull condition!"

"Hull 100% intact, Sir. Deflector array normal. Gravitational envelope suppressed at 50%. Trajectory to Hahl off course by zero point three two. Ready to correct on your order."

Dan Morris stroked his chin as if waiting for inspiration.

"Okay," he said noting the readouts on his own screen. "Commence course correction and initiate negative gravity output."

"Aye aye, Sir!" said Glenda in acknowledgement.

"Commander," interrupted Mat. "Don't you want a status report from the science station?"

"Not really," he huffed. "I've heard enough from you already. I will ask for a report if I want it Mr. Kemel. Please don't interrupt whilst a navigational operation is ongoing."

Mat continued to study his readouts and concentrated on searching for gravitational distortions that might indicate the presence of an uncharted asteroid. He flicked a glance at Glenda, but her attention was fixed on her navigational adjustments.

"Ready to initiate gravity drive on your mark, Captain!" she said.

Commander Morris rubbed his head. She wondered if he had heard her.

"Engage on a count of five," he then said.

There was another pause as he rubbed his forehead. Glenda was about to say something when he started counting down.

"Five, four, three, two, one. Engage grav drive!"

The sensation of weightlessness came on as the ship's gravity envelope was altered to negative. Mercury 4 was travelling at a huge velocity. It would take months if not years for the vessel to reach Hahl if a breaking orbit was all that was used to stop. Generating a negative gravitational field would enhance the braking force considerably and the stopping time would be greatly reduced.

"Lieutenant Gold transmit data stream to outpost TC1: "Objective one achieved. Entering Tau Ceti system. Preparing for first orbital pass of Hahl."

"Aye aye, Sir!" Jenny replied.

"Shouldn't we mention the evidence of G9?" said Glenda.

"What evidence?" said Morris cynically. "Our science officer wasn't sure."

Mat and Glenda exchanged glances.

"Okay, from now on, the Bridge will be manned by two people!" declared Morris. "First watch will be Glenda and Robbie Taylor."

He tapped at the intercom button on his seat pad.

"Engine Room, Bridge!"

Alan Young's taut sounding voice replied.

"Chief, we are running a two man Bridge watch. Send up young Robbie if he's there and you'd better knock off as well 'cause you're on in four hours with Ami Wilson!"

Alan grumbled under his breath, but acknowledged and then hung up.

Dan Morris shifted in his seat again as a stab of pain shot through his head. He almost cried out, but then all traces of headache suddenly disappeared completely.

"Jenny, you will be on with Mr. Kemel in eight hours!"

"Aye, aye," she replied.

"Okay," he said. "Stand down when you're ready!"

He moved to nimbly get out of his seat, but as his feet landed on the deck, he realized too late that internal gravity had dropped to just 10%. He bounced off the deck and narrowly avoided smashing his head on an overhead display.

"Miss Gold!" he yelled. "Reset internal gravity to normal! Godammit!"

"Sorry!" she replied.

With his arms, Morris thrust himself downwards only to land on the deck on one leg and topple forwards toward the science station. He swung a clumsy foot out to steady himself against Mat's console just as the internal gravity began increasing.

"That's why we have drills!" he barked. "To make sure these sort of cock ups are eliminated!"

Regaining his composure, he departed with a wounded ego, leaving Jenny and Glenda giggling like schoolgirls. But Mat was not for laughing.

"He can be a real pain in the ass," he sighed. "What's with him anyway?"

"He's just trying to ensure deep space protocols are adhered to," explained Glenda.

"Yeh, but we could do without the Hitler stuff," added Mat. "And....."

"What?" said Jenny.

Mat moved to the Bridge door.

"Well why does he make such a saga out of showing his contempt for me?" he said bowing his head. "Have a good watch!"

The first pass of Hahl took the ship 200,000 kilometres passed the planet, but close enough for the ship's telescopic array to take a mass of photos of Hahl's realm.

Of all the orbiting moons and debris, the rock that was of most interest was a 5 kilometre long slab that circled the planet. The eccentricity of its elliptical path suggested that Hahl's hold on the satellite was only very tenuous. The 'half baguette' shape with one side flat and the other rounded and craggy, tumbled in its orbit.

The flat side, although littered with small and medium sized boulders, presented itself as an attractive site for a landing platform and a good location to set up a signal station.

"Sebastian!" said Jenny excitedly.

"What?" Dan replied.

"The rock has not been formally named," explained Jenny, "so I'm suggesting we call it Sebastian."

"Why the hell Sebastian?"

"It was the name of my dog on Earth."

"Oh, God!" exclaimed Dan cynically. "We're not naming things out here after a damned dog!"

"Why not?" said Mat. "Sebastian is a good name. We're the first humans out here, so why not name objects after things we have some attachment to?"

"We should put it to Sharon to pick a name!" said Dan.

"Why?" argued Mat. "Why can't we pick the names we want?"

Dan Morris pensively glowered back at Mat.

"Sharon, is there any other astronomical object in the explored systems named Sebastian in your data banks?"

"Stand by!" replied Sharon. "Searching."

After a few seconds wait, she answered: "Negative."

"Very well," Morris continued. "In future we'll have a vote on names, with me having the final say. On this occasion we'll go along with Jenny's suggestion. The name of the rock we will call Sebastian."

He typed the name into his personal log and entered it into Sharon's database by hand as was the custom for captains to do when naming a new astronomical body.

As Mercury 4 closed on Hahl and with each orbital pass, Mat carried out sweep after sweep in search of G9, but found nothing. A full scan of the surfaces of Hahl and its moons revealed no impact with any of them, so that a planetary collision seemed to have been very unlikely.

However, just when Mat was about to call it a day, the forward pulse scanner detected something of significance. Mat was about to dismiss it as another spurious contact. It was a solid object no more than about ten centimetres long. The analysis reports then gave a 50% chance that the object had belonged to G9.

"Sharon!" called Mat.

"Yes, Mr. Kemel?"

"Contact Commander Morris and inform him that scans have detected a small object that has a 50% probability of being part of G9! It may be confirmation of my hypothesis."

"Very well," she replied.

"Are you sure?" said Jenny.

"Nothing is certain," he responded, "Look, you'd better work out how to intercept this object for retrieval."

"We can't just stop in mid space and go after a tiny bit of rock in the middle of nowhere!" protested Jenny.

"I'm not saying we should, but there's no harm in calculating what's required. I'll mail you the coordinates."

The Bridge door slid open and Dan Morris stormed in.

"This had better not be yet another of your red herrings!" he blurted.

"See for yourself!" Mat gestured to his console. Commander Morris examined the analysis results.

"Give the data to Jenny and see if we can rendezvous!" he said.

"She's making the calculations as we speak."

Jenny smiled. "On our current trajectory we need to adjust course 1.3 degrees to pass within 50,000 kilometres. That's the closest we're going to get."

"Get Glenda up here!" ordered Morris. "She can organize a retrieval bot."

Hahl was every bit as frozen as expected. They conducted a full surface scan, but Commander Morris decided that the main priority now was to set up a nav guidance beacon and to deploy the Temporary Space Conduit (TSC) equipment they were carrying.

The establishment of the first full wormhole between the Tau Ceti system and Outpost TC1 would mean the end of the extravagant use of wormhole rings that currently caused ships to expend enormous amounts of energy to hop short distances through a series of mini-wormholes. A permanent and functioning full wormhole would facilitate the rapid development of Tau Ceti and, with it, colonization and the further extension of man's influence and presence across the galaxy.

Commander Morris assigned Mat and Jenny to oversee the assembly of the TSC in shuttle, Sparrow 2. Shortly afterwards, the little ship was detached three hundred thousand kilometres from Hahl to carry out its task.

Meanwhile, Glenda programmed and launched a retrieval bot. The small bot would home in on the G9 object, recover it and then pursue Mercury 4 to bring it back. It was hoped the piece may yet reveal how the probe met its end and, bring with it evidence that alien life had met human technology. It would probably be the only thing ever found from G9.

After the bot's launch, Glenda put Mercury 4 into a tight orbit around Sebastian and synchronized with the moonlet's twisting rotational spin. Commander Morris, with Ami, Alan and Robbie aboard, then descended in Sparrow 1 to the surface.

Glenda monitored their descent, calling out every 10 metres until Sparrow 1 had landed safely.

Sparrow 1 lurched as it touched down causing Alan to sigh with relief. He had never been a fan of shuttle flights. In training, he mentioned more than once that in a shuttle you were always a few seconds from "catastrophic cellular disruption".

"What's the matter Mr. Young?" snorted the commander seeing Alan's apprehension. "Had your doubts that we'd make it?"

"N-No, of course not. It's just that if things do go wrong we're all alone out here."

Dan Morris was not impressed, but held back further comment.

Suited, the commander with Ami Wilson following closely behind, opened the airlock and floated down to the surface; the first humans ever to set foot in the Tau Ceti system.

"Remember, walk carefully!" he warned. "No jumping about or you'll bounce right off this rock!"

Ami tried not to moan. She looked up towards the far end of Sebastian to an overhang and then, she was over. She scrambled to regain her footing but ended up crashing into Morris and bowling him over too.

"Watch what the bloody hell you're doing, you clumsy...."

"Sorry, I tripped on a boulder."

"For God's sake, Wilson!" he exclaimed, standing upright once more and peering down at Ami on her hands and knees. "You know the place is littered with crap, so take care! You could have ripped our suits, God damn it!"

"Everything alright down there?" Glenda's voice crackled over the com.

"Yeh, we're fine," grumbled Morris. "Where's Alan and Robbie? They're supposed to be out by now."

"We'll be with you shortly," responded Alan. "Just having a final check to see if we've got everything."

"We've done all that!" snapped Morris. "Just get your asses out here and let's get moving!"

"I don't think Alan's too keen on space walking," suggested Ami.

"Well, he shouldn't be on the bloody space program if he's got a problem," he retorted. "You're all as bad as Kemel!"

"Commander, Mercury 4!" called Glenda.

"Glenda, you don't have to be quite so formal. We're the only humans out here."

"Sorry, Commander," replied Glenda. "Just wanted to let you know that the recovery bot has recovered the G9 fragment and will be docking in 25 minutes."

"So soon?"

CHAPTER FIVE

"Amazing isn't it?" said Mat gazing in awe as the giant circular hoop slowly began to take shape.

The TSC had been manufactured and stowed in such a way that it would deploy automatically with very little assistance from humans. Jenny and Mat sat comfortably in the pilot seats inside Sparrow 2 and watched as the TSC slowly and gracefully unfolded and began constructing itself as if by magic.

Jenny said nothing for several moments, but took time to covertly gaze at Mat.

"Mat?" she said finally.

"Yeh?"

"You can call me Jen if you like."

"You're going to ask me something personal aren't you?"

"Err well, I just wanted to know if you're interested in women?" she said falteringly.

"Of course I'm interested in women," he retorted.

"Oh, I thought you might have other interests."

"If by that you're implying that I might be gay, then the answer is I'm not. I'm bisexual."

She did not answer, but he could tell from her expression that she wanted further explanation to his comment. He smiled warmly.

"Everyone is bisexual," he explained. "By that I mean in terms of sexuality, we all appear on a bisexual scale; some are inclined towards same gender; some towards opposite gender relationships."

They shuffled as close to each other as the arms on their seats would allow.

"Both genders have sexual merit," he continued. "Both have attractiveness and repulsiveness. Understanding that, means that I can see the beauty, and ugliness, in both genders without prejudice. It makes me free to fall in love with a person for who they are rather than what they are. It frees me to love without penalizing myself because they're the wrong gender and, I don't have to love them because of my sexual interest."

She rested her head on his shoulder and looked meaningfully up at him. His heart raised a beat.

"If you must know," he said affectionately. "I'm towards the hetero end of the scale. Does that answer your question?"

Their mouths closed to exchange a kiss.

"Mostly," she replied softly, running a caressing hand over his chest.

Their eyes locked and the hand slid down to his arm.

"How many times have you been with a man?"

Mat shifted uneasily, breaking eye contact.

"I'd rather not talk about it."

"Please, tell me the truth."

Mat squirmed, but her gaze was persistent.

"Once," he said quickly and looked away. "I guess I was drunk or something at the time. I didn't know much about it. It just happened before I realized what was going on."

"Were you …?"

"I don't want to talk about it."

"Did you enjoy it?"

Mat was uncomfortable with the question.

"It wasn't like that," he replied curtly. "I'd prefer not to talk about it."

She patted his arm reassuringly.

"It's okay," she said. "Really, it's okay."

They locked eyes again and smiled. She leaned toward him and pulled his mouth to hers.

Glenda ran through some routine internal checks to help overcome the monotony of being alone. Then, she started sensor sweeps of the sector around Hahl and Sebastian to search for any other moonlets or asteroid chunks.

An object, the size of a small office block approached Hahl. She dismissed it as an inbound meteor at first, but when it altered course to take up an orbital path her heart skipped a beat. She diverted more sensors to the object, but it disappeared around the far side of the planet.

"Sharon," she said.

"Yes First Officer?"

"Sharon, could you address me as Glenda from now on?"

"Is that an instruction?

"Err, yes."

"My address to you has been adjusted."

"Thank you," answered Glenda. "Sharon?"

"Yes Glenda?"

"We just detected an object that approached Hahl. Could you analyze the data collected on it to assess whether it is moving independently of gravitational forces? I'll give you the coordinates."

She pointed her cursor at the object shown on the view screen and clicked it.

"Data provided is inconclusive," said Sharon after just a few seconds.

Glenda waited anxiously for the object to re-emerge from Hahl's far side. As it emerged it did not remain in orbit, but had used Hahl for a slingshot and was now heading directly for Sebastian.

Glenda, normally calm and unruffled, found her hand trembling as she adjusted the screen display and magnified. It took a while for her to assess what she was seeing.

"Looks like a …," she struggled for words, "… a giant pine cone."

She regained her composure, swallowed and reached for the radio.

"Sparrow 2 this is Mercury 4."

"Sparrow 2 this is Mercury 4." she repeated.

"Mercury 4, Sparrow 2, is there a problem Glenda?" replied Jenny.

"I don't know yet," Glenda said with an edge of concern in her voice. "I'm picking up an unidentified object on an approach course from Hahl. I have no confirmation as to what the object might be, but judging by its behaviour it could well be alien."

"What?" blurted Jenny in disbelief.

"The object could be alien," she repeated. "How long have you got before construction is complete?"

"Another 3 hours at this rate," said Mat. "How long before the UFO is in range of us?"

"I didn't say it *was* a UFO," argued Glenda.

"Possible alien suggests UFO to me," replied Mat.

"And how long before alien contact?" said Jenny.

"Err, 6 hours I estimate."

"Bags of time," Mat replied. "We'll be back in time for tea."

"Have it your way," replied Glenda. "Anyway, thought you'd be interested to know that the bot has returned with its space debris."

"And?"

"And, I'm running analyses tests on it. Initial indications indicate that it *did* come from G9 though, but I don't think the tests will tell us what happened."

"What is it?" said Mat.

"A pinion bolt from one of the probe's sensor arrays," she replied. "At least that's what the HC's definition of it is. It's incredible that we found anything."

Glenda switched to view the object.

"Mind you, I reckon it looks more like a small data capsule," she murmured.

"We'll finish off here and return to Mercury," said Mat.

He returned his attention to Jenny. "Now, where were we?"

Jenny kneeled naked astride Mat, their spacesuits and undergarments cast aside.

"This is huge!" said Jenny sensuously as she brought her lips to his.

"Thank you," Mat mused. "I thought it was just normal size."

"Silly, I mean, it'll be first contact with anything alien."

She nibbled his chin and their mouths engaged.

"Oh yeh," he replied returning her affections. "I hope they're friendly."

"Like us," she smooched.

CHAPTER SIX

On Sebastian, Commander Morris planted the customary aluminium Earth flag. It did not flutter in the airless environment but, through his efforts to straighten it, stood out crinkled and wavering gently.

A brief ritualistic announcement claimed Sebastian as a possession of Earth. The use of artificial light enhanced the flag's blue background; the rainbow coloured circle representing Earth, and the olive leaf-carrying white dove. Together, the crew saluted and took a few moments to contrast the flag's colourful presence with its surroundings. If aliens ever visited this place, what would they make of such a gesture by humanity?

Commander Morris, ever conscious of duty, broke up the ceremony. He ordered Robbie back to the shuttle to prepare for launching and their return to Mercury 4. In the mean time, he and the others set about carrying equipment to various sites on the planetoid.

Even with the low gravity and the hover cart, it was difficult work hauling gear. The terrain was littered with all kinds of rocks, some the size of a large motor car.

At the end of Sebastian, furthest from where Sparrow 1 was parked, they discovered a prominence. It took the form of a thick horn several metres wide that overhung the plateau at a height of about three metres. It was a curious design that left a small, natural cave-like shelter beneath.

Commander Morris had been taking seismic readings and collecting debris samples everywhere he went. He did the same here.

"It's okay!" he said. "Stable enough! We'll plant the main beacon on top and the power equipment can sit in the shelter."

"It's not as if we're expecting high winds," mused Alan.

"It's tidier that way," Commander Morris grumbled.

Alan and Ami worked on top of the horn, setting up power cables and computer equipment. A sensation of something passing nearby distracted them. They looked up into the blackness to see Mercury 4 flying over their heads like a peculiar space bird. Its sleek form gave it a racy appearance.

"Wouldn't see it at all, but for the night lenses," squawked Alan.

Glenda's voice reverberated in their suit coms.

"How you getting on down there?" she said enthusiastically.

"I expect we'll probably be all done in about an hour," replied Dan.

"Don't take too long," she said. "We may have company."

"Company? What sort of company?"

"I've detected a possible alien ship heading from the direction of Hahl."

"What? Why didn't you say something before?"

"I tried, but you weren't receiving any of my transmissions."

Dan Morris winced as a twinge of pain stabbed his temple. The headache had returned.

There was a cry. He looked around to see Ami tumbling off the overhang and drift down toward the equipment he had just laid out.

"Jesus!" he exclaimed and leapt at the slowly descending body. They collided, 2 metres from the surface. Ami spun away to crash forcefully against the rock face, whilst he bounced off her and ended up almost 10 metres from his original position.

She screamed with pain and Alan jumped off the rock to float down to her. Dan hauled himself up grumbling bitterly at her clumsiness, but Ami remained lying face down, clutching at her midriff and whimpering.

"What's the matter?" called Alan anxiously. "It wasn't that bad a fall."

"Am hurt," she rasped. "Think suits pierced. Ribs hurting bad."

"God's sake!" Morris complained. "Told you to be bloody careful!"

Ami did not want to move, but they eased her over to look at the damage. A sharp jag of rock penetrated Ami like a dagger at her midsection. Blood boiled away steadily from the suit breach.

Alan rummaged around in her pockets until he found the suit repair kit. He pulled out an aerosol and shook it.

"Okay, pull your hands away!" he said. She reluctantly took her hands away.

"Hold her!"

Dan Morris held her wrists and Alan sprayed the can contents over the wound sealing it instantly with the dagger still embedded.

He quickly glanced at her face and noted her bulging eyes and running nose, then immediately turned his attention back to the damaged suit. The sealant had worked.

"We have to get her back!"

"I know," Dan scowled. "Help me get her on the cart!"

They cleared the cart of its goods and placed her on to it. She groaned, drifting in and out of consciousness, as they lifted her.

"It's okay," said Alan. "We'll soon have you back on the shuttle."

"We have to finish the construction," said Dan.

"Surely our priority is to Ami?" argued Alan.

"It doesn't need both of us to get her back," he replied. "You stay and finish. I'll get her back to the shuttle."

"But it's against regulations for one person to be left alone."

"Well, I'm countermanding the regulations," he explained. "We have a mission to complete! I want this gear set up and working! That's what we came all this way for and that's what we're bloody well going to do! If *we* don't succeed someone else is going to have to haul ass to get out here and do it!"

Robbie had the auto doctor online long before Ami was on board, but by then she had slipped into unconsciousness.

He cut around the wound area just below the ribs on the right side, then promptly removed the rest of the suit and extracted the razor edged shard. The auto doctor lid closed over Ami's body and he keyed in for the device to run a full bodyscan.

The Hypo 172 Auto Doctor had a relatively limited capacity for dealing with complicated medical procedures. The initial assessment indicated there was extensive skin damage and that Ami's liver had been badly affected. She had blistering and swelling over 25% of her thorax. It recommended rest and plenty of fluids, further liver tests and skin grafts, but also suggested referral to a higher grade auto doctor than itself.

Nevertheless, Ami would be kept safe and in a stable condition until the opportunity arose to repair her damaged body.

"Sparrow 1, Sparrow 1, this is Mercury 4," called Glenda.

It took a few moments for Dan Morris to reach the radio.

"Sparrow 1, Sparrow 1, this is Mercury 4," she repeated.

"Mercury 4, respond!"

"Commander we've received a broadcast message from TC1."

"What does it say?"

"The construction vessel Taj Mahal passed TC1 ahead of schedule and is due to arrive in the Tau Ceti system in about six days."

"My God!" exclaimed Dan. "They're supposed to wait until we've completed our mission and set up the conduit. What the hell's the rush? Ask Sparrow 2 how the TSC gear is getting on."

"I did a few minutes ago. Jenny told me the construction part had almost finished and they were about to power up and run a full diagnostic."

"Well ask them again for an update!" he snapped.

"Will do Commander," she replied. "I think you should tidy up down there and return to Mercury. The alien ship will be with us in less than an hour."

Dan Morris exploded.

"What! I thought we had three? Why the hell didn't you say something sooner?"

"You were busy. The craft or whatever it is has increased velocity and is on an intercept course."

"We've still got the chief on the other end of the rock! It doesn't give much time. Patch me up with Jenny Gold and that amateur space idiot."

"Sparrow 1, Sparrow 2!" Jenny interrupted.

"Sparrow 1 go ahead."

"The conduit ring construction is complete," Jenny explained. "However there is a problem with the power unit. The power converter has a malfunction."

"And yes, Commander," added Mat curtly. "The vortex generator itself has a program fault. It'll take a long time to sort out."

"Well it'll have to wait," he replied. "Return to Mercury 4 immediately! We have guests arriving shortly!"

"We're already on our way back now. Be with you in about 45 minutes."

"Chief, Sparrow 1!" Morris continued. "Shift your ass double quick! We're lifting off in 10 minutes!"

"I can't make 4 Ks in ten minutes!"

"Do your best!"

Both sparrows arrived at Mercury 4 within seconds of each other, but the alien vessel was also upon them.

"We can't dock until the alien's intentions are clear!" said Dan.

"Commander, I have tried calling them on a range of frequencies, but have had no response," said Glenda.

"I tried as well," added Jenny, "and got nothing back but static."

"All I can tell you is that it's ovoid in shape, less than a quarter of the mass of Mercury 4," said Glenda. "Bit like a big egg. Basic colour is brown. It has a dappled, sort of warty, hull surface."

"What about life forms and energy readings?" asked Dan.

"Commander, I could do with a hand here," replied Glenda. "It's difficult navigating and doing analysis readouts at the same time."

Commander Morris sighed. "Okay, Sparrow 2 will dock. I will observe from Sparrow 1. Maintain course Mercury 4!"

Jenny fired thrusters and docked Sparrow 2, but before she had secured, the alien vessel had arrived in visual range and had passed ahead of Mercury in a flash. It closed on Sebastian. Spurts of flame burst from small thrusters at its stern and then it swung and disappeared around the far side.

The locking clamps finally secured Sparrow 2 into position and the bay doors closed around it as the alien craft burst out from the far side of Sebastian and headed back in the direction of Hahl.

Mat tried a variety of scans when he arrived on the Bridge, but these only produced limited results.

"Odd," said Mat. "It's as if the alien is blocking the scans. I wouldn't have thought it possible."

He tried and retried, but each time proved fruitless. More than once Commander Morris expressed dissatisfaction at Mat's failure to gain anything useful and the two exchanged angry comments with each other.

After completing a single orbit of Hahl, the alien set off in the general direction of Tau Ceti and soon had disappeared from sensors altogether.

Ami was transferred to Mercury's Hypo 180 Medical Lab and Robbie remained with her. The rest of the crew gathered in the mess room to watch the viscorder of the whole alien encounter.

"What kind of ship is it?" Glenda asked again as they played the recording for the second time.

"Well, the infra red sensors detected the possibility of two life forms aboard the vessel," said Mat. He held up a videchip. "I think we should look at this next."

He slotted the small disk into the player and they sat in silence as the same scene they had just watched was replayed, but this time as seen by heat sensitive scanners. All they could make out were smudges and glows coming from within the vessel's hull.

"There must be something the aliens were emitting," said Mat shaking his head. "Virtually every sweep I tried bounced back as if it had been blocked."

"How do you work anything out from that?" snapped the Commander.

"Well I have used a few technical tricks to get something," replied Mat and paused on a side view of the ship. "Let me clean up the image first."

With a number of taps on the keyboard, the still picture showed more differentiated glows, and as the viscorder re-started on very slow speed, the two creatures could be made out more clearly.

"It's still a bit fuzzy," said Alan.

"Patience!" retorted Mat. "I'll add 3-D effect."

Once more, they watched the sequence. This time the two forms, one at the forward end and the other amidships, became more distinctive. They were decidedly not humanoid. Instead, their bodies appeared elongated, though no physical features could be made out.

"What the hell are they?" said Alan.

"Let me alter the view a bit more," said Mat. Again he tapped at his keyboard.

"Right now, this sequence has computer enhancement based on all data received. It's about 60% accurate on what you'd see as if you were able to look directly at the two occupants."

The clip was re-shown with magnification on the two aliens.

"They look like…" began Glenda.

"Like maggots?" added Mat.

"Maggots with arms and legs," said Jenny.

"So we're going to call them maggots?" scowled Dan Morris getting to his feet. "That's a great start for making our first contact with intelligent life. Begin by insulting them!"

The tension between Dan Morris and Mat was obvious to all. Glenda felt obliged to try to diffuse things.

"So what name should we give them?" she said.

The commander sat down again, but glowered cynically at Mat before answering.

"We'll ask the computer," he said. "Sharon! Based on all available data select six names that we could choose from to name the new alien species.

After some debate, the name decided on was "Mago".

"Sounds a bit too much like maggot to me," said Mat. Commander Morris gave him a dark glower.

"I think we should work out how to communicate with them," said Glenda.

"Why?" Dan Morris asked. "Jenny tried to contact them using the standard calling pattern. They just ignored it."

"I even tried using mathematical patterns, but it had no effect," added Jenny.

"Did we not get any kind of signal or radio pattern from them at all?" asked Mat.

"What have we just said?" Commander Morris barked. "We have nothing from them. They ignored us. They are hostile."

"We don't know that. Maybe they transmitted something, but we haven't realized it yet," replied Mat.

"What kind of talk is that?" retorted the commander with undisguised incredulity in his voice. "Alright, you're the Science Officer, analyze whatever we may have received and see if you can come up with something!"

"Loosen up Commander," said Mat.

Commander Morris rose from his seat, his face deep red. "Do not tell me how to behave, Sunshine!"

Mat stood and faced him down.

"You may be captain on this vessel, but it doesn't mean I have to take this shit from you!"

Commander Morris's face changed from sternness to that of a smile. He spoke with controlled venom in his voice.

"Of course not Mr. Kemel. I want you to carry out the tasks that are required of you or you'll find yourself floating back to Earth in a spacesuit. Deep space is no place for tourists!"

Mat's anger surged through him, but Alan's firm hand gripped his forearm.

"Let it pass," he said.

Both men sank back in their seats and said little more throughout the rest of the meeting. The discussions moved on as the others grappled with how to deal with the faulty TSC assembly; the condition of Ami and back to what to do about the aliens.

Mat had about 6 hours before he was to set off for an attempt at repairing the conduit assembly. He undressed, showered and lay naked on his bunk with lights on, thinking.

The door buzzer sounded. He stood up and secured a towel around his abdomen.

"Come in!"

"Sorry," said Jenny seeing him in his scanty attire. "I'll come back later."

"No, please," replied Mat. "Stay for a chat."

"With you like that?"

"It embarrasses you?"

She gave him a cheesy grin and flopped into his easychair.

"I don't know what you might do," she beamed.

"You don't think I'm trustworthy?"

"Based on past experience? No."

He sat on the edge of the table.

"What're you going to do?" she said provocatively. "Give me a peep show?"

"Is that what you want?" teased Mat. Their eyes met and held each other's gaze. Mat knelt between Jenny's legs and leaned forward to kiss her on the lips.

"We ought to get some sleep," said Mat softly.

"Do you think you'll sleep much with me here?"

"With you holding me, I'll sleep like a baby."

"I'm not coming on Sparrow 2 with you," said Jenny. "Alan and Robbie will be accompanying you."

Mat scowled.

"They're both tech people," he said. "Fine for helping sort out the conduit problems, but what if Mercury needs an engineer?"

"He figures the greatest need is the conduit."

"Nice of him to tell me," moaned Mat. "I don't know what's wrong with the guy."

"He's ambitious. Likes to achieve goals. To him, it's the number one priority."

"I guess, but why does he have to be such an asshole?"

"True, he makes no secret of his feelings towards you, but at least he's honest."

"Warped, if you ask me."

Mat stood up and took a couple of paces.

"You called on Ami earlier?" said Jenny. "How's she doing?"

"Robbie was with her."

"He seems to hang around her a lot."

"They're mech buddies. Anyway it'll take a while before she's fit again. Even with the Hypo 180 it'll be a week before she can resume duties."

"Why couldn't we pick up any decent data scans of the aliens? Why wouldn't they talk?"

"One of two possibilities," said Mat. "Either it's them or it's us. They could be using tech and material that prevents effective scanning or, there's something wrong from our end."

Jenny's clothing fell from her nubile body and she slid her lithe form gracefully over to the bed. Mat watched her lustfully. He felt passions arouse. He dropped the towel covering his abdomen and lay down beside her.

Tenderly, she slipped her arms around his back and embraced him. He watched her pupils dilate as she pulled him closer. Her moist lips pouted temptingly at him. Their bodies entwined and mouths locked together in a French kiss.

"Enough!" he whispered affectionately and lifted his head. "We need to sleep."

She pulled his face to hers again, and ran her hands down his back to gently clutch his buttocks.

"Think not, baby," she purred. "I won't let you."

After just a few hours of sleep, Mat, Alan and Robbie left in Sparrow 2 to attempt the repair of the TSC's power converter. It was expected to take several hours and would include a space walk; the one aspect of the job that Mat dreaded.

In the meantime, Mercury 4 set a course for Hahl.

"I sent the data stream," said Glenda.

"Good," Dan remarked.

"Well, if they can get the conduit open, we'll probably be home before it."

Glenda chuckled to herself and twiddled with her hair.

"If they get it working," she added. "We can always send another stream through the wormhole."

Dan said nothing but just brooded. He seemed in an unusually melancholic mood. Jenny eased Mercury 4 into a standard orbit around the frozen planet.

"Okay," he said finally. "We'll do 3 orbits and make detailed surface maps, before we take Sparrow 1 down,"

"We?" said Glenda.

"You and I."

The surface, like so many other billions of barren bodies, was yet another moonscape. Craters and boulders were littered all about. However, the suspicion of there being the trace of an atmosphere was confirmed. It existed as little more than a few wisps and clouds of freezing vapour that hogged whatever crater or pothole that happened to be near, but it was enough to qualify as an atmosphere.

"Difficult to find a decent landing site," confessed Glenda.

"Every planet is difficult to land on. Just find something."

"If it were that easy," muttered Glenda. "The whole surface is a mess."

"What about there?" said Jenny pointing at the screen map.

"Well it is something of a plain I suppose," replied Glenda. "But there's rock debris everywhere like everywhere."

Commander Morris was visibly impatient. He rubbed his forehead.

"It's my hunch that the rocks on that plain are smaller," said Jenny.

"Hunch!" he snapped. "We can't set down on a hunch, for God's sake!"

Jenny flushed but said nothing. She magnified the area and tapped in for a closer examination of the terrain.

"This area is part of a shallow valley," she explained pointing the cursor. "It's like a bowl with gently sloping sides. The ice clouds are plentiful and what I think has happened over time is they have frozen and thawed the rocks causing them to crack into smaller pieces."

"How can there be any thawing on an ice world?" argued Dan.

"Well that's what closer studies might just reveal," Jenny replied. "Even at extremely low temperatures there may be different expansion rates."

"Okay, enough of the school lessons, that's where we'll set down," Dan declared tapping at the graphics display screen. "Looks like the shuttle will have to use extended landing legs though."

"Shall I prepare it?" asked Jenny.

"No, I want you to stay here to monitor from orbit."

"But I'm pilot trained and specialize in Geology," Jenny protested.

"Look, I'm fed up with every decision I make being questioned. Glenda will do just fine."

"I don't mind being Orbiter," said Glenda.

"What have I just said?" replied Commander Morris. "This time I want you with me."

Jenny was not happy. "Well at least I'll get some lone time."

"Yeh, you can dream about your boyfriend," he sneered.

"Wha ..?"

"It's no secret Lieutenant! You know the mission rules. It will be in my next mission report!"

On board Sparrow 2, Alan, Robbie and Mat were working out their repair strategy.

"I think we can't do much more from Sparrow," said Alan. "We have to get into the circuitry in the power assembly if we're going to have any chance of sorting it out."

"Why don't we leave it until the construction boys get here?" suggested Robbie.

"There's no guarantee they'll do much better than us," replied Mat.

"Yeh, but they're supposed to bring additional equipment for the conduit," answered Robbie.

"That's meant to be to enhance the power and reliability of the wormhole when it's formed," said Alan. "Most of the stuff they're transporting is for establishing outposts and bases."

"Well we haven't had much time to find a cozy planet for them to pitch," said Robbie. "I don't see why the big rush."

"Budgets," Mat responded. The other two looked at him for an explanation.

"It's all to do with budgets," he continued. "ESO is under pressure to prove that the huge funding they receive is going to pay back dividends. They have ten years to start proving their economic worth or the United States of Earth Government is going to start cutting costs."

"So?" said Robbie prompting for reasons.

"So, before that happens ESO is pushing things faster. Why wait until results are returned from probes and explorers. Analyze data whilst the next stage is in progress. They're doing it before the dosh runs out. It's just a cash flow thing in the long term."

Alan coughed impatiently. "Very good on the politics, but we've got a naff wormhole conduit to deal with for now."

"Do you mind if I stay behind to keep an eye on Sparrow 2?" asked Mat.

"I think the shuttle can look after itself, don't you?" responded Alan.

Mat groaned.

"Besides, we'll get things done a lot faster with three of us working at it."

"You okay with space walking?" Robbie winked.

Mat swallowed.

"You know I hate space walking. I've been sick 3 times doing it."

"Yeh, I saw you in the training prog."

"Well, if you concentrate on the job to be done," squeaked Alan. " It'll take your mind off it."

Sparrow 2 positioned fifty metres off of the wormhole control station and magnetic clamps attached just in case the two vessels should drift apart. Navigation controls were switched to auto and the three men suited up.

The control station consisted of a rectangular block that housed the power assembly and all the controls to the systems needed to create and sustain a stable wormhole conduit. It was about 4 metres high, 8 metres wide and 12 metres long and had been the bulkiest of Mercury 4's cargo.

Robbie gave a short blast to his jump pack and drifted confidently across to the entrance hatch of the station. In moments, he deftly attached the safety line and activated the door controls. The door slid open and he imagined a hiss, as there had been in training, but in space all was silent. He startled as Alan touched him and held up a hand to acknowledge that all was okay.

Mat was noticeably apprehensive. Alan and Robbie beckoned to him, but he hung back reluctant and hesitant by Sparrow's airlock.

"Come on!" called Alan.

For a moment they didn't think he was going to leap, but as they contemplated fetching him, he at last pushed off and drifted towards them.

Inside, the station was dark and soulless. Alan led the way down corridors lit only by their suit headlamps. Mat withdrew a hand into his suit and switched on external sensors. The outside temperature showed - 207.4 degrees Celsius.

They drifted up a ladder to the next level with Mat just tagging along, not really knowing where he was.

"Glad you know where you're going," he remarked.

"You think I know, huh?" joked Alan. He stopped at an unlit panel and opened the cover. A small yellow light glowed, but otherwise the unit was lifeless.

"Ah ha!" Alan exclaimed and pulled down a lever. Mat's speakers crackled and the dark corridors were adorned with dim fluorescent lights. "Power on line!

"Power assembly controls are around the corner" he went on. "Robbie, you check out the vortex stabilizer unit! It's down the next level, Section 46."

"Aye okay!" came the less than enthusiastic reply.

At Power Control, Alan used his test gauge to check numerous different circuits whilst Mat just hung about feeling useless and bored.

"Anything I can do?" he asked. "Make the tea perhaps?"

"Not at the moment," said Alan concentrating. "Suppose you could flash up central computer and run a systems diagnostic."

"I did that on Sparrow."

"Well it might reveal more with a close up exam."

CHAPTER SEVEN

Commander Morris set Sparrow 1 down carefully on the surface of Hahl. One of the four extended landing legs sank deeper than expected into the carpet of shingle shards. The craft lurched sharply, but then steadied and listed at a shallow angle.

He wasted no time in descending the ladder to Hahl's surface and seemed overly keen on being the first human ever to set foot there. Glenda barely had time to join him before he had planted the metallic flag and was hurriedly rattling through the traditional ceremony that claimed the planet as another Earthly possession.

"On behalf of the people of Earth and the government of the United States of Earth," he announced. "I claim this planet!"

Jenny sat back in the command chair on Mercury 4, feet up, and gazed at the stars. The patterns they formed were very different from those seen from Earth. She allowed her imagination to wander and began creating new constellation patterns.

Unnoticed, a small yellow light began to wink from the navigation console.

"That one looks just like a horse," she muttered to herself, tracing the shape with her index finger. "I'm sure there was a horse constellation on Earth. Sharon, is there a horse type constellation on Earth?"

"Constellations do not feature on planetary surfaces. Such information is not contained in my data banks," replied Sharon.

"Oh of course not," Jenny huffed in irritation. "Pegasus! That was it, Pegasus!"

"Pegasus was a mythological winged horse," answered Sharon.

"I thought you…" Jenny's words were cut off by the proximity alarm. "Jesus!"

With a start, she fell forward and out of her seat then spotted another yellow light winking on the science console and lunged towards it.

"What the hell is it?" she blurted.

"Scanners have detected an object of unknown determination passing within minimum safety parameters," replied Sharon rather woodenly.

Jenny fought for composure and leapt into the navigation seat.

"Is it the Mago we encountered earlier?" she blurted.

"Negative."

She checked the course trajectories. "Well at least we're not on a collision course. Where did it come from?"

"It emerged from over the planetary horizon of Hahl," replied Sharon.

"Why didn't you warn me?"

"Light displays had been activated for two minutes and forty two seconds on the navigation and science consoles before proximity alarm sounded."

Jenny studied the readouts and gazed at the visual display.

"Have you learned not to give a direct answer to the question why?"

"I am unable to respond to your query."

Jenny frowned at Sharon's comments, but put them to one side in order to concentrate on the passing object.

"It looks the same as the other one, but the readouts make it about five times the size of the other Mago. Is that correct?"

"The new vessel is eighteen times the size of the previous Mago vessel."

"Then you can confirm that it is a Mago?"

"I have insufficient data on Mago, but on recently gathered data there is a 28% likeness comparison."

Jenny checked the visual and frowned again.

"Only 28%. I'd say it was a good 90."

She watched as the gap between the two vessels began to widen.

"It's leaving orbit in a hell of a hurry," Jenny murmured. "But where's it going?"

"Current trajectory suggests it is on an intercept course with Sparrow 2."

"Shit!" exclaimed Jenny and flicked on the transmitter. "Sparrow 2, Sparrow 2, this is Mercury 4 you have a Mago vessel approaching you!"

She listened, but there was no reply. She repeated time and again, but still no one responded.

"I think we should have conduit power available now Mat!" Alan shouted. "Do you want to test and power it up?"

"Wouldn't we be better waiting for Robbie to finish?"

"He should have been done by now."

"Another 5 minutes," said Robbie.

"Why's it taking so long?" cried Alan.

"The circuits are scrambled. I think the extreme cold got to them. The whole board could do with being replaced."

"It's supposed to be freeze shielded," complained Alan. "I'm coming down!"

Mat finished the diagnostics tests and confirmed that the fault lay with the vortex stabilizer.

"Do you need me?" he said.

"No, I think we can manage. You hang out somewhere or go make the tea," Alan chuckled.

Mat made his way to one of the few view ports on the station. He anchored himself and gazed out into the void. He was still bored and apprehensive and so began meditating.

An unusual vibration transmitted through his suit. It seemed very faint, but it was enough to make him break his mental routine.

"Did you feel something?"

"What?" Robbie answered over the com.

"Did you feel something? A kind of vibration?"

"No Mat, we didn't," said Alan kneeling beside Robbie.

They focused their attention on the panel configurations.

"You're right, it's kaput!" he admitted to Robbie. "How the hell did this get passed QC? If you go to the spares locker there should be a duplicate."

Mat tried to continue his meditation, but then, there it was again, a vibration. This time it was more of a very faint shudder. Acute anxiety crept into his veins. He began to feel very uneasy and very alone.

"There it was again!" he called.

"Are you freaking out?" squawked Alan. He looked at Robbie. "Now you can see why Commander Morris wasn't keen to have him on this mission."

"Commander Morris is an arrogant tosser!" answered Robbie.

Mat decided to join his two compatriots. He hauled himself along the corridor, and propelled towards the ladder. Nervously, he checked his readings again. The external temperature indicator showed -85 degrees. Something drew his attention to the right. A section of bulkhead glowed red and was melting. His heart raced.

"Holy shit! We've got visitors guys! Whatever you're doing, get done fast and let's get out of here!"

"God's sake Mat calm down! You're freaking out!" Alan scowled. "Should never have left him alone up there."

Mat shot head first down the ladder and rushed along the lower corridor.

Alan sighed with satisfaction. "All done. The whole wormhole generator should now be fully functional. Just need to boot up."

"We can do that from Sparrow!" cried Mat. "Right now we need to get out of here!"

"Mat calm down you've gone phobic!" shrieked Alan. "I'll power up from the control panel upstairs."

"No!" said Mat. "They're coming through the bulkhead up there!"

Mat's internal suit speakers crackled. A small red warning light flashed on telling him that there was a power supply fault to the comms system.

"Take Mat back to the shuttle," Alan said drifting off in the direction of the ladder. To Mat, the transmission came over like a slowed down gramophone. He tapped his helmet to try to correct the problem.

Robbie stirred to go, but found himself suddenly grappling with Mat's torpedoing body racing across the compartment.

"No!"

Robbie's hand gripped Mat's leg like a vice as he reached for Alan.

"Cool it man!" said Robbie, but Mat somehow shrugged Robbie's hold off and continued his pursuit.

Alan was already sliding up the ladder and had quickly reached the top before Mat got to the lower rung. A series of high pitched staccato sounds echoed in Mat's helmet. Something greyish-white flitted across the top of the ladder so fast that he wasn't sure he'd seen anything. Then he noticed that Alan's body had no head. The top of Alan's suit vomited blood, guts and gas like some kind of hideous volcano and Mat could do no more than stare in disbelief and horror.

Robbie grabbed at Mat to restrain him, blatantly unaware of what had happened.

"We have to get out!" Mat said weakly.

"For Christ's sake calm the hell down!" shouted Robbie.

"Look up!" Mat pointed.

A space boot banged onto Robbie's helmet and this time, it was Robbie's turn to freak out. Alan's lifeless form had drifted down the ladder, his innards continuing to spew from the neck of the suit like a garish firework. A vulgar brown mist had already formed into a cloud inside the ladder trunking.

Stricken with horror, panic took over. Robbie dragged at Mat's arm to haul him towards the station exit port. As they emerged into open space, the huge alien ship loomed ominously over them, hanging there like a monstrous threatening leviathan.

"We have to get to Sparrow!" exclaimed Mat.

The realistic terror of the alien presence put Mat's dislike of space walking into context. The two jetted over the short distance. They felt as helpless as ants before a praying mantis.

Frantically they scrambled into the airlock and it took forever for the air pressure to normalize. Gasping, they lurched out of the chamber, tearing their suit helmets free. Mat staggered to the helm controls.

"What do we do?" said Robbie. "What do we do?"

"Get away! Back to Mercury!"

Robbie powered up the thrusters, then the various lights on the control panels started flashing yellows and reds. Warning alarms bleeped.

"What the hell's happening?" Robbie demanded.

"Hull alarm! Oh, shit! They're on the fucking hull!"

Mat pressed the comms switch. "Mayday! Mayday! Mayday!"

"Mat!" exclaimed Jenny. "What's going on?"

"Jenny!" cried Mat trying to control his emotions. "Alan is dead! They're breaking through the hull! Don't know what you can do, but we're in a shit load of trouble!"

"Hull breach! We have a hull breach!" screamed Robbie. "Helmets on!"

Mat hit the thrusters and Sparrow 2 lurched forward.

"The engines aren't warmed up!" yelled Robbie. "There's only one firing!"

The stars whirled as the single thruster sent Sparrow into a spin. Mat gunned the throttle causing the spin to increase.

"What the hell're you doing?"

"Getting away from here," retorted Mat.

Two elongated light-grey objects flashed passed the cockpit view ports.

One by one Robbie managed to fire up the other thrusters and Mat brought the shuttle under control as Sparrow 2 moved swiftly away from the station and the Mago ship.

"Robbie, can you track the son of a bitch to see if it or anything is following?"

"I'll turn on the broadscope," he answered and pulled a broadscope helmet down slotting his own head into it in one movement.

Viewing through the broadscope was like floating in space with no obstructions to vision. The Mago ship was massive, but showed no immediate signs of pursuing. Two tiny objects drifted nearby, but were receding rapidly as Sparrow moved away.

"Nothing after us!" said Robbie.

"Thank God!"

Robbie focused on the two objects and magnified. A large ragged mouth filled the screen causing him to gasp and pull off the helmet.

"You alright?" said Mat.

Robbie rubbed a hand over his face. "Yeh, just got the magnification wrong."

"What did you see?"

"Why don't you look for yourself?" said Robbie.

"Will in a minute. I've just got to coordinate an approach path with Mercury."

"Sparrow 2, this is Mercury," Jenny's voice filled the cockpit.

"Jenny, we're alive and returning," replied Mat. "Where the hell are you?"

"Just emerging from the far side of Hahl. Alter course 043.6 degrees, elevation +24.8, should rendezvous in 14 minutes."

"Why are you over the other side of the God damned planet?" Mat cursed.

"We're in orbit, Dummy!" retorted Jenny.

"Where's Commander Morris?"

"He's on the planet with Glenda. They are returning to their shuttle and won't be joining us for about an hour at least."

Sparrow 2 docked with Mercury without further incident.

Soiled and sweating, Robbie and Mat clambered through the airlock. Robbie said nothing, but headed straight towards Engineering whilst Mat went for the Bridge.

Tears soaked Mat's cheeks. He forced composure before joining Jenny, but his distress was obvious.

"Want to talk about it?" she said firmly. He shook his head, opened his mouth, but couldn't say anything.

"Alan?" she prompted.

"Dead. They decap…" he muttered but stopped. "Not now, Jenny. Maybe later. We've got things to sort."

"Where's Robbie?" she asked.

"Gone below."

He moved to the science console and brought up a visual display of the station. The Mago ship was now moving towards Hahl, and them.

"They're coming!" he said with a level tone. "Get them off the planet!"

"Sparrow 1, this is Mercury 4," said Jenny urgently. "You must return to orbit immediately. A Mago vessel is approaching your position!"

A crackled and distant response was the only reply.

"Take over comms!" said Jenny. "I need to pilot."

She took over the command chair strapped herself in and donned a broadscope.

"You expecting a bumpy ride?" murmured Mat. She did not reply, but busied and orientated herself with displays and readouts.

"Mago ship on an intercept course," she said coolly. "Estimated time of contact 11 minutes. Am taking Mercury out of orbit. Tell Sparrow 1!"

"Aye aye! Should I deploy the laser?"

"What?"

"The laser in the nose, should I deploy it?"

"The laser is not designed as a weapon," said Jenny. "It's used for the possibility of having to break up small rocks."

"Right now it's the only thing we have to fight with if we need to."

"Let's hope we don't need to."

"Well? Should I deploy it?"

"You can do all the checks so that it's ready for use, but hold off on deployment."

There was an alteration of on-board gravity and a small jolt as the thrusters fired and Hahl began to diminish in size on the view screen. Minutes seemed like hours as they pulled away and the planet slowly receded.

"Are they following?" said Mat.

"They're launching something."

From small bulges on the Mago's hull, what had looked like warts, now became tiny launch ports as six small ships left. Two headed for Hahl whilst the others peeled off in pursuit of Mercury 4.

"We have four bogeys on our tail. Warn the captain that he has two inbound."

Jenny raised the throttle to bring Mercury to maximum velocity.

"Have you got through to the captain?"

"Not yet. He's not responding. I think they may be jamming."

"One of the Mago is gaining on us," cried Jenny. "I can't shake it."

"So far they haven't fired any weapons," said Mat. "Where are you headed for?"

"I'm taking us to Albert. Maybe we can shake him off there."

"Don't go to Albert," replied Mat. "Move away from all astronomical objects."

"But we'll be sitting ducks! We need cover!"

"Trust me on this one. I have a hunch."

"Jesus Mat, we need more than a hunch to live off!"

"Right now, it's all we have to go on and it may make the difference between life and death."

Jenny altered course, veering away from the approaching moon. They both studied the tracks and watched as Mercury 4 pulled away from the pursuers. Jenny sighed with relief.

"It worked!"

"For now," added Mat. "I'm going below to get Robbie. We need to get Sparrow 2 ready for flight."

"But she *is* ready to go. Call Robbie from here."

"I tried just now. He didn't respond."

"Well try again!"

Mat ignored her and strode to the Bridge access.

Jenny slapped her seat.

"Stop! For God sake slow down!"

Mat checked and turned.

"You have to explain what you're thinking and what you plan to do!" she said firmly. "You can't go charging off without telling others what you're up to. Communication is how ESO got out here in the first place; so just spend a moment, huh?"

"We need to get the laser operating on Sparrow 2 so that it can be used as a weapon."

"What's wrong with Mercury's? It's got a higher yield."

"Mercury is not as manoeuvrable as Sparrow 2."

"Tell me why we managed to lose those Magos?"

"I thought you'd have worked that one out yourself."

Jenny frowned and gave a pleading shrug.

"Humour me."

"Gravity," explained Mat moving back to the centre of the Bridge. "They use gravity more effectively than we do to control their velocities. By going towards Albert, it was helping them to gain on us. It may also mean that they are not as manoeuvrable as us away from planetary objects."

Mat headed for the exit again.

"How did you know?"

"I didn't. As I said, it was a hunch."

He winked at her and left.

"Could still have called Robbie from here!" Jenny muttered to herself after he had gone.

On Engineering Level, Mat walked quickly to Science Lab 1. He pressed the button and stepped in before the door had finished sliding open.

"Robbie!" he called. "Robbie? Where are you?"

He moved around the central test table. Robbie's locker door was ajar and slumped against it was Robbie.

"Jesus, Robbie!" said Mat with surprise. "I tried calling you from the Bridge. No wonder you didn't answer."

His head wobbled as he gazed up at Mat.

"Shlee's not goin' t make it," he stammered and slurred.

"You're drunk!" said Mat. "You know alcohol is forbidden on space flights. How …?"

The small still sat on a shelf inside Robbie's locker. It had obviously been a long term activity that Robbie had taken part in. Bottles and flasks of various shapes and sizes were stowed on the lowest level. Three empties lay strewn on the deck.

"A- A don't care wut 'appens now. She's goin' t die and us too."

Mat concentrated on what he was saying.

"Were gonna git hitched when this ride was over. Now nothin'!"

He began to weep. Mat pitied him, but puzzled over what to do. He stooped and put an arm around his back to help him up.

"Come on! I'm taking you to sick bay."

"Won't do no good."

"Robbie you have to get a grip on yourself! We need you! She needs you, but you're no good to anyone in this condition."

With difficulty and much burbling, they made it to sick bay.

"Bridge, this is Mat!" he called on the intercom. "Jenny, this is Mat! Any news on Sparrow 1?" "Sensors indicate Sparrow 1 tried to lift off, but didn't make it. I've lost contact."

"Holy shit!" Mat cursed.

Jenny paused, a quiver edging into her voice. "I don't know where they are or if they're alive. It looks pretty grim. It, it looks like we're alone."

Entering Sick Bay, Ami lay motionless in hibernation whilst the auto doctor continued to repair her damaged body. Mat eased Robbie onto a medical slab beside her.

"She'll not wake up again," Robbie blubbed. Mat held his face in both hands and looked into his wide, brown eyes.

"Robbie, you don't know that. We're still alive. She's still alive. We still have hope and there's still a good chance to go home, but to do that, we need you. More than ever."

The tension in Robbie's face seemed to lift a little.

"I'm going to detox your body," explained Mat, "and then we're going to rescue what's left of this crew, warn the Taj Mahal and go home!"

Mat rejoined Jenny on the Bridge to get the latest update.

"I don't know if they've still got us tracked," she said, "but they seem to have lost interest in us for the time being."

"How're we doing for fuel?"

"Still two thirds full. We're okay for now, but if we keep having to do evasive manoeuvres then we'll have problems before too long."

"We have to warn the Taj Mahal about the threat."

"How do we get through to them? Receiving transmissions in interstellar flight is very hit and miss."

Mat began to pace.

"We have to at least try," he said. "There are over 2,000 people on that ship. They'll be walking into a death trap."

"We didn't get round to testing all the equipment. Even so, the best hope we have is on Sebastian."

"Alan was a damned good engineer!" fretted Mat. "I guess we'll have to trust to him getting it right first time."

"How's Robbie?" said Jenny sullenly.

Mat stopped his pacing, hesitating to answer.

"Drunk," he said softly.

"Drunk! How the hell did he get alcohol aboard?"

"He has a still. He seems to have strong feelings for Ami. He feels kind of responsible for her."

Mat noted Jenny's mocking smirk.

"Her being as she is and the threat of the Mago, it, it kind of tipped him over for a bit."

"Jesus!" sighed Jenny. "That's an instant dismissal, having alcohol on board an interstellar space craft."

"Robbie is a good man. He cares for people. He'll be alright."

"It has to be logged," said Jenny.

"He needs compassion not punishment. I think future disciplinary action is a bit irrelevant at the moment, don't you think?"

"What have you done with him?"

"Sick Bay under detox therapy. He should be okay in about 20 minutes."

"This mission is a mess," complained Jenny.

"It's a challenge. I wouldn't say it was a complete mess yet."

"One dead, possibly three. One critical; one legless; one shuttle down; one space station wrecked, not to mention the potential deaths that are to come. I'd say that was a fair indication of a mess."

"We didn't know we were going to run into a new species like the Mago and," Mat exhaled. "We don't know about the station. It can be operated remotely. Alan fixed it before he…"

Silence fell like a curtain between them. Mat wandered aimlessly over to the science console and browsed the panel without any real purpose.

"Let's go then," said Jenny. "Without Commander Morris and Glenda on board, I am the senior officer and I'm making my first command decision. We go to Sebastian and send a message to Taj Mahal."

"Okay, but why not do a sensor sweep first to try to find survivors, activate the beacon on Sebastian then head for the station."

Back in sick bay, Mat removed the medical tubes from Robbie. He sat on his hands whilst Robbie hauled himself upright and swung his legs over so the two men faced each other.

"Sorry," he murmured. "I fucked up big style."

"No one got killed," said Mat sympathetically. "Feeling okay now?"

"Like an asshole."

Mat stood and slapped his shoulder. "We've got work to do, Buddy."

Fitting Robbie's modified laser to Sparrow 2, Mat felt he was no more use than a kid passing tools to his dad. Robbie was not as quick at doing things as Alan had been, but he was every bit as thorough.

Jenny carried out a number of long range sensor sweeps, but found no trace of human life, but what she did discover was that the Mago were now present in numbers both in orbit and on the surface of Hahl.

"Nothing so far," said Jenny. " I need to get closer to be sure of tracing them, but there are too many Mago to risk it."

Mat thought for a moment before responding.

"Why?" He puzzled. "Why the hostility? Why attack us? We've only just met."

"Maybe it's their way. Maybe they need to learn respect the hard way before they'll talk."

"It doesn't make sense."

"We can do no more. I'm breaking off the searching and heading for Sebastian. That is if your lordship doesn't mind?"

Orbiting Sebastian, Mat remained on Mercury 4 so that Jenny could pilot Sparrow 2 down to the surface with Robbie as company.

Mat was not idle in their absence. He constantly swept frequencies for any form of communication either from the Mago or from Sparrow 1, but all that greeted him was the background of stars and continuous static.

Jenny and Robbie had been gone an hour when the scopes picked up movement. The Mago were coming.

"You guys better hurry up!" he called. "They're back! Reckon they'll be with us in half an hour."

"We're nearly done," said Jenny. "Be with you in ten."

The scopes recognized the same four small cigar shaped ships that had chased them away from Hahl. Sparrow 2 was up from Sebastian in plenty of time to dock but, to Mat's surprise, it didn't. Instead, Jenny set off on an intercept course for the Mago.

"Jenny, this is no time to play heroes!" cried Mat. "We're already one ship down. We can't afford to lose another."

"If we don't take these geeks on we'll never know if we're capable."

"Jenny, Sparrow 2 is not designed for combat. You're armed with nothing more than a cutting torch. If you dock now while there's still time we can be away from here and powering up the station."

"It's my call," said Jenny, "and I'm going for it."

"Jenny!" pleaded Mat. "This is foolish and unnecessary!"

"Sorry, Mercury 4 your transmission is breaking up."

"Jenny! For Christ's sake!" cried Mat. "Don't try that old trick! Turn around and return to Mercury 4 immediately!"

Mat watched as the four Mago closed. Three of the vessels maintained course for an orbital pass on Sebastian, but the fourth one veered towards Sparrow 2.

"Sharon!"

"Yes Mr. Kemel?"

"Take over navigation control, break orbit and head for the conduit station via these coordinates."

He punched in the coordinates.

"Yes Mr. Kemel," a pause, a judder then. "Orbit of moonlet Sebastian has been disengaged. Setting new course of zero seven five decimal two, elevation minus zero three five. Course engaged. What ETA do you require, Mr. Kemel?"

"Uh? Oh," Mat looked at the nav data to give him a clue. "Make it, er, sixty minutes from now."

He was helpless to intervene as he watched the vide-screen and the drama unfolding before his eyes.

At first it looked as if Sparrow 2 and the Mago ship were going to collide at high velocity. Then with seconds before impact, Jenny jinked Sparrow 2 to one side and spun 180 degrees. She fired thrusters and moved in close on the Mago with breathtaking skill. The Mago ship glowed on a small spot on its fuselage. Gas spurted from its side and then it started to spin slowly, but very definitely out of control.

As the other three Mago passed around the far side of Sebastian, the damaged Mago glanced off the leading edge of the rock and disintegrated. Jenny brought the shuttle around to start to close Mercury.

Mat picked up the caller.

"Great stuff, Jen. You're clear to dock."

But there was no response.

"Sharon, send a test transmission to Sparrow 2!"

The computer's response was almost immediate.

"Test transmission to Sparrow 2 sent and received. All communications operating correctly."

The three Mago came out from behind Sebastian, on course for Mercury 4. Sparrow 2 bore down on the nearest one. Its nose came within a few metres of contact; then the same red spot as before appeared on the Mago's side. The same as before, gas vented from the hull. This time though, the whole ship split asunder like a popcorn. Immediately, the remaining two altered course to pass astern of Mercury and head back towards Hahl.

It drew a huge sigh of relief from Mat when Jenny finally docked, but once aboard Mercury she went straight to her cabin without so much as a word.

Robbie joined Mat on the Bridge.

"Why didn't she come up?" said Mat.

"She needed to wind down after that."

"Wind down?" Mat thought for a moment. "I guess the old adrenaline would be pumping after a stunt like that."

"Adrenaline!" cried Robbie. "I was having kittens out there. I'd heard she was a top fighter pilot, but that was the wildest ride I've ever been through."

"What about the comms gear?"

"Working normally and transmitting every ten minutes."

"Good," Mat became pensive. "Maybe I should pay her a visit."

Outside Jenny's cabin, Mat procrastinated; pacing up to the door then retreating. His hand wavered over the door buzzer, then pulled away. The door panel light was red. He walked to his own cabin and went inside. In his bathroom, he stared at himself in the vide-mirror.

Vide-mirrors gave a viewer a choice of seeing an image as a reflection or as they actually appeared to others. It took a bit of getting used to when combing the hair to those who had never used one before, since the right side was the right side.

His wavy, dark brown hair could do with a trim. Several strands were out of place. It normally looked like that, but it hadn't bothered him before.

He needed a shave too. He ran cool water in the basin and washed his face; dried and straightened his uniform, not as if there were any creases to straighten out in the first place. After three deep breaths he marched out into the alleyway almost colliding with Robbie.

"Robbie? What are you doing here?"

Robbie wore a guilty look on his face and shuffled nervously.

"It's okay. I'm not off for a tipple."

"No, I never suggested you were. I suppose Sharon is on watch?"

"Yeh, she's set to alarm us if anything approaches."

"You mean alert us."

"That as well."

"Ami?"

"Err, I'm just off to see her now," with that, Robbie strode off towards sick bay.

Mat decided to risk Jenny's wroth and buzzed her door, but the door light remained red. He held back from pressing again, then turned to leave. The light changed to green and the door slid open.

Mat cleared his throat. "May I come in?" He said sheepishly.

"The door's open, isn't it?" Jenny answered in a low stern voice from somewhere inside the darkened room.

She was sat with her legs crossed in her easy chair. Two towels were wrapped around her body and a third wound in a turban around her head.

"Sorry to disturb you, I…" Mat said falteringly.

"Oh, for fuck's sake Mat stop apologizing!"

"I just came to see if you wanted to talk."

"About what? I did what I had to do and that's that. What is there to talk about?"

"Well, it was an amazing piece of flying from where I was watching."

"I was top in fighter pilot training. Well, for the practical part anyway."

"I can see why. I just thought with the stress of combat you might need a chat."

"Now you're starting to piss me off. I don't need a psychotherapist and I especially don't need you as one."

"Good."

Mat reversed the desk chair and sat down with his arms resting on the back.

"I was given operational seniority by Councillor Morley for this mission."

"I know."

"You disobeyed orders. You didn't return to the ship when I told you to."

"So fucking court martial me! You may have that authority, but you are not ESO. You have no jurisdiction in battle conditions. I am combat trained it was my judgement call."

Mat changed tact.

"Okay, so what do we do from now?"

"Simple," said Jenny. "We power up the conduit generator. It will probably take a couple of days to create a stable wormhole. Whilst that's in hand, we find Commander Morris and Glenda; hole up some place until the construction boys show up, and then "haul ass" as they used to say."

Mat gave a wry smile. He could sense the tension in her start to lift.

"How long do you need to recover?" he said.

"I don't fucking know."

"I've never heard you so vulgar."

She didn't respond, but sat and hung her head. She looked as if she was going to cry.

"You felt dirty didn't you?" he said gently. "It was your first kill?"

She said nothing, but the tears began to flow. He moved to her and encompassed her with his arms. She drew to him and wept on his shoulder.

"It's alright you know," he said soothingly, stroking the nape of her neck. "You did what you had to do."

She remained silent, gave him a quick squeeze and then straightened herself.

"Twenty minutes?"

She sat in her armchair and looked affectionately up at him.

"Why twenty minutes?" he said.

It was Jenny's turn to smile. She uncrossed her legs. "That's how long you've got to make me a happy girl."

"Am I worthy of you?"

She pressed the remote door control. It slid closed and then locked.

"No, but you're the only man I want right now."

Robbie stood silently over Ami's cot as he had done many times already. Medical bandages covered her abdominal area as part of the treatment process. The bandages actively worked on wounds to keep them clean and promote healing.

With the threat of the Mago in mind, Robbie wondered if she would ever awake. He rubbed his chin. The goatee beard was well pronounced. He lay down on his side on an adjacent couch to watch her and let his mind drift away.

The sun was shining. The trees were green and fully leafed. Mat walked along the grass covered path into the first line of conifers and stood there listening. No bird song, no nothing, just a gentle rustle of wind through the leaves.

But then, there was something. Very faint, but distant, a low unearthly moan carried on the sweet breeze.

He continued his walk. The foliage was getting thicker on both sides of the pathway. He listened carefully to the distant sound. It became somehow disturbing and threatening and, it was drawing nearer.

Why was he doing this? Why was he here? The sound grew louder and more ominous. Something monstrous stalked him. He could sense it and was drawing ever closer.

The sun, where was the sun? He hadn't noticed it had gone. The calm and serenity was rapidly changing into a sensation of anxiety and fear.

The path was gone. He had been walking on it. How could it suddenly go? A hideous growl somewhere in the bushes ahead. A wolf maybe, or a bear? There should be no such wild animals around in these woods, so what was it? What woods were these? The beast was closing. There was nowhere to hide. All he could do was run and so, he ran.

It hunted him. His strides became heavy and awkward. The thing was behind him now, not far, and closing with every leaden stride he made. He ran in slow motion. It was closing. Terror filled him. He dared not look back, but he did.

A shimmering, spindly leg emerged from behind a tree, then another and another. The fiend rapidly took the shape of a huge metallic crab-like creature. It framed up and pursued him at frightening speed. His terror was complete as the V-shaped face with glowing evil eyes and savage teeth drew within a few metres. It howled with a pitiless voice then leapt at him with open claws.

He floated in mid air, just out of range as the claws snapped together. He spun to look downwards at the fiend. It prepared itself ready to leap again; then stood on two legs and reached. A claw dug into his right arm and he woke with a start.

"Jesus, what time is it?"

A check on the ship's clock told him what he feared. He had been asleep for over four hours. Jenny stirred next to him then sat bolt upright.

"God! The time!" she cried. "We should be on the Bridge!"

Mat was already dressing as she threw back the covers and stood up. He forced his shoes on and stumbled over the easy chair as he made for the doorway. He grappled with his tangled shirt, finally unraveling it and pulling it over his head as he left the cabin. The door slid closed behind leaving Jenny cursing trying to find her shoes.

Sharon had brought Mercury 4 to just 500 metres off the conduit station and held position to wait patiently for human instruction.

The station hung there, motionless and silent. Mat scanned for life signs, but found none. It seemed the creatures had left it. Jenny arrived sorting out her tangled hair.

"Looks clean," said Mat. "Alan said it could be operated from Mercury, but I'm not sure how to do it."

"Expect Sharon knows how," replied Jenny. "Sharon, we want to initiate a wormhole using the conduit station. How long will it take to establish a stable wormhole with Outpost TC1 and how do we do it?"

"From which control location do you wish to commence initiation?"

"We want to power it up from Mercury 4," Jenny explained.

"The function can best be initiated from Engineering."

"Robbie!" they said together.

"Where is Robbie?" cried Mat.

"Robbie is in Sick Bay," replied Sharon.

"What's he doing there?"

"Sleeping."

Jenny cursed.

"We can't blame him, we slept as well," said Mat. "Wake him up!"

Sharon responded after a few seconds.

"Robbie will not be awakened."

"I'll get him!" said Mat.

"Robbie! Robbie!"

Robbie cried out and woke with a fright. Mat Kemel was vigorously shaking his arm.

He sat up, feeling clammy with perspiration running down his face.

"Nightmare?" beamed Mat.

"Oh yeh, some scary spider thing," he replied rubbing his eyes and yawning. "What time is it?"

"0430. You took a bit of waking."

"Wh-what's happening?" he said with bleary eyes and yawning again. "Are we under attack?"

"You dreamed of a spider?"

Robbie swung his legs from the couch and stood.

"Yeh," he said rubbing his eyes. "Silvery beast. Nasty looking thing."

"Curious," was all that Mat would say. "Okay, we all overslept, but right now the ship is 500 metres off the station and we need to get the wormhole stoked up and on line asap."

"Alan was the …"

"We don't have Alan. We have you."

Mat followed Robbie to Engineering.

"The procedures are dependent on human factors," said Robbie. "The time to create a stable wormhole can vary."

"Sharon, there are three main stages is that right?" said Mat.

"Yes," replied Sharon.

"Once all the stages are complete, how long before a stable wormhole can be created?"

"Minimum expected time will be two hours thirty six minutes."

"As you can see," said Mat. "We've got a lot of time and effort and waiting to do."

It was long and painstaking work as Robbie loaded and checked program after program, but at last Stage 1 of the wormhole generation boot up successfully came on line.

"Stages 2 and 3 should not take as long as Stage 1," advised Robbie.

Mat prepared a simple meal of cheeseburgers and fries for them all and then buried himself in data analysis at the science station. He would mutter inaudibly to himself and then occasionally set off for some unknown destination in the ship.

Jenny maintained a constant scan of the region around Hahl for any sign of Mago presence, but it seemed they had vanished as quickly as they had appeared. Mat seemed unhappy with her report though, but would not say why. She pestered him for an explanation, but he stubbornly declined to give one.

As Hahl slowly revolved, Jenny found something interesting on its surface. In one area, two ranges of mountains met. Some peaks reached upwards to 30,000 metres, and in another area ran alongside each other before merging. The two groups of mountains created a raised and rugged elongated plateau between them. It was in this zone, at one of the many outcrops of mini peaks that characterized the geography of the place, that the scanners detected synthetic and metallic material.

Jenny zoomed in with Mercury's powerful camera and there, spotted the remains of Sparrow 1. It would have been a cause for celebration if it were not for concern over finding survivors. From their current distance, it was not possible to detect much detail since the site was still coming over the horizon as the planet turned towards them, but it seemed that, in spite of sustaining severe damage, the bulk of the ship had remained in one piece.

"We should take Sparrow 2 to search for survivors," Mat suggested. "You're sure there are no signs of Mago?"

"I can't be certain, but there is nothing within an hour from our current location."

"At least one of us should stay up here," said Mat. "And I don't want to leave Robbie alone up here."

"Don't you trust him?"

"I just think, he shouldn't be all alone. Mercury 4's a big ship to handle especially if the Mago show up. Besides, you're a pilot."

"Okay, I'll go alone."

"You sure?"

"God Mat! Stop patronizing me!"

Mat pulled a panel from beneath the nav console and disconnected the power supply. His action triggered red alarms to flash and buzzers to sound.

"What're you …."

"Shut up and listen," he said abruptly. "We have about 20 seconds. We didn't oversleep. The CO_2 levels were increased for all of us to make us oversleep. The Mago are still out there somewhere, but have been selected out of the scan data …."

The alarms stopped.

"But who …?

Mat held a finger to her lips then reconnected the power supply and restored the panel to its proper position.

"HC," is all he said.

Jenny eased Sparrow 2 from its docked position and away from Mercury 4.

"Don't fall asleep on me," she said over the comms. "I need you to watch my ass."

"I like watching your ass," Mat chuckled. "Anyway, I thought using terms like that over an open radio was against protocol."

"Book me!"

She over flew the crash site once, taking aerial footage for Mercury's logs to record before lining up on an approach vector. Mat confirmed the scopes were green and clear as she descended to land just 400 metres from the remains of Sparrow 1.

"Mat, I'm leaving 2. Keep a good watch. I don't know what I'm going to find, but time is what I need if there's any trouble."

"Just take care!"

As she strode away from Sparrow 2, she could not help but feel anxiety creeping up on her. She puzzled over Mat's earlier comments and constantly studied the black sky for any tell tale signs of activity. More than once she stumbled due to not watching where she was going.

In front of a triangular chunk of rock lay a jagged piece of hull plating, probably from the underside of Sparrow 1. As she progressed, more wreckage, mangled equipment, more hull plating, and then what could only be a section of wing protruding from a hollow filled with gravel. It was a grim sight and filled her with dread over what she would yet discover.

"You getting this?" she said as much for the comforting sound of her own voice. She knew that the suits in-built micro cameras would allow Mat to see everything she could.

"You bet," he replied solemnly.

"I'm fearing the worst. If you can pick up what I'm seeing, why can't you pick up the commander's and Glenda's suits?"

"I don't know, but we should at least get something from their locators and I'm not getting anything from them either."

It was as dark as midnight. Jenny cursed and plodded onwards. She set her suit light to wide beam so as to take in as much of the scenery as she could.

"Talk to me baby! It's spooky here. You know it's against regulations to space walk alone."

"I know," replied Mat. "I'm not happy about it, but we are out of numbers. Don't worry, I'm with you."

She rounded yet another mound of stones and rocks, and there, just twenty metres away lay the main body of Sparrow 1. It was lying like a smashed eggshell on a cold and unforgiving world. Its nose had splintered against a small cliff face. Half a wing was still attached, but the fuselage had been ripped open like a sardine can.

She approached it with in trepidation. Her heart raced and her eyes glued to what used to be the cockpit.

Both seats were still intact and secure to what was left of the deck. She clambered through the twisted debris, and nimbly sprang up to stand next to them. A long sword like rock had smashed between.

Half of the co-pilot's seat, obscured from the ground, had been sliced apart. Hanging there by its material was the arm of a space suit. She felt nauseous staring at it and found herself reaching out to grab it. Globules of blood flew off from the open end and a skeletal arm slipped out, flesh still clinging raggedly to the bone. Jenny then recognized the stains and bits of tissue that littered the shredded cabin. She looked around for the rest of the suit and a second one, but there was nothing else.

"Gruesome," said Mat noting the tension from Jenny's bio-readings. "You okay?"

"I'll be fine," she wheezed. "There's only an arm? There's still a chance they may be alive; even if they're not in one piece."

"Whose is it?"

Jenny checked for markings.

"Glenda's. She has to be dead, no matter where the rest of her is."

Swallowing hard to keep the bile rising up from within, Jenny moved to what was left of the nav console. She fumbled in one of her suit pockets and drew out a multi-purpose knife.

Savagely, she hacked at the panel until it broke free. Tossing it to one side, she prized clear the black data sphere inside then started as Mat spoke again.

"Don't bother with opening it."

"They don't make these things easy to put in your pocket."

"Are you bringing it back now?"

"I want to have a look around first. I've got to know where they are."

"Be careful. Oh, by the way, Robbie has reached Stage 2. The wormhole will commence powering up in thirty minutes."

"Well, that's some good news anyway."

For data recorder purposes, she surveyed the scene one more time. It was grim, but she played the suit camera over what was left of a fellow human being. A death so remote from others, it was the least that could be done to show people back home how rough it can get in deep space.

Her light danced over the ground below looking for a safe place to jump down to. It was the most light that these rocks had probably gotten for billions of years.

It was then that she noticed the drag marks. Someone *had* survived the crash.

"Mat, are you getting this?"

"Absolutely."

She dropped slowly to the ground near to the tracks. Footprints accompanied the drag tracks. They led off to the right, away from the wreck.

"I'd say from their size, it's definitely Commander Morris," said Mat.

"That means …"

"Yeh."

Eagerly, she followed the trail. The drag marks stopped near some boulders towards the base of a steep mountain path, but the footprints continued upwards. In spite of the low gravity, its shear sides and height of the mountain would be a challenge for any mountaineer.

The tracks disappeared across shingle, but then resumed by running into the mouth of a cave. Jenny bounded across the gap and stood at the entrance.

Two bodies lay face down on the cave floor, one with an arm missing. She went to it first and knelt besides it, then braced herself as she turned it over.

The visor was a mass of red where the body had exploded from the rapid decompression of the damaged suit. She gagged, trying desperately not to throw up, but could not stop herself. She doubled over as her suit filled with the contents of her stomach. Tears flowed, as much from the stench in her suit as from the grimness of her find.

"Uh! Sorry Mat," she panted. "I couldn't help it."

There was no response.

"Mat?"

There was still no answer.

She fought to calm and control herself, wriggling a hand free from its sleeve, she delved passed globules of vomit to the small control panel in her helmet and tapped in a code. A menu display reflected off her visor.

"Ah yes," she puffed. "Auto clean. That's the one."

She sat on the ground next to the corpse. There was no need to confirm its identity, she already knew who it was. Her light shone onto the breast area and a lump formed in her throat as the tag read: "Glenda Shaolin".

The foul air in her suit slowly freshened, although she had found herself becoming strangely accustomed to it. She drew slow, deep breaths as tears wetted her cheeks. The body beside Glenda's stirred.

"Dan?" she said feebly. "Dan? Are you…?"

She scrambled over to him. The body rolled onto its back.

Commander Morris gasped for air and stared up at her with wide eyes.

"We never picked your homer up on the scopes."

"Rocks," he strained to say. "Rocks block signal. Must get me outa here. Suit damaged."

She looked down and saw a tear in the left breast. A patch had been crudely applied, but seemed to be holding. She delved in a pocket and produced a tube of sealant.

Morris gripped her arm. "Let's get out!"

"When you're patched properly," she replied coolly. He tightened his grip and she stared into his glowering eyes. Alarmingly, they seemed to glisten with a green hue. She placed her free hand on his wrist. "Please?"

He shrugged it off and her grip relaxed and hand fell away.

"Can you walk?" She said, squeezing sealant along the furrowed edges of the patch.

"I got here didn't I?"

He rose to his feet.

"Pick up Glenda!"

"She's ..." Jenny stopped.

"We're not leaving her here in this God forsaken place."

Glenda's body was light in the low gravity, but Jenny was not keen on the idea of having her disrupted remains so close. Dan Morris carefully led the way as they left the cave.

"…coming, you must take off immediately," said Mat's frantic voice.

"Mat, what's wrong?" said Jenny.

"God's sake where the hell have you been?" said Mat.

"Silence you moron!" Commander Morris screamed. "Just tell us what the hell's goin' on!"

"Commander, how nice to hear you again. We have Mago vectoring us, and you have less than eight minutes to get your asses into orbit."

"We can't make it in that time," protested Jenny. "It'll take at least ten just to reach the shuttle."

A jet of fluid sprayed from Glenda's torn arm socket onto her visor. She gave a little cry, recoiling and stumbling backwards.

"What the…?" Jenny looked for the commander, but he was gone. His footprints led off in the general direction of the shuttle. "Commander! Wait!"

"You heard the guy," he said. "Eight minutes!"

"We'll never get into orbit in eight minutes. Wait!"

Jenny kept Glenda's body in her arms, but hurried as best she could. She flicked cautious glances to the sky and then a large, dimly lit, shape blotted out a patch of stars. It passed over in just a few seconds and was gone.

She stumbled and fell and Glenda's form skidded away from her and floated into a small crater. She left it, got to her feet, and rounded a final group of boulders in time to watch Sparrow 2 lifting skywards.

"You bastard!" She screamed. "You bloody bastard!"

"Jenny are you alright?" said Mat.

"He's left without me! He's left me behind!"

"He'll never make it!" declared Mat.

Sparrow 2 gained altitude just as several shapes flitted across from over the horizon. She heard Mat's voice shouting harshly.

"Commander there are multiple contacts vectoring your position. They'll be on you before you reach orbit."

"You said there'd be time!" he replied hoarsely.

A beam of light flashed from one of the shapes and Sparrow 2 glared on its port side. There was a second flash from another shape and the shuttle crumpled like melting plastic. A third flash and Sparrow 2 became a fireball plummeting back towards the surface.

"You asshole Kemel! You've killed me! You fucking asshole! Curse you to he...!"

Radio silence. Jenny didn't see the impact, but Mat recorded it on Mercury 4's scopes.

"Oh, Jesus," she fretted. "Mat, I'm marooned! Oh, God!"

"Jenny listen," said Mat. "Robbie has got to Stage 3. We're on a 5 minute automatic countdown to starting the wormhole. I'm coming for you and we're going home, together."

"The Mago won't let you." She fought to regain her composure. "Mat, I have operational experience. Break orbit! Go get the wormhole going; take Robbie and Ami and go home."

"There's time! They're in orbit! They've passed over! They'll be over an hour before they're back I'm coming for you!"

"No, Mat you have to go! I'll hide in the caves. I can last for days. You have to report what happened!"

"I can do it!" cried Mat desperately. "No one will come! You'll never survive before they do! They'll be..."

A moment's silence.

"Oh shit! I don't think there'll be any opportunity," he said.

"What do you mean?"

"The Mago are here! Coming right at us!"

He pressed the internal comm microphone.

"Robbie, the Mago are heading straight for us. Suit up!"

Robbie did not respond.

"Robbie, I'm not a pilot. I could use some assistance right now!"

"Mat, talk to Sharon," Robbie replied. "I'm with Ami."

"Can't it wait?"

"Mat, I'm not that …." he broke off.

Mat opened his mouth to speak, but held back. He cleared his throat.

"Sharon?"

"Yes Mr. Kemel?"

"Err, engage evasive manoeuvres!"

"You have to select Auto Navigation followed by Evasion Mode. Then to activate your selection," said Sharon.

Mat frantically tapped out the instructions and activated his selection.

CHAPTER EIGHT

Robbie leaned over the cot. He looked into Ami's tranquil face and smiled.

"Sharon, what is the status of Ami's condition?"

"Ami Wilson's injuries are currently reduced to affecting 0.15% of total body mass."

"0.15%? She had 6% previously. Does that mean she can get up and move about?"

"Ami Wilson's condition permits active movement, but for 100% recovery she will require another 5 hours of treatment."

Robbie toppled over the cot as the ship lurched.

"What was that?"

"Mercury 4 is under attack. Mr. Kemel has engaged HC to control evasive manoeuvres. The gravitational stabilizers take a few seconds to compensate. I apologize for any inconvenience."

The vessel jolted again.

Mat was intensely anxious. The huge alien vessel had launched dozens of fighters. They looked like smaller cigar shaped versions of itself and homed in on Mercury 4 like a swarm of angry bees. Sharon swerved the ship in a vain attempt to avoid their attack.

The carrier ship fired what looked like an intense narrow beam of light at Mercury's hull. Alarms flashed red on the command console: ***"Hull Breach! Hull Breach!"***

"Sharon! Damage report!" said Mat.

"Hull breach on Decks 3 and 4. Sections 6, 7 and 8 are open to space. Zero atmosphere detected."

Mat activated the laser controls and opened the external hatch on the nose cone. Mercury 4 had just one pulse laser. It was there to be used for destroying small meteors that threatened to smash into them during flights, but it could only angle at a radius of 20 degrees from right ahead.

"Sharon, bring us around into an attack position."

"Which vessel do you wish to attack?"

"The big battle cruiser!"

Sharon did not argue like a human might do and obediently swung Mercury 4 around for an attack run. The cruiser filled half the vide screen.

Meanwhile, Mago fighters closed and attached themselves like mosquitoes to Mercury's hull. Another red warning light flashed up on the command console. ***"Intruder Alert! Intruder Alert!"***

"How many intruders and where?"

"Two Mago creatures have entered Deck 4 Section 9. Section 9 is venting into space.

"I thought that area *was* just space?"

"Only Sections 6, 7 and 8 previously. Section 9 is now at space condition."

"Well how the hell are they surviving?"

"Initial analysis suggests the Mago creatures can exist in space without the need for protective suits."

Mat cancelled the warning lights and picked up the caller.

"Robbie, if you can hear me, you need to get away from the lower decks. We have two Mago on board. Get to the Bridge as soon as you can."

Mat passed an eye over the increasing number of red alarms.

"Is he still alive?"

"Affirmative."

More intruder alert warning lights began to wink.

"What is it this time?"

"Two more intruders have entered Deck 4 Section 5. Section 5 is venting into space."

Mat pressed the caller button again.

"Robbie! For God's sake get the hell out of the lower decks! The place is crawling down there!"

The Bridge hatch slid open. Robbie, with Ami hanging over his shoulder, staggered in.

"Ami?" Mat said with astonishment. "Is she alright?"

"She's not perfect, but she has a better chance here than in Sick Bay."

Robbie carefully lowered a very weary Ami and propped her into the seat next to the science console.

"I was getting worried about you," Mat began to say, but Robbie did not intend to stay and moved back to the hatchway.

"I have to go back to the labs. There's stuff there that might help."

"There isn't time, Robbie. It's too dangerous!"

"There's a laser rifle I was building. It might make the difference."

"Half that deck is decompressed and there's four Mago down there."

"I'll take my chances."

"Robbie don't be a fool!" But he was gone. "Robbie!"

Mat cursed and gave Ami a visual check. The ship bucked and shuddered from hit after hit.

"Sharon, display locations of intruders on the ship's layout," said Mat.

The ship's layout plan filled the vide screen. Four yellow dots were moving rapidly through different Deck 4 compartments. The ship lurched heavily.

"Mago cruiser has fired on us again," advised Sharon. "We have damage to Deck 3 Section 8. Compartment is decompressing."

"Close to within firing range of the cruiser! Reduce layout plans to 20% of screen!"

As the two ships closed, the screen was filled with the image of the cruiser. The layout at the side, showed Section 10 on Deck 3 as suffering decompression. It was where Robbie was heading.

"Mercury 4 within laser range of Mago cruiser," announced Sharon.

Mat leaned forward in the command chair and stared at the screen.

"Fire!" he yelled.

A series of molten spots appeared on the Mago's hull and plumes of gas spurted from two of the small holes that were created, but there was nothing more dramatic than that.

To his right, Ami groaned as if having a bad dream. She was wearing a spacesuit, but had no helmet on. He realized he was rigged the same. If the Bridge bulkheads ruptured they would both be dead in seconds.

He turned back to the screen. To his surprise, it indicated Sections 5, 8 and 9 had been sealed. Section 10 on Deck 3 was no longer decompressing, but then the deck sensors for that area failed.

"Fire again!"

Another molten spot and more gas erupting from the hole it made, but the first two holes had stopped venting. Then the Mago fired again.

It was a mortal blow. The blast shook Mercury 4 throughout. More red warning lights, more hull breaches, more damage. The fight between the two vessels was unequal and Mat's stomach sank. He knew when he was licked. He fired one more time then ordered Sharon to head for Hahl.

Robbie sprinted along alleyways towards Science Lab 1; each compartment had been sealed by airtight doors. Every door he opened and passed through took precious time and made him doubt the wisdom of what he was doing. As he reached the central stairs, the ship jolted throwing him off balance and sending him tumbling down them. The anti-grav safeties were off line and he landed heavily. He scrambled to his feet again and stabbed a finger at the manual door control before him. The airtight door hissed and slid open. The science lab was just a few metres away on his left. The ship bucked again. Alleyway decompression warning lights began flashing. He dove into Science Lab 1 and dashed for the escape suit locker. All he needed was a helmet.

Fumbling at the locker catch, he flung open the door and swept up the helmet, but just before he put it over his head, he heard the lab door hiss open. He swivelled to face it. The laser rifle lay on a side bench three metres away.

The fiendish Mago reared above him like a coiled cobra ready to strike. Its ribbed 'maggot' body tapered down like a worm's tail, but unlike a maggot, the body was supported by four legs. At its upper half, two tentacles extended as arms and on the end of each were four fingered claws that flailed menacingly over Robbie's head.

On the creature's head four emerald, glassy eyes surrounded an open bud like mouth with its four rubbery lips. Inside the hideous orifice, eight rows of angled and serrated teeth presented a fearsome visage. Robbie could understand how efficiently such a monster would have dispensed with Alan's head.

The creature hesitated, seemingly studying the puny human beneath it. Robbie edged away, fighting to control his nerve. Every centimetre brought him closer to the rifle. Without warning, the Mago's mouth closed again to a point and the beast lunged at him. In panic, Robbie tumbled backwards over a stool and sprawled across the deck.

The creatures 'nose' stuck momentarily between the stool legs. It bought Robbie precious time. He put an arm over the bench above him and found the laser.

The Mago flung the stool to one side and charged at him again.

Robbie fired the rifle at point blank range. Nothing happened. The laser was out of charge.

As the gruesome mouth bore down and within centimetres of death, a huge shockwave smashed through the lab. Bulkheads collapsed, equipment data pads, containers and the Mago were suddenly sucked into space as the compartment was torn apart. Robbie hooked an arm around a fixed table and hung on.

The blast from the cruiser was a hammer blow that had smashed right through the aft structure and completely taken out the engines. The mortally wounded Mercury 4, was now hurtling towards the cold and unforgiving planet of Hahl, out of control and with complete failure of virtually all systems.

"Sharon, where is Robbie?"

"I am unable to detect any life forms on Mercury 4. The only functioning systems are on the Bridge."

"Is there anything that can be done to avert an impact with the planet?"

"Collision between Mercury 4 and Hahl is now unavoidable," she said with a level tone.

"How can the crew survive?"

"The only functioning life saving appliance I can detect is the Bridge module."

He wished he'd paid more attention to the space survival lecture when in training.

"The Bridge module? Explain!"

"The Bridge module, when activated causes the Bridge section of Mercury 4 to detach from the rest of the vessel. Cushioning devices are built in to the design to minimize impact with an astronomical object. There are now two minutes to impact at current velocity."

Mat leapt out of the command chair to get to Ami and secure her helmet.

"There are now ninety seconds to impact at current velocity."

"That was never thirty seconds!" Mat protested.

"Calculations to impact are based on current velocity without taking account of acceleration. There are now sixty seconds to…"

"Take account of acceleration…, Oh what the hell? Launch Bridge module immediately!"

Frantically, Mat put his helmet over his head and sealed it. With all the strength he could muster, he hauled Ami into the science officer's seat and strapped her in. He found himself floating as the ship's gravity systems went offline.

"Sharon report on Robbie? Is he still alive?"

"There is no data."

Desperately, Mat fought to get back to the command chair as Sharon counted down for impact from twenty seconds. Balloon type bags were inflating all around.

At five seconds, he was finally secure and looked up to see the ground rushing towards them.

It was over in an instant.

Jenny could barely make out the small flashes of firing during the dual, but she watched as Mercury 4 fell towards the planet. She felt deep anguish and despair as the gallant but outgunned ship plunged groundwards with flame and smoke trailing behind it.

Where Mercury 4 crashed she could not tell, but it was a long way from where she was. All she could do was to feebly mutter "Mat" and hang her head in grief.

Next to the crash site of Sparrow 1, she scooped out a hollow with her gloved hands, then carefully placed Glenda's remains in it, treating it with the kind of reverence as if she were putting a baby to bed. She placed Glenda's severed arm across the chest and draped a dog tag over it. It would be the only badge of recognition left for the skeletal corpse of her shipmate and her friend.

Tearfully, she heaped up small stones to create a mound and knelt next to the grave to offer a silent prayer. A few metres away she found a slab of light coloured rock and dragged it over to place it on top, then she used one of the many strewn rock shards to scratch Glenda's name, dates of birth and death, and the simple slogan "Rest In Peace".

She plundered what she could from the wreckage of Sparrow 1, a ration box, the data sphere and the odd small tool. Everything else was either damaged or unusable or too bulky to carry.

She transported her finds to the cave where she had found Dan Morris and Glenda. Then, she set out, a lone figure on a cold and remote planet to find Sparrow 2 and to see what could be salvaged from it.

She had no exact location of where it might be. Her suit equipment was able to provide an estimated calculation of where the ship might have crashed, but it only gave a rough idea with about a 40% accuracy. If there was nothing of worth there, it would most probably be the last trek she would ever make. Her air supply could last for several hours, but there would be no way of renewing it when it ran out. Mercury 4 had been her only realistic hope for survival. By the time Taj Mahal arrived in the system she would have been dead for days.

CHAPTER NINE

Mat returned from unconsciousness wondering if he had entered hell. Darkness and unfamiliar shapes surrounded him. He had the most excruciating headache and his ribs and chest felt raw as if the skin had been peeled off.

He moved just to see if he could. His right ankle was painfully stiff. His right wrist was sprained, but seemed not to be broken. He could taste blood and the bitterness of bile in his mouth.

Each seat on the bridge of Mercury 4 had been fitted with an impact cushion that was designed to envelope the whole chair in the case of an extreme concussion. He was only alive because of it. He could make out rends in the material that had cocooned him for…. How long had it been?

Gingerly, he reached down to release his harness, wincing at the stabbing agony in his head. As the belt fell free, he tumbled forward, somersaulting through the torn cushion. Slowly, he drifted down and landed limply on his bruised and tender back on a shingle escarpment. He slid gradually down, but dug in his heels to halt the descent. His strained ankle sent a shooting pain up his leg causing him to cry out, but in spite of the suffering, he stood up.

His eyes presented him with double vision and it took several minutes for them to return to normal. He adjusted the night setting on his spacesuit and then surveyed the dark, frozen Hahlian landscape. The scene was one of black and barren rock. A tall, vertical faced cliff ran to his right for as far as the darkness would permit him to see and to his left the ground worked its way upwards in a series of craters and hills toward a mountain range. His headache did not ease and he soon found himself bent over and puking.

When he had recovered sufficiently from the trauma, he looked around to see what was left of the ship.

In spite of the night scope, it was difficult to see anything in the gloom and all he could make out were a few misshapen pieces of debris. He sank to his knees and flopped onto his back again and cried. The head pains were unbearable.

Immeasurable amounts of time passed as he slipped in and out of consciousness. It seemed inevitable that death would mercifully overtake him, end his torture and he could finally rest.

Eventually he awoke. The head pains had eased, but he was still extremely groggy. He was hungry and desperately thirsty. He sucked three mouthfuls of water from his suit supply. Although his suit would recycle all moisture, he had to conserve what he had. Constantly recycled water became less wholesome after several circulations and he could expect no replenishments in this place.

Aware of the potential pain brought on by moving, he rolled gently over on to his front and eased himself into a standing position. He waited for the agony to return, but all he felt was dull and dizzy.

He had to organize himself. He had to find out if anything could be salvaged from the remains of Mercury 4. He began to climb awkwardly up the escarpment. Maybe at the top he would be able to see more.

Ami? He'd forgotten her. What and where was she? His head stabbed a couple of times. It slowed him down, but he pressed on stumbling and slipping with every step, until he reached the top.

His suit's night vision ceased to function properly and he was forced to use up valuable torch power to peer into the darkness to try to locate more debris.

Right under his gaze on the other side of the slope he had just climbed, lay a section of the Bridge and further down he could just make out Ami's cocoon. He made a beeline for it, shuffling his way down the hill, ignoring the bouts of pain and dizziness.

Like his had been, the cocoon was ripped and when he looked inside he feared the worst. A narrow spear like rock shard had been driven right through the middle. Ami lay still with the rock passing through her side. He lowered himself down to her and peered into the helmet. Red effluent and vomit smeared the inside of the visor, but the suit monitor said she was alive!

He examined the rock more closely and could see that Ami was curled around it. Miraculously, there had been no penetration.

"Ami?" he croaked. His throat was sore and parched. "Ami?"

He had to rock her a few times before she responded. She was confused and delirious as she came round.

A bright glare defined the shadows all about and Mat shielded his eyes. Through his anti-glare visor he could make out a large vessel descending. He knew that their remote chance of survival would be reduced to zero if the Mago reached them and yet, perhaps they were the only realistic hope there was. Maybe it would be more prudent to be captured than to endure a prolonged and miserable death in this wasteland. Somehow though, the prospect of capture still remained unappealing.

"Ami? We have to go! We cannot stay here!" he explained.

Mat wasn't sure how much she understood. He gripped her arm and pulled her to her feet.

He shot a quick glance around to see if there was anywhere that afforded them cover. The hills on his left may offer some protection, but they were quite a distance. There was no choice. He decided; it was the hills or nothing. If the Mago came upon them in the open they would not stand a chance.

With Ami draped and leaning on his shoulder, they set off at an unsteady pace. He meditated to suppress the aches and pains from the various parts of his body.

He felt puny and vulnerable, like an ant scurrying away from a boy's shoe. They had no supplies, limited air and no chance of being rescued. The Mago could probably track them anyway. If they hunted for them the pursuit would not last long. Death or capture, neither option presented a savoury prospect. At least heading for the hills gave a purpose and made it feel that they might at least stay alive.

It didn't take long for the ship to land. Ami was starting to use her own feet better, but Mat pulled her to the ground at the top of a ridge. The position would provide a good view of the Mago as they emerged and would give them both a much needed rest. Even though the aliens were over a kilometre away, the huge ship seemed within touching distance.

They were partially concealed by the ridge, but Mat was afraid to use his radio in case it was detected. Ami lay motionless on her back. He leaned over to gaze into her soiled visor.

She was asleep again. The sight of her snoozing triggered waves of drowsiness to pass through him. His vision went double once more. He yawned and rested his head on her chest, lying there on his belly, as flat as he could and slept for a while.

When he came to, he studied the features of the mighty ship. His suit's faltering night sights made it difficult to focus on detail, but from what he could make out there were several hatchways open near its base.

Nothing seemed to have happened whilst he had slept then suddenly, scores of Mago started to pour out over the Hahlian surface just like maggots from a rotting carcass. He studied their movement and behaviour. It was true, they did not need space suits. Seemingly their rubbery hides were able to contain their innards and resist the pressure that would explode a human body.

It looked as if they were going hither and thither without purpose, but Mat began to realize that there was a method. They had organized themselves into groups and were searching the surface systematically, but for what he was not sure.

A few came across what appeared to be pieces of debris from Mercury 4. They paused, taking note of it and seemingly sniffed the wreckage. Most of it they left where they found it, but occasionally they would hook little tendrils onto a piece and drag it back to their ship.

A couple of groups were concentrating their efforts on another ridge the other side of the ship, but Mat could not see what it was that had their interest. Then, to his alarm, some started heading directly towards them. He was inclined to break cover and run when, quite suddenly they turned aside and he realized it was just part of their search pattern. Still, he knew that it would not be safe to remain where they were for much longer.

His head pounded though not as bad as previously. He felt incredibly tired, but desperately fought off sleep. He prodded Ami. She awoke drowsily again. He held a finger to his helmet indicating silence and then gestured that it was time for them to leave.

She was able to walk unaided this time. They kept close to rock formations and large boulders as they hurried towards the hills. Mat could not resist frequently looking back to see if they were being followed.

Reaching the hills seemed to take forever, but once there, they discovered a series of craggy caves of varying sizes. There was no time to be fussy, so they slipped into one of the first ones and hid.

Mat's exhaustion was overwhelming and he slumped against the cave wall. He shone his suit light over to where Ami lay. She was already asleep, so he lay back and soon drifted off himself.

When he awoke, it was with a fright. Something was on his leg and shaking him. He sat up with a yelp and could not believe his sight.

"Robbie! You're alive! How can it be? How did you find us?"

"Your homer was on," he replied. "And, it was easy to follow your footsteps. I've been here for ages, about three caves along. I watched you coming up here."

"The Mago?"

"They left about half an hour ago. Hopefully for good."

"What did they want?"

"Salvage, and my guess is they were also looking for minerals of some kind."

"Ami?"

"She's fine," Robbie said with clear satisfaction. "Thanks for saving her."

"I'm not sure if I've done her any favours if it's only going to prolong the inevitable."

"Maybe, but I haven't been idle. Can you walk?"

Mat gestured an 'okay'.

"Come!" Robbie beckoned.

Mat hauled himself up and glanced down at Ami before following.

"She'll be okay for a few minutes," Robbie added.

He led Mat along a rock wall for about thirty metres and into a larger cave. Inside, he shone his suit light over the floor. Dozens of artefacts from Mercury littered the place including spare gas bottles, emergency power packs, food rations and ice blocks.

"Whilst you two were sleeping on the job, I was out collecting all kinds of stuff."

"How did you manage to haul all that to here?"

"It took a couple of trips, but with low gravity, you can carry more. I loaded up broken panelling and dragged most of it."

"Robbie, I thought you were dead."

"The lab had all kinds of things stowed there including survival gear."

Mat's headache eased, but he still felt very groggy. He tottered a couple of times and felt a strong urge to stroke his forehead. Robbie stood in front of him and peered into his helmet.

"God man! You look a mess."

"I feel like shit," replied Mat. "What do I look like?"

Robbie studied him.

"You have had the mother of all nose bleeds."

"I must admit, it feels like I've been in the worst brawl imaginable."

Robbie closed so that their helmets touched.

"You've got bleeding from the ears. I'd say you're at least severely concussed. You may have a skull fracture, though I'd need to scan you to be sure of that."

"I've had a dreadful headache and nausea. Passed out a couple of times, but I'm okay."

"That's consistent with what I've said."

Robbie turned and gestured to the gear lying about. "I've got a med tent."

"D'you want me to help set it up?"

"If you're able."

"Ami should be first in."

"I don't know so much. Maybe the med tent will help her, maybe not. It's fairly basic. I'd say you need it much more than her."

"I'll be okay," replied Mat as if to stress a point.

Mat's vision altered, as if his eyes had somehow separated. He was seeing double again. Robbie caught him as he stumbled to one side and lowered him to a sitting position.

"Okay really?" he said sarcastically.

Mat patted his arm to reassure him.

"Somehow, we'll get out of this alive," said Mat.

"Wish I shared your optimism," replied Robbie checking the instructions on the med tent. "We're vulnerable to detection even in the caves. We should get Ami in here so that at least we're all together should they find us."

"The Mago or the rescue teams?"

"We don't have any rescue teams looking for us."

"It was an attempt at humour."

Robbie busied himself unpacking the med tent.

"I don't think they're that bothered about us as individuals," said Mat. "It just puzzles me why they've been so aggressive."

"Maybe it's their nature? Maybe we've been unlucky that our first ever encounter has been with hostile aliens?"

He spread the med tent out and started constructing supports.

"Great isn't it?" Robbie went on. "Our first ever contact has gone directly to a war footing."

Mat unsteadily hauled himself up again and immediately began checking items that Robbie had salvaged.

"That's just it Robbie," he said after a while. "We aren't the first contact that the Mago have ever had with humans. What about Mission TC002?"

"There wasn't a 002 into Tau Ceti."

"The official version was that it was merged with the setting up of the TC1 Outpost, but I suspect that G9 was not the only human object to enter the system."

"Pity your theories will never get heard by anyone off this planet."

"Jenny? What about her? Where is she?"

"I scanned briefly for her, but unless she's line-of-sight there's no hope of detecting her."

Setting up the med tent took their minds off the hopelessness of their situation. The tiny structure was tough and compact, made of synthetic metal alloys and thick skinned so as to be able to sustain Earth like air pressure. It was painstaking work to set up. Inside, its smooth walls were designed for capturing condensation that was then processed by the tent's life support system to be used for drinking.

"The power pack will last for about twelve hours after that it's just junk," said Robbie. "The whole unit is a clever feat of engineering. It's just like a big pressure bag."

Back in the small cave, they looked down at Ami's still form.

"Shouldn't we put her in first?" suggested Mat.

"I guess once she has had all the sleep she can pack in she'll feel a whole lot better. I'm hoping she'll get back to her usual self on her own."

"Do we need to use it yet?"

"I'd like for you to go in, otherwise we will have just spent precious energy for nothing."

"Not for nothing," said Mat. "It gave us creative thoughts to keep our minds healthy and towards the end, it may give each of us valuable extra hours; especially when we probably won't have the strength to build it by then."

"It won't be much use by the end."

"Before I go in, I want to have a check on things outside. We should set up a beacon for Jenny and the Taj if it ever gets here."

"Won't the Mago detect it?"

"We have no choice. The Taj Mahal is our only hope."

Mat played his torch over the ground that sloped down from the caves. The barren landscape seemed darker than ever.

"Look! What is it?"

In dozens of cracks and crannies, patches of ghostly white clouds were seeping out and flowing over the ground. It presented an eerie spectacle.

"Some kind of gas," replied Robbie. "I thought this planet had no atmosphere."

"Glenda found traces, but didn't get an analysis report. Have we got any gear?"

"Well no. I thought this was about survival. I didn't expect to run into a load of gas to be taking samples of."

"Of course not, but it's strange though how the gas is coming out now when it's supposed to be night time."

"Yes, very strange," answered Robbie.

"There's less sunlight when it's nightfall," Mat explained. "Everywhere the temperature should be lower, which should mean any gases would be denser and less likely to come to the surface. It's just very curious. The place is already frozen and, hell, there's sod all sunlight anyway at the best of times."

"Yeh, very mysterious isn't it? Now, Mr. Kemel as the only human medic on this mission, I'm ordering you into the tent."

"How's it going to fix me?"

"It uses medical nanites to carry out basic biological repairs to damaged tissues. It doesn't do cosmetics."

"No chance of a face lift then?"

"Not in your case. You're a no hoper."

So began their long and monotonous wait for the chance of a rescue. Realistically, there was little prospect of escape especially with the Mago around in such numbers. They knew that in all probability, they were in for a long, slow death either from starvation or insanity or both.

Ami was sitting up in a bewildered state when they returned to the cave. Robbie explained to her what had and was happening as Mat wriggled into the claustrophobic med tent. Inside, he removed his helmet and lay panting and wondering about the expenditure of energy. If he had untreated internal injuries then Robbie was right. He would be dead long before starvation finished him off.

The activated tent drew in around Mat's head momentarily inducing a sense of panic. It felt as though he was about to be stifled. Soon, a sweet aroma filtered into his nostrils and he found his mind drifting off without a care in the universe.

As Mat slept, Robbie examined him with a small manual scope. He found that he had endured severe physical trauma from the impact of the crash. Numerous blood vessels had been ruptured causing extensive bruising both internally and externally. Robbie suspected brain haemorrhaging and a fractured ankle, but the rest of his skeletal structure seemed otherwise intact. His own stiff elbow was very light punishment by comparison.

Ami joined Robbie outside the cave entrance and peered through the darkness.

"Do you think I should go in the tent after Mat?"

"Do you feel sick?"

"I've felt better, but I guess I'm okay."

"Using the med tent unnecessarily is a waste of energy. If you can get away without it so much the better."

"Thanks for standing by me," Ami said softly.

Robbie felt embarrassed.

"Do you think Jenny's alive?" Ami continued.

"I hope so, but whether she'll find us, who can say. And if she does, it'll just mean she'll die here rather than out there, somewhere alone."

"This place is so miserable and barren," said Ami.

They settled into a small indent in the rock wall and Robbie slipped an arm around her waist.

"Well, if it's worth anything," said Robbie, "if we're going to die, at least me and you will be with each other."

They moved as closely together as possible and hugged, then gazed into each others' helmets with an unfulfilled longing.

She rested her head on his chest.

"If only we could touch."

Mat's condition rapidly stabilized, but it was several hours before he emerged from the tent. When he did, he found Ami and Robbie lying asleep in each others' arms and so, sat apart from them. He set about working on programming the mini computer in his suit so that it could simulate the planetary noises that might be heard if there had been an atmosphere.

What came out was a weird and exotically alien drone. He linked the sound system with the proximity detector in the suit hoping that at least he would be able to hear a footfall if it were to happen.

It was solemn, bleak and lonely sitting there hour after hour effectively waiting for death. Ami gave occasional light groans. Robbie snored and stirred. He would tell them how to set up their own suits when they awoke. If nothing else, it would help break the boredom.

The suits catered for all kinds of physical needs, but the mental side had been sadly neglected. Should he survive, he would have to recommend that later suit models be fitted with some kind of entertainment device.

With the bottles that Robbie had salvaged, Mat estimated there was sufficient air to last about three more days. Water could be recycled, but there was only one day's supply of food rations. The prospect of survival was grim. It was too dangerous to return to the wreckage of Mercury 4 and, if they did, there was unlikely to be much profit from the expended energy. However, to stay in the cave would minimize the chances of ever being found. They would have to rely on Taj Mahal detecting them in order to have any hope of being rescued. And, in all of this, where was Jenny?

Mat checked the rescue beacon routinely and moved it to an outcrop. He was mindful to avoid concentrations of the white gas that skitted over the surface. He wasn't sure whether the gas was corrosive and what effect it would have on his suit. It seemed to behave like a timid creature with the way it formed in little pockets and flowed from one hollow to another as if fearing some kind of assault.

As he planted the beacon, Mat looked out across the dark valley below. Lights twinkled from across the landscape. He stared uncomprehendingly for several seconds before he realized. The Mago were back.

Depression welled up inside him, but he comforted himself with the notion that if they came now, then the death would probably be a quick one. He propped himself up against the outcrop, waited and watched the white gas as it seemed to expand then creep slowly across the landscape.

He tried to blot out negative thoughts. The bleak sensation of hopelessness and suffering would be the biggest threat to their sanity. He tried to think of all the nice things that had happened to him in life. He remembered his last walk across Campus Park two days before he left to come on this mission. He allowed his mind to close down and slip into sleep or unconsciousness. He could not tell which.

Hours passed, or was it days? The wait was interminably long. It gnawed on the spirit and tested to the limit the will to survive. The brain, starved of input and stimulation, can easily suffer an implosion of intellect and psychological stability.

Robbie supplied each of them with their own batch of psychotropic drugs and in the end it was that dependency that helped them hang on.

Whenever he awoke and the drugs wore off, all Mat could feel was hunger, thirst and growing despair. He found it difficult to ration his intake. The bliss of sleep and intoxication was a refuge from hunger and depression.

He took solace in meditation when he could, thrusting aside the onset of malnutrition and the torments of burning thirst. Robbie and Ami invited him to join them in making physical contact, but when he awoke from a drowse he would find the two separated from him and locked in each others' arms again.

Most of the time Ami and Robbie remained away from him, sitting and huddling, constantly together. They kept mainly silent, but occasionally it sounded like they were weeping, though the suits made it difficult to tell what emotions were affecting anybody.

The white wisps of vapour provided the only entertainment and continued to crawl like colonies of spectres across the foreground. The suit's audio system crackled as the super cool vapours split away chunks and splinters of rocks that they touched.

Mat noticed crystalline growths that had formed on under hangs. None of the gas came close enough to be observed intricately, but he puzzled about what type of gas it was that flowed over the surface with such abundance. He pondered whether the gas could possibly be a form of life, but that would be something that would have to remain an unsolved mystery.

Every six hours, a tiny bleeper told him to take some form of nourishment and also to apply another dose of narcotics. It became an event; to long for the little alarm that would permit the only pleasure available. However, in time, the longing evolved more and more into a craving and the only relief from numbness and boredom.

CHAPTER TEN

Was it hours, days or weeks when someone arrived? Mat could not tell who it was, but thought it might be Jenny who had found him. His mind had become numb and vegetative within his nihilistic state. He had lost all awareness of even the proximity of Robbie and Ami. Hunger and thirst had steadily and relentlessly gnawed at his resolve and become a part of his psychological condition. His thoughts had stagnated. He found it difficult to meditate anymore. He felt his sanity slipping from him and, towards the end, did not even know or care if he was alive at all.

The sounds in his suit suggested that someone was moving around and checking him. He was too weak to respond. His last memory was not of seeing anyone other than Ami and Robbie lying on their backs, side by side and motionless.

He was too far gone, such was the deterioration of his cognitive powers. Someone was connecting something to his nutrition pack and his supply of air, water and food all increased. Was he dreaming? It was all a blur. Had he passed over? Was this heaven? An angel of mercy visiting him and tending his needs?

"Thank you Jenny," was all he could whisper. He puzzled how she could have done it. Surely she would have been feeling the effects of malnutrition herself? She must have salvaged extra oxygen bottles, additional food and water rations from the wreck of Sparrow 2. Whatever, she was the angel of his salvation and he blessed her for her kindness.

"I just want you to know," he croaked. "Whatever I did wrong, I'm sorry for. It was great to have known you."

"Hang in there!" she whispered.

He could hardly make sense of what she was saying. His mind constantly drifted in and out of reality. He felt intensely weary. A voice inside told him not to sleep, but why not? What was the point in hanging on in such torment and suffering? His headaches were all but gone and all that remained was the ease of drifting into peaceful nothingness.

She seemed to go away without saying anything more. He didn't want her to leave him, but had no energy to object.

"How's he doing?" said an unknown voice.

"I think he's trying to come to," muttered another.

Why couldn't they let him be? All he wanted was to sleep. He felt so very tired.

"Jenny?" he tried to say, but his mouth was full.

"Mr. Kemel?" said one of the voices softly. It was male, but with a light tone.

"Mr. Kemel?" it repeated.

Mat just wanted to be left alone. He moved his mouth and felt the tube running into it and down his throat. He swallowed instinctively. It hurt like crazy.

"We'll take it out," said the man. "I don't think he needs it anymore."

Mat squinted, trying to focus on the man's face. A hand gripped the tube, and with a firm, steady pull, it slid out. His eyes stung and he gurgled as the tube cleared leaving his throat raw and painful. Hands slipped behind his back and helped him into a sitting position. Someone offered him a beaker.

"Here, drink this!" said a stern, matronly voice.

He drank slowly, enjoying every drop of the flavoured water. It had to be heaven to be woken up with a drink like that.

"Where am I?" he said feebly.

"Welcome aboard the ESS Taj Mahal," said the man. "I am Doctor Joseph Farnhurst and this is my assistant, Nurse First Class, Brenda Williams."

Mat shakily rubbed his forehead and eyes trying to revitalize them. His body was numb and stiff all over.

"The others?" He croaked.

Dr. Farnhurst sighed. "I'm afraid Mr. Taylor and Miss Wilson didn't make it, but I thought you would know that already."

"Already? How would I know? Jenny? Is Jenny alright?"

"We found Jenny Gold some forty kilometres from where we found you. We got to her just in time. She's up and about and doing well."

"Forty kilometres?" Mat was incredulous. "She was with me. How could she have been forty kilometres away?"

He puzzled for a moment then added: "Can I see her?"

"Err, a bit later. She's, err, doing some tests at the moment," Dr. Farnhurst gave a little cough to clear his throat before continuing. "I think you were in a state of delirium for several days before we found you. The mind can play funny tricks when you're close to death."

"Several days? How long have I been here?"

"The Taj Mahal has been in the system for six days now. We found you and Miss Gold on the first day."

"Ami and Robbie, didn't you find them?"

"Only their remains."

"Remains? What do you mean?"

"As I said, perhaps you could explain that to us."

Mat was puzzled by the remark.

"I don't understand."

"You were most probably delirious."

"The Mago?" said Mat. "Have you run into the Mago?"

"Mago?" the doctor gave a placatory smile. "Apart from your warning broadcasts, there has been no evidence of any alien presence in this sector. I expect the captain will want to debrief you in due course."

"You haven't encountered the Mago?"

"Please rest, Mr. Kemel. When you're ready I'll get the captain to come and see you."

"I've rested enough. I'm well enough now," said Mat though his body felt like it could use another ten hours sleep. "I don't understand. The Mago, where are they? I really ought to speak to the captain now."

"You ought to sleep."

"No, I have to talk to the captain now!"

Dr. Farnhurst shook his head.

"Only if you're sure."

Captain Sharp was a 'no nonsense' type, an ambitious man, the type that wanted to get the job done as efficiently as possible.

"We haven't been able to get hold of all the data from your crashes," he said gruffly. "Odd how you managed to crash all three vessels."

Mat felt the hackles rise at the dismissive nature of the captain's response.

"It's quite easy to crash when you're under attack and have nothing to fight back with," Mat replied sarcastically.

Captain Sharp folded his arms and glowered at the bedraggled and unshaven young man sitting before him. Dr. Farnhurst and Brenda Williams busied themselves in one corner of the room.

"Mr. Kemel," the Captain said, as if trying to carefully choose words to say. "I'm a little confused as to what went on aboard Mercury 4. It seems that you and Commander Morris didn't exactly get along."

"How do you know that?"

"I said, we have collected some info from Mercury 4's data sphere and received coded transmissions from the beacon on Sebastian but, moreover, we have his testimony."

"How can you have his testimony? He's dead."

Mat was bemused that a space transmitter should contain trivial information about crew personality differences, but for Captain Sharp to claim there was a testimony when the guy was dead was preposterous.

"Is that what you were hoping?" said Sharp.

"What?"

Captain Sharp went on, "Let me be blunt, Mr. Kemel. Did you mutiny?"

Mat was outraged. "Of course not! That's ridiculous!"

"Commander Morris said he felt threatened by you and feared for the safety of his ship and crew with you aboard."

"I don't believe it!" Mat protested. "Look, we are in grave danger whilst we remain here."

"From you or the Mago?"

"The Mago of course! Speak to Jenny! She'll verify everything I've said."

"We are unable to at present. She's undergoing treatment for possible brain damage. She has lost the power of speech. The doctor hopes she will make a full recovery, but for now you are all we have to work with."

"The doctor said she was up and about."

The doctor and nurse shuffled out of sick bay.

"Captain, search Mercury 4's crash site. The Mago cruiser landed there. There's bound to be evidence of the landing."

"We are unable to commit men to a full search of Hahl at present," Sharp explained. "We are four days behind schedule already. You failing to get the wormhole station functioning properly cost us two of those days."

"But if the Mago return we are all at risk. Let me head a team. I can show them where it pitched. I won't need more than a couple …"

"You are going nowhere," Sharp interrupted. "You have been diagnosed as suffering paranoiac schizophrenic delusions. Until your condition has been brought under control, you are confined to Sick Bay 3."

Mat felt the anger rising. "You think I'm nuts?"

"Think?" snorted Sharp. "After how you finished off Mr. Taylor and Miss Wilson?"

"Finished off?"

Sharp backed away to the door. The doctor returned with an orderly and moved in front of him.

"Yes, Mr. Kemel, you murdered them and stole their supplies. That's why you're still alive and they're not."

Mat's stomach knotted.

"No!" he cried in utter disbelief.

"You've suffered deprivations," said the doctor sympathetically brandishing a needle. "It's time for your medication."

Mat experienced something that had only affected him once before. He saw red flash across his vision. Although in a weakened state, he managed to find strength enough to swing a palm up and catch Dr. Farnhurst underneath his chin. The doctor flew backwards against Captain Sharp. The orderly pounced and delivered a well aimed blow to the side of Mat's neck.

CHAPTER ELEVEN

He was walking in the woods again. As previously, there were no sounds of birds or any other animal. The sun shone brightly and the wind rustled the leaves on the trees. Mat listened carefully in fearful anticipation.

There it was, that same unearthly sound he had heard previously; a base, mind-numbing rumble. It sounded like the devil breathing, full of menace and evil intent. It was distant, but whatever hideous fiend was making that sound was getting closer.

This time he did not foolishly and carelessly head off into the trees, but turned and started to run purposely away from the sound. At least he tried to run, but his strides were cumbersome and all he did was in slow motion.

The monster was getting closer and closer and the fear in him built by the second. He tried to resist looking back. He had no desire to see the onrush of horror coming for him, but in the end he could not resist the draw and he did look back.

A monstrous metallic creature, less crab like than before, but definitely insectoid, burst out from the trees behind and sprinted toward him. Its visage was covered in eyes, human eyes. He glowered in terror as it gained ground. He was moving far too slowly to get away. His legs strove as if through treacle.

As the creature got to him, he floated clear of it and hovered just out of reach. He hung there in mid air, his doom waiting beneath. The many red glowing humanoid eyes gazed lustfully up at him. A human face appeared in the middle of its head and mouthed words at him.

"Join me! Join me and be free!"

Then the face dissolved and was replaced by a fang filled mouth drooling blood and effluent. Suddenly, he fell. The hungry mouth opened wide to swallow him whole. He screamed and awoke with a fit.

His jaw ached, his head ached and his arms ached as reality returned. The ship's warning alarms were hooting loudly. A worried looking Nurse Williams was checking medical instruments to one side of sick bay. The door slid open and Doctor Farnhurst rushed in and joined her.

It was painful to speak. His jaw had either been broken or was severely bruised. He tried to get up but restraining straps held him in place.

"What's happening?" he muttered between clenched teeth.

The staff ignored him, so he repeated the question a little louder.

A worried Dr. Farnhurst turned to look at him.

"We, we are under attack," he said hesitantly.

"The Mago?"

"It's too early to say," Farnhurst replied. "It's probably just a drill."

"It's no drill. It's the Mago! They've come haven't they?"

Mat strained vainly to free himself from his straps.

"Get me out of these things!" he demanded.

"Only under Captain's orders can you be released," said Farnhurst.

"We have hull breaches on Decks 11 and 12, Sections 35 through to 38," blared an urgent male voice on the tannoy system. "Evacuate all adjacent areas. Damage Control teams close up!"

"Don't you think the Captain's got enough on his plate already? Make a decision, let me go!"

"Mr. Kemel," Farnhurst retorted softly yet firmly. "I *have* made my decision. You are to remain as you are until he instructs otherwise."

Mat tugged aggressively against the straps but to no avail.

"For God's sake...!" he pleaded.

Another announcement butted in: "Intruder alert! Intruder Alert! Two aliens have entered Section 39 on Deck 12. All personnel are to evacuate Section 39 immediately! Armed security to intercept."

Dr. Farnhurst left sick bay hurriedly with a doctor's bag in hand.

"Doctor, please! You can't leave me like this! I won't stand a chance!"

The nurse followed Farnhurst out and turned to say in passing: "You don't deserve a chance for what you did."

A cold chill ran down Mat's back. What was going on? How could they think him a selfish killer? Had Dan Morris survived? Sparrow 2 had been fried. There was surely no way he could have survived.

The ship shuddered from an impact of some kind. An intermittent alarm was interrupted by another frantic announcement informing the ship's company that there were more hull breaches and more aliens entering. Mat twisted his arms and body but still made no impression on his bonds.

The door slid open and in marched Commander Morris alone. He held a laser pistol in his hand. He took one look around sick bay, then walked straight up to Mat's bed.

"Commander Morris!" was all Mat could say. Morris raised the gun to rest the muzzle right at Mat's forehead. He watched the forefinger squeeze slowly on the firing button.

"Please no!" Mat pleaded and closed his eyes.

"I've always wanted to see how a brain cooks when exposed to laser treatment," said Morris

The hatch door slid open and Nurse Williams re-entered. In an instant, the laser was lowered and Morris had concealed it.

"Commander Morris," she said with some surprise. "I didn't think you…"

A red spot glowed on the left side of her chest. Her tunic smouldered in the same place. She had time to give a pained look of shock and a little yelp before she collapsed to the deck dead.

"Not much blood," mused Morris. "Wound must've cauterized with the heat."

Mat tugged hard on his straps, but his efforts were useless. Morris raised the muzzle of the gun to Mat's skull once more.

"Why are you doing this?" he said. "You've had long years of training and experience. You've been through all kinds of tests to get to your position. Why have you set yourself on this murderous vendetta against me?"

"All personnel are to evacuate Decks 11 and 12. Security teams to regroup in Section 30 on Deck 10!" the tannoy man announced.

Dan Morris leered, pressing the gun hard against Mat's head as if trying to push it through his skull.

"You are scum! People like you should be purged from space. You set off to corrupt good and proper astronauts. Your sort are no more than a virus in the system. You need to be eliminated at every opportunity. Your promiscuity was spreading like a cancer on my ship."

He leaned over to within a few centimetres of Mat's cheek and hissed like a snake.

"My ship was destroyed because of you!"

Mat was speechless. He studied the face before him, filled with hate and loathing and…madness. That was it! He had to be insane. Something must have got to him. Perhaps something *had* happened to him during hibernation.

"This is insane! Dan listen to me just this time!"

"Why should I listen to you trying to worm your way out of your destruction?"

"Dan listen!"

"Don't Dan me! We're not on first name terms!"

Mat pressed on.

"If you are only against me, then why did you just kill the nurse? What had she done?"

"I didn't kill her! You killed her!"

"I killed her? How the hell…?"

"You used your polluting thoughts. You must die to make it stop."

Morris gripped his own head with both hands, impressing the gun on his forehead, screwing up his face in a distorted grimace.

"Dan, you're ill."

Spittle ran from the corners of his mouth. He lowered his hands and screamed.

"Shut up, you bastard! You have to die!"

"But it doesn't make sense! Why did *she* have to die?"

Dan Morris began weeping and mumbling incoherently.

"I'll leave the gun here. They'll know you did it then."

"Maybe, but why did she have to die?" Mat insisted.

"She was interfering with my work to purify the fleet," he ranted angrily. "You know! You gave me the order!"

"Did you kill Ami and Robbie?"

"What?" he waved the gun unsteadily at Mat's head.

Mat stared fixedly at him.

"Did you kill Ami and Robbie?" He said forcefully.

"I had to, you had corrupted them. I found them together. They were sinners! Copulating on my ship! They were beyond redemption!"

"They were in love. That is not a sin!"

"You're twisting things again! They were sinners!"

"Why didn't you kill me on the planet? Why did you spare me?"

"You had to take the blame! You carry the mark of sin on you! You have to survive!"

"The mark of sin? What are saying?"

"You are …" Morris pressed the palm of his hands into his eyes and began to cry uncontrollably. "Ooooohhh!"

"Commander Morris, there are logs everywhere. They record everything you say and do. You'll never get away with all these killings. You must let me help you."

"You help me?" Morris scowled. "How can you help me when you're lying there unable to move and entirely at my mercy?"

"And Jenny? What have you done to her?"

"The Mago have broken through to Deck 10. All non-security personnel are to keep clear of Deck 10!" said the tannoy man again.

"Jenny? What of Jenny?" Mat repeated.

"Who?"

"Jenny Gold? What have you done to her?"

Dan Morris was deeply troubled.

"Jenny?" he said distantly. "You have condemned her. Twice she has escaped purification. Twice luck has prevented it, but she will be purged just like you."

"But if you kill me, they'll know it wasn't me!" reasoned Mat.

"All Emergency Crew Prep Teams close up!" blurted the tannoy. "All Emergency Crew Prep Teams close up!"

"Commander, the crew are losing control of the ship to the Mago. What we are doing here is irrelevant. We are all going to die here. What you do to me makes no difference."

"Now hear this! Attention all personnel!" It was Captain Sharp this time. "This is the Captain speaking. We are unable to contain the Mago intruders that have invaded our ship. The wormhole is now fully functional. There will be a staged evacuation of Taj Mahal. Those shuttles leaving the vessel are to head directly to the wormhole and return to Outpost TC1. Abandon Ship Stage 1! Abandon Ship Stage 1!"

Distracted by the announcement, Mat returned his attention to Commander Morris who was again stood with both hands clutching his forehead. The laser had dropped to the deck, but he seemed racked in pain.

"Uhhh!" he cried. "The voices they won't shut up!"

The door slid open and Dr. Farnhurst entered with two security guards besides him. They stared at Dan Morris in astonishment.

"This is your killer, doctor!" announced Mat. "He's sick."

Morris lowered his hands to glower insanely at the three arrivals.

"Are you in pain?" said Farnhurst.

"Of course he's in pain," said Mat. "Now cut me loose, so we can all get out of here."

Several things happened in quick succession. Dr. Farnhurst moved towards Mat. Dan Morris suddenly burst into life and with a loud "No!", shoved the doctor with unnatural strength to send him tumbling over a couch. He dove for his fallen pistol, reached it and fired into the head of one of the guards. The man dropped like a stone. As Morris rolled the second guard fired, searing the flesh in Morris's right leg. He yowled like a scalded animal, scrambled out through the sick bay door and was gone.

Farnhurst and the remaining guard went directly to their fallen comrade, but it was obvious there was nothing they could do for him.

"The Mago have control of all lower decks," said the tannoy. "Launch 13, 14, 15 and 16 immediately before the Mago reach the evacuation bays."

"Will someone get me out of here?" Mat screamed.

They freed him.

"Jenny? Where is Jenny?" said Mat.

"I had her transported to the shuttle, Skylark 1, at first stage," said Farnhurst in his customary soft tone. "She should be launching about now."

The three headed down a corridor on Deck 8, mindful of the threat of Dan Morris as well as the concern over running into Mago.

"Commence Abandon Ship Stage 2," said Captain Sharp's voice from a deckhead speaker. "Commence Abandon Ship Stage 2."

As the group reached an intersection, a shriek of agony struck their ears from the alleyway leading to the right.

"Wait here!" cried Mat and bolted in that direction.

As he rounded a corner, he found the upper half of Dan Morris' torso lying on the deck. His dead eyes stared upward at him.

Towering above, stood a still and solitary Mago. Blood dripped from its jowls and he could see a piece of garment hanging from a tooth. The creature examined Mat with its four round, cat-like eyes, but did not attack.

The Mago resembled a three metre long giant caterpillar on legs. Its tentacle-like arms and four fingered claws hung limply. The creature's green-brown hide was smooth like leather and marked with a series of thick ribs that ran around most of its body.

Mat slowly levelled his gun at the creature, but it did not attack. It just stood there resting unsteadily on its four legs with its tentacles remaining motionless by its sides. It seemed stunned. It twitched once and then again. The twitching increased and developed into muscular spasms. The affliction quickly intensified until the whole body convulsed. Mat backed off. The Mago's yellow eyes dulled and greyed. Its head sagged and the body slumped to the deck as the legs buckled and gave way. What a moment ago was a proud and threatening monster, now had been reduced to an enfeebled and wretched animal in its death throes.

From somewhere behind him, Mat could hear the others calling to him, but he was transfixed by what he was witnessing. He lowered his gun as the creature squeaked like a child's pathetic soft toy. Then, its body started to change. Grey and silvery veins appeared and spread rapidly across it. The eyes evolved into ovoids and the multiple teeth began merging.

Suddenly, there was a horrific explosion and the side of the alleyway blew away and into space taking the Mago with it. Mat would have been sucked out too except that an airtight damage control door instantly shut right in front of him. It almost sliced him in two, but nevertheless saved him from certain death. Even so, the temporary collapse of pressure had slammed his body causing him to sink to his knees with the shock.

Farnhurst was beside him in next to no time.

"You okay?"

Mat nodded and got up with the doctor's help.

"Lets get outta here," he said breathlessly.

Taj Mahal was fitted with four shuttle bays. Each bay housed four Skylark shuttles making sixteen in total. In an emergency the Bridge could detach to make a seventeenth rescue craft.

"Where're we going?" said Mat.

"Bay 3 is nearest," replied the guard.

A huge explosion from somewhere deep inside Taj Mahal rocked the entire ship. The sound of rending metal filled their ears.

Captain Sharp spoke with urgency. "Abandon Ship Stage 3! Abandon Ship Stage 3!"

"Three is just around the bend," said Farnhurst.

A ghastly sight greeted and sickened them as they turned the corner. Four headless bodies were strewn around outside of Bay 3. Blood and entrails were splattered all across the deck, bulkheads and deckhead.

"Abandon ship Stage 4! Abandon ship Stage 4!" said the tannoy frantically. "Launch all shuttles immediately! Everyone leave now!"

"We have to take our chances!" said Mat stepping forward taking care not to tread on any of the gore.

A short docking bridge connected to each ship, closed at each end by airtight pressure doors. They chose Skylark 9 to board since No.9's docking bridge doors were still invitingly open. At first it sounded like rubber grating on plastic, but then they realized it was a human voice, several human voices, at various levels of fear and suffering screaming from inside.

Farnhurst and the guard recoiled and started retreating, but Mat gripped the guard's forearm.

"Give me a weapon!" he demanded. "Let's at least try and make a difference!"

"Dr. Farnhurst," Mat stooped to pick up a dropped laser pistol as he spoke. "See if you can get into No. 10. There's no need for you to be here."

Farnhurst said nothing but went back towards the nexus where the four docking bridges met. Mat and the guard hurried cautiously toward Skylark 9's entrance. A woman's voice screamed as if she had just been discovered. They could hear her pleading fearfully.

Inside, more savaged corpses littered the entrance. The woman screamed again in terrible anguish. They rushed into an alleyway and there was the Mago. They had come in behind it and the creature had not seen them.

Ugly mandibles clutched a terrified woman, holding her in the air as if she were as light as paper. The guard stared in awe at seeing the creature, but it was Mat who fired first, searing the monster's upper back.

The Mago gave an unearthly trumpeting sound like that of a muffled elephant. It dropped the woman and spun round with lightning speed towards them. The guard fired his rifle, hitting the creature above its mouth, but it was at the man in an instant.

Mat was knocked to one side as it passed. There was a 'thunk' noise and the guard stood with his head in the monster's mouth.

It took a moment for Mat to realize that the man's head was no longer attached to a body. The creature turned on Mat and he fired his pistol again at the fiend.

From nowwhere Farnhurst dashed in brandishing a rifle and fired from no more than a metre away, straight into its mouth. It trumpeted defiantly for a few seconds waving its jaws around and then dropped dead.

The frightened woman scrambled on all fours towards them as the death rattle of a man from elsewhere in the ship struck their ears.

"There's another one," she snivelled looking down the alleyway to the next compartment.

"Oh God!" she shrieked in a high pitched voice.

Mat lunged for the guard's fallen rifle, rolled over and came up in a crouching position. He was just in time to see an enormous mouth closing on him. He fired as the beast smashed into his thorax with a crunching impact.

Agonized, Mat lay there dazed and spitting blood. The creatures hideous, heavy mouth lay over him. Long, needle-like curved teeth pierced his tunic and flesh. Another second and they would have sliced right through.

He winced, realizing that he had probably collected more broken ribs. Nevertheless, the second Mago was dead.

Gingerly, he prized each of the creatures bony teeth from him. They reminded him of a lobster's antennae. It still took a few seconds to regather his wits, but he managed to force out the words: "Close the goddamned doors!" before slumping to the deck and clutching his bleeding wounds.

The ship swayed in its dock as the Taj Mahal was hit by something heavy.

Farnhurst tended Mat and the young woman who, from her small lapel badge, indicated she was called Maria.

Mat got himself into a sitting position to help his breathing.

"How many others on board?" He gasped.

Maria was still clearly distressed from her ordeal, but managed to compose herself sufficiently to answer.

"228, but …" she broke off.

Farnhurst patted her arm to console her.

"Where are they?" said Mat.

"Most are in the cargo hold," she replied.

"Any pilots amongst them?"

"None are shuttle trained," she sobbed. "They're mainly scientists, engineers and architects."

"What about you?"

Maria was awash with grief for a few moments.

"Maria!" he prompted. "We have to get away from here. We need someone to fly this thing."

"I'm in charge of ration distribution and air quality control," she said rubbing blood shot eyes. "I've never flown anything."

"So the Mago got the flight crew?"

Maria nodded and broke down again.

"They killed my boyfriend," she wept. "He was a pilot."

Mat recalled that a couple of the bodies they had passed earlier had flight insignia on them.

"I'm sorry," he said.

Farnhurst placed a comforting arm around her shoulders.

"Would you like a sedative?" he asked.

She nodded.

"Before anyone starts shelling out pills," said Mat. "Get me to the cockpit."

He clutched his damaged ribs and tried to suppress the discomfort as they got him to his feet.

When he had taken his seat in the pilot's chair, Farnhurst returned to the rear compartments to gather more medical supplies.

Maria flopped in the navigator's seat and just stared. She watched as Mat ran through pre-flight checks and typed in a couple of command codes.

A panel light flashed green: "Clearance for launch granted".

He activated auto control and the launch sequence began as the bay doors opened.

Another huge shudder jolted them as the countdown reached eight then, at zero, Skylark 9 broke free and the side thrusters pushed it away from the Taj Mahal and into space.

The view that greeted them was like that of a mini asteroid field. Indefinable pieces of debris of varying shapes and sizes floated and whirled around the main body of the Taj Mahal. Wide rifts had opened up along several sections of its side.

Dozens of small cigar ships buzzed the beleaguered vessel like angry hornets. Many had latched onto its hull and Mago were burrowing through it to gain access to the interior. The Taj Mahal looked like an undignified fallen animal being eaten alive by hungry insects.

Above and behind, sat three Mago cruisers constantly spewing cigar ships and periodically flashing energy weapons to inflict additional damage to the doomed colony transport.

Then, to his horror, Mat realized that the Taj Mahal was not the only vessel suffering. Two Skylark craft, tiny by comparison to the mother ship, lay listless and without power at the mercy of the Mago. Two more seemed to be caught in some kind of web emanating from one of the cruisers and were being hauled in to some indescribable fate.

The auto pilot engaged rear thrusters and Skylark 9 edged forward allowing Mat to inspect the extent of the damage on Taj Mahal's starboard side. A small shape uncannily like that of a human skeleton whipped passed the cockpit window and was gone.

The proximity alarm sounded. Mat steadied himself in the pilot's seat and gripped the helm.

"Switch over to manual control!"

The ship lurched as the controls transferred over to manual.

"Damn that was close!" he said.

"What was it?" asked Maria timidly.

"That was us being fired on by that cruiser."

Mat pushed the helm down and veered to starboard. The cruiser fired and missed a second time. A small piece of debris struck the starboard wing as the shuttle passed underneath Taj Mahal. Mat donned the broadscope and witnessed volcanic type eruptions as they passed.

When they emerged from underneath, the sight he most wanted to see greeted him; the faint glow of the wormhole. Between them and the wormhole however, another cruiser blocked their path, but it had ensnared another skylark and seemed distracted by its efforts to drag it in.

Mat pushed the helm over and down sending Skylark 9 into a roll. It was a timely manoeuvre as a jet of what looked like steam shot past. He pulled the helm up again and straightened the roll. They cleared the cruiser and now lined up on an approach vector for the wormhole.

"Skylark 1," murmured Maria almost inaudibly.

"What?"

"I think that's Skylark 1 that's what the ID signal says. I thought they would have made it if any one would have."

Maria shook her head.

"Skylark 1? Isn't that the one Jenny Gold is on?" said Mat.

"I don't know. Who's Jenny Gold?"

Mat pulled on the helm and the shuttle looped around to head back for the cruiser.

"We can't go back!" she exclaimed.

"What weapons has this thing got?"

"None I think," Maria replied. "It's only got the standard cutting laser in the nose. It's not much use in combat."

Mat looked at his control panel, but couldn't see anything resembling a laser control.

"Computer," said Mat. "Indicate where the laser controls are on the pilot's console!"

Although they could understand voice commands skylarks' hyper computers were not fitted to reply verbally.

A small black covering illuminated in front of him. He lifted the flap to reveal the controls underneath. A red light shone advising that the laser was offline.

"Computer, prepare laser for operation!" The red light changed to green indicating that the laser was ready.

Mat felt his anxiety grow as the cruiser loomed before him. Skylark 9 was closing, but too fast. He flicked a switch to change the helm over to HC control.

"Computer bring the ship to within optimal laser cutting range of Skylark 1."

The ship reverberated violently as the computer used maximum reverse thrust to slow the approach.

"They'll web us as well!" cried Maria.

Mat opened the laser port.

"We'll have to take that chance!"

A small light indicated "Optimal laser range achieved".

Mat wasted no time. He targeted the thready material ensnaring Skylark 1 and activated the laser, splitting the web like a knife running through butter.

"Good work Skylark 9," the radio crackled.

"Is everyone alright?" answered Mat.

"No casualties to report," replied the pilot. "We've lost our port engine but are able to compensate. Let's get out of here!"

"How's Jenny Gold?"

No one answered as Skylark 1 accelerated past and headed directly towards the wormhole.

"What about the others?" cried Mat, but still there was no reply.

Three other skylarks left Taj Mahal just as a massive explosion from the mother ship blew the aft end sections away in fragmented chunks. The Taj Mahal was breaking up.

The last skylark of the trio was caught broadside with loose debris. It immediately lost power and vented gases from four different points.

Mat checked the I.D. readout: "Skylark 8".

"Skylark 8 this is 9 what is your status?"

There was no response.

"Computer why are they not answering?"

"Scans indicate that Skylark 8 has lost all power," said the readout. "Communication systems have failed. Life support is at 10% capacity and failing."

"Bring us in to dock with Skylark 8," said Mat.

"Clearance to dock from Skylark 8 has not been granted," said the computer display.

"Over ride requirement for clearance. Approach Skylark 8 to within docking range!"

Computer display: "Manoeuvre inadvisable due to random nature of Skylark 8's trajectory."

"Oh for God's sake!" Mat exclaimed. "Give me manual control of helm!"

Mat eased the joystick to close on Skylark 8. He was not a trained pilot, but if any on board were still alive then he was all the hope they had.

Suddenly, they pitched and stopped. Maria was thrown out of her seat and up against the command chair.

Mat guessed what it was immediately. They were caught; one of the cruisers had cast its web over them and now it was their turn to be hauled in. He tried thrusting forwards, backwards and rolling the ship, but nothing could free them. He cursed with frustration.

"Caught like a bug in a web!"

He looked down at the Taj Mahal. It was speckled with the Mago ships clinging to it. Their lethal occupants had infested every deck. God help anyone aboard her now. His plight would soon be just as desperate though, once Skylark 9 had been pulled inside the ominous cruiser.

Mat's thoughts of survival were rapidly turning to preparing to meet the inevitable doom when, from nowhere, Skylark 1 appeared like a flash into his vision. With deft accuracy it sliced through the binding web in seconds.

"You're back!" was all Mat could say.

"Couldn't expect to leave you all on your own!" cried Jenny cheerfully.

"Jenny! I thought, I mean what? How did…?"

"No time to explain fly boy, we've got some rescuing to do!"

Mat watched as she swung Skylark 1 with brilliant accuracy and docked with the troubled Skylark 8.

"Jenny, you've got one coming in!" cried Mat. "What do you want me to do?"

"Just go home, babe," she replied. "You'll only get into trouble if you hang about."

"I can't just…"

"Go Mat! Otherwise I'll have to rescue you a second time. Take your people home!"

Mat moved his shuttle away from the incoming cruiser and then lined up for the wormhole.

"Computer, prepare for entry into wormhole! Transfer helm to HC control!"

The change was smooth and unnoticeable. Periodically, the HC swept the entrance to the wormhole with a lazdar beam in order to monitor navigational progress, but Mat's attention was elsewhere.

"Jenny, this isn't right!"

"Live for us both, honey!" said Jenny and then comms were cut.

The multiple ships and space flotsam were receding rapidly behind. Mat tried frantically to restore the link and to see No.1 one last time but all he could make out were the huge cruisers and the shape of the stricken Taj Mahal lying there like a dying animal being devoured alive. Flame and explosions continued to rip the mother ship apart and it was impossible to distinguish Jenny's shuttle from all the mayhem.

Mat kept the radio receivers on to listen to the terrified voices of those they were leaving behind. The mouth of the wormhole appeared all round Skylark 9 as the one-sided space battle slipped from view and vision became increasingly obscured.

"God bless and protect you my darling," Mat muttered to himself.

As they slipped into the wormhole, he felt that he was leaving a part of himself behind with Skylark 1. He felt dirty, and it pained him that he was running and leaving behind someone he cared about so deeply. He closed his eyes and uttered a silent prayer, then removed the broadscope hood and sank into the pilot's chair to reflect.

He hadn't noticed Maria leaving the cockpit cabin, but next she was pushing a mug of hot coffee into his hand.

"I thought you might need that," she said with a warming grin.

She recognized his grief as he clutched the drink. He smiled back.

"Thanks," he said.

"Jenny Gold?"

"You know her?"

"You mentioned her earlier," said Maria. "I assumed you had some connection."

"You could say that."

"You feel ashamed."

He felt pierced by the words.

"It's your masculinity wanting to protect her and you couldn't," she continued. "You couldn't do anything to save her and it makes you feel ashamed because you feel you failed as a man."

He said nothing. Maria made him feel raw and vulnerable.

"It's difficult I know, but if she's still alive back there, knowing you made it will give her an incentive to go on living and surviving. You have to go on for her sake."

Mat fought back the urge to cry. Maria could see it in him.

"It doesn't make you less of a man to cry about someone you care about."

"I lost too," she added.

The dam burst and they held each other in grief and anguish as the tears flowed.

"You're English?" Mat snuffled after a while.

"How can you tell?" she blubbed.

"Well the accent is a dead give away, but you're also from the North of England."

"I'm from the North West of England," she replied. "What used to be called Cumbria. I thought I'd lost my northern accent."

"It was a guess," said Mat wiping his eyes. "It's just that you made me a coffee without me asking. I thought that only Northerners did that sort of thing."

"How did you get that bit of knowledge?"

"I know a few English guys and gals. It was something I picked up about their behaviour."

"I have a few Southern English friends who have made cups of tea for me," Maria retorted.

"Yeah, but did you have to ask first?"

Farnhurst appeared in the cockpit.

"How are things, Doc?" said Mat.

"Well, young man," he replied. "Just one more casualty to take care of and… Where are we?"

Mat leaned over to read the nav screen.

"In the wormhole heading for TC1. Computer, what is the ETA to Outpost TC1?

"Just over eight hours," read the screen.

The stabbing in his ribs made him wince as he glanced back at Farnhurst.

"You said you had one more casualty to take care of?"

"Yes," replied the doctor. "You."

CHAPTER TWELVE

"Seven dead?" Mat sighed sitting tentatively on the edge of the couch. "How come security weren't able to take them out?"

"They have tough hides," said the cadet. "The lasers weren't powerful enough. They moved so fast as well."

"Mr. Kemel, I advise you take it easy for a few days," said Farnhurst. "You must give the damaged tissue time to heal."

"Are there any other officers or technicians amongst the escapees?"

"There are two other cadets besides myself, sir," said the cadet, "but they are juniors."

"What's your name?" said Mat.

"I am Cadet Mohammed Salem," the cadet replied smartly and pointed to the name badge on his lapel.

"Of course," said Mat belatedly noticing the badge and wincing again. "What do they call you?"

"My friends call me Ham," he smiled.

Mat stood up briskly and wobbled unsteadily.

"Mr. Kemel, I …" began Farnhurst.

"Yeh, okay doctor," said Mat flinching. "Ordinarily I'd take as much rest as you recommended, but there is no time for that now."

Maria and Farnhurst enlisted Ham to help them set up an emergency clinic.

The small room they used was cramped, but adequate. Three beds were tightly set against the outer bulkhead. A small work surface was cleared and a makeshift cabinet set above, stocked with basic medical supplies. The cabinet could be detached from the bulkhead and used as a carrying case should the need require it.

Two of the beds were soon occupied. One by a man with head and neck trauma he had suffered after being flung to one side by a Mago. He had remained comatose since the incident and Dr. Farnhurst privately expressed concerns for him.

In the other bed, lay a young woman with a suspected spinal injury. She had been knocked to the deck by someone fleeing the attacking Mago and had landed with her back across a small upturned table. She remained sedated and under observation.

"I have to get back to the cockpit," said Mat.

"I'm sure the HC can handle things," said Farnhurst.

"The Hyper Computer should not be left unattended whilst passing through a wormhole."

"Maria's up there presently. I'm sure Maria can oversee perfectly well."

"She's not pilot trained."

Mat tried to hurry. Giddiness slowed his movements and a stabbing pain in his head brought him to a halt.

"Well who else can fly it better in a wormhole than an HC?" replied Farnhurst moving to grip his arm.

Mat shrugged him off and stumbled towards the door.

"I have to get back out there."

"You're in no fit state Mr. Kemel," said Farnhurst blocking his path.

Mat felt his hackles rise.

"Doctor, not so long ago you were about to have me thrown in the loony bin. I'm sick to death of people, especially medical staff, ordering me about and trying to restrain me. There is still an ongoing danger. Someone needs to be at the controls. So please stand aside!"

Farnhurst stood aside reluctantly and watched as Mat hobbled off.

A burly, overweight man almost collided with him on the way out. The man gave one look up and down at the slighter build of Mat and then turned to Farnhurst.

"Doctor," he said pleadingly, "those carcasses are stinking, let's dump them before the whole ship goes down with some kind of alien plague."

"Mr. Sanderson," replied Farnhurst. "They may be unpleasant, but they are an important biological find. We have to take them back with us for scientific research. We'll have to freeze store them for now."

"There are no such facilities for freeze storing on skylark shuttles," replied Sanderson in a more surly manner. "Doctor, I must inform you that as Chairman of Skylark 9 Survivors' Committee we consider the carcasses to be a serious hazard to human health and must insist that they are disposed of forthwith."

Mat stopped in the alleyway and returned at hearing the man.

"Survivors' committee?" he said incredulously.

"That is correct," replied Sanderson straightening himself. "If you don't mind, this matter is between the doctor and the committee."

Mat could not help himself.

"We've only been off the ship about three hours and you've formed a committee?"

"Of course," retorted Sanderson with some irritation. "This work force prides itself on its efficiency."

"Doctor, aren't there plasticising guns on board?" said Mat.

"Our members will not go near the creatures without proper protective clothing," Sanderson stated.

"Didn't you go 'near' them to come here?"

"Only out of necessity."

"Look, we'll be out of the wormhole in about four hours," said Mat. "Surely you can wait that long?"

Sanderson swung around and his eyes flashed. He stood threateningly close to Mat to glower at him.

"I'm afraid not and who the hell asked your opinion anyway?"

"Well, I am or was the Science Officer on Mercury 4, so I guess that should give me some say."

"I think Mr. Kemel is correct," said Farnhurst.

"There's your answer," Mat said looking up into Sanderson's face.

"That is not good enough," said Sanderson raising himself up to his full height and peering menacingly down at Mat.

"Look, I'm not in the best of shapes to slug it out with you right now," said Mat pointing at the man's chest, "so please don't come out with all this macho shit."

Sanderson was clearly offended by the remark. He burned with unconcealed hostility, then leaned forward to speak right into Mat's face. Mat smelt the foulness of his breath, but did not flinch.

"I will go back to the hold and tell the committee that the carcasses are to be removed."

"I don't think that was what I said," retorted Mat.

"The committee has decided," said the big man and moved off.

"Just one thing," said Mat. "If you won't go near them without protective suits, then who's going to do the removing?"

Mat saw Sanderson's fists clench.

"That is your problem, Science Officer!"

"Where did you find a gorilla like that one?" said Mat when he'd gone.

In the cockpit, Maria helped Mat climb back into the pilot's seat. He thanked her.

"Let me know when Sanderson is in the hold again. There should be a viewer to monitor him."

"He's there now," Maria replied.

"Good! Computer, seal the cargo hold from the rest of the ship. Allow no access from it to the forward section without this code authorization. That should give Mr. Sanderson and co something to discuss at committee."

He typed in a personal code and entered the data.

"How can you have authority?" said Maria. "You're not the recognized pilot."

"Earlier, I assumed command," he explained. "That was sufficient protocol."

"I didn't hear you say anything."

"I typed it in when I did the pre-flight checks."

Mat felt haunted by thoughts of not staying behind to wait for Jenny. He fought to clear his mind and took his time scanning readouts and gauges. He wondered how much quicker a trained ESO pilot would have been.

"Long range emitters are fried! Well, apart from short range comms, it looks like we're unable to talk to anyone," he said. "Wait, what's this?"

Maria moved closer to see what he was looking at.

"What's wrong?" she said.

"We've got a bogey on our tail!"

"I beg your pardon?" Maria said in puzzlement.

"I don't mean a lump of snot hanging off your nose. I mean there's a Mago on our rear and gaining."

He took a few seconds to assess the data.

"God damn! It's one of those cruisers! Looking at the calculations, we had a two hour head start, but it'll be on us in less than an hour."

"Why are they following us?" asked Maria. "Why did they take so long to give chase?"

"Who knows? Maybe they decided to give us a sporting chance. We're going to have to push this crate to its limits if we're to have a chance at all of making it."

Mat eagerly studied his readouts.

"Computer, can you increase velocity beyond maximum limits?" said Mat.

The computer gave its answer on the screen:

"An HC may not take a spacecraft beyond its operating capacity. The manoeuvre can only be performed whilst in manual control."

"Okay give me manual control," said Mat. The shuttle slewed slightly as Mat orientated himself. He pushed the throttle levers forward, but the velocity altered very little.

"This isn't working!"

"Perhaps the limits are still in force," suggested Maria.

"Good thinking! Computer remove safety limits to engines."

The computer replied on screen: "Override functions cannot be operated by voice."

Mat swore but then apologized after remembering Maria was present. He typed in the command and then entered his own personal code. The screen flashed red, warning that safety protocols had been removed.

"This is Sanderson here!" cried an angry voice. "Open the access door at once!"

"What the hell?" said Mat with amazement. "How the hell did he get patched in here?"

"There are technicians on board," said Maria nonchalantly. "They probably hooked in to the power cables and used them to carry a signal to a speaker."

"I'm impressed, I didn't expect you to have such a quirky mind."

"I specialize in electronics."

"It's going to be a tedious next hour or so," said Mat wearily. "You couldn't fix me up with some more coffee could you, please?"

"I'm not your servant you know," Maria said with mock indignity. "However, as you're sick, I'll make allowances."

"Thank you nurse. Oh, and see if you can get that cadet, Ham, up here!"

Maria left to carry out her errands.

"I suggest you let us out of here!" exclaimed a red faced Sanderson. "You're in enough trouble as it is, Kemel."

"Kemel?" muttered Mat. "How did they get to know my name?"

"You'll get more than sectioned when we get out of here!" Sanderson ranted on.

"Enough of this crap!" said Mat and turned on the intercom to the cargo hold.

"Mr. Sanderson and co, I suggest you shut up and cooperate if you wish to survive this little trip."

"And I suggest you let us out of here immediately!" roared Sanderson.

"Not a chance! I am in command of this ship and unless you want to find out what it's like trying to breathe in a vacuum then I insist you sit quietly for the rest of the trip."

"How dare you threaten us!" raged Sanderson.

The hubbub of other angry voices could be heard in the background.

"Mr. Sanderson," continued Mat calmly. "You have already established that I am to be sectioned which means I am mentally unstable. I have control of life support and can open the cargo bay doors at any time I like. If you annoy me I may just lose what little bit of self control I have and do it just for the hell of it. Don't tempt me!"

For once Sanderson was stumped for words. His comms channel flicked on for a couple of seconds and then went dead. Mat turned off his own intercom and blew a sigh of relief.

The nav display readings showed thruster power to be operating at 110%, but the instant diagnostic readings were still only in the yellow. He checked the Mago vessel.

It was still gaining.

"Here's all or nothing," he muttered and removed the limit bar on the throttle lever, then steadily pushed it all the way forward to beyond maximum.

Ham arrived and Mat motioned him to sit in the co-pilot's seat.

"I assume you've passed your basic pilot training certificate?"

"Yes Sir," Ham nodded.

"Well then, you keep an eye on any gauges and tell me if you see anything abnormal or in the red."

They watched the diagnostic dial as it edged towards the red zone.

"What happens when it gets to the red?" said Ham.

"I don't know," replied Mat. "I've never been there before."

Coffee arrived. Mat set the helm to auto pilot and left the pilot's seat to sit elsewhere.

"Sure you can handle things?"

"Excuse me, sir?" said Ham politely. "Shouldn't you stay here?"

"Why? There's nothing more to do for now except worry. That's what you're here for. You're ESO, I'm not. You're certified, I'm not."

He tapped his skull and winked at Maria as if his last comment was meant as a joke.

"But what do we do when it gets to the red?" complained Ham.

"Worry some more," answered Mat. "If that thing catches us, it'll be the least of our problems."

Mat sat in the nav seat and held his head in his hands.

"Can't we ditch something that will slow the aliens up?" said Ham.

"You mean like Sanderson? There's nothing here that'd have any more effect than a gnat on a windshield."

"So, you're not an ESO officer?" said Maria.

"That's correct," replied Mat. "I'm what you might call "under contract". It means I come under ESO rules, but I have no jurisdiction when taking on command decisions. In other words, when people are falling off the perch, I'm the last one to be captain."

"So, how come you've taken charge here?" she asked.

"Lack of anyone else, I suppose. Someone's got to do it."

As the minutes passed, Mat and Maria exchanged stories with occasional interjections from Ham. Eventually though, Ham's concerns about the engines caused Mat to resume his position in the pilot's seat, but sharp rib pains kept him reminded of his injuries.

"Let's see now," he said assessing the situation. "I reckon we've probably got about ten minutes before we lose everything and even if we don't, the Mago will still catch us in twenty.

It's nearly an hour before we leave the wormhole. Most of the other skylarks are approaching the exit mouth now."

He paused, staring at the forward scanner screen.

"What the hell is going on?" he said with amazement. "There's something entering the wormhole from the outpost end!"

"Is that bad?" said Maria.

"Well I don't think it will affect the stability of the wormhole," explained Mat. "But when you're being chased by the devil, the last thing you want is someone blocking your path."

"It's coming at us!" exclaimed Ham.

"I'm taking the helm back into manual control!" declared Mat.

"But Mr. Kemel sir, the engines are going critical!" Ham warned.

"Mat! The name's Mat!"

The object approached at high velocity. Mat pushed the helm down. The ship lurched and closed on the wormhole side. One touch would mean disaster. The oncoming object whipped by in less than a blink and was gone. Mat fought to get the ship back to the middle of the wormhole.

"Did you get a chance to ID it?" said Mat.

"It was an ESO maintenance cutter," answered Ham.

Mat pulled the broadscope helmet over his head to see what was happening astern.

"What the hell's it ….Uhhh!" a brilliant glare seared his vision and blinded him. He ripped off the helmet, but could barely see enough to recognize the warning gauges blinking red all over. Skylark 9 rocked as the starboard engine exploded.

"The wormhole is destabilizing!" screamed Mat. "I can't see! I can't hold course! We're going to hit the side!"

"Let the HC take over!" yelled Ham.

"Are you kidding?"

"Trust me!"

Mat moved the throttle back to nominal position and re-engaged computer control.

"Okay, it's your call!"

The HC immediately shut down the port engine. The ship rolled and spun careering towards destruction.

"My God we're going to die!" screamed Maria.

"Have faith!" replied Ham calmly.

The HC waited until the ship's stern was closest to the wormhole's side and then initiated a two second burst with the port engine. The distance to the side held as the engine shutdown again.

"The wormhole's collapsing!" cried Ham.

"Where's the Mago?" said Maria.

Ham studied the scanners. "It's gone! Destroyed!"

A gigantic shock wave struck Skylark 9 from behind hurtling the ship towards the tunnel exit. The panel controls flashed warnings of imminent depressurization. The HC initiated another thrust. The port engine came on line again and thrusted for another three seconds before shutting down once more.

"We're out of control with no engines and spinning like crazy," said Mat hitting the general emergency switch. "Are there enough suits for everyone?"

"On Taj Mahal there were," shouted Maria. "But not on here. There wasn't time to get everything."

The stern struck first ripping it from the fuselage. Then the port wing hit and it too sheared off. Everyone and everything, not secured was hurtled about like carrots in a blender as the ship whirled wildly.

Ham strapped in and gripped the armrests as if he was going through some crazy fair ground ride. He watched Mat flung like a rag doll against the deckhead and knocked senseless as his head struck hard on an overhead panel.

Maria, ghostly pale, glowered in complete discomfort, spewed and passed out, stomach contents splattering everywhere including across the right side of Ham's face.

PART TWO:
CHARON BASE

CHAPTER ONE

Commodore Maximus Leopold Vogel stood, feet apart, hands clasped behind his back and gazed out of his office window. He was a romantic and had always savoured the view of Pluto rising over the Charon landscape. He preferred the plain view of Pluto to some artificial and hologramatic wall display of the home world.

For years debate had raged over whether Pluto should retain the classification of being called a planet. For those stationed on Charon Base, which numbered just over three hundred people, opinion of Pluto and its co-planet Charon fell mainly into two categories. There were those who regarded them as forbidding, desolate worlds and those who could see charm, mystique and even beauty in the arrangements of the planetary surfaces.

Vogel stared blankly at Pluto, deep in thought, as its dark disk hung with the faintest of light falling on its surface from a far off sun. It presented a ghostly and shadowy image in the black sky.

As with many other barren worlds, Charon's terrain was scarred by the impact of thousands of meteorites that had fallen over countless millennia. Fissures from ancient volcanic activity had added to the vista, creating mountain ranges and valleys.

In the last few million years the cooling core had caused considerable contraction and had folded the surface giving the plains a wrinkled appearance.

In the grand scheme of things, man had only just arrived. Charon Base had been established and commissioned only fifteen years ago. The base had been constructed largely from minerals found on Charon, but its survival was still dependent on shipping energy creating materials from the inner worlds.

Earth Space Vessel Mariana, on its way from the Alpha Centauri system to Earth, was due to arrive in three hours time to collect him. Vogel had been scheduled for a personal interview on Lunar 2 in front of the Earth Space Organization Council about his performance and the operational efficiency of the base.

Lunar 2 had been lauded as mankind's first off world wonder and the essential stepping stone for establishing an empire amongst the stars. Vogel would normally enjoy such a visit to Earth's primary space station, however, he was tired of the bullshit of bureaucracy that plagued his job these days and was more looking forward to the eight weeks of leave that would follow his interview.

He felt a touch of sadness about leaving Charon. During his two years of command he had become accustomed to Charon being his home from home; a world far away from the hustle and bustle of Earth.

He was not expecting to be returning after his leave and it had been strongly hinted by senior officials that Captain Jonathan Bridely, currently the base's Deputy Commodore, would be assuming the post of full Commodore.

Vogel was not keen on Bridely, an austere man, he saw as wanting to succeed for himself rather than do what was right. Bridely believed that rules were there to be obeyed and that chaos came about when they weren't but, what Vogel disliked mostly about him was his arrogance and vision of his own self importance. Rules were for others. Bridely believed that those in power had a right to privilege. It was one of his definitions of power.

In the eyes of the ESO Council however, it was believed that people like Capt. Bridely were key to increased efficiency and productivity in space exploration and exploitation.

Vogel's office buzzer sounded, waking him from his thoughts.

"Come in!" he bellowed and turned away from the window to move to the centre of the room. The office door slid open. Lieutenant Carol Young entered carrying a batch of electronic files in her hands.

"The reports you asked for, Sir," she said.

"Oh yes," he replied. "Thank you."

Carol Young was the shortest person in the whole of ESO. In her socks she stood at 4 feet 10 inches (147.3 cm). But for all her stature, she was very talented in many ways.

In her teens, she had won gold and silver medals for gymnastics and now, in her mid twenties, had applied her agility to off world space development. She was one of the fastest space walkers on the base and had been assigned as Officer-in-charge of the base's surface rescue team.

She held her dark hair in a ponytail. Her facial features were symmetrically apportioned and, with her broad mouth and dainty nose, she was much admired for her looks by most men on the base.

Vogel was old enough to be her father, but he could still appreciate aesthetically pleasing looks in a young woman. He found it difficult to suppress his paternal instincts toward her and sometimes had to overcompensate in order not to display favouritism.

The files thudded onto his desk as she unloaded her burden.

"Will that be all sir?" she said standing to attention.

He took a moment to study her expression before replying.

"You're looking a bit, err, grey, Lieutenant," he smiled.

"Sir?"

"Have you been taking sufficient time in the solarium?"

"I think so, Sir. It's not the same as natural sunlight though."

"Natural sunlight can be very damaging to the skin," he replied. "Besides, you won't get much out here on Charon. The solarium was developed to produce the correct proportions of solar radiation for our needs. You should…"

He realized he was starting to lecture her and stopped before he got in too deep. He turned towards the window to once more gaze at the view.

"I'm going to miss this place," he went on. "It's not everyone's cup of tea I know, but it has a lot of good points."

"Have they told you where you are to be posted next?" she said.

He shot a smirk at her.

"So the rumours of my leaving for good are true," he exhaled. "No, I expect they know, but prefer to keep me guessing."

An awkward silence fell. Vogel was not sure whether to continue talking or to get stuck in with the files.

Lt. Young stood patiently waiting to be dismissed.

"Err, you may go, Lieutenant," he said with a little cough of embarrassment.

"Thank you sir," she replied, saluted, swivelled and left in military fashion.

He looked at the mini mountain of documents on the desk and sighed, then sat down and began to wade through each one. There were reports on ore extraction and work productivity levels carried out on Charon and Pluto; the number of ships passing by and using the base; and status reports on the new colony being established in the Alpha Centauri system.

The call buzzer sounded.

"Vogel!" he answered.

"Commodore, Control Centre, Sir," said the voice. "The latest transmission from the Tau Ceti system has just been received."

Glad to be saved from admin work, Vogel replied cheerfully: "I'll be right there!"

Control Centre was spacious and circular, 30 metres in diameter. The domed roof was made of a molecularly complex material known as Pleximglass that allowed its opacity to be adjusted as desired. Below the dome, hung a transparent concave ceiling where light could be reflected downwards in a diffuse form. It meant there were no glaring reflections of lamps that would interfere with the view of the heavens and yet hardly any of the light provided was lost upwards.

Acoustics were excellent, a shout would be heard only a little more than a pin dropping. It was an eerie experience for those visiting for the first time and took some getting used to. Most functions were automated and controlled by Robert, the base's hyper computer.

Only five people were in Control Centre when Vogel entered. Lt. Young was sitting at an astronomical data console on the far side, but Vogel was interested in the station manned by Second Lieutenant Amos.

Vogel placed his hands on the console to read what Amos had on display.

"Do you want it put in the daily Charon Bulletin?" asked Amos.

"Let me read it first," replied Vogel.

Amos leaned back in his seat in a casual manner. He glided his hands over his shaven scalp and clasped them at the back.

"Hmm," Vogel remarked. "So, Mercury 4 may have found our lost probe."

"Hardly, Sir," said Amos. "I wouldn't call a bolt "finding it"."

"No, of course not, but it's on the scent and I think to have found anything at all is quite remarkable."

"So what should I put in the Bulletin?"

"You're keen on your Bulletin aren't you?" commented Vogel. "Do you wish you'd been a reporter rather than a computer boffin?"

"Mmm, not really," said Amos thoughtfully. "Computers have always been fave. Reporting is just a hobby."

"You should get out more often, my boy," smiled Vogel patting his shoulder approvingly. "Amos, you should know by now, as long as you're not going to liable someone, you can put what you like in the Bulletin."

He patted Amos on the shoulder again then stood up straight and began his customary and, what would probably be, his last ever tour of Control Centre. Everything was immaculately clean and functioning at optimum efficiency as it had been when he had taken over as base commander. He had complete confidence in Robert's management of the base systems, although at times it did make him feel surplus to requirements.

"Latest ETA on the Mariana indicates she will be arriving in two hours time, Sir," said a young man at a console as Vogel passed.

Vogel glanced at his watch.

"Thank you Graham. That's thirty minutes earlier than scheduled," he moaned. "Better let Captain Bridely know."

"Aye Sir," said Graham.

"Err, where is Captain Bridely?"

"One moment please," Graham spoke to his console: "Robert, show us the location of Captain Bridely!"

Instantly, a map of Charon's surface surrounding the base came on screen and a flashing yellow blob of light indicated Captain Bridely.

"Captain Bridely is on a surface walk approximately two kilometres from the base," said Graham. "Should I recall him, Sir?"

"No, that won't be necessary son," replied Vogel. "Just patch him the information."

Vogel returned to his office. He had hoped to hand over any last issues and at least say goodbye to Bridely before he left. However, not meeting him would allow the opportunity of avoiding any last minute unpleasantness. Even so, there was still plenty of time for Bridely to return, and he knew Bridely would probably be only too delighted to witness him finally leaving.

Six months ago, there had been a mining tragedy where one man had died and another had been seriously injured. The nozzle of a cutting tool had frozen causing a fuel cell to explode. The incident had been investigated by Captain Bridely who had criticized the work unit for not checking their equipment properly before use.

Vogel felt that Bridely had not been thorough enough in his inquiries and had been too ready to blame human error for the accident. He had engaged Young and Amos to carry out a separate investigation. They had found that the nozzle was a component of a batch of faulty equipment that had somehow been reintroduced to work units. Captain Bridely had been the authorizing officer and corruption was suspected but never proven.

Vogel had privately reprimanded Bridely, but higher authorities had ideas for Bridely and Vogel's confidential report got buried. The relationship between the two men had always been awkward, but from then on there was unconcealed hostility between them. Bridely's ego had been wounded by Vogel's stance and he would never forgive him for that.

Vogel poured himself a coffee and sat down to plough through more admin. The door buzzer sounded.

"Jesus!" he cursed. "Is there no peace?"

He changed the door opacity and could see Carol Young with Amos.

"Come in!" he called.

They trooped in and stood before his desk.

"Commodore Vogel," said Carol. "It is of urgent importance that you accompany us to Control Centre immediately."

"But I've just come from there," Vogel complained. "What's wrong?"

"I'm sorry sir, but something has just occurred that needs your attention right away."

"But what is it?"

"It's easier if you see for yourself."

Vogel became worried and followed them back to Control.

When he entered, the centre was in complete darkness.

"What in the blazes!" he exclaimed.

The lights returned and there was a roar.

"Surprise!" shouted over a hundred people.

Vogel was stunned.

"We got as many as we could to present you with a going away gift," said Amos.

With that he offered Vogel a crystalline statue of a sailboat. There was huge applause all round as the gift was accepted.

"This was carved from Charon rock and hopefully will be a lasting memory of this place," said Carol.

"I, I, I'm stunned," Vogel stammered. "I-I'm really grateful to you for going to all this trouble. I can only say thank you for such a wonderful piece of memorabilia. But I have one thing that I will take with me that is more precious than even this."

He swallowed and everyone waited. His eyes glistened with held back tears as he searched as many faces as he could.

"It is the memory of each and every one of you that I will keep here."

He touched his breast.

"For the rest of my days."

Amos took photos of Vogel and Carol with the trophy and also of Vogel and as many others as he could get in.

"It's for the Bulletin," he explained. "And I expect it will annoy old Bridey like hell."

Vogel laughed aloud at the thought. They chinked glasses and drank to the future and to Commodore Vogel's longevity.

CHAPTER TWO

ESV Mariana darted out of the Alpha Centauri wormhole and lined up for final approach to Charon Base. Commodore Vogel watched on the dome screen in Control as the sleek vessel manoeuvred and closed.

As it swung above the landing pad, one of the doors in Control slid open and Captain Bridely burst in. He spoke loudly with a perfect Oxford English accent.

"My apologies for being late, Commodore," he puffed, trying to regain his breath. "I must say, there are some fascinating rock formations the other side of Bailey's Ridge. It's a pity you won't be seeing them again."

Vogel eyed him briefly and noted his neatly pressed uniform with it's pristine, gold insignia embroidered on the shoulders and the lapels. Bridely followed the other's gaze and stood with a gape to his mouth. His shiny and greased dark hair never had a strand out of place.

"I know the ones you mean," replied Vogel. "There's one that looks just like a horse's head and another that they call the saddle."

He held back the compulsion to say "horse's ass". There was no point getting drawn into a row in front of base staff at this stage.

"Yes," Bridely nodded. "Wonderful. It's as if they've been crafted."

"They were," Vogel noted the surprise in Bridely's face. "By one of the technicians overseeing the base's construction. Did you see the little dog as well?"

"No," said Bridely in a subdued tone.

It was cheap, but Vogel felt a certain satisfaction at exposing Bridely's ignorance. Bridely had been here for 18 months and had learned remarkably little about the background of the base.

They watched in silence as the Mariana descended and settled onto the landing pads with minimum thrust.

"Oh, that's a computer landing!" remarked Vogel disappointedly. "I'd have thought the pilot would have had a go himself."

Vogel turned to Lt. Young. "How long before take off?"

"She's scheduled for 1800, Sir," replied Young. "That's just over an hour."

"What's the big rush?" said Vogel.

"She's a crew transport," said Young. "They normally don't like to hang around."

"That's the trouble these days," moaned Vogel. "Nobody wants to take time and enjoy anything. They've all got to rush off to eke out their little existences in some hovel they call home."

Vogel realized he was rambling on and stalked off to his quarters to await the visiting pilot and any officers that chose to call by.

His cases stood inside the entrance. He switched on the wall TV to watch the latest Solar News broadcast. Even though it was being transmitted through the trans solar conduit, it was still an hour behind real time.

The Servants of God (SOG) had devastated a part of Inner London when they had detonated a bomb inside a mega block. The report suggested that as many as five hundred people were expected to have died with hundreds more injured or missing. Vogel had heard of such a group, but they had never carried out quite such a devastating attack as this before now.

An earthquake in the Pacific, 100 kilometres off of California had produced a tsunami that had smashed into the American West Coast. Sea defences had been breached. There had been wide spread destruction and many lives lost. A fault with the disaster early warning system had meant no broadcast was made. By the time most people received information of the approaching tsunami, the coast was already being battered. Few had a chance to escape.

The door buzzer rang. Vogel held down a button on his desk and the door turned transparent. He could see a slimly built young man in pilot's uniform on the other side.

"Enter!" he bellowed.

The news reports continued as the door slid open and the young pilot stepped inside and saluted.

"Lieutenant Delware reporting, sir!"

"Did you dock yourself, son?"

"Err no, sir," Delware said a little apprehensively. "The HC did it."

"Hmm, disappointing," said Vogel gruffly. "I had hoped to see you take the opportunity to practice docking on manual."

"Safety regulations, sir," replied Delware. "Hyper computers are to carry out docking manoeuvres unless special dispensation has been granted for training purposes."

"What the hell...." Vogel stopped before he could embarrass himself by revealing that he was out of date with the regulations. He remembered the report after there had been a succession of shuttle craft crashes and the loss of a couple of deep space transports where human error had been blamed.

Directive 2105-0033 had been issued shortly after 15 people had been killed in one such accident. All docking was to be done under HC control. Pilots were to be regularly sent on simulator and refresher courses in order to keep their skills up to scratch.

The news reports were still coming in.

"Okay," sighed Vogel, "lead on, Macduff!"

Delware puzzled at the remark.

"It's from Shakespeare," Vogel explained. "It means lead the way. Have you not read Shakespeare?"

Delware shook his head and picked up Vogel's bags without replying.

When Vogel reached the door, he opened his mouth to tell the vide screen to shut down, but then saw the next report come up.

"A leaked report from ESO has been received of how one man died and another was injured in an incident on Charon. The report has been kept secret for several weeks and suspicions of a cover up have been voiced by many of those concerned with safety issues on the base. The commander of the base, Commodore Vogel, has been recalled for questioning over the incident and is expected to be relieved of duty as a result."

Vogel erupted in fury.

"How the hell did that get on the news?" he roared.

The pilot was clearly perturbed by the outburst. Vogel jabbed at his call button.

"Send Captain Bridely to my quarters immediately!"

"Should I carry on to the ship, Commodore?"

Vogel fought to control his temper and glowered at the young man.

"I'll wait outside," Delware added meekly.

He met Bridely in the doorway and saluted him as he passed.

"Have you seen the news?" Vogel started before Bridely had gotten through the door.

"No, I haven't," said Bridely smugly.

"They've come out with the mining accident. After six months!" cried Vogel. Bridely muttered something inaudible.

"What's more! They've pointed the finger of blame at me!" he snarled.

"Oh," said Bridely wearing a fake smile. "Well, as base commander, such things are ultimately your responsibility."

Vogel's eyes bored into Bridely's face as he tried to measure the weight of what he had said, but his expression remained flat, and he suspected that underneath all his smugness, Bridely was laughing loudly.

"You wouldn't happen to have some knowledge of this, would you Jonathan?" said Vogel trying to contain his emotions.

"Commodore, I do not engage in such petty politics as timing your departure with the news of an unfortunate error of judgement."

"Well, I think by that remark it seems you knew something was going on."

"I resent that comment!" said Bridely with a raised voice.

"Especially if it's the truth!" retorted Vogel. The door buzzer sounded.

"Yes!" yelled Vogel angrily.

The pilot entered again.

"Sir, I apologize for interrupting," said Delware, "but we are on schedule to take off in less than half an hour."

"Can't you bloody well wait five minutes?" bellowed Vogel.

Delware started to apologize, but Vogel held up his hand to stop him.

"Very well," moaned Vogel. "I'll be along in a minute."

"I'll take your cases and wait for you at Mariana," said Delware.

"Thank you," said Vogel with controlled venom. "I won't be long."

After the pilot had left, Vogel closed the gap until he was nose to nose with Bridely.

"Something is going on," he said. "It feels like no one is in control anymore. You are just a cheap opportunist, Bridely. Something is happening to ESO command and I do not like it."

"You're sounding paranoiac," said Bridely flippantly.

"There have been too many subtle changes. ESO is not what it was. When I get back, I intend to find out what really is going on. I have new data that, once it gets out, will blow this whole thing apart."

"What data?" challenged Bridely.

Vogel leaned forward on his knuckles and met Bridely's gaze squarely.

"Things are not what they seem," he said slowly. "ESO is being taken over by somebody or something. I intend to get to the bottom of it and find out what is really going on. I will expose the truth!"

Bridely grinned wryly, but said nothing. The two men eyed each other as if the other was carrying a dagger.

"You are history," Bridely said eventually. He turned away and gave an almost triumphant smirk. "You know nothing."

"That is another admission in itself," retorted Vogel. "I know a lot more than you think!"

Mariana was primed and ready for take off by the time Vogel boarded her. Bridely did not accompany him to the ship, but watched from Control.

Most of the passengers on board were returnees from Alpha Centauri. There were just three from Charon Base. Vogel sat alone and plugged his ear phones into a 'music only' channel. He tried to relax, but was agitated by the thought of how an element of malice had crept into ESO. He wondered if he really was becoming paranoiac as Bridely had suggested, but the look on Bridely's face at the end of their exchange betrayed some deep inner secret.

Vogel had been a loyal and dedicated servant of ESO all his working life. In a few hours, he would be at Lunar 2 and answering press questions. His leave would have to wait. He had to find out what was happening to the organization but, where would he start? All he had was a handful of suggestions and hunches, but he could sense when something was wrong. No doubt he was more than likely to be declared mad or bad if he asked the wrong questions to the wrong people. He closed his eyes in an attempt at sleep.

Watching the Mariana disappear into the conduit to Earth, drew a smile of satisfaction from Capt. Bridely. He was now effectively base commander. His elevation from the rank of Deputy Base Commodore to Base Commodore would be a formality. He thought it wise to remain with his old title just for a short while so as to avoid accusations of being presumptuous. He would start with a complete tour of the base, just to show his face and let the inhabitants know that he was the new boss now.

He made his way to the Base Commodore's office where, less than an hour before, he had had his stand up row with Vogel. He inspected the décor and shook his head with disapproval, then sat down and logged into the computer.

"Robert, put on line the ESO's new build star ships!"

Instantly a list appeared on his computer screen. He filtered out the freight and passenger carrying vessels and soon was left with four military ships that were nearing completion. He ran through the specs of each one and noted when they were due to be delivered.

"Robert, give me a secure channel to Lunar 2. I want no recording of this transmission. All log references to the communication are for my eyes only. Acknowledge acceptance of these conditions!"

"Conditions accepted," said Robert in a calm baritone voice. "Secure channel available. Please enter personal code to activate."

"Robert, when I activate this channel, you will cease to monitor this room or this channel until I have instructed you otherwise! Acknowledge acceptance of these conditions!"

"Conditions accepted," said Robert.

When he was satisfied that no one was eavesdropping, he clicked a small box on his screen that said "Connect".

ESV Mariana left the conduit with the usual effect of seeming to appear out of nowhere and began its approach to Lunar 2.

Lunar 2, the most prestigious space station ever built, orbited Earth like a second moon. It even had its own history museum detailing and holding artifacts concerning the construction of the first world space station more than a century before. The historical and interactive displays were hugely popular exhibits for tourists. The station had been the number one off world attraction since it had opened for operations nearly twenty years before.

Lunar 2 was not just a monument to space construction, it was also home to almost a million people and man's first metropolis in space. Control over world communications, solar radiation, and regulating global temperature were just a few of its contributions to the welfare of mankind and planet Earth.

As a passenger, Vogel could view the station on his seat monitor, but he much preferred to see it with the naked eye. The real sight was far more awe-inspiring. He strained to peer through the porthole for just a glimpse of the massive station.

Mariana adjusted its course and then, there it was, a huge ovoid shape sparkling with lights and activity. The jewel and heart of man's future space empire; Earth's second moon, Lunar 2.

Its mass filled the view ports as Mariana drew closer. Other ships: maintenance scutters, shuttles, explorers and freight transports were docking or undocking and orbiting the station continuously like bees servicing a hive.

Two military escorts approached. They were relatively small 2-man vessels and it looked at one stage that collision with one of them was imminent, but then it pulled away and clear. Vogel presumed it was satisfied with Mariana's authenticity.

Bay doors opened and Mariana entered Dock 2 to berth. All went smoothly and without hitch.

Within a few minutes there was a brief judder and thunk as the docking clamps engaged and Mariana was secure.

As the airlock doors opened, Vogel spotted his cases waiting for him at the end of the gangway. When he took his first step on to the station's deck, he found to his surprise, there were only four news reporters to greet him. He had expected there to be a posse.

They made straight for him and immediately began bombarding him with all kinds of awkward questions. He remained tight lipped and unperturbed and walked swiftly to the nearest available transport car. Inside, silence reigned supreme as the door closed.

The small, automated runabout vehicle ran on magnetic strips under the deck. Vogel read from his briefing pad details of the quarters that had been assigned to him and asked the cab to take him there. The on board computer verbally acknowledged, and the vehicle set off at a modest running speed away from the troublesome reporters.

It turned into a tiny, enclosed bay. Doors closed behind and the cab locked itself into position with a few clicks and whirrs and then was injected into the transportation tube system.

Vogel did not care to know the kind of speed the car travelled at. It worried him to think about it. If he became aware he feared it might put him off travelling in it ever again.

In spite of the vastness of the station, it didn't take many minutes for him to reach his destination. The car decelerated almost imperceptibly, then turned neatly into another small bay before emerging once more onto a walkway.

It drove for several metres, turned a corner and there, outside a residential door, stood over thirty reporters.

"A number of persons are obstructing the normal parking position, sir," said the computer in a friendly voice. "Would you like to alight early or would you prefer another destination?"

"Err no," answered Vogel swallowing at the prospect of having to run a gauntlet. "Here will do fine."

The car slowed to a halt. "My apologies sir, for failing to deliver you to your requested destination."

Vogel pressed the door button. "That's fine. Thanks for the ride."

Damn, he was being courteous to a computer!

He stood erect, and stiffly walked towards the mob. The reporters swarmed around him with their numerous, unanswerable questions. They jostled and bumped to get a glimpse, but he kept his cool, said little, and pushed his way towards his residence and hopeful safety.

Something bit him. It felt like a sharp pinprick on the back of his head. He raised a hand to touch the spot. He looked at his fingers and, to his surprise, found blood. Dizziness overtook him, then the world around him faded as he fell to the deck, dead.

PART THREE:

THE OUTPOST

CHAPTER ONE

Outpost TC1 revolved constantly. It was not that it needed to in order to create artificial gravity, that function was taken care of by the grav generator at the heart of the station. The revolutions were more for the psychological nourishment of the four crew.

The changing background of stars as the station slowly spun gave some kind of semblance of night and day as it completed one revolution every 24 hours. At this distance both Sol and Tau Ceti were but very bright stars, but the timing of the revolutions was such that Sol would appear in the centre portal of the station's sun lounge at 1200 every day.

Being located between two star systems, there was no real daytime, dawn or dusk, just perpetual cold and darkness. The fusion reactor provided almost limitless supplies of power and energy, and was more than adequate for the station's inhabitants.

Although small by comparison to the metropolis station, Lunar 2 orbiting Earth, the interior of the outpost was still huge. Its botanic and agricultural gardens produced far more fresh vegetables and herbs than could ever be consumed by the inhabitants. In fact, most of the produce was preserved and packed ready to supply any spacecraft that would soon be passing to or from the Tau Ceti system.

It was a lonely existence, but not at all monotonous. There was always some system to overhaul or crop to tend to or astronomical research to conduct. Nevertheless, it was the kind of life best suited to those seeking peace and solitude and not at all for socialites.

Earth Space Organization maintained the policy that a supply vessel would visit every 50 days or so and, when it did, it would bring a relief crewmember to join and take one back to Charon base. A posting to TC1 therefore, meant a 200 day stint for each person.

When the Taj Mahal had passed by several months ago, there had been no stopping at TC1. The ship had dropped off a domestic container carrying personal items for the crew and collected a food consignment in return. Mail was usually sent electronically on a carrier wave through the wormhole to the Sol system, but it was still a pleasing old custom to receive a quaint handwritten letter. It gave the reading of it a much more personalized touch.

Although only four manned TC1, there were sufficient facilities and accommodation on board to cater for over 250. As it was, the crew were all women. Lieutenant Clare Roberts was in command; Medical Officer Dr. Fiona Benjamin was also a herbologist; Stellar Cartographer Paula Savage also held responsibility for communications and tracking; and then there was First Technician Kelly O'Hare who was kept fully occupied coping with maintaining all on board systems to optimum levels. She was the next one due for relief on the arrival of the next supply ship, but for personal reasons was not looking forward to returning home so soon.

Kelly's additional project was to try to stabilize and monitor the entrance of the new wormhole to Tau Ceti that had just begun forming. She had detected that the generator set up by Mercury 4 in Tau Ceti was creating a phenomenon that was causing the conduit inside to fluctuate in diameter. It made it very dangerous for any ship to transit to and from the system. ESO were to be sending additional technicians on the next supply vessel to try to rectify the problem.

Kelly had no doubt that one day TC1 would become obsolete. Wormhole technology was still in its infancy. Scientists had not yet perfected wormholes with sufficient stability that would allow safe transition directly from one star system to another. The distance of leaping across space had been limited to the extravagant use of wormhole rings that would allow ships to hop a parsec at a time. Hence the need for half way houses such as TC1 which acted like a base camp before the final push.

Kelly had managed to send a re-sequencing pattern to the Tau Ceti generator and had had to reinforce the distortion field around the wormhole using TC1's excess power. It was not an ideal situation and it was doubtful that such an arrangement could be anything but a short-term solution. If there was any disruption to the power supply or a fluctuation in the reinforcing wave pattern then the wormhole might collapse fairly rapidly with disastrous consequences for any vessel in transit. Her efforts bordered on the genius for having achieved what she had done and Lt. Roberts, unbeknown to Kelly, had recommended her for a citation.

Clare Roberts entered Lab 1. Kelly, wearing goggles and a long white science coat, was concentrating avidly on one of her laser tests. She had been at it for hours and seemed completely absorbed with her work and oblivious to Clare's presence.

Clare knocked on the bulkhead to gain Kelly's attention.

"Time for a break," she smiled.

Kelly looked around, startled by the sound and removed her goggles. She swished her wavy, black hair, partly held in place by a dark brown hair grip.

"I've had lunch," replied Kelly bluntly in her broad Irish accent.

"Lunch was over eight hours ago."

"Oh, was it? I guess I must have lost track of time. I wondered what the tummy rumblings meant."

"I've come to persuade you to take dinner," said Clare.

"I'm not hungry," answered Kelly. "Anyway, you're just in time to give me a hand."

"Err, sure. What d'you want me to do?"

Kelly mentally blotted out Clare whilst she focused on making adjustments to a pistol shaped device clamped to one end of a long table. She waved an arm horizontally with a finger pointing downwards, but did not explain what her gestures meant.

"Kelly, you ought to have a break," Clare suggested firmly. "I don't know what the heck you're doing, but you've been obsessed for weeks over this and I'm genuinely worried about you."

"Are you going to help or just stand there and give me lectures and hassle?"

She pointed downward again.

"There!" she said. "That is the phase converter."

Clare moved closer in order to see what she was referring to. It was a small cubic box, 8cm along each edge.

"This is the phase converter?"

"What's the reading?" Kelly went on.

Clare examined the box without touching it. She could not see any readout on the box itself. Connected to it, by a small socket and lead, was a keypad with a switch, but there was no indication on this either.

"What am I looking at?"

Kelly tutted impatiently then looked up.

"Here!" she said and passed a hand sized meter along the table. "You'll have to hold it fairly close, the range is very limited, but don't obstruct the aperture on the converter box."

"Okay," said Clare sardonically. She didn't have a clue what she was doing, but had decided for now to go along with whatever Kelly was up to.

"What's the reading?"

"Just a moment! This gauge isn't switched on yet."

Clare noted Kelly's barely controlled impatience. She turned on the device and waited for a few seconds whilst it warmed up.

"Have you got anything yet?" Kelly prompted.

She moved it closer to the converter box until a series of numbers showed.

"Err, it's reading 136.39."

"Oh shit!" Kelly muttered with dissatisfaction. "I'm at 142."

She marched around the table and leaned over to the box almost knocking Clare out of the way. Now it was Clare's turn to display impatience.

"Kelly?" she started and placed her hands on her hips. "Kelly? What are you doing? What is all this about?"

Kelly again ignored her whilst she fiddled with the keypad attached to the converter box. Clare grabbed her forearm.

"Stop!" she ordered.

Kelly came to attention and stood face to face wearing a fierce expression. She was shorter than Clare by about 5 centimetres.

"Kelly, tell me what this is about or I'll be forced to mention your behaviour in your appraisal."

Kelly flicked a hand at her fringe and shrugged her shoulders.

"Just a little pastime activity. You know, harmless fun."

"Most people play games or take up painting for a pastime. This is more than that. What is it?"

Kelly leaned over to the digital keypad again.

"Kelly?"

"This damn things got a calibration error in it," she cursed.

Clare moved away from the table. A letter, probably from the last mail drop, lay open on a side bench. She picked it up and instantly got a response.

"Leave that! It's private!"

Clare dropped it again.

"Are you going to tell me what you're doing?"

"I'll show you if you care to hang about just a few more seconds."

"Is this an actual letter or an electronic one?"

Kelly mumbled something.

"Well for what it's worth, the data mail arrived about half an hour ago," said Clare. "There's one for you."

"You haven't read it?" Kelly answered abruptly.

"Of course not. It's encoded. Only you can open it."

Kelly gave a grunt of satisfaction.

"There! That's as close as we're going to get!"

She carried on muttering inaudibly to herself and then declared: "142.34."

"Besides your personal mail," Clare continued. "There's one about you that I *was* able to read."

"Probably bloody Lance with some grovelling excuse why he's ditched me," Kelly ranted.

"What? I don't know anything about that."

Kelly paused for thought.

"Men!" Clare scowled under her breath.

"Just a few more seconds," she hissed. "Surprised you hadn't heard about it. I must have muttered a few expletives that you would have picked up."

"Men are such assholes!" said Clare.

"Not all of them," corrected Kelly.

"Well, I haven't met one yet that was worth bothering about."

Kelly afforded a quick smile.

"That's 'cause you don't give any a chance."

She tossed Clare some goggles then began gesturing again.

"Put these on and watch this! Stand back over there!"

She flicked a switch then, with another smirk on her face, stood with Clare behind a protective screen next to a side bulkhead.

The two women peered through the screen window. Kelly activated the unit and a red laser beam shone across the table from the pistol. The box became illuminated and the laser beam split into dozens of thinner beams that deflected off at different angles and the lab bulkheads quickly became peppered with laser impacts.

The display lasted for about ten seconds, then the box ceased deflecting and the full power of the laser focused on the metal side.

"Fuck!" cried Kelly and rushed out to cut the power. Smoke seeped out from a small hole in the converter box. More expletives followed.

"Kelly!" shouted Clare, but there was no holding her back.

"It's taken days to get the damn thing to this stage and now look at it!" she complained.

"That was amazing!" said Clare trying not to sound sarcastic. "What just happened?"

Kelly glared at her with a sour expression.

"Not the correct choice of words when describing a failed laser experiment."

"I'm sorry," replied Clare.

Kelly donned thick gloves and then proceeded to unscrew the box from its mounting. She fumbled the screwdriver, then removed a glove to get a better grip, subsequently burning a finger in the process.

"Shit!" she cried sucking her burnt finger. "The damn things fried!"

"Kelly! It's going to take hours if you're thinking of setting this thing up again. Come and have some lunch."

"I've had a sandwich. I'm alright!" she barked.

"Kelly, you will stop for a break! That's an order!"

There was stillness whilst Kelly pondered on the meaning of the words, then she threw the box down on the table like a child disposing of an unwanted toy.

"Fine! Let's go and eat!" she said slapping down her remaining glove. She folded her arms, adopted a fraught expression and stormed passed Clare for the exit. Clare followed.

They sat opposite each other in the mess room. Clare sipped coffee and nibbled on a piece of cheesecake watching Kelly savage a cheese and lettuce baguette.

"Amazing how the dispensers manage to produce such fresh stuff," said Kelly with full mouth. "Not enough mayonnaise in this one though."

"Don't you want to know what the mail said about you?" said Clare. "Stavros will be here in seven days!"

"Stavros?"

"The supply ship Stavros. All the way from Earth," said Clare trying to sound excited. "You're going home early."

Kelly showed no emotion.

"Early? Why so soon?"

"You know why," answered Clare. "Your Mum's ill. It's customary to get you back home asap if a close family member is taken seriously ill. You could be back on Earth in two weeks. Isn't that good?"

Kelly still showed no emotion.

"What's the matter, Kelly?" Clare said softly, touching Kelly's forearm. "What's the experiment all about?"

Kelly pulled out a crumpled piece of paper from her pocket. Clare recognized it as the letter in the lab, though she hadn't noticed Kelly picking it up. She pushed the letter over to Clare then picked up a glass of milk and drank long and hard.

Clare read the letter.

"I remember that accident," said Clare looking up. "Happened about a month ago."

She studied Kelly's features and noted the moistening eyes.

"Michael Hocking and I were ...." Kelly blubbed. "We were close."

"He was your boyfriend?"

"He was my fiancé," a tear ran down her right cheek betraying her emotional pain.

Clare felt a twinge of sympathy. Kelly had been on station ten weeks and this was the first time she had displayed any such feelings.

"I'm sorry," said Clare. "I haven't much time for men."

"You didn't meet Michael," Kelly retorted.

Kelly dropped her half eaten baguette, buried her face in her arms and broke down.

"Men are all the same to me," said Clare, "more trouble than they're worth."

"Fuck you!" exclaimed Kelly and moved to another table.

"I ...," Clare stopped. Now was not the time to say more about her views on men. "Kelly, I'm sorry."

She wiped the tears from her eyes then directed an angry gaze at Clare.

"You wouldn't understand! You and your hate! You treat all men the same! Yeh, well maybe a lot of 'em are losers, but not all and, believe it or not, some of them really do care. Maybe if bitches like you helped them rather than condemned them there wouldn't be so many you call bastards!"

Clare said nothing. She went over to Kelly to try to comfort her, but Kelly shrugged her off.

"He was the only man I really loved," she confessed. "He actually cared for who I was as a person. Now he's …"

"No man is worth that kind of pain," said Clare.

"Fuck off! How dare you say that?" snapped Kelly. "You're just a bitch dyke! Michael wasn't any man. He really cared."

"I'm sorry. I didn't mean to upset you."

"You've never had any time for men have you? That's why you got yourself stuck on this station."

"I can live without men. They cause nothing but misery."

"I thought I was feminized! You're just a bigot!"

Clare said nothing more and moved away to avoid eye contact.

Eventually Kelly calmed herself and became more reflective.

"Death stalks me," she went on. "It took me years to track down my dad. When I eventually found him, he was lying in a pauper's hospital terminally ill from cancer."

"I thought they could cure cancer?"

"He'd let himself go," she explained. "Men are often like that. They will let things go on, leaving things until it's too late. By the time he was hospitalized, it was already too late for him. He wanted to die."

"How come you hadn't seen him before hand?"

My bitch of a mother made it awkward, kept me and my sister away from him."

"You shouldn't say things against your Mum."

"Why not? She was a selfish bitch and that's the truth!"

A tear ran down Kelly's cheek. There was stony silence whilst she brought her emotions back under control.

"But your mother is ill," said Clare, "and you're due to go home to her soon."

"Out of duty rather than compassion!"

Clare sat opposite her again. She could think of nothing more to say.

Kelly cleared her throat and wiped a hand over her face.

"Mike and I were working on deflector shield technology before he was posted to Alpha Centauri. He went six weeks before I was sent here."

"Why didn't you ask to be posted with him?"

Kelly grunted resignedly.

"I don't have too many friends in personnel, I guess. They don't appreciate my style."

Clare had read Kelly's personnel file and how her hot temper had gotten the better of her on more than one occasion. She hated queuing, couldn't stand paper work and bureaucracy, and could flare up at the drop of a hat. Twice she had been sent to anger management therapy.

On one occasion, her entry into ESO's personnel office had been barred when she had forgotten to bring ID with her. The guard barring the door had suddenly been subject to a tirade of punches, kicks and claws. It took two other guards to restrain her. She was dragged away and had been suspended for eight weeks with a month's pay deducted.

"So, if you and Mike were close, who's Lance?" queried Clare.

"Lance? Oh, him!" she took a deep breath before carrying on. "After Mike had gone, I felt like crap, so I went out and got shit faced. Lance was some guy I picked up on the rebound."

She paused to reflect.

"I needed a shag. He seemed okay, so we had a couple of sessions. Lance thought he was in love and then I got sent here."

She glowered at Clare, seeking understanding in her face.

"It was just a one off thing. I was never in love with him. I just used him. I know it was wrong. I had a need. People do it all the time! Now Mike's gone it doesn't matter any more."

"Men do it to us."

"So, does it make it right we do it to them?"

"It's okay, Kelly. You don't have to justify yourself to me."

Clare thought for a few seconds before continuing.

"That's what the experiment was about? What you did with Mike?"

Kelly's enthusiasm returned.

"Mike was a genius. Most of the stuff I've been working on is based on his research and ideas. He just got careless I suppose. He pushed the power beyond its capacity.

"In the lab, the converter box was able to stand a full laser charge for about ten seconds. Mike was dealing with much larger outputs."

Kelly searched Clare's face for a response before continuing.

"Don't you see? If we could get this thing to work, ships fitted with it would be able to withstand impacts from Class C meteors without damage. They'd have power shields."

"Scientists have been working for years to perfect shield protection for ships. Are you really that close?"

"Mike was. I just hope I can finish what he started."

"If it's dangerous, you shouldn't be doing it. I could have you confined for carrying out what you did today. You had no authorization!"

"But you won't?"

Clare smiled reassuringly.

"I have problems with power inputs," Kelly explained. "You saw that in the lab. Mike seems to have had problems with getting his hands on reliable equipment. If we'd been allowed to work together though, I'm convinced we would have succeeded."

"Kelly, forgive me, I'm just a simple woman. Explain the basic principle how it would work on a ship."

Kelly broke into a broad smile at the prospect of sharing her knowledge. She placed the tips of her fingers together and formed a bridge.

"A ship's hull would be fitted with small nodes all over. I guess they'd look like warts. From each node would pour countless numbers of phased high speed particles. The nodes would be like fountains. These particles would flow like water over the hull. Any impact with physical objects or energy weapons would deflect off the hull thus minimizing any damage that otherwise would have been caused. At least, that's the theory."

"If you're close to achieving that, it would be a tremendous breakthrough."

"There are a few problems. The set up in the lab is limited."

"How so?"

"Well the particle shields won't totally prevent hull damage for one thing; only reduce it. Secondly, the nodes will draw enormous power when activated. Thirdly, the deflected rays from energy weapons could go anywhere and end up striking other innocent vessels. You saw that today."

Clare's bleeper squealed suddenly. She read the message.

"Incoming transmission," she said getting up to leave.

"Can I come with you?"

Clare smiled at her. "Of course."

The Control Room was adorned with many kinds of instruments, most of them dedicated to communications and astrophysics. Perhaps the most striking thing though was the view. The all-round window was spectacular and a little agoraphobic.

Paula Savage looked up as they entered and sneered at the sight of Kelly. Clare was aware of the animosity between the two. Never a day went by without some difference being aired between them.

"We're getting all kinds of transmissions from the Tau Ceti wormhole," said Paula. "It's very confusing."

"What sort of transmissions?" said Clare

"Much of it's pretty frantic."

"Can you clean them up?"

"The first one was from the Taj Mahal saying that they had reached the system. They had just managed to establish a comms link through the wormhole. Then there was a coded message that carried through from Mercury 4's monitoring station on Sebastian. There were all kinds of noises and messages not long after that; mostly from Taj Mahal. It's difficult to make out. One of them said that they had recovered survivors from Mercury 4. There's a great deal of distortion and interference to the signals. It'll take a while to process them to get any more detail."

"What's causing the interference?"

"I'm not certain at this time, but it is probably radio transmissions from the wormhole vortex itself."

Meters monitoring the wormhole suddenly jumped.

"Something's inside the wormhole!" said Kelly. "Someone's trying to come through!"

"Perhaps they're sending a probe," suggested Clare.

"No," replied Paula concentrating on a dial and the scanner screen in front of her. "It's bigger than a probe. Probably a shuttle from Taj Mahal. Err, Skylark 16 according to the ID transmission."

"That's not within the mission's parameters," said Clare. "They're supposed to get clearance before going into the wormhole. The wormhole isn't stable enough to use for ships."

"Something's wrong!" declared Kelly.

"We have other shuttles entering," continued Paula. "Skylarks 2 and 12."

"My God!" exclaimed Clare. "What's going on?"

"They must have abandoned ship!" said Kelly.

"There's more!" added Paula. "Skylarks 4 and 13 have also entered and, Skylark err, Skylark 11 and, err Skylark 9."

"How long before they get here?" said Clare.

"You mean if they get here?" corrected Paula flicking a glance at Kelly.

"She means when they get here, horse mouth!" retorted Kelly with eyes flashing venomously.

"Kelly! Cut that talk out!" growled Clare.

Paula casually picked up a glass of water sitting beside her and flung the contents into Kelly's face. Kelly launched herself, but Clare intervened quickly.

"Stop it! Damn it! Just save the cat fight for later!" demanded Clare.

"Cat fight?" the other two chorused.

"How long before they're through?" reiterated Clare.

"Approximately eight hours I estimate," replied Paula.

She shot another hostile look at Kelly. Kelly couldn't resist the opportunity to stab.

"Is that a day or two either side for error?"

Paula began to mouth a response, but Clare slapped an authoritative hand on a console to try to maintain order.

"Enough!" she screamed. "If there's a distress on, the last thing we want is a war on our hands in the control room!"

She moved into the command chair and spoke sternly.

"Now, Paula keep monitoring for transmissions! Kelly, contact Charon Base and retransmit all incoming comms to them! They've got more people there and will hopefully be able to analyze things more thoroughly even with the time delay."

Clare moved to the internal comms system to make a station wide announcement.

"Who're you calling?" said Kelly. "If you want Dr. Benjamin just bleep her!"

"She might be on one of her cycling expeditions and not hear it."

Clare flicked on the mike.

"I'm sounding General Quarters!"

"There's only four of us on the station and three of those are here."

"Just following correct procedures."

"Who're you expecting, the marines?"

Clare ignored Kelly's comments and made her announcement.

"This is an emergency! This is an emergency! Dr. Benjamin report to the control room immediately! Dr. Benjamin report to the control room immediately!"

"My God!" cried Paula.

Clare whirled around.

"What?"

"They've been attacked!"

"What?" said Kelly and Clare together.

"That's part of one of the messages," said Paula. "Three large alien vessels appeared and opened fire.... Heavy damage....casualties.... Aliens boarding .... Losing control of ship... unable to contain them.... Many deaths.... Abandon ship."

All three women sat dumbfounded as one of the control room doors burst open and a breathless Dr. Fiona Benjamin rushed in.

"What's the emergency?" she said panting hard.

"It's going to be a few hours before the first of the skylarks exits the wormhole," said Clare. "Fiona, prepare quarters to receive casualties and survivors!"

"Charon Base are putting together a team and will be dispatching them through the Charon-TC1 wormhole as soon as they're ready," said Kelly.

"Okay," said Clare. "We need to organize a duty system, otherwise the whole thing will turn into a mess."

She brushed her hand through her hair as if to think.

"Kelly, prep Finch 1 for launch! You'll probably need to pack additional medical supplies. We're all going to be exhausted before this thing is over."

She consulted the time: "23:18".

"Okay, we'll maintain current manning levels until 0100," she went on. "I want no more arguments between you two! Is that clear? We don't have the staff as it is and we can't afford fights especially during an emergency."

Kelly and Paula exchanged hostile glances.

"Paula, you stand down at 0100 and return at 0500 if there are no significant developments. Dr. Benjamin will stand down when she has finished her preps and can relieve you at 0100. Kelly, go and prepare Finch and come on duty at 0300."

"Should have had more on station in the first place," moaned Kelly.

"Well, we haven't!" Clare snapped, "so we'll have to live with it!"

"Someone will have to continue to monitor transmissions," droned Paula.

"Well, that's why we'll be doing duty watches," answered Clare.

"They won't be able to do it as well as I can!" Paula retorted.

"Oh, hark at her now!" cut in Kelly sharply. "Missus Special thinks she's indispensable does she?"

Anger welled up in Paula and she flew across the room towards Kelly. Clare leapt between them for the second time and struggled to hold Paula off.

"Stop it!" she yelled. "Stop it right now, the pair of you!"

"I want a piece of her!" snarled Paula.

"What have I just said! We have a real fucking emergency and all you two want to do is scrap like thugs. This will be mentioned on your reports! Kelly button it! Get a grip or you'll be drummed out of ESO before you can blink!"

"Why pick on me?" Kelly whined.

"'cause you started it, cow!" said Paula.

Kelly took a step toward her, but Clare remained between them and they backed off.

"You will do as you are told!" cried Clare. "Paula, you will monitor all transmissions from the wormhole and remain at your post until 0100. Kelly, you are dismissed to other duties and will come on watch at 0300! Now leave!"

Clare paced, brushing her cropped hair as she did so.

"Control, this is Finch 1!" called Kelly from the station's service craft. "Finch 1 is prepped and ready to fly!"

"Very good Kelly!" replied Clare. "You may stand down!"

"All cabins have been inspected and are available for immediate use," reported Dr. Benjamin. "I will set up all medical droids for immediate deployment."

"Very good," answered Clare. "Stand down when you have completed your task!"

"Lieutenant?" said Paula with some urgency.

Clare swivelled in her chair to see what the problem was.

"Something big has entered the wormhole."

"Big? What do you mean big? Be more specific!"

"Well, whatever it is, it's not of human construction. It doesn't match any known ID patterns."

"How long before the last shuttle arrives?"

"Skylark 9 will be the last. She's due in about eight and a half hours."

"How long before *it* arrives?" demanded Clare.

"At it's current velocity, about nine hours but, the alien vessel is increasing velocity."

Paula studied her readouts avidly.

"ETA, eight and a half hours. It's gaining on them quite considerably! Skylark 9 won't make it!"

"Kelly, this is control," called Clare. "We may need to launch Finch 1 earlier than expected."

The door slid open. Kelly and Fiona entered.

"I'm here," said Kelly and Clare quickly explained the dilemma.

"What difference do you think taking Finch will do?" said Kelly.

"Obstruct them, talk to them, anything that will delay the aliens until our people are out."

"Come Kelly, you're with me!" she added and marched out.

"Wow, she looks like thunder," said Fiona meekly.

"Everything ready?" said Paula.

"Ooh yes," she replied. "Most of the preps were about being a chamber maid."

"You mean getting rooms organized? I thought that cabins were ready for use anyway?"

"If we are to expect casualties, then I can't care for them all by myself. I've had to program the four service droids to prioritize their duties to the cause of Sick Bay."

Clare returned, wearing a space suit and with Kelly trailing behind.

"Paula, patch me up with Charon Base!"

"There'll be at least a five minute time lag for communications," said Paula.

"Just do your best!" snapped Clare. "Tell them what's going on and ask for advice on what action to take."

"Charon Base! Charon Base! This is Outpost TC1," said Paula. "We have a new situation. A large unidentified spacecraft has entered the Tau Ceti wormhole and is gaining on the shuttles still inside. Their intentions are not known, but are possibly hostile. Am attempting to contact the escaping skylark vessels. Please advise on action to be taken?"

"You know, I've always said that they should have set up the subspace comms link system," said Kelly.

"It's not been fully tested," answered Fiona. "Anyway, mini wormholes inside wormholes. It sounds freaky."

"What's freaky about it?" snorted Kelly. "All it is, is creating miniature energy vortices inside each other and allowing radio transmissions to leap through at considerably reduced time delays, that's basically how probes send their data from deep space."

"Doesn't it require huge volumes of energy?"

"Yes, but wormhole technology is a developing science, and is…"

"Girls!" interrupted Clare. "Less chatter please, more action!"

"What action?" blurted Kelly. "It's not exactly hot stuff at present."

"Kelly, don't you do anything without spoiling for a fight?"

Clare concentrated on a small vide-screen and eventually slapped the console in frustration.

"Nothing!" she exclaimed sounding acutely disappointed.

"What are you looking for?" asked Kelly.

"Nothing apparently," Clare huffed regaining her composure. "I was trying to find something that could be classed as a weapon. There is nothing."

"You're planning to do battle with it?"

"Well, if that thing is hostile I think we're going to need more than a gloved hand and a welcoming smile when it comes through. Looking through the stores there's not even high ex."

"Well there wouldn't be," replied Kelly. "We're not a mining colony."

"They didn't send us out here with the idea of starting an interstellar war with the first aliens we meet," added Fiona.

"This isn't about starting anything," said Clare. "It's just having something to defend ourselves with."

"It comes under the same package," replied Fiona glibly.

"There speaks the true pacifist!" said Paula.

"Violence never solves anything," retorted Fiona.

"Oh, I don't know," mused Kelly. "Punching Ms. Savage on the nose would be quite satisfying."

"Kelly!" exclaimed Clare.

"They do say that history is written by the victors," added Kelly, "so winning at violence must count for something."

"Men's talk!" grumbled Clare.

"Is there nothing we can do?" said Paula.

"Wait for orders," replied Fiona.

"Kelly, is there no way we can use the grav generator from TC1 to speed up the shuttles' approaches?" asked Clare.

"Probably if we had a team of engineers working for a week. But, we don't have that luxury."

Every one became pensive and silent.

"May I speak?" said Kelly sarcastically.

"Isn't that what you've been doing non stop?" sniped Paula.

"If you must," sighed Clare.

"Well I won't if you don't want me to."

"Oh for God's sake Kelly!" Clare snapped. "Say what you have to say!"

"Well, unless we've got something bigger than a blow torch to fight this alien ship with, I have an idea about how to destroy it if we have to."

"Let's hear it!"

Kelly seemed to savour the attention.

"We collapse the wormhole."

"What!" cried Fiona. "That would destroy everything inside, including the shuttles!"

"Told you she was psycho!" said Paula.

"It would also cut off any hope of rescuing those still in Tau Ceti," added Clare.

"Precisely!" nodded Fiona.

"But it is an option, nevertheless," Clare replied pensively. "One that can't be ruled out."

"You can't seriously contemplate…" Fiona protested.

"Just how do you intend to collapse the wormhole?" said Paula. "It's being powered from the Tau Ceti side and has been for the past 12 hours. We have very little control over it."

"We detonate a bomb against the conduit wall," replied Kelly.

"Where have you been?" scalded Paula. "There's nothing on station to explode."

"Oh, yes there is," retorted Kelly. "The station's reactor. Dump the reactor! We'll pick it up with Finch 1."

"You can't be serious?"

"Life support would fail!" added Fiona. "We'd be dead within hours!"

"Days, to be more accurate," replied Kelly. "There are several power generating gizmos around the station. It'd be ages before the station totally conked out."

"Let's hope it doesn't come to that," Clare said as a note of appeasement. "Kelly, make the preparations, but do nothing without my command! Is that understood?"

"Crystal!" replied Kelly enthusiastically.

Paula cursed when Kelly had left.

"That fucking woman!"

"Clare you must get authorization from Charon Base before collapsing a wormhole," said Fiona. "And, especially if you're going to dump the reactor."

"She's right," added Paula. "It would be willful destruction of ESO property.

"We've had very little advice from Charon so far," said Clare.

"You'll be court martialled if you go ahead with it," said Fiona.

"Better still, so will that looney Irish bitch!" added Paula cynically.

"She has a touch of genius," remarked Clare drawing a scoff from Paula. "At least that's what I'm relying on."

With a maximum capacity of four people, the seating on Finch 1 was cramped.

Clare joined Kelly in the cockpit.

"Kelly, take control of comms and tracking! I guess your watch started a bit sooner than anticipated."

Clare adjusted her space suit.

"Kelly!"

"Yes?" Kelly replied nonchalantly.

"Put and keep your helmet on. No one knows what is going to happen."

"Finch, Control," called Paula.

"Finch, go ahead Paula," replied Clare running through all the preflight checks.

"I've managed to make contact with all shuttles except Skylark 9," said Paula. "They are maximizing their velocities. Skylark 9, appears to be damaged."

"The way that thing is gaining on them, Skylark 9 doesn't have a chance!" said Clare. "Eject the reactor!"

"If you initiate a collapse of the wormhole," Fiona said sternly. "You will be condemning them to death. They won't last a second!"

Clare glanced at Kelly.

"Kelly, I told you to put your helmet on!"

"I'm busy!"

"Do it!"

"Fine!" grumped Kelly. "It's not so quick doing things wearing all this gizmo!"

Finch launched and waited for the reactor. There was a puff of gas from the base of the station and a small white globular object emerged.

"Reactor ejected!" said Paula.

"Clare think what you're doing!" pleaded Fiona. "It's not worth it! We don't know that they're hostile!"

"The decision's made! Now button it!"

Clare swung Finch around to intercept the sphere. In one movement she closed to within a few metres extended clawed arms and ensnared it. The additional mass greatly reduced Finch's speed and manoeuvrability, but Clare rapidly edged the little ship towards the wormhole.

"Why are you suddenly so quiet?"

"I'm concentrating," replied Kelly.

Clare pondered for a moment.

"We have no delivery system," said Clare.

"Oh, you've realized at last! Well it so happens that I have the solution!"

"Which is?"

"It's all down to my concentration, you know."

"Kelly!"

"I tethered Junior and Minor to Finch ready for use before we launched."

"Junior?"

"Huh, the outpost's two external service droids. Don't tell me you didn't notice the additional mass?"

"And?"

"And we attach them to the reactor; run at the wormhole to gather velocity; detach the reactor and bingo!"

"You're hoping the service droids will act as the guidance system? How can you be sure of accuracy?"

"They don't have to be accurate. Unless the reactor flies a straight course, which is extremely unlikely, then it should hit the wall easily."

"And what of Skylark 9? Suppose it hits them or hits the wall too soon?"

"Well, you're always bragging about how good a combat pilot you are. We'll see how good a shot you really are when the chips are down."

"There's still going to be a slice of luck needed."

"Isn't there always?" said Kelly.

"How will they survive with the wormhole destabilizing all around them?"

"Surf!"

CHAPTER TWO

"Don't you love space walking?" Kelly proclaimed cheerfully.

Clare was in a serious mood.

"No," she replied.

They worked feverishly to weld Junior and Minor to the reactor. Paula, in TC1's Control Room, kept them updated with the progress of the approaching skylark craft.

"What if this doesn't work?"

"Well then," chirped Kelly, "me and thee will be spending the next ten years in a prison stockade on Ceres."

"Not my idea of fun," Clare moaned.

"Oh yea of little faith!"

"How can you be so cheerful?"

Fiona and Paula observed from the comfort of TC1's control room as Clare took Finch to 100,000 kilometres from the wormhole entrance. Mindful not to create undue stresses to the hastily done welding jobs, Clare cautiously turned Finch to line up for a direct run at the vortex.

"Control, what's the status of the escape craft?"

"Skylark 16 will be emerging in 12 minutes!" replied Paula. "No. 2 will be another minute behind that!"

The wait seemed interminable. Clare put her hand to her head to rub her brow, but then realized the helmet prevented it. She looked across at Kelly who appeared to be dozing.

"Kelly, your suit's not plugged in."

"These suits don't need to be plugged in. You can be out in them all day without worrying about running out of air."

"Still, it's standard practice to …"

"Stuff standard practice!"

Clare tried to rub her head again.

"You okay?" said Kelly glancing over.

Clare yawned.

"Fine! Just a bit of a headache coming on that's all."

Paula commentated on the coming of Skylark 16.

"…will be exiting in 10, 9, 8, 7 …."

Clare and Kelly sat, staring with fascination, as one by one the skylark shuttles appeared. Each bursting out like tiny fireflies from the blackness of the wormhole into the blackness of star-studded space.

"How far behind is 9?" asked Clare.

"30 minutes to clear. Alien vessel will be on them in 15," answered Paula.

Skylark 11 was the last one out when Finch began accelerating towards the wormhole.

At 40,000 kilometres from the mouth, Finch had reached its maximum velocity. Clare steadied her aim and switched her broadscope to view from Junior's on board camera.

"30,000 Ks," said Kelly. "When do you release?"

"Dunno, I've never done this before."

"20,000."

The sight in Clare's right eye suddenly went causing her to utter a little cry of dismay.

"Clare?"

Her vision quickly returned.

"I'm okay!" she said firmly.

"10,000," declared Kelly. "Are we goin' inside?"

Clare didn't answer. The read out reduced to 5,000K.

"Clare?"

Still no response. Kelly leaned forward, trying to peer into Clare's helmet. Clare ignored her and just stared blankly at her nav screen.

"Clare? Are you alright?"

The distance registered 1,000.

"Clare! Release Clare! Release for God sake!" yelled Kelly. "We're off line! We're going to hit the wall!"

The distance reached 100 and rapidly diminished towards zero and certain destruction. Kelly swung a gloved left fist and pounded it into Clare's chest.

"Pulling out!" Clare suddenly exclaimed and yanked the helm upwards.

"Release!" screamed Kelly. "Release!"

She reached across Clare and slapped a button. There was a jolt as explosive attachment bolts detonated and the reactor was away.

Finch veered across the mouth of the wormhole just centimetres from destruction as the reactor whirled ungainly inwards.

"Clare, you have to steer the reactor!" Kelly reminded her.

"I feel sick."

Clare shakily switched the joystick control to remote and adjusted the reactor's course. Kelly flicked Finch's nav to auto and typed in a basic instruction for the craft to stop.

"Clare? What's wrong?"

Again Clare did not answer. The reactor assembly quickly disappeared from visual and the proximity alarm buzzed.

"Shit!"

"I can't tell whether it's the wall or the skylark," Clare complained. "I'm losing control."

Panic etched into Clare's voice.

"I don't know what I'm steering and where!"

"Just do your best!" cried Kelly.

"I'm losing it! It's slewing!"

Kelly stared intently at the readouts.

"There's too much interference!" exclaimed Clare. "Minor's offline! I've lost control! It's going into the side!"

She jerked at the joystick then pressed and held down a boost button. Junior fired its tiny booster and the reactor began to move away from the wormhole wall.

"Phew! Nice piloting!" sighed Kelly, now back in her seat. "Just a few more seconds!"

"I'm going to crash it!"

"No! It's too soon! They'll all be killed!" yelled Kelly.

"Indicators show that Skylark 9 is still mainly intact but her engines are going critical!" announced Paula.

Clare's gaze burned into the monitor. Her hand nudged the joystick deftly. Beads of perspiration ran down her tense cheeks.

Junior responded, but Skylark 9 was yawing wildly. Clare pulled firmly on the joystick to avoid collision and, somehow, Skylark 9 skimmed passed in an instant.

"They're both out of control!" cried Fiona onTC1.

The huge alien vessel bore ominously down on 9, dwarfing it in size.

"Reactor's on overload!" cried Kelly. It'll go in less than 30 seconds!"

"I've lost it for good this time. There's nothing!"

The Mago cruiser fired a spectacular array of weapons.

"Large radiation emission detected from the wormhole!" Paula announced.

For a moment there was a fateful pause and then, the cold dark of space was pierced by a blinding white light. All view screens whited out as a bright glare radiated from the mouth of the wormhole. For a few seconds the swirling energy vortex lit up spectacularly.

"The wormhole is collapsing!" exclaimed Paula.

"Skylark 9? The alien ship?" demanded Kelly.

"Am detecting numerous fragments," Paula replied after her instruments regained their data inputs.

"I'd say the alien ship has been completely destroyed!"

"Skylark 9?"

Fiona slumped in her seat in the control room expecting the worst. The news of the aliens' demise disturbed her. She hated death and suffering of any sort.

"Am unable to …" began Paula.

"Look!" yelled Kelly pointing, but Clare showed no interest.

"Clare?"

Clare's head lolled in a listless gaze towards her. A glint of green flashed in her eyes that caused Kelly to start with shock.

"Yeh, I got her!" cried Paula. "Bit beaten up, but she's there. Scan reveals there are people still alive on her."

Skylark 9, with pieces flying off, tumbled away from where the wormhole once used to be.

"We have no means of rescuing them," fretted Fiona.

"Doctor?" called Kelly. "Doctor, I don't think Clare's too well."

"I'm fine," replied Clare. "Just a bit tired that's all."

"I'll direct one of the other skylarks to go to them," said Paula.

"Don't ask them," snapped Clare. "Tell them! Don't forget we're the On-scene Coordinator in this situation."

Kelly stared uncertainly at Clare, puzzled by her shifting temperament and erratic behaviour.

"Finch, this is TC1," called Paula. "Two messages from Charon Base coming through, Lieutenant."

"Finch!" responded Clare. "What do they say?"

"One says we are to wait for technical support to arrive. The other's a coded one just for you!"

Clare smiled wryly.

"Patch the coded one through to my comm position."

"What's it say?" said Kelly.

"It's not for your eyes," said Clare reading it aloud anyway. "Lieutenant Commander Spink, currently on board Skylark 4, is tasked with the responsibility of assuming immediate command of Outpost TC1 on his arrival at the station."

Spink was an experienced astronaut and had worked his way up the ranks through years of steadfast and loyal commitment. Although a capable pilot, he had never been one who had demonstrated any exceptional behaviour patterns.

"TC1, TC1 this is Skylark 4, this is Lieutenant Commander Spink. Request immediate clearance to dock?"

Clare spoke to Paula using a scrambler frequency.

"Deny permission and direct him to Skylark 9 to rescue persons on board!"

"TC1 this is Skylark 4," said Spink. "Am transmitting new orders from Charon Base! I am to assume command on boarding TC1. Request permission to dock?"

"He only takes over when he has boarded," said Clare. "You will deny him permission and order him to rescue 9!"

"Commander, I am instructed by the officer in charge," said Paula firmly and politely. "That you are denied permission to dock and must intercept Skylark 9 with the intention of effecting a rescue!"

"Lieutenant Roberts! What the hell's your game?" scolded Spink. "I have been given command of this station!"

"Not until you have set foot on it," replied Clare. "Right now, you are needed to rescue Skylark 9. You are the most experienced pilot and have a better class of ship than mine."

Spink was not happy with her direction.

"You'll not hear the last of this Lieutenant!" he scowled, but said no more.

Skylark 4 peeled off.

To dock with the whirling Skylark 9 presented itself as a very tricky task and Spink was concerned that his flying skills would be shown to be not up to it. He took his vessel within 20 metres and increased thrust to compensate for the rolling motion. Twice he almost succeeded in matching the movement, but each time he closed the gap, the two craft lost synchronicity and, in the end, his frustration got the better of him.

"TC Control, this is Skylark 4!"

"Skylark 4 this is TC1, go ahead," replied Paula.

"TC Control, we have a problem here. The rogue craft is rotating too quickly to be able to dock without risk. I suggest we wait for a salvage team to attempt the rescue. In the meantime an experienced medical team should scan the vessel for life and the health status of those aboard."

Paula thought for a moment.

"Skylark 4, this is TC1. It could be several days before that is possible. May I suggest you use antigrav to slow the rate of turn of Skylark 9?"

It was not the answer Commander Spink wanted to hear. He felt pressured.

"It's a very risky strategy," he sighed with a measure of frustration. "If there is a fluctuation in the power grid we could have a major disaster."

Clare could sense his reluctance and felt compelled to butt in.

"Commander, if you're not up to it, then say so!"

The provocative outburst did not sit well with him.

"Lieutenant!" He barked. "With remarks like that, I'll see to it that you're busted to a decommissioned rank! However, I'll give it a go, but I'll not put my passengers at risk!"

Clare docked Finch and flew out of her seat to run for the Control Room. She stood near the entrance to survey the situation.

Her headache worsened and, unnoticed by the others, her entire left leg suddenly went numb and buckled beneath her. She grabbed a nearby seat to prevent herself falling. The sensation passed almost as quickly as it had come and she managed to straighten up just as Kelly entered.

"Still no comms with 9," said Fiona. "There are people alive, but there's no activity. It could mean they're all incapacitated. They're probably desperate for medical help."

Skylark 4 moved cautiously closer to the rotating Skylark 9.

"Engaging anti grav," declared Spink.

"He's too far off," said Clare. "Commander, you need to get in close for this to work!"

"I can't get much effect with anti grav!" yelled a frustrated Spink. "I'm just putting my own passengers at risk."

"We have Skylarks 2 and 16 docking," said Paula. "The others wish to continue to Charon Base."

"Negative, they dock here first!" said Clare.

Clare twisted a short strand of hair and drew a deep breath. She rubbed her forehead. The headache eased slightly.

"You're still too far off!" she chirped.

"It's too dangerous to get closer," argued Spink. "We'll end up losing both ships!"

Clare's anxiety grew.

"Kelly, do you think you could possibly assist Paula, without getting into a fight?"

"I'm going to have to break off!" exclaimed Spink. "It's too dangerous! We'll lose both ships if we get any closer!"

Clare leaned between Paula and Kelly to study the situation.

"Commander, you have a three metre gap. You need to reduce to one metre distance to be effective."

"It's too dangerous!" was all Spink would say. "I'm aborting!"

"Chicken shit!" cursed Kelly.

Skylark 4 pulled out from the approach and lined up to dock with the station.

"I have considered all factors and am making the decision to dock at TC1," said Spink. "We will wait for the appropriate teams to arrive! Any further obstruction to my orders will bring a charge of gross insubordination with it!"

"Which skylark docked first?" asked Clare.

"Err, Number 2," Paula replied.

"Okay," said Clare decisively. "Paula, you remain Controller. Kelly, get down to the bay reception areas and send a team up here to help her out."

Kelly opened her mouth.

"And don't argue! That's an order! Do it!"

Kelly didn't move, but Clare had turned and nodded at Fiona.

"Doctor Benjamin, Skylarks 16 and 13 are just completing docking manoeuvres, shouldn't you go to the bays to meet them?"

"Skylark 11 is making its approach and will be docked in approximately eight minutes," said Paula. "Number 4 is also now making a new approach. ETA twenty four minutes."

"Status of Skylark 9?" said Clare.

"Latest analysis report just coming through!" said Paula

"And?"

"Scans indicate that life support will fail completely in thirty two minutes. Scanners also indicate that there are casualties on her. Some are alive. I can't tell yet how many dead there are."

"There's another message through from Charon Base," said Kelly. "It's from Deputy Commodor Jonathan Bridely."

"What's he say?"

"Just that Lieutenant Commander Spink is to assume command of TC1 and all operations."

"Skylark 4, this is TC1!" said Clare. "Skylark 9 will be losing life support in about thirty minutes."

"Lieutenant Roberts I presume," replied Spink, "I have orders to relieve you and am on my way to carry out those orders."

"Commander, surely those orders can wait a few minutes for the sake of the people on Skylark 9?"

"Lieutenant, I am unable to help those people. I have tried. I am therefore to dock at TC1 and assume command of the outpost as per orders issued by Deputy Commodore Jonathan Bridely."

"Hmm," was all Clare would say. "Kelly, come with me!"

Clare leapt from her seat and left with Kelly trailing behind.

"Err, where are we going?" asked Kelly seemingly relishing not being the only bad girl for once. "Err, it wouldn't be the shuttle bays by any chance?"

"It would and Kelly," she said, gripping Kelly's arm. "When I ask you to do something I expect it done!"

"You mean follow orders, just like you do?" she laughed.

"Kelly," Clare spoke as they hurried along. "From now on, you don't have to obey anything I ask you to do, but I need your help to pilot one of the shuttles. Will you help?"

"You know me," smirked Kelly. "I'm always one for a bit of fun."

Dozens of people crowded out of the docking areas and filled the broad alleyways. Clare moved with singular purpose, not stopping for chit chats or to gaze at this or that.

They fought their way past to reach the open hatch of Skylark 16. Fiona was stood in the doorway talking to a man clad in overalls.

"Doctor! Come with us!"

"But I have casualties …" Fiona protested.

"Well send someone to Control to help Ms. Savage!"

Clare did not wait for her answer, but stormed on board Skylark 16.

A teenager stood looking over the control panel in the cockpit compartment when she clambered into the pilot's seat.

"Get out or stay!" she snarled abruptly. "It's your choice, boy! I've no time to barter!"

"I'll stay, Ma'am," he replied nervously. "If it's alright with you?"

"I haven't time to nursemaid a kid," she barked angrily.

The boy began to back away and bumped into Kelly.

"You better do one or the other when she's in that sort of mood kid," Kelly grinned.

Clare frantically flipped switches and tapped command pads and the ship quickly came to life as hums, vibrations and clicks resounded throughout.

"You're taking this one out again?" said the boy.

"That's the intention," said Kelly. "Is everyone off?"

"I think there's a couple of engineers and a junior officer doing checks, I think," he replied.

"Don't think! Find out!" said Clare. "Batten the hatches!"

"I'll do it," said Kelly moving into the utility seat behind the pilot. "You get yourself sorted out, kid."

"I, I'll leave then," stammered the boy.

"Too late," Clare said abruptly. "The hatches are closing. We're unberthing in one minute."

"What? Where are we going?"

"If you want to stay in one piece, boy, you'd better strap in!"

"Err, okay, I'll…"

Clare ran through final pre-flight checks in record time as the boy slid into the co-pilot's seat.

"Lieutenant Roberts!"

It was Spink. Clare ignored him.

"Lieutenant Roberts!" repeated Spink. "You take that shuttle out and it'll be the last thing you do. You'll be facing a court martial for gross insubordination!"

"You abandoned them!" declared Clare. "You've left them to die!"

Kelly made an onboard announcement.

"Lieutenant Clare Roberts," said Spink drawing a deep breath. "I hereby relieve you of command of the Outpost TC1. You stand relieved of duty!"

"That officer scrambled off before the shut down," said Kelly. "That leaves us an engineer, I think."

"Great," Clare mumbled trying to show interest. "How many on board then?"

"Err, five including us."

Clare started the engines and initiated the unberthing sequence.

"Five? I thought you said one got off?"

"Yeh, there's three here, an engineer called Tate, and …."

"Dr. Benjamin," said Fiona taking over the fourth and last available seat in the cockpit."

"Glad you could make it, Doctor," chuckled Kelly. "Well we have a full Bridge team! So let's do it!

"We'll probably all be civilians by the time the day's out," replied Clare.

"TC1 this is Skylark 16 requesting clearance to depart?" said Clare over the radio.

Paula responded. "Skylark 4 will be making her final approach in twelve minutes and Skylark 11 is two minutes from berthing. Please standby!"

"Let me talk to her," said Kelly.

Clare nodded her approval.

"Ms. Savage, Skylark 11 is clear is it not?" said Kelly.

"Affirmative, but I have been instructed not to allow any movements until Skylark 4 has berthed," retorted Paula.

"Paula, we're leaving with or without authorization!" stated Clare. "Breaking links in fifteen seconds!"

"You know you'll be charged with contravening safety procedures?" advised Paula.

"Screw the rules!" cried Kelly. "Just add it to the list of charges."

Clare looked sceptically across at the boy.

"Thought you'd need a co-pilot," he smiled.

"I need a co-pilot, not a child with a dummy," said Clare venomously. "I certainly don't need a boy to hold my hand."

"I am top pilot in my year!" he replied calmly and assertively.

Clare sneered and was about to say more, but Kelly interceded.

"Clare you need a co-pilot! Give him a break! What *is* your name kid?"

"Cadet Oliver Stenson, Ma'am."

"No Ma'mmy stuff here, Olly. Call me Kelly or nothing at all."

Clare and Oliver donned broadscope helmets.

"Co-ordinates are on screen!" called Kelly.

"I got 'em," replied Oliver.

Kelly smirked at the boy.

"Tate, whatever you're doing, strap yourself in securely," announced Fiona over internal comms.

Clare counted down: "Eight, seven, six ….."

"Skylark 16 eased into the blackness with the twinkles of TC1's lights merging into the starry background behind them.

"We're getting a call from Skylark 4," said Fiona switching the speakers over to broadcast.

"Lieutenant Roberts," Spink said sternly. "Departing a station without proper authorization is tantamount to criminal negligence. You realize you're finished for what you've just done?"

"Screw you, Spink!" snarled Kelly.

"Thank you Kelly," said Clare calmly. "My sentiments exactly, though I wouldn't have put it in quite the same way."

Spink started to reply, but Fiona switched off the speakers.

"Enough of that babble!"

"Fi? I'd never have taken you for a rebellious type," said Kelly.

Fiona forced a smile.

"Well, I suppose I'll be lucky to be washing dishes at the local coffee house when this is over," said Kelly.

At full throttle, Skylark 16 rolled and slipped passed the other approaching ships, rapidly closing on the stricken 9.

"There's barely ten minutes left!" warned Kelly.

"Well, we'd better get this thing right first time," replied Clare.

Skylark 9 spun in an endless rotation as they drew near.

Kelly checked over the ship's systems.

"Anti grav unit is online! Err, aren't you coming in a bit fast?"

"I'm doing one pass first."

"Roberts….!" Clare switched off her display and comms feeds. "Wish he'd shut up!"

She focused on the approach to Skylark 9. One false move could mean death for them all. A spear like pain stabbed through her head and her vision went totally. She cried out and lost control.

A collision seemed unavoidable, but Oliver was quick to respond. He immediately took the helm and reversed thrusters. Skylark 16 closed to within 3 metres of 9 and all but stopped. Then, he rolled 16 so that both vessels spun in tandem and with deft touches closed the gap to less than a metre. Kelly and Fiona sat tense and silent as both vessels uncomfortably came within touching distance, but Oliver gently halted the approach just in time.

"Activating ant-grav!"

There was a slight wobble as the anti-grav started to take effect. Clare had been still for a while, but then moaned as if stirring from a sleep. It triggered a response from Fiona. She unstrapped herself and leaned over to tend her.

Clare slipped her hand inside the broadscope helmet and rubbed vigorously at her forehead.

"You okay?" said Fiona.

"Headache and tired," Clare yawned. "What are you doing boy?"

Oliver ignored her. He gently nudged the bow of Skylark 16 using the repulsing force of anti-grav to push on Skylark 9.

"Don't ignore me, boy!" said Clare provocatively.

"Clare, give him a break!" said Kelly.

Oliver still did not respond. The tumbling movement of Skylark 9 began to dramatically reduce.

Clare shoved Fiona hard and then struck out at Oliver pounding him high on the chest. The blow caught him unawares and for a few seconds he lost steerage. Kelly leapt forward and flung her arms around Clare's torso in a clasping hold. She responded by flailing her arms dramatically and screaming wildly.

"Just a few more seconds!" puffed Oliver.

Clare was becoming demonic.

"Fucking boy!" yelled Clare in a deep, distorted voice. "I'll rip your fucking eyes out!"

With ease she prized Kelly's arms away as if they had the strength of a mere child. Fiona, quick to recover, stabbed a syringe through Clare's suit and into her neck. Clare's body stiffened for a second and then fell back still.

In spite of the distractions, Oliver had maintained his concentration throughout most of the commotion and soon the corkscrewing actions of the two ships were evened out and the spinning stopped.

After that, the docking became a formality. The magnetic clamps locked the ships together and Oliver shut down the engines as the docking attachments were secured. Kelly gave a whoosh of relief, but it was the teenager who was first to spring from his seat and get to the hatch and, for the first time, they met Tate. Tate, tall and lean with a receding hair line and a hunched, skeletal frame grinned toothlessly at them when they met him. He was supposed to be in his mid thirties, but his drawn features and almost anaemic complexion made him look twenty years older.

Donning helmets, Tate swung the hatch wheel and wrenched the lid open, but it was Oliver who pressed passed him and was first down the ladder.

As soon as they were inside No. 9's hull, their feet drifted off the ladder and they started floating free. Debris lay everywhere and the glow worm emergency lighting provided barely sufficient light.

"No gravity!" Kelly mumbled. "We need magnetic boots!"

"No time," replied Fiona over the com. "You'll have to swim through it."

"You not coming?" said Kelly.

"I have to make sure Clare is alright first. I won't be long."

Oliver typed something on his arm control and his boots activated. The puffy suit gave little indication of the gangly body inside. His broad, cheerful smile beamed out from his helmet.

"All Senator Mark 8 suits are fitted with magnetic soles as standard," he said smugly. "That's what we're wearing."

He confidently took the lead and soon found the first person. The badge read: "Dr. Joseph Farnhurst". Kelly, following up behind him played a bio-scanner over him.

"He's alive!" she announced. "Unconscious, concussed, possible fractures."

"The power systems are off line, including life support," said Oliver. "This place is rapidly turning into a deep freeze. If we don't get power back on, these guys will all end up just frozen meat!"

"I've got oxygen packs," said Fiona joining them and handing them to the others. "Just give everyone a whiff of oxygen so that when they come round they can swim themselves out of here. If they're too badly injured I'll get to them when I can."

Inside the cockpit, Oliver found three people. An ashen faced Maria strapped into a side seat, was otherwise in a good medical condition. The same was so for Cadet Mohammed who was also strapped in. He was already conscious, but dazed, pale and bewildered.

Mat Kemel's limp body drifted afloat and had settled up against the deckhead. Fiona joined Oliver and quickly revived Maria with oxygen.

"How are you?" she said soothingly.

"Thank God you're here," sobbed Maria and looked up at Mat. "Mat needs attention!"

"See to him later," said Clare over the comm. "Get her out first!"

"Clare?" said Kelly. "I thought you'd sedated her?"

"I did," replied Fiona. "She's also got a restraint on her."

"He's alive!" exclaimed Oliver checking Mat. "But doesn't look too good."

"Leave him!" called Clare.

Kelly moved to the bottom of the connecting ladder to help propel people into 16.

"Clare what is it with you?" she cried.

Fiona quickly examined Mat and then gave the nod for him to be moved.

"He'll need a rhesus pack. Get him back to 16 asap! I'll be right behind you!"

Ham unstrapped himself and helped Maria propel herself towards the exit.

"Get her out and leave him!" ranted Clare bullishly. Her speech slurred and she was starting to sound more and more like a drunk.

"Clare? You're starting to scare me!" retorted Kelly.

"Leave him!" Clare snapped. "He'll survive. Men always do!"

"What the hell's wrong with you?" yelled Kelly. "Doc, you'd better go and check on her again."

"I told you, she's restrained. It may be unpleasant her talking like that, but at least it indicates she's alive."

Tate and Kelly moved aft in the direction of the hold. They reeled in disgust on discovering the two dead Mago. The corpses were decaying rapidly even in the chilled conditions of the ship. A pool of slime had collected about them and a thick layer of putrefaction spread, clinging to the deck and bulkheads in spite of the zero gravity.

Warily, they edged passed, trying not to get too close to the melting carcasses in case some terrible evil was unleashed upon them. Nevertheless, they reached the cargo hold, but with no power, had to open the door using manual pump controls.

The doctor warned them about the possibility of more unpleasant sights inside. They prized open the door and found several floating bodies. Many were bloodied and injured.

At seeing the open door, there was a surge towards them as the more able bodied ones scrambled to get out. Tate and Kelly could do nothing and were thrust aside as about a dozen men and women fought to escape.

Kelly tried to instruct them what to do, but they moved with gaunt, determined expressions and singular purpose, sliding through the entrance like crazed divers.

"Mob on the way!" was all she could say in the end as they passed.

"My God!" said Tate, peering into the hold. "It must have been like being in a laundry spinner."

Inside the hold, were scores of drifting forms, mingled with personal possessions, tools and flotsam. Globules of blood and spew of varying sizes rotated and spun like miniature planetoids. Some had suffered horrific injuries. One man was impaled through the chest, another two had died from severe head trauma. There were at least half a dozen with broken limbs and many had suffered head injuries. More than a few displayed clear signs of physical assault. Most had vomited and soiled themselves and all had lost consciousness.

"God, if they're all KO'd it'll take forever to get them out," said Kelly. "There's no time to examine everyone. Fiona where are you?"

"I'm back on board 16," announced Fiona. "You're right, there isn't time to gawk. Just get them out the best you can."

"We need you here!" insisted Kelly.

"I'd be no better than a first aider. I'm setting up a triage unit on 16 with Oliver.

"Are you getting this through our monitors?" said Kelly.

There was no response.

"Can you link life support from 16?"

A hammering sound echoed throughout the ship.

"The mob has reached the access hatch," said Oliver.

"We've closed the hatch to Skylark 16," said Fiona. "They can't get in."

"The temperature's down to minus 12 and falling rapidly," declared Tate. "Life support has failed!"

"How's Clare?" called Kelly.

"I've dosed her up again," replied Fiona.

"Fiona, you have to let them in!" called Kelly. "They'll freeze if they stay here."

A cluster of men banged ferociously and fruitlessly at the access hatch.

"They are aggressive!" said Fiona. "They may attack us!"

"They're trying to live, for God's sake!" cried Kelly. "Let them in!"

"I daren't," said Fiona.

"We need Oliver to help us shift the casualties in the hold! You're going to have to open up."

At the access ladder to Skylark 16, the figure of Tate appeared silently behind the desperate gang.

"Okay guys!" boomed Tate. The sound was muffled slightly by his helmet, but his voice was enough to get their attention.

"No one's getting out unless they cooperate and calm down!"

"We've been through hell!" yelled a shivering, wild-eyed woman at the foot of the ladder. Straggly blond hair was matted across her dirty face. Her cheeks were white with cold and tinges of blue etched her lips. "We just want to get out!"

"We're fucking freezing!" said a man, panting and clutching his chest. Others echoed his words.

"We need help to get the others out of the hold," explained Tate. "You go up there and I want your asses back here booted and spurred to do the job."

Tate's steady baritone voice seemed to have been enough to remove the panic from them. Their aggression was waning, but some of them were also starting to wilt with the cold. There was a clunk from above and the hatch swung open. Oliver dangled an arm down and one by one each was pulled clear.

The only gravitational influence was coming from Skylark 16. It was mild, but everything that was loose was slowly migrating towards the deckhead.

Fiona had thermal suits ready for those making it on board, but there were not enough for everyone. She had managed to revive Dr. Farnhurst who helped her rig rhesus packs for the more badly injured.

Kelly returned to 16 leaving Oliver and Tate leading teams of the more able bodied to evacuate the cargo hold. She made straight for the cockpit where she found the hatch locked from the inside.

"Clare?" she banged. "Doc, I thought you said she was dosed up and restrained?"

"She was," replied Fiona.

"Clare?" hammered Kelly. "If there's something wrong you can tell me!"

The ship rocked.

"Kelly!" shouted Oliver. "We're moving! The access link to 9 is becoming unstable! I don't think it's going to hold much longer!"

Kelly pounded her fists on the hatch.

"Clare! Open the hatch! Clare! Open the fucking hatch!"

The ship shuddered causing her to lose her footing. She grabbed a rail and hung on.

"Disengage the link Oliver!"

"There's just six more to get on!"

"Well, better get them in now or we'll all be space meat!"

The ship jolted severely, throwing her against a bulkhead.

"The connection ring has a fracture!" cried Tate. "We're venting! Pressure is falling!"

"Disconnect! Disconnect!" yelled Kelly.

There was another jolt and the screeching sound of rending metal.

"Oliver? Tate?"

For agonizing seconds there was no answer and Kelly feared the worst.

"All aboard!" panted Oliver finally. "We've broken free! Ship integrity restored!"

The lighting flickered as Kelly regained her composure.

"That flicker," she panted, " probably means the power plant is struggling to maintain life support. Tate, check it out!"

"Have it in hand!" he replied.

She straightened herself for another assault on the cockpit hatch, when suddenly it slid open. Clare appeared in the entrance. Her eyes emitted a faint green glow. Kelly stared at them apprehensively.

"Clare? What is .. what are you?"

"Men!" cursed Clare. "They're nearly all men!"

"It was probably the work corps in this one," Kelly explained. "Most tend to be men."

"Selfish bastards!" said Clare.

"Life support has been shut down!" said Tate.

Kelly gave a puzzled look at Clare.

"Clare what are you doing?"

"We must purge the system of men!"

Clare pulled out a laser pistol, and caressed it pensively.

"After I have purged them, I will restore life support!"

Kelly stared at her in disbelief.

"Clare, we are here to save lives! This was your idea! It doesn't matter whether they are men or women. We are here as rescuers!"

Clare shuffled passed her. Kelly moved to intercept, but an outstretched palm propelled her backwards with unnatural force and she slammed into a bulkhead.

Sanderson appeared.

"Are you in charge?" he said angrily.

Clare levelled the gun at his chest and fired at point blank range. His thorax exploded.

"Clare!" screamed Kelly.

Mat Kemel was dazed and nauseous, but conscious again. He tore at the rhesus pack, much to the dismay of Dr. Benjamin. She placed a steadying hand on him.

"You must stay calm. You could bleed to death if the pack is ripped away."

"I have to get to the cockpit!" he protested.

"Easy now," she said firmly.

"Doctor, we are all in danger," he explained as calmly as he could.

"Right now, you are in no fit state to go anywhere," she replied. "Tell me what the prob…"

Clare entered the bay. Her face was blank, but the green glow in the eyes was more prominent and conveyed pure malevolence.

"Clare?" was all Fiona could say.

Clare raised the laser and pointed it at the nearest man.

"All men are to be purged," she said in a strange monotone voice and pressed the fire button.

The rhesus pack splatted into her face, enough to spoil her aim.

"Ham!" yelled Mat.

She re-aimed at Mat as Ham delivered a powerful kick to her chest that sent her spinning back through the bay entrance.

Blood pouring from his chest, Mat stumbled towards her as she sat up abruptly. For a moment they locked eyes. There was no green glow. She mouthed and hissed a plea to him: "Help me!" and then the glow returned, and with it the malevolent stare.

Mat's strength was ebbing fast and blood poured from his wounds and mouth. Fiona tried to prevent him falling, but he crumbled to the deck before she could grab him.

"'lectric! 'lectric!" was all he could say as Clare stood over him. This time with the gun directed at his head.

There was a blue flash and a scream, but Mat's mind was already fading into unconsciousness by then and knew no more.

CHAPTER THREE

Back in space dock, Fiona Benjamin noted how much more alive TC1 had become since the Taj Mahal survivors had arrived. But in spite of Spink having taken command, there was little evidence of coordinated activity. Dr. Farnhurst joined her in providing and organizing medical assistance to those who needed it.

Spink had ensconced himself in the TC1 control centre where he sat in the central command seat pontificating over the theories of how things should be run, but without offering any positive directions or instructions.

"We have two Mago carcasses on Skylark 9," explained Mat. "They are decaying rapidly. We have to retrieve what we can of them for research purposes!"

"Nothing is to be brought here! They will remain quarantined on 9," replied Spink. "It is far too risky to bring anything belonging to them on board this station."

"But if they are properly sealed in air tight containers…"

"Mr. err…"

"Kemel."

"Mr. Kemel, I have made my decision and that is final. Skylark 9 can be recovered at the discretion of and with the resources of Charon Base. They are organizing a team. It may be some time before they get here, but it is best left to trained personnel."

"Commander, those carcasses are crucial to understanding the anatomy of an alien species. We may never get such an opportunity again."

Spink huffed and puffed and procrastinated.

"Mr. Kemel, I will ask Charon for further direction in this matter, but my inclination is that if no decision is forthcoming, then we should destroy Skylark 9 as it poses a risk to both health and navigation."

"You can't …"

"I will do what I see fit and you will not question my judgement!"

Spink gently rotated back and forth with his hands over his chest to form a bridge. His paunch betrayed his reputation for indulging in sweet foods.

Mat was still feeling groggy and week on his feet. He sat on one of the console seats to rest.

"Commander," said Mat wearily. "I think you should place the outpost under quarantine restrictions then."

Spink stopped his movement and glowered questioningly at Mat.

"Quarantine the outpost? You mean the alien's have been brought on board against my authorization?"

"No, they haven't, but there is another virus at large," Mat began. "I don't have enough evidence yet, but Lieutenant Roberts is the second person to be infected by a new strain."

"Lieutenant Roberts is facing a court martial," retorted Spink. "And I will see to it that she gets what she deserves."

"But …"

"No buts, Mr. Kemel. She has not come into contact with these aliens, yet you wish to claim that she has an infection of some sort? It will not stand in the way of justice being done."

"Commander, I believe this virus does not come from the aliens. I know that a full medical examination has been done and that Doctor Farnhurst found nothing wrong with her. She doesn't even have a cold virus in her, which is strange in itself, but her behaviour is something I have seen before."

"Mago?" said Kelly. "Is that what you call them? I saw the ugly bastards in 9's assembly area."

"You saw the rotting remains. We needed those carcasses so that we can learn all we can about them," explained Mat.

Kelly looked around at the others present.

"I'm not used to seeing so many in this mess room."

Mat supped his tea.

"I'm gravely concerned about Clare Roberts."

"So am I. What's happened to her? I've never seen anyone with eyes like hers? I can't believe it! D'you think the docs will find a cure?"

"No, but I have a theory that might help her. I have to see her."

"Hi," said a woman standing over them.

"Maria?" replied Mat standing up to greet her.

"Don't get up," she replied and took a chair beside Mat.

"Maria, I'm sorry," said Mat. "I forgot to check you out…"

"Check me out?" she retorted. "What's that supposed to mean?"

"I mean I got side tracked, and well I .."

"Mr. Kemel, we've only just met," she said mockingly "You make it sound as though we're an item."

"I'm sorry."

"And stop saying you're sorry."

In the sick bay, nylon webbing secured Clare to a bunk. Fiona and Farnhurst were unsure whether she was sleeping or comatose. All readings indicated that she was wide awake. She lay on her back, peaceful and still with eyes closed, but all attempts to communicate with her had drawn no reaction.

"She hasn't moved since she was brought here," Farnhurst explained to Mat. "I gave her a mild sedative as a precaution, but I don't think it's made much difference."

"May I see her medical charts?"

"I didn't realize you were a doctor?" said Kelly.

"I'm not, I'm just a scientist."

"Only a doctor should be allowed to view another person's medical charts," protested Farnhurst.

Fiona ignored Farnhurst's protest and handed Mat an electronic pad.

"It's a bit vague on initial detail," he murmured.

"Vague!" exclaimed Farnhurst. "What do you mean vague?"

Mat smiled at him.

"It's not a personal attack, Doctor. It's inconclusive for what I was looking for."

Lieutenant Commander Spink entered on one of his rare excursions outside of Control. Mat mused whether concern over developing piles had compelled him to leave his comfortable throne. He looked directly down at Clare with a stern, disapproving expression. She remained still, emotionless and slumbering.

"Lt. Clare Roberts, you are hereby placed under arrest and will be escorted back to Charon Base. You will undergo an inquiry into your conduct and will be prepared for court martial."

"What the hell are you saying, man?" demanded Mat tapping his head. "She's not here. Can't you see she isn't well?"

Spink turned on him.

"Your request to retrieve Skylark 9 has been refused by Charon Base. By order of Acting Commodore Bridely. Skylark 9 is to be destroyed. A team from Charon will be arriving shortly to carry out those orders."

Mat mouthed a protest but Spink blurted on with his sharp staccato voice. It reminded Mat of Alan, only Alan's was a higher pitch.

"The team will also debrief survivors and organize transfers to Charon base. That will include you, Mr. Kemel."

Spink turned to leave, but looked down over his shoulder at Clare.

"She will be escorted in a security cell. When you have seen as many fakes as I have, you learn to spot those seeking sympathy over genuine ones. Playing the victim doesn't work with me!"

He glanced across at Kelly.

"I trust you to get her belongings together so that the both of you will be ready to be escorted back to Charon within the hour."

"Am I under arrest as well?"

"That remains to be seen on how well you co-operate!"

Spink swivelled melodramatically on his heel and left abruptly.

"Asshole!" said Kelly.

Kelly childishly pulled faces in the mirror of her bathroom before picking up her toiletries and packing a couple of travel cases. It didn't take long.

At the entrance she paused to survey her room for the last time then made her way to Clare's quarters to do the same there, treating her personal effects with the reverence as if she were packing her own.

In a drawer, she found a recently received printout and read:

"Please inform First Technician Kelly O'Hare that it is with deep regret that her mother, Felicity Anne O'Hare passed away on the morning of the 6th October."

Kelly slumped on the bed, staring at the script. She felt unable to move or do anything. All she could do was stare and try to understand what was going on. Clare had had this news for three weeks and had only mentioned that her mother was ill. She never said that she had actually died. Why hadn't ESO personnel told her directly anyway?

Kelly found Clare sitting on the edge of the bed and smiling when she returned to Sick Bay.

"Clare?"

Kelly could tell from her eyes that Clare was not 100%. There was no sign of green glows or anything seemingly sinister, but she held the look of someone high on something.

"I gave her a cocktail of psychotropic drugs," explained Farnhurst. "It seems to have done the trick. At least she will be fit to travel without so many restraints."

"Can she talk?"

"Kelly, of course I can talk," said Clare sounding like her old self.

Kelly pulled a chair up in front of her and sat down.

"Doctor? Can I have a couple of minutes alone with her?"

Farnhurst looked wary.

"Two minutes is all you'll get," he said and left with a nurse following behind.

"Kelly," huffed Clare. "I'm sorry, I should have told you a couple of days ago, but I just didn't get round to it."

Kelly was puzzled and became grim faced.

"Well, it's just that your...."

"Mum is dead?" Kelly finished.

"You know?"

Kelly remained dumb. Her face was frozen as she bored straight through Clare. There was no emotion.

"I'm sorry," Clare growled and gave a strain at the holding straps.

"Two days ago?" said Kelly dryly.

Clare nodded and grinned oddly at seeing Kelly's consternation.

"How did she die?"

A kaleidoscope of expressions crossed Clare's face, but she said nothing.

"How did she die?" Kelly pressed.

"Stroke I think. Could have been a fall. You didn't care."

Kelly ignored the jibe.

"Do you know or don't you?" asked Kelly.

"You didn't care for her anyway."

"Are you going to answer me properly Clare, or not?"

Clare struggled to speak. It looked as if she was trying to regurgitate something.

"Don't remember," she croaked.

"How can you not remember something as fundamental as that?"

"You didn't care."

"Stop saying that!" Kelly screamed. "Stop fucking saying I didn't care! She was my mother!"

Kelly wanted to shake her. She stood clenching and unclenching her fists.

"Go on!" urged Clare calmly. "Why not do what you want. I am still restrained. I can hardly fight back."

"Tell me what you know!"

Clare seemed to savour Kelly's angst.

"She was found at the bottom of the stairs in her home on Tuesday morning. They didn't know whether she fell or whether it was a stroke."

"Tuesday? Tuesday?" Kelly said with dismay. "4 days ago? When did you know?"

"11 days actually. Or was it 18?"

Kelly leapt up and grabbed Clare's shoulders then shook her as tears brimmed.

"How did she die?"

Clare smiled wryly, but didn't answer.

"Don't touch her!" cried Mat. "She's infected!"

He strode purposely over to the couch with a small handheld box in his hand.

"What's that?" said Kelly wiping her eyes.

Mat played the device over Kelly's hands and face and then studied the reading on a small display on top.

"Hmm," he said studying the numbers. "Hmm, I think you may have gotten away with it."

"What's that?"

He moved towards Clare. The box set off a squeal that startled both him and Kelly. The lighting went off momentarily and then flickered back on again.

"This is Eric!" He shrugged.

"Eric?"

"Electronic Resonance Impulse Contraption."

"Contraption?"

"Yeh, I'm not very good at word games. I had to think of something for the letter C," he checked the readings again. "She's heavily infected with a nano virus."

A tear trickled down Kelly's right cheek.

"What does that mean?"

"It means we have a problem and the virus has migrated off world."

"Migrated?"

The intercom blurted with Spink's voice.

"First Technician O'Hare and ex Lieutenant Roberts are to be made ready for shipment to Charon Base in 15 minutes. Transport is due in 30 minutes."

Mat stormed off and met Farnhurst returning.

"Don't walk away!" Kelly blubbed. "This is important!"

"We have a ship to catch," replied Mat. "I'll be coming with you. We can talk more then."

The lights flickered again. Mat looked up pensively.

"Although," he added, "I think our trip is about to be delayed."

CHAPTER FOUR

"How long have we got?" asked Spink.

"If we shut down non essential systems and areas of the station we could survive 48 hours," said the technician.

"48 hours? I thought the station had all kinds of back ups?"

"It does, but there are faults cropping up all over the place."

"Faults? What sort of faults?" said Spink getting out of the command chair.

"There are electric generators located at each level around the station," explained the technician. "For some reason we can't get them started. When we stripped two of them down, we found key components were seriously corroded."

The entrance hatch slid open and Mat entered. Spink scowled at him.

"Your hostility towards me is misplaced," said Mat.

Spink could not hold back displaying his distaste.

"Oh really?" he said sarcastically. "Then what am I supposed to do? Show you gratitude?"

Mat ignored the witticism and boldly approached the on-board systems console. The young man sat at the position glanced up at him.

"Do a full analysis of the metallic structures of the station!"

"Belay that!" bellowed Spink. "I am in command here!"

"You may not be for much longer unless you listen to what I have to say," retorted Mat.

The verbal slap silenced Spink, at least for the moment.

"Do it!" Mat urged the young man and then turned his attention to the technician.

"You said you were having problems with generators?"

"Err, yes sir."

"Are the generators hooked up to the station's HC system?"

"Everything is."

"Then disengage the remaining generators from the HC; carry out whatever essential repairs are needed and then start them up unconnected to the HC."

"What are you saying?" said Spink, finding his voice again.

"The station has become infected with a nano virus and is using the Hyper Computer as a carrier."

"But that's preposterous!"

"Commander, this station needs to be quarantined until we can purge the HC."

Clare was lying on her back, quite still, but with eyes wide open. Her chest rose and fell as she breathed gently. She smiled; not a warm, cheerful smile, but a far off, artificial one.

Kelly examined her face. It was like someone peering out from behind a mask; the face of some emotionless android. It was not the face that Clare used to have. Something else was there inside her, influencing her thoughts and directing her mind.

"This ain't Clare," she muttered. "Not the Clare that I know. There's something else in there."

For a moment, the pupils of Clare's eyes glowed faintly green. It was just for the briefest of instances and then it was gone. Kelly took a step back in shock. She was not sure that she had seen anything.

"Kelly," said Clare softly. "I could …"

Fiona Benjamin entered with a nurse pushing a trolley laden with all kinds of medicinal supplies.

"Unfetter me or I'll break your fucking arms!" Clare growled with cold menace.

Kelly stumbled backwards at the outburst knocking over a tray of surgical instruments.

"My God! What are you?" she said sniffling her nose and wiping away tears.

Clare's head turned mechanically toward her and the face beamed an unnatural, clown-like smile.

"Don't you know me, Miss O'Hare?" the face said. "Why, I am Lieutenant Clare Roberts and I have a flight to catch. Take any concerns you have about me to Lieutenant Commander Spink. Let him deal with your snivelling grief."

"Okay! That's enough!" cried Fiona.

Clare's eyes rolled back into their sockets and her head lolled to the side, but Fiona was right to her.

"She's having a seizure!"

The mouth sagged open and a fountain of foamy white sputum erupted from it. Her body shivered, shook and convulsed.

"What's happening to you?" shouted Fiona and, for the first time in her career as a doctor, she was at a loss as to what to do.

"Nurse! Get Doctor Farnhurst!"

The nurse had hardly left when Clare suddenly sat bolt upright as if she had been awoken from a sleep.

Although slight of build, Clare's strength became gigantic. Her muscles and sinews cracked audibly. She tore at her restraints, snapping them as if they were made of flimsy tape. With one massive heave she tossed Kelly and Fiona aside, sending them hurtling through the air and crashing over benches and into walls.

Kelly snatched up a scalpel lying on the floor. She hauled herself up from behind a trolley, but the trolley slammed against her with furious power pinning her as if it weighed a ton.

Clare was there, up close. Her green glowing eyes stared right into hers with a gaze filled with pure malice. Kelly knew that Clare could kill her there on the spot if she wanted to, such was the difference in strength but, for some unknown reason, she did not. Instead, she hissed triumphant defiance and walked promptly out of sick bay and was gone.

In the control room, Clare circled around the back of the command seat. Spink and Mat were absent and the four control staff seemed oblivious to her presence. They concentrated on their displays and readouts as she stalked them.

She produced a curved blade and promptly sliced the top off a man's head in one stroke emitting an insane throaty laugh as she did so. A young man at comms spun in his chair and was filleted in a second. The remaining two crew leapt from their seats and fled in terror.

Spink appeared from the control room toilet, adjusting his attire, and stood flabbergasted at the blood bath that greeted his eyes. He rushed to a comms station.

"Security! Security! Security to Control immediately!"

Clare lunged at him with the reddened, blood dribbling blade, but an electric bolt struck her arm and the weapon fell from her hand.

From nowhere, Mat stood between her and a horrified Spink. His contraption "Eric" smoked ominously.

"Damn!" he cursed. "That was my favourite one!"

Fiona and Kelly stumbled into the control room nursing bruised anatomies. They recoiled at the carnage that confronted them.

For a moment, rationality returned to Clare's face.

"You don't think I could do a thing like that?" she said meekly backing around towards the exit.

"If you didn't then who did?" Mat retorted indignantly.

"You are a man," she said pointing an accusatory finger at Mat. "You would know!"

Mat fumbled with Eric, but kept a watchful eye on her.

"Why would I know?" he said, struggling and hammering the device in his hands.

Blood speckled Clare's face and dripped from her clothes.

"You stay back from us!" said Kelly moving nervously away from her.

"Clare, let us out of here," pleaded Fiona.

"I don't hurt women," said Clare. "You're safe with me. All I want from you is for you to join me. Feel the strength and pleasure of our plurality."

"Plurality?" said Kelly. "What do you mean?"

"Join me and we will become 'us' and you will know."

"Don't go near her!" warned Mat.

"Together we can show the human race how things should be!" Clare continued.

"You're talking bullshit!" exclaimed Kelly boldly. "Say what the hell you're talking about."

"Join me and you will know! You know my hatred for men. Join me and their scourge will be gone forever. You will understand when we become as one."

"What have you got against guys?"

Clare's eyes glowed green more brightly than ever before. Mat gestured at Kelly and Fiona and the two women retreated leaving the exit clear, but Clare moved swiftly to them.

"Please Clare," Fiona trembled. "We're your friends. Please don't…"

Clare opened her mouth and they watched in horror as her canine teeth began to extend before them into vicious, pointed fangs.

Without warning she nimbly sprang at Mat and undoubtedly would have reached him, but for the dart that embedded in her neck. She dropped like a stone and landed limply in front of Mat's feet.

"Thought you might need a hand," said Farnhurst.

Fiona rushed to her.

"Have you killed her?"

"Don't touch her!" shouted Mat.

He fiddled about in his pocket and produced a screwdriver.

"This woman needs help!" argued Fiona. "In spite of what you may think about her!"

"Yes, and so will you if you touch her!"

He flipped open a lid on Eric and began working intently on repairing it while Fiona hovered anxiously above Clare's still body.

"She needs physics rather than biology," he said, "if she's ever going to be okay again."

"No!" shrieked Kelly.

Mat pulled Spinks arm upwards and the laser scoured the ceiling. He held the bigger man with what strength he had. It was barely enough just to get Spink's attention. The two men wrestled and faced off.

"She has slaughtered two innocent members of my crew in cold blood!" yelled Spink. "She should die for what she has done!"

"Commander, that body lying there is not Clare Roberts. She has been taken over. We must win her back if we are to have a chance of saving others."

Spink was wild eyed with rage and Mat's hold on him was weakening.

"We don't have much time," strained Mat. "The tranc will only last for a short period. I'm surprised it worked at all."

Spink shoved him away. They both breathed hard, but Spink did not try to fire again.

"You are weak Mr. Kemel," said Spink.

"I was never an all in wrestler."

"What are you proposing we do?"

Mat looked at Farnhurst.

"Doctor, isolate and treat her as you would someone with a bio-haz. Get her back to sick bay asap."

Mat stomped to the main door.

"Where are you going?" said Kelly.

"I need some gear," he answered. "I'll be back as soon as I'm ready."

He turned in the doorway and stared firmly at Spink.

"Commander, this station is quarantined until I say so!"

Spink mouthed a protest, but Mat was gone.

"Death seems to follow me around," Kelly mourned and grimaced at the sight of the bloody remains of the two crewmen.

CHAPTER FIVE

Mat worked swiftly on his equipment, studying wiring, checking connections and testing power outputs. Unnoticed, Maria appeared next to him.

"Do you need help?" she said softly.

He afforded her a quick smile but continued.

"Thanks, but no."

"You haven't bothered with me since our escape," she said smoothing herself down.

"Maria, I'm sorry, but there hasn't been the time."

She observed him, but held back speaking.

"Do you think," she began again. "When all this is over, we could …"

"Who knows?" he replied dismissively.

She turned away disappointed and ambled reluctantly toward the door.

"Look, I'm sorry Maria," he said standing up straight. "As you said earlier, we've only just met and not in very agreeable circumstances. Right now, this is urgent."

She hung her head and left without further comment or expression.

The control centre team watched as the Marco Polo came within weapons range of Skylark 9. It was all over in seconds. A burst of pulsed laser fire initially split the shuttle asunder and a single missile turned its remains into space dust.

"The Marco Polo has requested permission to dock, Commander," said Paula. "What are your instructions?"

Spink twisted and wrung his hands. He looked about the control centre to try to find any evidence of the murders that had taken place barely an hour before, but the cleaning droids had done a thorough job.

"Commander?"

Spink still procrastinated.

"Commander? What are your instructions?"

The hatch slid open and two cadets entered and stood to attention side by side in front of Spink.

"Cadet Oliver Stenson reporting for duty, Sir!

"Cadet Mohammed Salem reporting for duty!

Spink glowered at them as if he was having trouble acknowledging their presence.

"Cadet Stenson," he said suddenly. "We have a ship from Charon Base requesting clearance to dock, do we let it or not?"

"Not Sir."

"Do you concur?" he asked Ham. Ham agreed.

"Ms. Savage, tell the Marco Polo that she is to take up a holding position 1500 metres off the station and wait for further orders!"

Spink leapt down from his seat and almost careered into the two cadets. He straightened his tunic and then examined a gauge.

"Damn it!" he cursed. "Gravity's dropped 20%."

Mat wheeled his trolley into sick bay and found a semi-naked Clare chained and manacled in a cage. He felt huge pity for her. She stood like a zombie, her head pressed against the bars, rigidly staring out at the world beyond.

Kelly was transfixed, looking at the woman she had come to regard as a friend in the time they had been together on TC1.

"That's not Clare!" Kelly blubbed. "That thing is so cold; so unfeeling! That's not her!"

"Well, I hope she's in there somewhere," said Mat organizing a tangle of wires, junction boxes and a variety of gadgets.

Farnhurst and Fiona expressed curiosity at Mat's gear.

"What do you intend to do? Fry her?" said Farnhurst.

"Something like that."

"You are not permitted to do anything without our approval," added Fiona.

"I wouldn't dream of it," replied Mat.

The lighting flickered on and off.

"We don't have much time," said Mat. " Can you help me?"

"First Technician Kelly O'Hare to the Control Room on the double!" Spink called over the tannoy.

"Damn Spink!" cursed Mat.

"Don't worry! I'll see what he wants and be back in a jiff!" said Kelly.

"….order has come from Commodore Bridely himself," said Paula as Kelly entered the Control Room.

"Commander?" said Paula. "How should I reply?

Spink sat in his seat and ignored her. He instead turned his attention to Kelly, to whom he was unusually polite.

"I'm sorry to hear of your loss Ms. O'Hare. I've only just learned of the passing of your poor mother. Right now we need you. Any inquiries into your conduct will be suspended for the time being."

"What are you after, Spink?" she said sceptically.

"There's not enough power at all now with the main generator gone," Spink continued. "The situation is rapidly deteriorating. Emergency power will only last, at the most, about six hours. Your skills are needed more than ever. Already onboard gravity is dropping at a rate of 1 centigee per minute. We'll be floating within an hour. With no gravity and no power, this place will be just like a big dark deep freeze."

"There are guys on board who can deal with the power problems."

"May be, but we need every technician we can to sort out the station's system controls. We could be on the brink of an interplanetary conflict and *we* are in the front line."

"Transmission from Charon Base," said a young man at comms. "Another coded message."

"Patch it through," answered Spink.

Kelly just stared and said nothing, contemplating the things happening around her. Her mind was plagued by her grief for her Mum and the weird affliction that seemed to have grasped Clare and transformed her into something alien and other worldly. She felt a compulsion to get away from this place. She needed to go somewhere quiet; a private place to think and to grieve.

"Excuse me. I'll get down to Biophysics," she said. "There might be something that I can conjure up that will ease the heating problem."

Clare was once again strapped to a couch, though not with synthetic webbing. The imprisoning bars had been removed, but this time she was secured with arachinium. Arachinium, a molecularly complex and expensive material, the strongest substance that mankind had ever produced. It used the innate strength and elasticity of spider silk fused at the molecular level with the highest quality steel alloy. The combination of the organic with the inorganic made it virtually unbreakable, light and easy to handle as well as non corrosive.

Mat finished off adjusting connections to Clare's head and feet.

Fiona, as ever filled with compassion, studied Clare's blank facial expressions with concern.

"Why did you kill them?" she asked mournfully.

Clare croaked a response.

"Told you they were…."

"No! That's not it! You were never murderous. What's gotten into you?"

"Join me and you will understand."

"It's not Clare you're talking to," said Mat.

He tugged at a couple of cables to satisfy himself they were secure.

"There! All done!"

Clare's face suddenly changed to mauve and then deepened into blue as if she were badly bruised all over. Her neck tensed and her arms strained at her bonds, but the arachinium held. As before, she turned her head mechanically sideways. Pure malevolence possessed her. Her eyes glowed green and then changed into a burning red. The jaws opened wide revealing a mouth filled with extended teeth both top and bottom.

"Hit the switch, Doc!" shouted Mat. "Now!"

Farnhurst pushed up a lever. The overhead lights flickered on and off a few times.

They watched as waves of electrical energy surged through Clare's body. A cloud of vapour exuded from Clare's mouth and hung in mid air like a ball of steam. Mat produced Eric, directed it at the mass and fired into the cloud. Clare emitted a shrill, ear-splitting and high-pitched whistle-like scream. The cloud diminished in size and deposited what looked like rain on the deck beneath.

The acrid smell of burning electrics permeated the air and then the lighting failed completely. Flashes, cracks and sparks pierced the darkness in a confusing and blinding array of pyrotechnics.

All fell silent and dark except for a faint turquoise hue from somewhere near Clare's couch. It took a few more moments before lighting was restored and they were able to take stock of what had happened.

Clare lay at rest anaemically white and limp. At first Fiona feared she might be dead, but managed to detect a faint pulse from her gauges. She reached for the Hypo Doc, but Mat stopped her.

"No equipment can be trusted just yet until it's been checked out."

Mat examined Eric. The power level had been badly drained, but he was satisfied there was enough to carry out a sweep of Clare's body.

"Eureka! She's clear! Let's hope she stays that way. She's all yours doctors!"

And with that he left.

CHAPTER SIX

"I've done all you've asked," said Spink. "Though it has been against my better judgement, but what you're asking for now is going too far."

"Commander, I appreciate you trusting me. You have been very courageous in the face of things. All I ask is that you trust me one more time."

"But I have had specific instructions from Commodore Bridely that this station is to be boarded forthwith. The order was received more than half an hour ago."

"Have you acknowledged it?"

"I did," said Paula.

Mat paced with a limp from one side of the circular control room to the other. Spink eyed him, consternation etched across his face.

"Evacuate the station," said Mat.

"So you don't want us to stay here after all?"

"Now that I know that Eric works, I can screen everybody as they leave, it won't be necessary for them to stay."

"Eric? Who the hell's Eric?"

"Electronic Resonance Impul…" Mat began then tapered off. "Never mind, it's a device that can be used to detect and combat this nano-virus."

Another message flashed up on the screen.

"Direct Order from Commodore Bridely: "You are to facilitate the docking of Marco Polo immediately and without further delay. A team of decontam engineers is on board and will deal with the crisis."

"I'm sorry Mr. Kemel," Spink said frankly. "I have gone further than I should have done. I cannot delay any longer. Give the signal, Ms. Savage!"

"Commander, they don't know what they're dealing with here. This virus is not like any other."

Spink leaned forward and fixed a firm and unshakeable gaze on Mat.

"Mr. Kemel, those boys have pedigree. They said they would never stop Crypto Syndrome when it broke out in Latin America three years back. It took them just ten days. Last year, there was the threat of Super Plague in London, just four people ended up dying after they moved in. If anyone is going to stop this, this nano-virus, it will not be you, it will be them!"

Mat recognised a wall when he saw one and decided to return to his laboratory.

The temperature outside the control centre was already plunging when he left. In the alleyway a young woman staggered and fell forward. Mat caught her and eased her down onto her back. Her face was gaunt and full of fear.

"What's happening to me?" she gasped, fighting for each breath.

Her lower jaw fell wide open in an exaggerated gape. Mat recoiled, staggering backwards against the other bulkhead. He watched in disbelief as all the woman's teeth grew into extended canines that rapidly filled her entire mouth. She hissed trying to breathe. Her eyes became blood shot and bulged excessively.

Mat slid a few steps along the bulkhead wanting to run, but his attention was held in horrified fascination at what was happening.

The woman reached out to him appealing for help, but could not get up. Her fingers began elongating into thin needle like digits. She fell forward desperate, terrified and gasping. One of her fingers snapped like a dry twig as it struck the deck.

Mat slapped a hand to his mouth and fought to resist the panic. He dug into his pockets for Eric, but the woman gave out a shrill whistle like cry. Her body raised up like curling paper, savagely arching her back. Silvery blotches became manifest across all exposed skin and began to spread. Mat could only imagine the terror and agony the poor woman suffered in those last moments before she slumped down still and unmoving.

It took a few seconds to overcome the shock of what he had seen. He cautiously approached the lifeless form with the head lying face down on her arm. The silvery blotches continued to spread, giving her skin a strange shimmer. He passed Eric over his own shaking hands and found he was clear, but as he stooped over the woman's body, she suddenly rolled over onto her back.

Mat grunted at seeing the whole of her eyes completely black. Her shrivelled lips parted to reveal the huge teeth but, as he watched, they yellowed and then turned brown. A mist poured from her nostrils and mouth to form a small, white cloud above her face.

"Not again," he moaned to himself trying to contain his horror.

He prepared to discharge Eric into the mass, but then to his further revulsion, her entire body startlingly collapsed in on itself as if it had suddenly become hollow inside.

He fired Eric at the cloud. He thought he heard a very high pitch searing note and then as before, it diminished and was soon gone, leaving behind the empty wet skin of what used to be a woman's face.

He stumbled back into Control shaking and traumatized. Fear and shock had seized his mind.

"How long before the Marco Polo berths?" he heard himself struggle to say.

"6 minutes," said Paula.

"What are you up to?" said Spink. "You look like you've seen a ghost."

"Maybe I have," he replied. "A woman has just died outside of this compartment. There's nothing but skin left of her. The disease is here outside that door!"

"All will be set right in just a few more minutes," said Spink.

"Those men will be joining a death station with their name on the toll list like ours already is."

"Control! Control!" yelled Kelly over the intercom. "We're under attack! They're hammering on the door! They're breaking in!"

Thunderous bangs could be heard in the background as she spoke.

"We can't get out! Everyone's gone crazy! We can't get out!"

"Six minutes will be too late!" cried Mat. "The virus has already swept through the station. Those people are not in control of their bodies. The virus is! It won't take long before it works out the manual override to that door and then we're all finished."

"How can a virus think?" said Spink.

"It's a nano virus," explained Mat. "It's programmed to think."

Spink froze.

"5 minutes to docking, Commander," added Paula.

"They come on board," explained Mat. "They will become infected or take us back with them and others will get it. It'll be a plague that'll spread across the stars, but more than a plague; one that can think and adapt and plan. We'll never stop it!"

The hatch slid open and Maria rushed in. In her hand, she waved an aerosol.

"Good God!" cried Spink.

She pressed the nozzle and a spray with a bluish tinge gushed out. It collected and formed a cloud that rushed toward Paula. Paula screamed and fell backwards out of her chair to get away.

"Hold your breath!" yelled Mat and fired Eric at it. A lightning charge leapt from the device and into the cloud.

Maria, her eyes glassy, swung her spray-can towards Mat. In an instant she had been floored with a high karate kick and the can was sent spinning across the deck.

The cloud actively pursued Paula as she scrambled desperately to escape. Jon, one of the two other controllers on duty, pulled her toward him and swiped a data board at it.

It evaded his efforts and took on the shape of an elongated plume and then seemed to be sucked in to the board. Jon dropped the device like a hot potato.

Maria gathered herself up and sprang nimbly at Paula and Jon, but he swung a chair and held her off as she gnashed at him with long, savage teeth.

"You will join us!" she shrieked

A blue, electric shock leapt along her body. Maria screamed and Jon pushed her away with the chair and retreated together with Paula. Then she curled info a fetal position, clutching her head in her hands.

"Uggh!" she exclaimed. "The pain! I can't stop! Help me! Help me! ..."

Silence fell as she drifted off into unconsciousness. Mat adjusted Eric and checked the atmosphere.

"That worked better that time," he said.

Spink sat, unmoved in the command seat and simply stared in wonderment; his chubby face gaunt.

"All clear!" Mat declared. "Now close and lock that damned door and let's purge this station!"

"Docking in less than 3 minutes!" said Martin, the other duty controller.

A panicked plea came over the intercom.

"They're in!" shrieked Kelly. "Oh, God! Their eyes! Oh ....."

The intercom went dead.

On Marco Polo, fifteen Decon Team members, armed and fully dressed in bio-war suits, stood by the airlock ready to burst into action as soon as the door opened.

"Standby teams!" called the Captain. "Docking in 60 seconds!"

On this occasion, and rarely done these days, the Captain had authorized manual docking. The station filled their screens, but the mooring links had their own cameras and distance readouts to enable the most precision of berthings.

Suddenly, and to the Captain's astonishment, TC1 blacked out; a complete power failure; not even a twinkle shone from the station.

"What the ..?" was all he could say.

"Lost comms as well, Captain," said someone."

"Life support has shutdown completely!" said another.

"Docking in 30 seconds," said the Navigator. "Do you wish to abort?"

"Negative," said the Captain. "Engage magnetic clamps!"

He adjusted the intercom mike on his head piece before he spoke again.

"Decon Teams, this is the Captain. TC1 has lost all power! You will be entering the station in blackout conditions. There will be a short delay before you get the green light to board."

The magnetic clamps fired and attached to the station. Slowly, Marco Polo was drawn into position and adjusted to marry up the docking ports.

"Okay team," said the Captain. "We're in position and ready for you to board! Standby!"

"Captain! We'll have to force the station's access door!" said the team leader. "The external manual override has been jammed."

"What the hell's going on in there?" muttered the Captain. "It's as if they don't want us to rescue them."

TC1 was completely lifeless when the Decon Teams finally entered and internal temperature levels had already plunged below freezing.

Their first find was to come across a scattering of chilled and freezing bodies here and there in an alleyway.

"Marco Polo, this is Decon 1. Have found 8 people. All unconscious, but alive. Clear for removal!"

The med teams were quick to follow up once the vanguard had checked them for contamination.

Decon moved on and reached sick bay. There they found the hatch lying twisted inwards. Mindful of the jagged edge that protruded dangerously upward, they stepped over and entered.

The temperature inside still read +5° Celsius but, as was the case elsewhere, it was cooling rapidly. About twelve lay in close proximity as if they had just collapsed where they stood.

"Marco Polo, Decon 1. Are you getting these pics?"

"Roger, Decon 1," came the reply.

"Looks like some kind of battle. The place has been stormed."

More med team members returned to collect bodies as soon as they could. A torch shone over the face of Clare Roberts, lying motionless, but breathing shallowly on a couch. They noted the strapping on the woman's half naked body.

"Wonder what's wrong with her? She's tied with arachinium. What is this?"

They pondered as to how they would release her, but then one of them found that the bond had already been released.

Decon 2 reached Control, but not without discovering their own share of incapacitated bodies en route.

A small explosive device was used to breach the hatch. They rushed in brandishing their weapons and instruments, but inside they found everyone sitting patiently and awake.

"Don't move!" exclaimed the team leader.

Mat was stooped over Maria's body lying still on the deck.

"I wouldn't dream of moving," he said.

"Stay where you are! Don't move!" repeated the leader.

"We are clear," said Mat. "Just Maria. I've not checked her thoroughly, but I think she's okay."

He looked down at Maria.

"What you do to her?" said the leader.

"She's okay! She's clear as well! I checked her out!"

The leader clearly did not understand and was not convinced by Mat's posture.

"Okay on the ground! Right now, you son-of-a-bitch!"

"Deck," replied Mat. "It's called a deck!"

The leader waved his weapon at Mat in a threatening manner. One of the other men thrust his foot into the back of his knee and forced him down.

Mat appealed to Spink, but all Spink did was to point an accusatory finger at him.

"I am Lieutenant Commander Spink. He's the one you want, if you want to know what this is all about!"

Two men grabbed Mat's arms and roughly cuffed his wrists behind his back.

"Gee thanks for your support, Commander," Mat grunted.

Half a dozen guns trained on him as he was then unceremoniously hauled to his feet and dragged away.

PART FOUR:
CHARON BASE TO LUNAR 2

CHAPTER ONE

Captain Bridely had received good news from Lunar 2. Admiral Antyuk had informed him that his promotion to full commodore had been approved by the Board of Directors of ESO. The documentation for his award was being prepared and he was to attend Lunar 2 in ten days time to participate in the official ceremony.

A specially assigned transport ship had collected most of the survivors of the Tau Ceti and TC1 incidents and had taken them directly to Lunar 2. It was not expected that they would remain there long. Rumour had it that after a brief stop, they were to be shifted to the Aldrin base labs on the moon to undergo full medical and psychological evaluations.

One of Bridely's first tasks as the new number one was to promote Lieutenant Commander Spink to Full Commander and assign him to the construction vessel Omega 9. His assignment was to oversee the re-establishment of TC1's primary systems and then take over as station commander until a suitable relief could be found.

Commodore elect Bridely had insisted on meeting what he termed the "Renegades" before they were sent on to Lunar 2 for further questioning.

He sat rapping his fingers on his desk waiting for them to arrive. Eventually, the buzzer sounded and he could see through the opastic door that his wait was over.

He pressed the green enter light, the door slid open and in they trooped. First in was Kelly O'Hare. Dr. Fiona Benjamin was followed by Lt. Clare Roberts in a wheel chair pushed by Mat Kemel. Six security guards brought up the rear and took up positions near to the prisoners and by the door in case anybody attempted to escape.

"The prisoners will stand at attention!" bellowed the sergeant.

Fiona was the only one to obey. The guard moved to enforce his order, but Bridely waved him back.

"Insubordination!" grumbled the sergeant.

Bridely got to his feet, clasped his hands behind his back and moved around the desk so as to look into each of their faces.

"Well," he began sternly. "Where do I start?"

Kelly moved her lips to speak.

"Ah!" he exclaimed, holding his finger in front of her for silence. "Outpost TC1 has had to be temporarily abandoned due to extensive damage. A full team of engineers and construction scientists has been assembled and sent to carry out, what amounts to a virtual rebuild of the infrastructure. So, Charge 1 will be: wanton destruction of ESO property and equipment."

He leaned over Clare. She blinked up at him.

"She's sick…" started Mat.

"Shut up!" roared Bridely right in Mat's face.

He returned to focus on Clare.

"Where do we go with you? Murder? Wanton destruction? Insubordination?"

He straightened himself and paced with his hands again behind his back, but he also kept a cynical eye on Clare.

"Sick or not, you should be made an example of. You were instructed by your superior officer to systematically shutdown the wormhole conduit. Instead, you chose to collapse it in the most destructive manner and without any regard for it reopening in the near future. Huge resources have been squandered due to your action. You have set the space program back months if not years!"

Kelly tried to speak again, but he held his finger up in front of her once more to keep her silent. He moved to Mat and glowered contemptuously down at the shorter man.

"Mercury 4? Taj Mahal? I don't know what will happen to you laddie by the time they've done with you. A life in the ore mines of Mars would be one appropriate place I could think of!"

"But …"

"Silence!" roared the sergeant and drew his stun stick in readiness.

"Charge 2, murder!" Bridely continued. "Charge 3, disobeying a direct order from your superior officer. Charge 4: Sabotage."

"This is …," began Kelly, but Bridely was in no mood for interruptions.

"Quiet!" he roared. He paused before continuing. "Charge 5: Mutiny. We could go on and on."

"You are," said Kelly before she could stop herself. The sergeant brought his stick to bear across her shoulders. There was a sharp crack that dropped her to her knees in a yelp of pain.

Mat moved to intervene, but the guard pushed the end of the stick under his chin and held his finger on the shock button. Bridely continued to pace in front of them ignoring the sergeant's actions.

"I am a lenient sort of person," he went on.

He stopped in front of Fiona.

"Doctor Benjamin, although you participated, I have been instructed to tell you that charges against you will not be made and you are to resume your duties. But you will be required for the inquiry so you will be travelling to Lunar 2 on the next passenger ship."

Fiona remained where she was.

"Dismissed!" he shouted causing her to jump.

When she had left, Bridely moved in front of the small figure of Kelly. She had gotten to her feet again. He then looked up and down the three of them.

"A bunch of dwarfs!" he scoffed.

"Fuck off!" Kelly got in.

"Gag her!" Bridely directed the guards.

"Sir?" said the sergeant.

"Gag her or slug her!" he cried. "I don't care which."

The guard raised his stick, but Kelly landed a side thrust kick to his abdomen and doubled him up. In an instant, Bridely caught her on her jaw line with a slapping blow and she sprawled to the deck again. Mat swung a fist, but another guard delivered a stun shock to his neck and he ended up beside Kelly. A third guard menaced them with his stun stick in case they tried to retaliate and seconds later they were cuffed.

"Take them away!" snarled Bridely. "Keep them restrained until they're off the base!"

CHAPTER TWO

"So, what you claim in your statement, Mr. Kemel," said Councillor Morley, "is that Commander Morris suffered some neurological deterioration whilst in hibernation on passage to Tau Ceti?"

The twelve directors of ESO sat behind a large curved table, the locus of which centred on one padded black armchair; the chair that Mat Kemel was now sitting in.

"What I am suggesting," replied Mat, "is that what happened to Commander Morris was a clear sign of mental degeneration and that one possible cause was that something happened to him on passage to Tau Ceti."

Mat was dressed in a smart grey civilian suit minus a tie, but in spite of the temperature controlled environment perspiration seeped from his brow.

"Mr. Kemel," said Councillor Morley. "The hibernation chambers have all been thoroughly tested. They have served numerous astronauts for many years. They have a 100% fail-safe record. There has never been any problem prior to this. Where is your evidence?"

"Well, Councillor," said Mat. "All I'm saying is that Commander Morris, as with all of us, had to go through extensive screening and profiling before we went on this mission. I believe that, unless the results of the tests were false, then something happened to Commander Morris that should not have happened."

A bead of sweat trickled from Mat's forehead and down his right cheek. The councillors' heads moved as if they were talking to each other, but Mat could not hear anything they were saying. He surmised that a sound block device was being used to prevent unauthorized eavesdropping.

He checked his watch.

He had been there for nearly an hour being grilled over various aspects of his report. How much longer did he have to endure this?

"Councillors," he said. "I don't know if…"

The twelve heads simultaneously turned to gaze at him.

"I have been asking," he continued, "if a rescue mission is being planned, but no one is giving any commitments."

"Mr. Kemel," said Councillor Mulaudzi. "We are not at liberty to reveal future ESO plans at this time. This is an inquiry about gross misconduct, so far you've produced no substantial evidence other than hearsay."

"Then what about Lieutenant Roberts?"

"What about her?" replied Morley.

"She seemed to be displaying similar symptoms to Commander Morris when she killed the men on TC1."

"Tell us what you know of that incident?" said Councillor Lyndhurst.

"It's in my report," replied Mat. "I was there. Remember?"

"We'd like to hear it again, in your own words."

Mat stirred in his seat. He was frustrated and more than a little annoyed by all the formalities.

"Well, she apparently started acting out of character when she was on TC1. Whatever had infected Commander Morris I believe also contaminated her. The link is TC1. It has to be. We stopped there for three days before going on towards Tau Ceti."

The councillors began talking inaudibly amongst themselves again. Mat had had enough. He had been interrogated, tested, imprisoned, isolated from friends and family and no one seemed to be listening to him.

"Damn it councillors!" he cried. "Whilst we're sitting here on our asses people like Jenny Gold are fighting for their lives. We don't know what kind of torments they are going through or even if they are alive at all! What has happened to Morris and Roberts could already be developing into some deadly viral plague! We have to do something!"

The councillors allowed him his rant.

"Mr. Kemel," said Councillor Morley calmly. "If there was to be a rescue mission mounted, would you be willing to volunteer for such a mission?"

For the first time, Mat found something to smile about.

"Absolutely," he said firmly and on a quieter note.

More silent conferring ensued. It had become comical. Mat tried to work out from their expressions what they were discussing, but it appeared there was some division of opinion between them.

Councillor Morley did most of the talking and sat toward the middle of the table which probably meant he was the chairman. He cursed himself inwardly for not knowing these things. They didn't after all, live as a secret society. It's just that he never bothered with political things. It had never interested him to know who was who.

"Mr. Kemel," Morley said finally. "If you would be prepared to join in a rescue mission, then you will need to report to Crew Allocations after leaving this room. Would you be willing to do so at such short notice?"

Mat was bewildered by the statement. He had expected nothing but harsh discipline and this offer had come out of the blue.

"I would be more than happy to, Sir," he replied timidly.

"In that case we won't detain you any further," replied Morley. "All charges against you are suspended due to lack of evidence. You are released. Have you any questions before you leave?"

Mat felt dumbfounded. He struggled to think straight.

"Well yes," he said without really knowing what he was going to ask.

"Go on," Morley prompted.

"What is going to happen about the possibility of some kind of viral disease spreading throughout humanity?"

"We will be looking into it," came the reply.

"Will I be able to influence who may join me on this expedition?"

"Who did you have in mind?"

"Err, well, Kelly O'Hare, for one."

"Miss O'Hare has currently been charged and is facing a court martial," advised Councillor Lyndhurst. "Why would you want her?"

"I am allowed to express an honest opinion?"

"Of course," said Morley.

"I think to court martial Miss O'Hare is a gross error when she demonstrated loyal support for Lieutenant Roberts and was pivotal in saving so many lives. She showed that she is a cut above average. She has intelligence, spirit and the ability to think on her feet. To charge her is completely wrong. She should be given a medal for her behaviour not condemned for it."

"Your opinion is noted, but is not sufficient for a court martial charge to be dropped," said Lyndhurst.

"But," continued Mat. "Her ability to think on her feet is not that common and if we are going back to Tau Ceti, it is someone like her that may make all the difference between life and death."

"A moment, Mr. Kemel," said Morley. Yet more silent debate. More serious expressions. Mat found it so amusing that he was struggling not to start giggling.

"Well, Mr. Kemel," said Morley. "We are not at liberty to grant anything just yet, but we will look into your request. Anything else?"

"Lieutenant Roberts?"

"What about Lieutenant Roberts?" said Mulaudzi.

"No evidence of infection of any kind has been found on Lieutenant Roberts. She has been formally suspended," Morley responded firmly. "She has been charged with murder."

"But she clearly was not acting herself," replied Mat. "I treated her. I cured her."

"We do not know that she was infected with anything," argued Morley. "She is in good care. She must face justice."

"But it wasn't her!"

Morley was exasperated.

"You are beginning to sound paranoiac, Mr. Kemel. Drop the subject!"

"And Maria Hastings? Where is she?"

"She is being kept under observation," said Mulaudzi

"Nothing has been found," added Morley.

"But the equipment may not be up to the job," replied Mat.

"She has been looked at by the latest state-of-the-art Hypo 240 doctor. If there was anything wrong with her, we would know."

"Then what if there is something wrong with the equipment?"

"What are you saying?"

"I believe I am on to something; a cure; a treatment."

"For an illness that is not recognized and for which there is no evidence that it even exists except for your testimonies."

"You can't disbelieve us after what happened."

"Let us say, we are giving you the benefit of the doubt," replied Morley. "That is why you have been given your new assignment."

"If Maria Hastings is still infected, she should be quarantined and if she has been in contact with several people, they should be quarantined too."

"She is being kept under observation, as I have said. We have found no evidence of any infection."

"May I see her?" said Mat. "I would like to try an experiment that will tell us whether she is infected or not."

"Are you a medical doctor?"

"No, but this is as much to do with physics as biology."

"Mr. Kemel, if you have in mind using one of your Ernie gadgets then I have to advise you that such equipment has not been analyzed and approved by the board."

"Eric," retorted Mat. "It's called Eric, and I can assure you it leaves no long term after effects."

Another silent conversation took place amongst the council.

"Do you have any preference for pilots on your mission?" asked Morley.

"I would have liked Clare Roberts, but I suppose…"

Morley shook his head disapprovingly.

"Would it be too much to ask to allow that cadet, Oliver Stenson to be the pilot?"

"He is inexperienced," answered Morley, "but if you want him then it will be arranged."

"Let me take Lieutenant Roberts with us as a stand in. I can monitor her condition on passage. She is the first to be cured so far."

"Of a disease that is unproven to exist," added Morley. "Taking her on this expedition is out of the question!"

Mat got up to leave.

"Mr. Kemel," said Morley.

Mat stopped at the door and waited whilst the council carried on with their silent tête-a-tête. Morley stood and straightened himself.

"We will grant you a specialist visitor's pass to go to Lieutenant Roberts. But whatever you do, nothing will prevent her from being court martialled."

Morley sighed. "Will that be all, Mr. Kemel?"

"Err, just one more thing," said Mat. "When are we due to launch?"

Mat decided to walk the distance to the Crew Allocation Office. Walking helped him to think. He also felt the desire to take in and enjoy the view of Earth. There were many observation points en route. Nearly all of them had groups of people, mainly tourists, gazing in wonderment.

Lunar 2's roads and pathways consisted of a web of walkways going to and from different levels. Auto cabs cruised along 'cab tracks'. The station was an amazing feat of engineering and design, home for over a million people. It was not simply a stepping stone for the stars, but monitored and acted to control climate change on Earth. Huge arrays, known as "Directors", orbiting the sun drew positive feeds of solar energy and redirected it to provide power to the station, the wormholes and to Earth. Solar particles were drawn off from the received energy and used to bolster Earth's and Lunar 2's electromagnetic fields.

Mat leaned on a railing to watch everyday events unfold. A boy, probably about six years old, came out of a shop with his parents. His father tried to snare his hand, but the boy had other ideas and ran off. His mother screamed as the boy ran onto the cab track lane right in front of a cab. The car halted immediately, much to the consternation of its two passengers. One of the men inside the cab hurled abuse at the boy's father, but the cab carried the men away before any unpleasantness could develop. Mat wondered if a human driver would have reacted so well.

He strolled over to one of the huge view ports. From it, the moon was rising from behind the Earth; an impressive sight, half in nightfall, half in daylight. The blueness of the oceans always filled one with awe and the white whirls of super typhoons added a fierce beauty to the Earth's visage.

Many habitations were now constructed sub surface and thus most people were shielded from the worst of nature's effects.

The Earth had faced environmental catastrophe but, with Lunar 2, man's marvel of technology, climatic deterioration had been checked.

Far over to Mat's right, the sun shone as powerfully as ever. Mat ran through a revision exercise in his head about all that he knew about Earth's closest star. It was just entering its latest eleven year cycle of sunspot activity. It had been one of the main hazards that space workers had had to cope with during the construction of Lunar 2.

Nowadays, the field generators in the station were more than capable of deflecting whatever the sun spewed out, but what had fascinated him in the last few years was the use of four Director stations to enhance the energy gathered from the sun.

Directors were unmanned satellite arrays placed close to the sun. They created gravitational eddies to attract the power produced by solar prominences. From these, radiation could be processed and converted into different forms of energy to be used according to man's needs.

In spite of all that was promised, Mat had been publicly critical of the Director Project when it was first initiated, and it was ironic that soon after voicing his opinion, his post at the University of Houston had been abolished.

"Mr. Kemel," said a voice.

Mat broke from his concentration with a start. He turned to see who could possibly know him.

"Councillor Morley," Mat said with unconcealed surprise. "What are you doing here?"

The councillor smiled warmly. He was no longer draped in his toga styled clothes of office, but was attired casually.

"I thought I would enjoy the sight of moonrise," said Morley cheerfully. "May I join you?"

"Of course," said Mat. "It's a free world."

"Is it?" replied Morley stroking his greying beard. The two stood leaning and gazing from their vantage-point.

"Are you questioning that it's a free world, councillor?"

"Hmm, perhaps more whether we are on or in a world," came the reply.

Morley looked at his watch.

"Expect you're off on some duty, aren't you?" said Mat.

"No, not really," he paused and studied Mat's face. "Mr. Kemel ..."

"My friends call me Mat. That is if it's not too presumptuous to be on first name terms with the Chair of the Council."

Morley chuckled.

"Mat," he said. "Would you care to join me on my private launch for an orbital tour of Lunar 2?"

"You're not after some kind of kinky sex are you?"

Mat blushed and regretted making the remark as soon as he had said it, although Morley displayed no reaction.

"I'm sorry," said Mat immediately. "I shouldn't have been so flippant."

Morley continued to say nothing, but just smiled.

"Okay, I'll take up your kind offer. Would tomorrow be alright?"

"Tomorrow is impossible, I have several appointments booked. I was hoping you would come with me now. There are some things we need to discuss that should not wait."

The two walked to a nearby cab track and secured a ride. The cab took them to Docking Bay 2 where Morley's launch 'Eagle 1' was berthed.

Mat stood beside the gangway and cast an eye over its small, sleek shape. He reckoned it was capable of carrying no more than a dozen or so people at a time.

"Neat," said Mat. "I'd have thought someone in your position would have had something a bit grander."

"Believe it or not, I am a modest person."

Morley opened his arms and gestured for Mat to step aboard.

Mat found himself in a small, but elegantly decorated lounge area with few fittings and no computer terminals at all. The only gadget visible was the universal dispenser, built in to the bulkhead. Luscious seats adorned the sides and the whole décor gave an impression of comfort and relaxation.

"Would you like a tea or coffee or maybe something a little stronger whilst we wait?"

"That's kind of you," replied Mat trying to think of what he would prefer. "I don't suppose you'd have that old English beer they call "Bitter", would you?"

Morley chuckled. "As a matter of fact, I do. I even drink some myself once in a while."

Morley produced two large glass tumblers and poured out a measure of medium brown ale into each. They settled down on the comfortable side couches beside a table to sup their brew.

Mat took a tug of his beer and, savouring the malt flavour, sighed softly in satisfaction as he swallowed.

"You said we were waiting?" said Mat.

"They shouldn't be long now."

"Who?" asked Mat.

"The other guests."

"I didn't know we were having a party."

"A small meeting, not a party."

"Excuse me Councillor…"

"Morley, call me Morley!"

"Err don't you have a first name?"

"Yes, but I thought you'd prefer not to get too chummy with the Chairman of the Council?"

"Err yeh, you're right," Mat took a moment to recall the question he was about to ask.

"Our guests are to join us on this orbital excursion."

"Who?"

"Ah, here's one now," said Morley with mild approval. "I'd like you to meet Professor Elijah Kim."

A small-built, bespectacled Asian man marched, without hesitation, in through the open entrance portal, shook hands with Morley and Mat then found a spot to sit down.

Morley moved to the entrance in time to greet an elderly man in a Muslim headdress. He was introduced as Ayatollah Maahti, the head of the Mosque on Lunar 2 and the only Muslim cleric residing off world.

Closely following behind was an athletic, solidly framed man in a newly cut suit.

"Hi," he said in a casual English accent as he shook hands. "Luke Overton. Just Overton will do."

Morley closed the hatch as soon as Overton was inside, then moved into the cockpit area to initiate a program sequence before returning to issue beverages and take his place with the others.

"I guess we are not here just to enjoy the sites then?" said Mat.

"You are correct," said Morley, "but please wait a few more minutes until we have cleared the station.

They watched as Eagle 1 cautiously and flawlessly cleared the docking bay. It drew away, exchanging communications with the station's dock master hyper computer in indecipherable techno-language. Much was inaudible to the human ear, but that which could be heard was just a cacophony of computer talk.

Mat admired the view and craned his neck around to get a glimpse of Earth astern of the vessel and a half-lit moon just abaft the beam. The ship steadied itself into a slow orbital path around Lunar 2.

"Attention!" said a soothing computerized voice. "Attention to all personnel on board this vessel. A series of simulated emergency tests will now be carried out. There is no need for action on your part. These tests do not require any human involvement. I do apologize for any inconvenience that may be caused."

The background hum of power and engines faded and went silent. Mat realized how much he had taken those sounds for granted.

"Well," said Morley with a sigh. "Shall I begin?"

"Please do," nodded Maahti politely.

"You may wonder why I have invited you here in this manner," began Morley.

He took time to ponder over his next set of words and his guests eagerly listened in anticipation. He cleared his throat before continuing and clasped his hands together as if he were about to pray.

"The thing is that I believe we are on the verge of an extremely serious crisis."

"Crisis?" said Mat. "For ESO?"

"Not just ESO," said Morley. "For Earth itself. For all humanity."

He paused to swallow a gulp of beer.

"It's rather complex," Morley continued. "The systems we have in place are containing many of the Earth's environmental problems. The nano-chems implanted on Antarctica have arrested and even started to reverse the big thaw that had been getting out of control a few decades back and; although there is still a lot to do, more secure habitation is being constructed for those who live in 'hive' blocks. But there are underlying problems that are threatening to get out of control completely and all the good work is in danger of being undone. World leaders say one thing to reassure people, but are powerless to stop the chain of events that threaten our very existence."

Morley stopped to sup more beer. They were all hanging on to what he was going to say next. He swallowed a second mouthful of beer before continuing. Mat amusingly wondered whether he was going to get drunk and start ranting and singing bar songs. He had to fight back a giggle.

"You have no doubt heard of an organization called "The Servants of God"," he continued. "Now on the face of it, it seems they are like many other fundamentalist type groups we have encountered in the past."

"Fundamentalist was originally a Christian term," interjected Maahti.

"I'm sorry, Caliph. There was no intention to insult Islam."

"Islam is not insulted by misunderstandings," replied Maahti.

"Quite," continued Morley. "Unlike previous religious factions, it seems this one is a kind of hybrid. It includes people from different denominations."

"Why is that so serious?" said Overton who spoke with a powerful masculine voice that seemed to command respect.

"Well, this bit sounds like paranoia, but please, bear with me," Morley took another mouthful of beer. Mat copied and observed as Morley's eyes seemed to sharpen.

"They are united on a common theme," "They believe that the 'Final Battle', Armageddon, is within our lifetime."

Maahti stirred at this point and raised a hand to speak.

"What sources do you have on this organization?" he said.

Overton was not impressed by the discussion.

"We've had crank sects before," he complained. "There's nothing new about them."

"This one may be different," said Morley.

"In what way?" Overton challenged.

"This group is believed to have infiltrated ESO and is suspected of using ESO technology in a search for the Messiah. They believe that Dajjal has arrived and that finding the Messiah is the only hope for mankind."

"Da, who?" said Mat.

"The anti-Christ," answered Maahti. "You would perhaps be more familiar with him being called Satan."

"Oh, you're kidding?" scoffed Overton. "This is all just fairy tales and folk law."

"It may well be," said Morley. "But to these people it is a serious business and if they believe it, we cannot ignore what they may do to achieve their aims."

"How is this group likely to affect the environment and aren't the security forces more than adequate to deal with this matter?" said Mat.

"Ordinarily yes," replied Morley. "However, we believe they have compromised security and have access to all security data files. They can even rewrite the data within those files."

Mat felt incredulous.

"But surely that can be overcome? You say they have been using ESO technology? ESO data is open to everyone, I thought?"

Morley grunted in acknowledgement.

"They have targeted ESO to gain control not just for information. The data that is available to the public is essentially scientific. The SOG are using our technology to search for the Messiah and this, this anti-Christ."

"Well can't we just change pass codes?" said Mat.

"If it were that easy, we would have done it."

Overton was clearly losing patience with the topic. He stood up and paced up and down in frustration, then went to the dispenser to get himself a soft drink.

"Maybe it's time for a film show," suggested Morley.

"Before we start that," said Mat. "Tell me, how can using ESO data banks be a threat?"

"They are not simply using our technology," answered Morley. "Our systems have been so infiltrated that we are forced to doubt their integrity. Accidents using technology are now likely to happen more frequently. As I said, they are attempting to take over control."

"ESO Hyper Computers have massive capacities," argued Mat. "How can they take over control and what happens if they find this Messiah and Daj whatever?"

"If they find what they believe to be Dajjal, then he and all of his associates will be in mortal danger."

"But again, surely this matter is for the security forces to sort out and the civilian authorities?" said Mat. "How can those of us here help in any way?"

"We have lived with terrorist threats for centuries," said Overton returning to his seat. "Why should this bunch be any different?"

"Let me show you this film I've had put together," said Morley. "Maybe it will help give some perspective to things. It only lasts about ten minutes."

They settled down and the vide-screen came to life.

The film consisted of a series of news reports and bulletins; all highlighting various disasters around the world from bomb explosions to earthquakes. It was a catalogue of the misery of modern day man. Everyone watched what many had seen previously broadcast on current affairs and news programs.

After several minutes, the screen came up with the caption "E.S.O. CLASSIFIED. FOR AUTHORIZED PERSONNEL ONLY".

"Are we authorized to watch this part?" enquired Mat.

"You wouldn't be here if you weren't," replied Morley.

"Oh, I don't remember signing any agreement on secrecy."

"You signed when you were contracted by ESO," said Morley. "You should always read the small print."

In the film, Councillor Morley appeared and began to explain that the number and intensity of global catastrophic events had been steadily growing for decades until about fifteen years ago when ESO had implemented "The Environmental Control Plan", the ECP as it became known as. The story went into all kinds of impressive graphical displays as Morley continued to commentate.

Director stations had been set up 60 million kilometres from the sun to tap, guide and process the sun's energy. They were able to convert the raw power and radiation into a range of energy commodities that would serve mankind's every need on a permanent basis.

Since the ECP had been implemented, there had been a steady decline in global events until a year ago when, it seemed, the Earth had somehow revolted against all efforts to control it. Natural disasters had doubled in the last six months compared to the same period the year before. Global authorities had played down concerns by claiming that it was a temporary blip that would settle down over time.

Nevertheless, it had been a mystery as to why these phenomena were happening. Then, a few weeks ago, a scientist working for ESO revealed that he was a member of a group known as the 'Servants of God'. He uncovered some of the inner, sinister secrets of that organization. S.O.G had been able to use a nano-virus to infect all of the HC s at Alpha Centauri. This new strain of nano-virus was able to infiltrate and bypass the security systems of an HC with impunity. Data banks of all hyper-computers had been compromised. It had undermined the precision with which these computers were able to operate, and one of the first examples of the virus's effect was believed to have been the first deaths outside of the solar system at Alpha Centauri.

It had been thought that the accident was caused by an experiment that had gone wrong when power settings were erroneously misaligned whilst testing shield harmonics. However, ESO specialists had gone through every check and diagnostic they could, but had found nothing.

There was great puzzlement. The safety protocols for the experiment had been strictly observed and the fail-safe devices were all operating normally. The equipment had been safety checked by the HC prior to the experiment starting and had been given the 'green light'. Either there had been human interference through some neglectful act or sabotage, or the computer checks were wrong. All the investigators could officially conclude in the end was that the incident must have occurred due to undetermined human error. However, in reality and to the consternation of ESO senior management, it pointed to a probable fault of the HC.

Morley pressed a control button and stopped the film show. He swept his gaze over everyone.

"Let me introduce our defector," Morley said with obvious glee. He held a hand out, palm up, to indicate. "Professor Elijah Kim."

The slightly built Asian man shifted in his seat and fiddled with the bridge of his large, thick rimmed glasses. He had said nothing the entire time he had been aboard. Mat had wondered where he came from and also, with modern optical treatment, why he chose to wear spectacles that had long been outmoded. Morley nodded to prompt him into speaking.

"Greetings to you all," Kim began in a quiet tone. He was well spoken though his accent betrayed his oriental background.

"I have worked in the field of nano-technology since I was at school. It is a hugely complex subject especially with the ethical questions that it poses. I am also a member of the Servants of God. I joined them many years ago when I was a young student at university. There were many religious issues that put my interest in nano-science in conflict with ethics, but I used their ideology as an ethical guide.

"Whilst in university I received a sponsorship award from a company called Jameson-Lewis Enterprises and have risen to the position of Chief Scientist for them. They have been world leaders in nano-science for many years. For me, joining them was an opportunity to develop my knowledge in the field with a world market leader. How could I resist?"

He stopped to take a sip of water and fiddled with the bridge of his glasses again before continuing.

"It was at Jameson's that I stumbled across a new type of nanite."

"Explain what you mean by nanite?" said Maahti.

"Yes, a nanite is little more than a miniaturized robot or bot as they are called now," Kim explained. "They can be incredibly small. The new version was for me a sensational breakthrough. It was revolutionary in its design. It…"

"Yeh, okay," interrupted Overton impatiently. "Just cut to the chase and tell us what's so special about this new one."

"I had created a super nanite, an SN, that could bypass any security system in the world.

"Super Nanite?" said Mat.

"The new nanite was not only molecular in size. It could reproduce, assimilate other nanites and commandeer organic cells. It could link with others to create a collective consciousness.

"For nanites to act effectively they normally have to be directed. Usually in medicine it means providing them with a bio-chemical impetus or implanting a nodal transmitter in the body. It gave us enormous breakthroughs in combating disease and reducing crime, but of course there were some terrible set backs."

"Please," said Overton. "Spare us the history lesson."

"The SN operates without the need for a nodal implant. It is a great step forward, but the consequences could be devastating if such devices were to be acquired by hostile forces."

"Oh, I get it, someone wants to sabotage Lunar 2 by infecting the HC," said Overton, "but doesn't the station have detectors in place for any encroachments by nanites?"

"Please gentlemen," said Morley. "Let the professor finish."

Kim sipped his water again.

"Not against these ones," he continued. "Their collective intelligence will use whatever method it can to accomplish an objective. SNs can adapt and mimic acceptable behaviour patterns. It means they can legitimately and innocently pass from one system to another and later mutate into a more malevolent form."

"So, SOG intend to attack the station with these SNs, but why?" said Mat. "What do they hope to achieve?"

"They believe that Armageddon is near and inevitable," Kim continued. "They see Earth as being doomed. They believe that Dajjal is already here. They have not yet unmasked him, but they feel it imperative that they prepare. We have already seen how in the 21st century the internet infiltrated every aspect of human life. SOG believe that Dajjal will use

HCs to seize power on Earth and that makes Lunar 2 a prime target."

"But if Lunar 2 were destroyed or even damaged," said Mat. "Hundreds of thousands of lives could be lost on the station and on Earth."

"Millions," added Morley. "We are barely containing the environmental problems the Earth is facing. Over the last decade, solar energy input has risen 5%. The numbers of super storms are continuing to increase at an alarming rate. The density of the atmosphere has risen 1% in the past six months alone. There has been an increase in volcanic disturbances. All these factors are combining and burgeoning together. The control measures are struggling to cope."

"For SOG, the sacrifice, though regrettable, would be worth it," Kim explained.

"So where do you stand?" said Mat. "If you are a member of this terrorist organization, why have you turned?"

"The Servants of God were originally a force for morality and goodness. They have become corrupted and narrowed in their view to the point of being psychotic. I could no longer support the cause. But to leave would be to invite retribution."

"Animals!" exclaimed Overton in disgust. He turned on Morley. "We should strike at them with all the forces at our disposal! Why don't people like you do that?"

"If only it were that simple," replied Morley. "They operate in cells and are well organized. They are difficult to infiltrate. Even so, Special Forces have carried out thirty raids on suspected SOG terrorists in the past few months with many notable successes."

"If they knock out Lunar 2," Kim continued. "They believe they will damage Dajjal's interests and hinder his chances of gaining global control. It may force him to emerge before he is ready and, it will give more time for the Messiah to be found."

"This is absolutely ridiculous!" huffed Overton.

"May be for you, a non believer," said Maahti. "But for some it is serious, deadly serious. It gives them purpose; a cause; a crusade!"

"That's strange to hear that word coming from you," said Mat. "But what does it all mean?"

"The encounter you had with the Mago in Tau Ceti," said Kim. "Has been interpreted by some as a sign that the Messiah will come from off world."

"I can assure you," replied Mat. "There is nothing messianic about the Mago. If they were to come here in numbers it would mean the end for everybody."

"So what are S.O.G. going to do after destroying Lunar 2?" said Overton. "Set a nuke off on Antarctica? Hell, they might as well finish the world off themselves if they're going to go round destroying everything."

"When the time is right, they will expose Dajjal and the final battle will begin," explained Kim. "S.O.G. may intend to establish themselves away from Earth in order to provide a triumphal return when Dajjal has been slain by the Messiah."

"But what forces do they have? Who is their leader?" said Overton.

"As Councillor Morley has explained, they have a cellular formation," answered Kim. "They are numbered in the thousands and have infiltrated just about every level of world government including ESO. They are powerful and they are ready."

"Who is their leader?" persisted Overton.

"A man called Ahmad Abd al Qaadir," replied Maahti. "He came to me once for spiritual guidance. He is regarded by many as a holy man; revered by tens of thousands; a bringer of light and hope."

"So, why are we here?" said Mat exchanging glances with Overton.

Morley grinned.

"Mr. Kemel you are to be sent on a mission back to Tau Ceti. Mr. Overton will accompany you on that mission. There, you will attempt to learn as much as you can about the Mago. Rescue anybody that may still be alive of course and, if possible, do what you can to neutralize any threat the Mago might pose."

"You are expecting a lot of one ship," retorted Mat.

"We are not expecting you to fight a war single handed. If anything, it will buy us time and, if you make it back, hopefully you will bring invaluable information about the Mago to us."

"How will that affect Dajjal?"

"Probably very little," said Morley. "We are trying to deal with a real and credible threat not a mythical one."

"And how are we supposed to neutralize the Mago single handed?" scoffed Mat. "So far they've proven to be pretty invincible. We have no weapons to match anything they have and there are an unknown quantity of them in the system."

"Let me finish, please," said Morley impatiently. "It is not an easy mission, but the public are demanding that something be done. You're not expected to take the system by force. That would be ludicrous. Neutralize can mean that, but it could also mean finding a peaceful solution to the problem. The most important thing you can do is to gather data about them. We are building warships, but it will be some time before they are ready. Indeed, if the SOG get their way, they may never be ready."

"How many warships?" asked Overton.

"That is classified," replied Morley.

"I thought we had clearance to know classified material?" added Mat.

"Not to that extent."

"Where do I fit in?" said Overton. "Mat is a scientist, but what about beef cakes like me? Why have I been brought in?"

"Surprisingly modest," commented Morley. "You, I regard, as completely trustworthy Mr. Overton. You have an enviable combat record. Twice awarded the UN golden star for bravery. You have demonstrated your abilities on numerous occasions. You're there for when things get difficult and to try to keep Mr. Kemel alive."

Overton felt uncomfortable with the outpouring of compliments.

"How will our mission to Tau Ceti help with what is going on here?" he said.

"This problem with compromised HC s," added Mat thoughtfully, "Why don't you send an uncontaminated HC into a remote part of the solar system and, if things go pear shaped, reboot the entire cybernet system?"

"That is precisely what we are doing, but we cannot be sure that any HC is not already contaminated. The professor and ayatollah will be working here with our scientists and security to find a solution to the problems. You are but one arm in this struggle. We need people we can trust in the field and away from contamination. When you return, things may be very different from when you left."

"So *we* are the back up disk?" replied Mat.

"Something like that."

Morley paused to drink his beer and gaze out of a portal. He tapped out a sequence of numerals and letters on a hand held keypad. The onboard computer acknowledged that tests were complete. There was the tiniest of jolts as the thrusters engaged and they were moving again.

"You may have wondered why a senior figure in ESO is divulging this information."

Morley was directing his words at Overton and Mat. He sighed and stroked his beard before continuing. "It's because, if things go wrong whilst you're away, you'll know why. You have a right to know."

"Just one thing," said Mat. "It'll take years to get back to Tau. Suppose we're not welcome by the time we return? What then?"

"Not years," replied Morley. "As we speak, a new wormhole generator has been set up as near to the Tau Ceti system as we dare go, but your new ship will not need it. It is the first vessel to be fitted with its own wormhole drive generator."

"But we only just got out by the skin of our teeth last time!"

"So it would seem, but Taj Mahal was not the only vessel to enter the system. Hard on her heels was a small maintenance vessel, ESS Beaver. She was instructed to remain silent and monitor Mago activity. It seems that shortly after the collapse of the wormhole the Mago withdrew from the region of Hahl. Beaver was able to re-establish the wormhole link and is still there now."

"Do you mean you knew about the Mago before we got there?"

"We were aware of an alien presence, but Commander Morris knew as well. It should have been no secret."

"And what if the Mago come back whilst we are there? What do we do?"

"Then you will carry out your mission as you see fit."

There was a moment's silence as Morley's words were absorbed.

"Allah will protect you," said Maahti. "What ever will be, will be. It is in his hands now."

"Mercy be," said Overton dejectedly.

"I have one last concern," said Mat. "The professor might be able to answer this one."

He had the others attention.

"I want to know for sure, can this SN virus be transmitted to humans?"

Kim shifted uneasily and stammered to answer.

"Well?"

Kim rocked forward and was clearly finding words difficult to say.

"Yes or no?" Mat pressed.

"Yes."

CHAPTER THREE

The promotion ceremony was basic and formal. A four-man quartet was all the pomp and circumstance given to the occasion. Bridely savoured the moment though. A lifetime of dedicated service had been recognized. He had taken an important step forward in his career and was now much closer to his ambition of becoming an admiral.

There had been a body of opinion who had been unhappy about the rank of Commodore being brought in to the command structure of ESO. It had been argued though that command of a base did not warrant the posting of an admiral and yet a rank higher than a captain was needed to wield authority over ships within a base's sector.

Bridely presented himself at attention whilst Councillor Morley stood at the podium to address the thirty strong audience.

"….it is a position of considerable responsibility and trust that we garnish you with…" he went on.

Bridely tried to maintain concentration. The ceremony was for him, so he ought to pay attention out of respect. But there was a lot to do whilst he was at Lunar 2 and his mind began to wander. It was warm. Maybe the air conditioning was set incorrectly.

He had to attend a preliminary hearing with Admiral Hawksley in an hour's time. He hoped they threw the book at the woman. People like Clare Roberts had no business being in space. Psychos like her should be rooted out. She should not have gotten past vetting. Instead, the system had allowed a whacko to hang out on a remote space station and commit cold-blooded murder.

"Commodore?"

As for the O'Hare woman, she was just a lesbian shrew. Society had become too tolerant with the likes of her. For all he knew Roberts and O'Hare were lovers anyway. It was bound to cloud their judgement.

"Commodore?"

Why had they dropped charges against Kemel? He must be up someone's ass to get away without any charges being levelled at him.

"Commodore?" said Morley. "Are you alright?"

To his embarrassment he suddenly realized that it was the third time he'd been called to the stand. It was time to give his acceptance speech and thank everyone for his promotion.

"My apologies Councillor." he flushed. "Space travel lag."

Morley nodded a doubtful acceptance of his excuse and Bridely boldly took the rostrum. He cleared his throat and then began.

"Thank you councillors, Chairman Morley, admirals and all those who have supported my promotion.

"It has not been an easy journey to get to this position, but I have learned a lot along the way. Charon Base is a crucial waypoint on our journey to the stars. It is a stepping stone to our future, for now we are reaching beyond the boundaries of our former existence and today are standing on the verge of empire. An empire that will be so unimaginably vast that it will extend from one edge of the galaxy to the other and with it will come new challenges, new opportunities and new discoveries ...."

An hour later after a few snacks and brief words with those at the ceremony, Bridely was taking his seat on the prosecution benches to one side of the admirals. ESO had three appointed admirals and all three sat on the tribunal - Admirals Hawksley, Carter and Antyuk.

When everyone was settled, Hawksley called out: "Bring in the accused!"

The double door swung open. Clare Roberts, pushed by Kelly O'Hare, was wheeled in. Both looked weary. Each woman was shackled at the ankles and cuffed and wore unmarked navy blue overalls. Kelly shuffled along as best she could.

Four muscle bound security guards flanked the women. Their comparative sizes made the prisoners look like children. Clare sat and stared blankly and without emotion.

"Where's Kemel?" said Admiral Carter.

A court sergeant stood to one side of the admirals' table. He was clearly uncomfortable with the situation.

"Err, Mr. Kemel has been reprieved," said Admiral Antyuk.

"Yes I know, but he was still required to attend."

The door burst open and Mat Kemel entered in a breathless state.

"My apologies for being late," he gasped.

"Mr. Kemel, we pride ourselves on punctuality in The Earth Space Organization!" said Carter.

Mat lined up beside Kelly.

"Mr. Kemel and the prisoners will stand to attention!" bellowed the sergeant.

Kelly lamely straightened herself and stamped her foot in acknowledgement.

Mat fumbled in a breast pocket. His action drew concern from the sergeant who placed his hand on his holster and drew his stun gun, but all that Mat produced was a scrap of paper. He uncrinkled it and placed the note on the table before Admiral Hawksley.

"I think you should read this before continuing," he said.

Hawksley sighed and scooped it up. Consternation passed over his face as he read. He then slid it along for his colleagues to read.

Mat caught Kelly's eye and winked reassuringly. The admirals' heads came together in an inaudible conference and eventually, Hawksley sat up and drew a deep breath before speaking.

"Miss O'Hare, all charges against you are hereby dropped and you are free to leave."

Hawksley nodded to the sergeant who then moved to Kelly and freed her from her bonds. She rubbed her wrists and ankles then looked around in bewilderment.

"You are dismissed from the hearing!" called Hawksley.

Kelly thought to stay, but the sergeant ushered her out and secured the door when she had gone.

"Mr. Kemel," he continued. "You may also leave the court."

"May I stay to help Ms. Roberts?"

"No you may not!" exclaimed Hawksley and gestured to the guards.

The sergeant and one of the guards grabbed each of Mat's arms and removed him unceremoniously from the court before he could protest. The admirals then turned their attention to Clare Roberts.

"Now, Ms. Roberts," said Hawksley. "You are here today to face serious charges of murder and extreme misconduct. I want you to declare whether you are guilty or not guilty after each charge is read out. Do you understand?"

Roberts had sat listless and zombiesque until now, but with all the attention focussing on her something seemed to stir inside her. Suddenly she began tugging at her restraints and unleashed a tirade of obscenities.

"You are vile filth!" she growled with spittle flailing from her mouth.

"Answer the court!"

"You will never take me! You fucker! You ass licking piece of shit!" she wrenched against her restraints, but they held. "Filthy male animals. I'll kill you! I'll kill the whole fucking lot of you!"

"Gag her!" Hawksley ordered. As the gag went across her lips the sergeant noticed her mouth starting to emit foam. She spat right in the sergeant's face. Her eyes bulged wildly when he secured the gag behind her head. For a moment he felt light-headed and tottered. Everything sounded very distant.

"The first ....," began Hawksley but he never got the chance to say more. The courtroom door swung open and in marched Councillors Morley and Lyndhurst.

"I am sorry to interrupt proceedings, Admiral" said Morley. "But I must ask this hearing be adjourned until a later date."

"Under whose authority?" said Admiral Carter.

"The Council of the ESO," replied Morley. "The Council has voted unanimously that charges against Ms. Clare Roberts be held in suspension until a later date."

"This is most irregular, Councillor," snorted Hawksley. "She is charged with murder. There is no precedence ……"

"I am sorry admiral, but these are extraordinary times."

Morley and Lyndhurst stood before the admirals' table and placed a certificate of authority in front of them.

"I'll admit," said Morley, "that as far as delivery is concerned, it is a little unusual, but there are numerous examples where hearings have been suspended."

Hawksley studied the document as if to find something wrong with which he could challenge its authenticity, but could find no fault. His compatriots leaned over to view it, but remained grim and silent.

Finally accepting it, Hawksley laid the certificate flat and cleared his throat. Clare Roberts continued to wrench at her restraints and snarl like a wild animal.

"This tribunal hearing is hereby suspended," Hawksley announced. "A date will be set as and when circumstances permit."

"This is outrageous!" protested Bridely. "This woman is a monster! Look at her!"

"Thank you Admiral," beamed Morley, ignoring Bridely's outburst.

"Ah, yes," Hawksley coughed nervously. "The accused is to remain under your control in the meantime until summoned to appear before the court. She is your responsibility Councillor."

"Admiral, you can't let them both go unpunished!" protested Bridely. "It would undermine all discipline throughout ESO!"

Roberts gave a loud shriek and slumped back wide eyed and still, but her heaving chest indicated she was still alive.

"She needs medical attention," said Lyndhurst. "A trial serves no purpose with her in this condition."

"No one is going to escape justice," said Morley. "The hearing is merely adjourned. Justice will be done, but not here; not today."

Roberts was wheeled away by one of the guards closely followed by Morley and Lyndhurst.

Outside the courtroom, Kelly was waiting with three more ESO security guards. She caught a peek into the courtroom as the group emerged and took a quick note of the sergeant rubbing his forehead. She tried to enter the court, but the security door locked as soon as it shut.

"I didn't realize we had friends in such high places," said Kelly.

Roberts bucked and arched in her chair.

"There was purpose in our act," said Lyndhurst looking at the distressed woman.

"What is wrong with her?"

Morley issued instructions to two people in white coats.

"I would say it looks like a relapse," said Lyndhurst.

The white coats wrapped her in synthetic medical sheets and removed her to an ESO marked ambulance.

"Where are they taking her?" asked Kelly.

"Treatment," answered Lyndhurst.

"Wouldn't have something to do with our special assignment?" Kelly queried.

"Mr. Kemel has told you already?"

"It was just a hunch. I figured it's the only reason you'd bother to save anyone from the ordeal of a trial. Besides, I've not seen Mat Kemel since we arrived until just now. Then, he just scurried off without even saying hello or goodbye."

"Funny you should say that," said Morley flagging down an empty group carrier taxi. He instructed three security men to follow in the next cab as they climbed into the carrier. The computer voice asked politely about their welfare and where they wished to be taken.

"Sunset Boulevard Space Crew Accommodation for a stop and then transit to Dock One," said Morley. "Disconnect speech. I want silent running until we reach our final destination."

"Why are we going to Sunset?" said Kelly.

"To pick someone up of course," answered Morley.

"Oh, yeh? Who?"

The councillors avoided answering.

"You can report to your new ship at Dock One right away," said Lyndhurst.

"Already?" said Kelly. "Don't we have time to go home?"

"Of course," answered Lyndhurst. "She's not quite ready to go yet. One or two modifications are needed from the original design plan. In between training sessions, you'll be granted leave."

"Suppose we don't want this assignment?" asked Kelly.

"Well then, we just continue where we left off with your misdemeanours."

"That's blackmail," said Kelly.

"It's reality," said Morley. "The law of barter. We do something for you and, in return, you do something for us."

"Okay, deal!" said Kelly.

"Personally, I would not have selected you for this mission," said Morley. "But Mr. Kemel wants you along. He vouched for you because he believes that you played a significant part in the rescue operation from Tau Ceti."

"I didn't do much," mused Kelly. "Why should he think I'm good enough to bring along?"

"Well I thought a lady of your disposition would have worked that one out," Lyndhurst replied. "Someone who can think on their feet and has character is what he said."

"I'm no lady," declared Kelly mournfully and peered out of the window at the streets and the scores of people they were passing.

"Sunset Boulevard, you think they'd think of some original names for these places."

"We have a lot of American personnel on the station," said Morley. "It makes them feel more at home."

"Most Americans don't live in Los Angeles," remarked Kelly. "You should name places up here after stars. Get them looking outward at space and beyond, not back down at Earth."

"You forget, Miss O'Hare," said Morley. "The purpose of this station is 90% for the benefit of Earth and its needs. The use of Earth names therefore is more appropriate."

The cab glided to a stop at Sunset Boulevard.

"How long do you wish me to wait, Sir?" said the cab.

"As long as it takes, chip brain," said Kelly.

"I'll tell you when we should continue," added Morley more politely.

There was a tap on the windscreen. Lyndhurst opened the door and Mat Kemel and a huddled hooded figure got in.

"Cab, you may continue the journey," said Morley.

"Why didn't you wait outside the court?" said Kelly.

"I had to collect something," he replied nodding to the hooded figure. "I also had a problem with my check out card."

"They still use check out cards?" said Kelly. "I thought they ditched them two decades ago?"

Kelly looked with curiosity at the hooded person. Carefully, Mat removed the hood.

"Clare!" said Kelly. "How can it be you?"

"A clone," said Mat. "Well, the one in the court was a clone. They are viral carriers."

"They?"

Clare suddenly lurched forward at Mat, her arms extended towards his neck "You must die!" she growled and grasped his throat in a vice like hold.

He felt immense strength crushing his windpipe and toppled backward in the cab to try to ease the pressure. The others tussled with her to try to free him, but already his mind was closing down.

"Violence is forbidden!" yelled a mechanical voice. "Violence is forbidden!"

Mat tried desperately with his waning strength to break the hold, but it was no use and his consciousness deserted him.

He woke up lying on the floor of the cab with faces peering over at him and checking his condition. It didn't take him long to reorient. The Clare Roberts figure was hooded again, but slumped back against the far door of the cab. Her hands were cuffed and Lyndhurst wielded a stun stick over her. She sat still and silent.

"Violence is forbidden! Violence is forbidden!" repeated the cab voice.

"Cancel alert!" called Morley. "Override code 194326Xray."

"Violence is…," the broadcast ceased.

"Welcome back," said Lyndhurst cheerfully. "You okay?"

Mat rubbed his throat. It was painful and bruised.

"I've felt better," he said huskily.

He looked over to a lifeless Clare. Her head drooped as if she were asleep.

"Thank you," he said to Lyndhurst.

"I'm afraid it wasn't me who saved you from a broken neck."

Kelly smiled in a girly sort of way and held up a long dildo like device.

"It's my self defence gadget," she boasted mockingly. "Delivers a 240 volt shock. Never thought I'd be using it on another girl though."

Mat frowned and slipped back on to his seat.

"Continue journey!" Morley instructed the cab.

It took a few more moments for Mat to regain his composure.

"Is she alright?" he gasped.

"Aaw, she'll be fine," replied Kelly, "though usually they're over it by now."

"You mean you've used it before?"

"Not on maximum setting."

"She was okay before," said Mat. "She was very compliant. No warning of aggression at all."

"If she's still got it," said Morley, "then why did you bring her in here? We might all be infected."

"I don't think it's reached the airborne stage yet."

"The guard," said Kelly. "The guard at the court room. He looked a bit rough as we left. He was rubbing his forehead as if he wasn't quite with it. You don't suppose she, the other Clare, infected him somehow?"

Lyndhurst touched his wristwatch.

"Why didn't you say so before?"

"I didn't think it was that important."

"This is a biohaz alert! Security to isolate the Admiralty Court," he said to his watch. "Isolate all guards in Court 23 as well as the three admirals and court staff. They are to undergo full medical diagnostic scans! I repeat: this is a biohaz alert!"

Mat plucked up courage to check Clare's vital signs. She was comatose and not responding to stimuli."

"So how many Clare's are there?" said Kelly.

"I don't know," replied Mat.

"Come to think of it, are there any more me's?"

"Now there's a thought," he chuckled.

"So what have you done with the other Clare?" said Kelly. "Err, the one that was in the court?"

"She is being taken to Aldrin Medical facilities on the Moon for observation," replied Lyndhurst. "She'll be well looked after. I hope this procedure you're proposing works, Mr. Kemel."

"Using the ship's labs gives me a chance to test the ship's effectiveness and if anything goes wrong it will be easier to isolate the ship than to isolate the whole station."

"The Roberts in the court was screened for alien contamination," replied Morley. "She was given the all clear?"

"She *was* all clear," said Mat. "She and this one have both been re-infected."

Clare's head sagged and nodded as if she was having a disturbing dream.

"It means that," he continued, "either whoever re-infected these women targeted them specifically, or else the virus is already at large amongst the population. Whatever, this thing is, is getting out of our control."

"SOG!" cursed Morley.

"From the evidence so far, most probably it is them, but it is by no means certain."

"We should activate the pandemic containment protocols immediately," suggested Mat.

"We'll do that right away," said Lyndhurst.

"Woah!" exclaimed Morley. "We start restrictions, word would get out and God knows what panic it would create."

"Not to do anything would be irresponsible," said Mat.

"These things have to be decided on by the ESO council," said Morley. "We are not allowed to just do things by dictat."

Mat huffed in frustration.

"Speed is of the essence. If this thing is loose, then it is probably spreading with every minute that passes."

Mat produced Eric and scanned Clare Roberts.

"Well, Miss Kelly's little device might have done some good, even if it is only temporary."

"Is she clean?" said Lyndhurst.

"No, but viral activity is dormant."

"Why are there clones of Clare and was she specifically targeted to be a carrier?" said Kelly.

"Cloned humans are not as rare as they used to be," replied Mat. "As for why she's a carrier, who knows?"

"Well now, Councillors," said Kelly in her broad Irish accent. "I know you picked us to join you on a mission. The question that no one has answered yet is, where are we going?"

"Tau Ceti," Lyndhurst responded.

She looked sceptically at Clare Roberts.

"I'm not happy with her tagging along."

"I thought you were best of friends?" said Mat.

"The Clare I knew on TC1 was my friend, but now I don't know who she is or who is the genuine one."

"Why did you change your mind and allow Ms. Roberts to go with us?" said Mat turning to Morley and Lyndhurst.

Lyndhurst grimly shook his head.

"There is nothing that our doctors have been able to do for her. If you believe you have an effective treatment that works on her then you may be our best hope. In the meantime, scientists on the Moon will be working on the clone, and the others."

"Sending us back to Tau, the place will be crawling with Mago," said Kelly. "Why should anyone want to go there after last time? We'll be going to our deaths. What good will it do?"

"It has been predicted that if we do nothing, then death will find all of us when they come here," replied Lyndhurst. "There are no other ships ready for this kind of mission and we desperately need to find out more about these creatures."

"Clare is hardly someone to take on a dangerous mission, she has a psychotic hatred of men and she'll just be a liability."

"Her feelings and attitudes are accentuated by her illness," explained Mat. "It's one of the symptoms. Emotions are enhanced by the nanites altering the body's chemical balance. One thing they are vulnerable to is a powerful magnetic field which is why your little device was so effective. It disrupts their systems, but seems not to be permanent. If I can cure Clare, we can probably develop a serum that could save millions. Besides, she'd be an excellent reserve pilot."

"Can this one fly?"

"You should know, this is the one you were on TC1 with."

"How do you know?"

"Each clone is genetically marked. This Clare is not. She is the genuine article. For her sake she has to come with us to keep her safe. She's the Clare Roberts blue print."

"What if you can't cure her? I don't see what you can do that scientists on Earth can't?"

Mat nursed his damaged neck and swallowed painfully, but did not answer.

"If she stays here," explained Morley. "She will spend the rest of her days in a secure unit and will be a permanent health hazard to all."

"I am hopeful that she will be cured before we leave base," said Mat.

"What's this ship called?" asked Kelly. "If we're going to stand any chance of making it out alive from Tau Ceti, we're going to need a ship with a lot more clout than anything we've had so far."

"Woden," said Morley, "and I hope it will satisfy at least some of your desires."

"Woden?" queried Kelly. "The Norse God of War?"

"In a manner of speaking it will be Earth's first purpose built warship."

"I should point out that I am a pacifist," declared Kelly. "I don't feel easy about serving on a killing machine."

"Killing machine or not," said Mat. "The fire power of that ship may be all that stands between us and annihilation."

"I haven't agreed to go," said Kelly.

"You know what awaits you if you refuse," warned Morley.

The cab stopped outside the dock entrance. Morley showed his security ID, but the doors remained closed until the vehicle had completed a self scan for suspicious devices.

Eventually though, the dock gate opened to allow them in, and Morley and Lyndhurst exchanged smiles at the sound of their guests' unanimous gasps of awe.

Woden completely filled Dock 1 with its dark grey, streamlined hull. Its arrow like shape gave it an overly sporty look that suggested both stealth and speed. Technicians, construction workers, engineers and bots crawled all over it like ants in a frenzy of activity.

"You can see the amount of effort being put into it, Commander," said Morley. "Look after her and she will look after you."

"Commander?" puzzled Mat.

"Yes, Mr. Kemel. You have been assigned a field commission to the rank of Commander. You will be second in command to Captain Singh although you will leave shipboard operations to Commander Willis."

"Captain Singh?" Mat shook his head. "I don't know the guy."

"Can't say I've heard of him either," added Kelly cynically.

The cab pulled up beside a boarding ramp and they alighted. Three men dressed in protective suits emerged, placed Clare Roberts in a secure mobility chamber and wheeled her on board. Morley credited the cab which responded with its pre-programmed gratitude and pleasantries.

An austere looking meatloaf of a sentry blocked the access to the ramp. Morley again did his bit with security arrangements and seconds later they were stepping onto the gangway.

"Thought they'd know who you are by now," commented Kelly.

"If they had not challenged me, heads would have rolled," replied Morley tersely.

The smell of celluloid and newness filled their nostrils. Mat felt the thrill of excitement like a little boy going for a visit to the fairground. At the entrance, they were met by a tall, fair young man by the name of Lieutenant James Ruddle. He courteously saluted and then politely offered to take them on a tour.

"I'd like to see my quarters to start off with," said Kelly.

"Of course, Ma'am. I have you as being allocated the 1st Techno-Engineer's suite."

"Who has the Commander's quarters?" said Mat.

"Err, Commander Willis. You have been designated the Science Officer's suite, Mr. Kemel."

"This is what happens when no one has been formally introduced," muttered Morley. "Lieutenant, the person you're talking to is Commander Kemel. He will be second in command."

"Oh, my apologies," replied Ruddle. "I didn't realize you had a rank."

"Neither did I until a minute ago."

"Would you like to change over cabins?"

"No, that won't be necessary. Commander Willis needs to be nearer the Bridge than me. Can you take me to the science lab where Lieutenant Roberts has gone?"

"Yes sir, this way," said Ruddle belatedly as Mat peeled off.

"I'll come too," said Kelly.

"Can we have a cabin allocation plan?" called Lyndhurst.

"Err, yes sir," said Ruddle clearly divided on whether to go or to stay. "I'll get one to you as soon as I can."

"You look after Miss O'Hare," smiled Lyndhurst. "We'll find our own way around."

"Yes sir. Thank you sir."

Morley and Lyndhurst made their way to one of the personnel centres and took time to greet as many of the crew as they could. It would be the last chance they would have of seeing many of them before the mission began.

Clare Roberts had been laid in a large, transparent sarcophagus with two medics dressed in white standing over her. The hood was still draped over her head, but she was completely motionless.

Kelly recognized one of the medics instantly.

"Fiona!" she cried.

Dr. Benjamin turned and smiled radiantly.

"How come you're here?" said Kelly as the two embraced. "I thought you'd be on leave?"

"I was meant to be, but I couldn't miss out on this opportunity," replied Fiona.

"How is she, Doctor?" said Mat solemnly.

"The Hypo 400 is analyzing her condition. It's remarkably quick, but it's already produced confusing results."

"I thought the 240 was the thing?"

"The 400 is essentially the same model, but is designed more for ships. It has programming that allows it to learn about alien biology."

Fiona referred to the data expressed on her screen.

"Initial evidence showed Clare had a nanite infection, but then further investigation showed her to be normal, although there was a substantial amount of inexplicable foreign bodies in her blood stream. They looked like dead bacteria, but none that I could identify."

Lt. Ruddle excused himself and left.

"Okay," said Mat. "Are we set up for the treatment?"

"Mr. Kemel," replied Fiona. "I think it's a highly dangerous practice. It will put her life at extreme risk."

Mat held both of Dr. Benjamin's arms in a plea.

"Fiona, if we do nothing she will die anyway and thousands of others also. If we do this it could save her and give the world a fighting chance."

"It didn't work before. She relapsed."

"I don't think she did."

"What is this treatment?" asked Kelly innocently.

Mat turned to her to explain his plan.

"To send an electro-magnetic pulse through her body. The nanites are vulnerable to it. But because we are dealing with SNs we first …"

He moved Kelly into the viewing room and secured the door.

"Bridge!" Mat called on the intercom.

"Sci One, this is Bridge, Commander Willis speaking."

"Good afternoon, Commander. This is Mat Kemel. I would like to carry out Program Kemel 462. Do I have permission to proceed?"

There were a few seconds of hesitation before there was a reply.

"Councillor Lyndhurst has authorized you to proceed."

The hood had slipped from Clare Robert's head. Mat worked on the medical console, but kept a watchful eye on her.

Her eyes flickered open and with that, she began to struggle and fight and beat furiously against the sarcophagus lid, although the obscenities she yelled were muted by the lab's sound suppressant system.

"It's as if she's possessed!" cried an anxious Fiona.

"An apt description, Doctor," replied Mat. "You could say the virus is aware of our intentions."

He gave a cursory inspection of the scene.

"Rig the terminals!"

Dr. Benjamin and Lauren, her assistant, burst into life. Monitors and equipment were moved into place at each end of the sarcophagus whilst Mat set up a series of antenna dishes around it.

Clare continued to thrash and buck. She thrust her knees against the container trying to force it open. Kelly shivered at watching Clare's nails snap one by one as she tried to gouge into the sides.

"Okay! Ready!" cried Lauren.

"Ready!" exclaimed Dr. Benjamin.

Everyone donned protective goggles. Mat nodded to the other two, then pressed the start button. There was a short whir as the program was initiated. He pulled down a small power switch and immediately blue and white electrical charges leapt around the sarcophagus.

The lab lights went off and a bluish sheen emitted from the dishes and enveloped the whole container. Between these dishes, small blue sparks could be seen at various points flashing and arcing. It looked as though dozens of little flies were striking a power point from inside and were being incinerated for their efforts.

Clare's assault on the sarcophagus became hysterical. Her vital signs displayed serious fluctuations. Fiona took a step forward, but Mat put a steadying hand on her arm to restrain her.

"She's dying! We're killing her!" she pleaded.

"That's the point!"

The sarcophagus creaked.

"She's breaking out!" screamed Lauren.

"Stand back everyone!" yelled Mat.

Fracture lines appeared on the transparent walls of the container. The force field between the dishes became an ever-increasing cascade of sparks and electrical discharges.

The pounding and writhing continued incessantly. They stared in horrified fascination as Clare's mouth opened jaw breakingly wide. She emitted an unearthly banshee-like scream, that 'curdled the blood'. The sound even penetrated the muting effect of the sound suppressors then she convulsed violently and her eyes bulged hideously as if they were about to burst from their sockets. Finally, she puked a geyser of green and brown fluid; arched her back and collapsed back and still.

The eyes remained wide and blood shot and the spew trickled and dripped down the ashen and bloodless face. The Hypo 400 went into red alert mode, displaying all vital signs as failing and the gape of her mouth indicated she was dead.

Dr. Benjamin tried to move forward again, but again Mat restrained her. Suddenly, in one final convulsion, Clare's body arched upward in one more back breaking contortion. She cried out a final scream of defiance and fell back limp.

"When the sparking stops," said Mat holding on to Fiona's arm. He pointed to the blue sheened force field. The sparks carried on for another minute and then abruptly ceased.

Kelly looked at him through the view window with complete contempt.

"You've killed her!" she wept.

"Do your bit doctor," he said softly.

"She, she," he stammered with a dry mouth. "She's not beyond hope yet."

As soon as Mat released her arm, Fiona rushed to Clare's attention. She moved to unclip the security locks on the sarcophagus.

"Wait!" said Mat. "Let the Hypo do its job!"

"It's a bit late for that!" barked Fiona.

"Please, trust me a little longer!"

Reluctantly, she waited as did they all, for what seemed like hours. Then, there was a twitch, and another, and another. Monitors showed heart activity restarting. There was huge relief as the display changed from flat-lining to a weak pulse and one by one Clare's vital signs began to restore.

Mat satisfied himself that she was alive and then spun on his heels and marched out of the lab without another word.

CHAPTER FOUR

Mat's and Kelly's quarters were not far from each other. Their cabins were not overly spacious, but had compactness and style. Wood-look panelling and impressions of plants and animals on the mural displays gave the décor a pleasing ambience, but these could be altered easily to suit the particular taste of the inhabitant. Each cabin had its usual entertainment systems with vast amounts of musical, virtual reality and 2-D movie inputs.

Lieutenant Ruddle stood very patiently and waited for Kelly to try out every seat and seemingly every sitting position in her quarters. It was like watching a teenager moving into a new apartment. Mat stood beside him, hands on hips, bemused at her ranging.

"How did you know it would work?" said Kelly.

He turned away, not wanting to answer, but she could tell by his agitation that he was uncomfortable with the question.

"Well?" she prompted.

He drew a deep breath.

"I didn't," he replied. "It was a, a, ar, a hunch."

She stood up and thrust her face at his.

"You mean, you took a gamble on the woman's life?" she said venomously.

"It was a calculated risk," he replied. "It was that or she would have died for certain."

"You don't know that!"

"What would you have done?"

She turned away and grinned at Lt. Ruddle standing upright and as near to the door as he could get.

"How about that familiarization tour of the ship, Lieutenant?" she asked.

Ruddle took them to deck after deck; through engineering, astro, horticulture, sick bay, armoury, power plant, exercise and gymnasium courts, labs and yet more labs. By the time they had returned to their cabins, their luggage had arrived and was in place.

"Just like a hotel," Kelly remarked. "Care for a drink off ship, Lieutenant?"

"Err, no thank you ma'am," he replied courteously. "I'm on duty in an hour."

He politely said his goodbyes and excused himself.

Captain Singh, they discovered, was not yet on board. He had been attending a conference on Earth and was due to be arriving on the early morning shuttle for a meeting of all officers and crew at 10.00.

Commander Willis was acting as Captain in his absence. It did not take much to convince him to permit shore leave for the crew, a concession he would probably regret.

Central Bar was packed with revellers that evening, but Kelly seemed to be in her element and led Mat and Fiona into the thick of it. Mat felt completely out of place.

"Is it always this crowded?" he shouted over the din.

"It's Friday night! Party night!" yelled Kelly. She grabbed Fiona's hand and pulled her into the middle of a jostling group of boogying people.

"What do I do?" called Mat feeling left out.

"Get the drinks!"

"Oh yeah fine!" he grumped.

Mat wormed and squeezed his way passed the vibrant throng to the huge circular bar, wondering how ever he was going to get service with so many in the way. Hell, he forgot to ask the girls what they wanted.

When he finally made it he found all the bartenders were too busy to serve him. A neon sign shone overhead saying: "Step up, give your order and wait, please".

"Two Bacardi Breezers and a litre of bitter!" he called uncertainly.

To his surprise, a small display in front of him lit up: "Please deposit your credit and your drink will be served."

He fumbled to slot his credit disk into a small slot, but no sooner was it in than a little hatch opened to deliver the drinks on a tiny tray.

"Anything else?" read the display.

"No thank you," he replied. It was then that he noticed that there were dozens of these little hatches all around the bar. He realized that most of the people were just standing there to lean and not get served at all. The tenders were present just to make idle conversation and provide a human touch.

"Mat Kemel!" cried a woman's voice. Mat spun to try to see who was calling him.

"Mat!" a young brunette woman, slightly shorter than Mat enveloped his shoulders with her arms. "Mat, you surely remember me! It's Francine!"

"Francine, of course I, I remember you," he waffled. "It, it's just I, I didn't expect to see you here."

"Well, it's a surprise seeing you in a joint like this," she beamed, sensually gyrating her belly against his. "Didn't think you liked these sort of places?"

"Well, I don't actually" he shouted. "Far too noisy. Can hardly hear myself think."

She noticed the drinks.

"You're not alone I see."

"No, I'm with friends. Would you like a drink?"

She clearly had had a few already. She didn't answer, but pulled herself into him and slowly worked her body into his. He felt awkward and embarrassed.

"Oh, don't be such a stiffy," she cried and then roared with laughter after realizing what she had just said.

She sensed his unease and crushed their bodies together. He felt really awkward and looked about nervously. She savoured his discomfort and pressed her body against him harder, pulling his face to hers and kissing him full on.

He remembered his previous fling with Francine in science college. She'd hooked him for four days. He ended up missing lectures and finishing his assignments late. He'd been forced to lie by saying that he'd been sick. It was only afterwards that he found out that she had a boyfriend who wasn't too chuffed at having his girl sleeping with another guy for the best part of a week.

Francine affectionately nibbled his ear.

"Are you with anyone?" he said.

She chuckled and pulled his head down to hers again and began a slow deliberate French kiss. A heavy hand fell on his shoulder and whirled him around.

"That's my chic you're messing with!" growled a tall and wiry, pale man with a goatee.

Mat held up his hands, palms outwards.

"I'm sorry. We were just passing."

"Looked like you were doing more than that from what I saw!"

Mat moved to collect his tray of drinks and to try to ignore the man.

"You'll find yourself in a world of pain, asshole!"

"Really?" Mat retorted, his temper starting to bubble. He squared up and stood eyeball to eyeball. "Yours or mine?"

A fight seemed inevitable, but two large-framed security staff stepped between them.

"That'll be all, gents," one said sternly, arms folded.

"How did you get here so fast?" said Mat.

"The auto bar doesn't just receive drinks orders," said the man.

Fiona and Kelly had moved into a dimly lit alcove when he found them again.

"Where the hell have you been?" said Kelly.

"I ran into traffic," replied Mat, moving in beside her.

"Cheers," said Kelly curling the 'R' in an exaggerated Irish dialect.

They slurped their beverages as the noise and activity outside the booth increased to fever pitch. More and more people packed onto the dance floor as the music pulsated.

"There must be some safety regulation somewhere that prohibits the number of people allowed on a dance floor at a given time," remarked Fiona.

"Oh, lighten up!" shouted Kelly. "I'm going out for some more. Excuse me!"

With that she sidled passed Mat and was soon lost in the crowd.

"Haven't you got someone you know?" said Mat.

"I did have a guy called Daniel back on Earth," Fiona shouted to make herself heard. "He's into bio research. Keeps himself to himself. Haven't spoken to him for about three months now. It was never likely to go anywhere."

"Well, I expect not. It's hardly the best place to be chatting someone up on a single sex outpost stuck in interstellar space."

"I guess I'm a career woman when it comes down to it. What about you?"

"Nothing too serious until Mercury 4."

Mat sipped at his drink.

"Jenny Gold, lost in space. I, we were getting on really well when it all went so wrong. Some relationship, huh?"

"I thought you were gay? I mean the rumours I'd heard. Not that it bothers me, you know."

"Something happened in college," sighed Mat. "I think I was drunk or something. It just happened. I'd rather not talk about it."

He took a gulp of his beer. Fiona stroked his forearm.

"I *am* a doctor," she said smiling, "and a friend."

"I have no hang ups about homosexuality," Mat went on. "This other guy; we were both a bit drunk. I don't know what happened; it just happened. I don't remember how."

He felt very uncomfortable. Fiona just continued to smile and listen. He gulped some more beer.

"I don't know why things happened. I didn't realize I was like that. I just woke up and found this guy in bed with me. It scared the hell out of me. It was probably a testosterone thing, you know; mixed with drink. He's the only time it's happened and I don't remember any of the detail."

"Mat, you don't have to justify yourself to me. I'm okay whatever your preference."

"I've had three longish relationships with girls in the past and just this one-off with this guy. The reason everyone knows is because he boasted about it afterwards, so everyone labels me as gay. I don't know why everyone seems to know. Who cares anyway?"

"Were you drugged?"

Mat hung his head. He could not meet Fiona's gaze.

"I felt so ashamed and dirty at the time."

"It happens to women as well," she said.

He got up to leave, but Fiona held on to his arm and urged him to stay.

Kelly emerged from the crowd panting and hyped up and carrying a fresh tray of drinks. Alongside her stood another woman, Francine.

"Guess who I ran into?" yelled Kelly excitedly filling the table with glasses.

"Mat!" cried Francine.

"You two know each other?" cried Kelly.

"Matty and I go back a long way," said Francine cheerfully.

"This is my old room mate at college, Francine," beamed Kelly.

"I know, we've met," said Mat furtively as Francine slid in beside him. "Where's your meat loaf protector?"

"Randy? He's gone out to pick up some mates. He'll be back in about half an hour. Gives me a chance to catch up on old times."

"He seems a real knuckle dragger, spoiling for a fight."

"Oh, he gets a bit jealous about other guys. He's quite sweet really."

"Yeh, well he may be sweet to you, but it's not so sweet having a fist land on the end of your nose."

"So, that's what you meant by traffic," said Kelly.

"Are you going with Mat?" asked Francine.

"No!" Kelly answered curtly and dropped into a solemn mood. "We're just ship mates."

"Oh, you're still thinking about err, what's his name?" Francine pondered.

"Michael Hocking," said Fiona. Kelly flicked a pained expression at Fiona then downed two glasses of drink in succession.

"I'm sorry," said Francine gripping Kelly's arm in an attempt at sympathy.

Kelly took a third glass, but Mat steadied her hand.

"Easy Kelly, you'll be …"

"Fuck off! I'll do what I want!"

"I didn't realize you still missed him so much," said Francine.

"You don't know what I miss!" Kelly snapped with a faint slur. "But I'm getting over it."

"Let's talk about the ship," said Fiona trying to change subjects.

"You're going on Woden?" said Francine.

"Don't say you are too?" said Mat.

"Crewman Francine Waterfield at your service," she saluted.

Francine's hand slipped beneath the table and onto Mat's leg.

"But I'm not sailing on her. Just a C and M," Francine went on.

Mat drew a sharp intake of breath as Francine worked her fingers towards his crotch.

"C and M?" said Fiona.

"Construction and Maintenance crew.

Mat saw a flash out of the corner of his eye and moved his head just in time as a beer glass smashed against the booth partition.

"I told you, you bastard!"

Angry Randy blazed with hatred.

"Lay off my woman!" He roared and charged forward.

Things happened very fast. Someone swung a stool down at Mat's head. He ducked so it missed him smashing against the table. Broken glasses and spilt fluids splattered over everyone. Fragments of wood and plasti-glass flew in all directions. Randy lunged at Mat's throat, but another man grabbed him from behind and received a fist in the face for his troubles. He and someone else wrestled and sprawled backwards cannoning into others. Fists and kicks began flying from all directions as more joined in the mêlée and, within seconds, the whole place had erupted into a brawl.

A bald man landed on the table in front of Kelly. She scooped up one of the last remaining drinks just in time. The man's face trickled blood from a cut to the eyebrow. A bearded man leapt on top of him and began pummeling his face. Kelly's eyes flashed with anger. She delivered a well placed punch to the side of the man's head that knocked the attacker tumbling to the ground.

"Thanks lady," said the bald man.

"Get off my table!" she slurred.

He didn't hesitate.

"I think we should leave whilst we can," suggested Fiona politely.

"If we can," corrected Mat.

Kelly's 'dark cloud' lifted and her face beamed with pleasure.

"Leave?" she slurred. "I'm just getting started. It's party night and no one should leave while things are still hotting up."

Several security men armed with stun guns arrived and were immediately set upon.

"Kelly, I think things are just a bit too hot at the moment," declared Fiona.

Mayhem reigned. Mat grunted as Francine's hand clutched and squeezed his privates. He put his hand down to steady her and smiled sheepishly at her.

"Let's crawl out," she whispered.

"And then what?"

"Well, I don't know, your place or mine?"

"Francine, we've not seen each other for two years."

She grinned impishly.

"Yeh, but it was so good last time."

A man sprawled across the table in front of them, his face a bloody mess.

"Come on Kelly!" exclaimed Fiona. "We're leaving!"

As they got up a weight crashed into Kelly's back almost toppling her over. With surprising strength, for someone of her stature, she tossed the form aside and stepped over the body. She seemed to have an instinct to protect Fiona and kept herself on the danger side of the skirmishing.

A woman swung a fist at her. She ducked and caught the woman's arm and then kicked her in the groin. The woman went down groaning.

"I didn't think that worked with women," said Fiona in her ear.

"Believe me, it hurts!" yelled Kelly.

A gorilla of a man gripped Kelly by the throat. There was an insane anger etched in his face and he clearly intended to throttle the life out of her. She was lifted off the ground gasping for air and fighting to retain consciousness. She swiped a hand at him, but could not reach. Her fingers vainly clawed for something to grab. Mat delivered a punch to his kidneys, but to no effect. Fiona placed a bottle in each of Kelly's hands and with considerable force, she brought them together with the man's head in between. He dropped like a sack, leaving her on her hands and knees gasping for air. Mat rabbit chopped him on the neck and he keeled over.

A banshee woman shrieked and flung herself headlong. Kelly nimbly stepped aside and merely helped her crash through tables and glasses.

More security arrived and began driving their way deeper into the bar room. An opening to the entrance loomed. Mat grasped Francine's hand and pulled her forcefully to the exit. He almost made it, but three figures suddenly blocked his path. To his dismay it was Randy and two of his friends, built like mountains.

"I fucking told you mate!"

"I'm just getting Francine to safety," he argued lamely.

Randy was clearly not impressed.

"I guess we're going to have to teach someone some manners the old fashioned way."

Together, the three thugs took a step forward. Someone thundered into Mat's spine causing him to lurch forward. His head cracked onto the bridge of Randy's nose in an inadvertent head butt. Randy's nose split spurting blood everywhere.

Mat did not waste time, and followed up his unexpected advantage with a shoulder charge into the heavy on Randy's left. The mountain stumbled backward and over Kelly who was crawling towards the exit. He fell backwards, thundered through a table, struck his head and stayed down. Randy's other henchman raised his hands to back off as Mat took a free style karate stance and prepared to take him on.

Yet more security arrived and were now using their stun batons to drop more and more people further inside the bar.

Haphazardly, the escapees somehow made it outside Central Bar and pulled away from the entrance to draw breath and to contemplate their next destination.

"Can't we just go for a quiet coffee?" Fiona suggested. They agreed and cautiously sauntered off in search of a quiet stop.

Two streets away they reached The Bistro Café. There were few others inside and so they were able to give their orders to the waiter with little delay and settled down in seats next to the window to admire the setting. The scene was stunning and filled them with wonderment. Earth partially filled the view, shining in half darkness, half light.

"Beautiful!" muttered Fiona.

"It always is," mused Francine. "I've been posted here for a year and I never get bored with it."

"Well, that was interesting," sighed Kelly still slurring her speech.

The waiter brought the coffees and smiled courteously before scuttling away.

"You're pissed," Fiona grinned.

"What if I am? At least I'll be able to say I've had a good time."

She supped on her Irish coffee and grinned.

"If you're able to remember it," added Fiona.

"Just to change subject for a minute," said Mat. "What do you think about the extra bits that Woden's got? Do you think we'll be able to achieve anything?"

Francine's hand was sliding along his leg to his crotch again.

"Francine?" he said gently, moving her hand away. "Please behave yourself."

"Oh, I forgot that you are a gay boy now," she teased.

"I am not a gay boy!" he retorted.

"Francine!" said Fiona. "We don't want anymore scenes tonight."

She looked across at Kelly basking in, what appeared to be, a merrily drunken state. The marks on her neck were mauve and ugly. However, the drink seemed to have anaesthetized her to any discomfort as well as to any rational conversation.

"That guy," muttered Kelly.

"Which guy Kelly?" Fiona said.

"The one tried t' top me. Somethin' funny 'bout 'im."

Then she stared as if in a distant world and said no more.

"Going back to Woden," said Fiona. "I'd like to be optimistic and say we have a good chance of survival. Whether we'll achieve anything positive other than survive, is another matter."

"Do you think anyone might be alive back in Tau?" said Mat.

Francine squeezed his thigh, but he ignored her.

"I really don't know," replied Fiona.

"I don't believe it!" All except Kelly turned to see who had spoken. "Mat Kemel! Here, of all places!"

They looked around to see a man with cropped blond hair sitting two tables away.

"Steiner?" replied Mat unenthusiastically. "What a small world!"

"Well, there's nothing like getting down to business right away," said Steiner and pulled up a chair to sit at the end of the table.

"What business is that?"

"A little matter of a hundred credits, if I recall."

"What hundred credits?"

"Don't play ignorant with me!" said Steiner soberly. "You were meant to pay your dues before you left. Instead, you did a runner and have been playing hard to get ever since."

"I resigned my membership of the lotto club two weeks before I left. I owe nobody anything."

"I vouched for your entry into that club. You dropped out without the one month's notice. That made me liable for your tab."

Mat plonked a ten credit bill on the table in front of him.

"Here, that's all the change on me. Now do you mind? I'm trying to have a chat with my friends."

"You insulting bastard!" growled Steiner. "You can transfer the full amount with your disk these days. Don't try to cheap skate me! There's interest to pay after all this time!"

"Interest?

"Doubles every year," Steiner sneered.

"Excuse me," complained Kelly. "I thought we were having a quiet cup of coffee?"

"Business is business lady, wherever it is."

The familiar flash of anger flickered through her eyes. She drained the last drop of her Irish coffee and then in one movement slammed the mug straight into Steiner's forehead. The material in the mug prevented it from breaking, but Steiner sprawled head over heels and ended up on his back.

Dazed and completely surprised, he heaved himself onto his elbows, blood already oozing from a deep cut to his brow. Kelly looked intently down on him.

"That's for patronizing me, you son of a bitch!"

Two coffee shop staff approached.

"And, for ruining a quiet few moments," she added.

"I'm afraid I'm going to have to ask you all to leave," said the manager.

"On our way," sighed Mat, hands up.

One of the staff stooped to tend Steiner's wound. It gave sufficient time for Mat's party to make an escape.

"Another quiet drink somewhere?" chuckled Kelly.

"Back to the ship and bed!" declared Fiona. "I've had enough excitement for one night, thank you."

Fiona led off with positive strides in the direction of Dock 1 then stopped and turned to Francine.

"You said you are a CM to the Woden mission?"

Francine nodded.

"What about that boyfriend of yours?"

"Randy? He's maintenance too. Who are you anyway?"

"She's Dr. Fiona Benjamin the ship's senior medic on board Woden," answered Mat.

"I'm sorry, I had no idea who's who on the ship."

"Of course not," replied Fiona, "but as you're unfamiliar with everyone, let me introduce the others properly."

She gestured firstly to Kelly and then to Mat. "You know Kelly. She is First Technical Officer on board and is ranked as Lieutenant. Mat is signed on as Commander. He is also Science Officer and second in command of the mission."

The formalities seemed to have a sobering effect on Francine. She drew away from clinging on to Mat's arm and stood separately.

"I'm sorry," she said.

"No problem," he smiled. "We were casual. You weren't to know."

"There they are!" came a shout.

"Oh, God!" cried Fiona angrily. "Is there no let up to this?"

Five men, Randy amongst them, ran towards them and behind them Steiner appeared with two others. The eight charged, brandishing sticks, chains and belt buckles. Unexpectedly, a catlike figure leapt from a side entrance and, in a stunning display of martial arts skills, laid each one of the attackers out in quick succession. Steiner was the only one left untouched, but after witnessing the demise of the others, backed off and fled.

The figure faced them, smiled and bowed politely.

"Luke Overton, Woden's Chief Security Officer at your service."

"Luke!" phewed Mat. "Are we pleased to see you."

"I told you, call me Overton. I prefer it that way."

Some of the mobsters stirred. A couple took to their heels as soon as they were able to stand, but Overton made no effort to pursue them.

CHAPTER FIVE

Back on board Woden, Fiona checked on Clare sleeping in the infirmary and satisfied herself that she was still stable and recovering. She then quickly made her way to Kelly's cabin and let herself in with her med pass.

She found Kelly fully clothed and sprawled across her bathroom, face down. From the trail of spew, it seemed she had barely made it to the toilet and had fallen asleep where she lay.

Fiona set about undressing her and cleaning her up as best she could. Kelly was too far-gone to object to anything. With some difficulty, Fi managed to drag her to the bed and got her tucked up under the duvet. She then propped herself in a chair to try to get some rest for herself. It was not unnecessary to watch over Kelly; medi-scans were fitted to all cabins and most compartments, nevertheless she felt it was the human thing to do.

Captain Singh arrived in the early morning and called for a briefing of all ship's crew at 0600, four hours earlier than the original time.

He was talking with Admiral Carter when Mat and his fellow revellers paraded into the briefing room in Dock 1, ten minutes late. The only vacant seats were at the front where Overton was sitting. Everyone else had already arrived and were seated.

Carter and Singh had been chatting informally and now turned simultaneously towards the new entrants, their faces austere and disapproving. Carter beckoned to them to leave with him via a side door before they could get comfortable.

Mat led the way, followed by Kelly, Fiona, Francine and Overton. Carter briskly ushered them in to a small empty office and slammed the door. He swivelled on his heels and glowered thunderously at them.

"I've had reports coming in all morning about your activities last night!" he said angrily. "Most people who go station side manage to enjoy themselves without incident."

Kelly's mouth moved to say something. He choked her off with a loud, startling bellow.

"When I am talking you button your lip until I'm finished!"

The flicker of temper within her simmered, but she held her tongue.

"If I had my way," he continued. "None of you would be anywhere near this mission or any other space going craft! You are *supposed*, and I emphasize "supposed", you are *supposed* to be officers. You are *supposed* to represent civility, control and discipline. You are certainly not *supposed* to get involved in drunken brawls in bars and street fights."

Francine gingerly raised a hand to speak. He ignored her and ranted on.

"I do not know what the Council's game is, nor is it for me to try to second guess it. All I can say is that they must have some pretty strange reasons for allowing lowlife like you scum on board at all, let alone as officers."

Francine waved her hand slightly to draw attention to herself. He turned savagely to her.

"What?"

"I'm sorry admiral, but I don't believe that what happened last night was their fault."

"Their fault?" he shrieked. "Their fault? Are you saying *you* weren't implicated?"

Francine shut up.

"What the hell are you saying?" Carter pressed, bearing down on her.

"Well sir, all the trouble that happened, came to them," said Francine. "They didn't go looking for it."

"Really?" he replied cynically. "It is the responsibility of an officer ashore to conduct himself in a fit and proper manner. This includes avoidance of trouble should it arise."

"Bullshit!"

He swung fiercely to Kelly. His anger at her was reflected back with equal venom.

"How dare you speak to an admiral like that!"

"Bullshit!" she sputtered unable to hold back her boiling temper.

"I'll have your butt off this ship and hauled away in irons for gross insubordination!"

"Up your ass, admiral!"

"Kelly!" Fiona said meekly.

"Shut up!" barked Carter then continued to direct his ire towards Kelly. "I cannot imagine what scheme the Council has planned, but *you*, young lady, are definitely not part of it any more."

"And you can …..!" but she stopped herself saying anymore.

Unheard, the door had opened and someone had entered, noticed only by Overton. There was a polite cough, and the others looked to see who had arrived.

"Eyes to the front!" bellowed Carter. He pointed directly at Kelly, frowning at the visitor.

"She's off the mission! I don't care what protocol I have to bust to haul her ass out of it!"

"My apologies, Admiral Carter," said Lyndhurst. "I'm afraid the decision to send her stands. Although, you can prepare fresh charges for her for when she returns."

"What is so special about her that she has to go?" Carter said incredulously. "There are dozens of others better and more deserving than her."

"She's going because I want her," said Mat.

Carter stood eyeball to eyeball with Mat and looked daggers down at him.

"And who the hell are you?" he said fiercely.

"I am not an official member of ESO," Mat calmly explained. "I am under the directions of the Council and am answerable to them only."

Admiral Carter looked at Lyndhurst.

"What's the meaning of this?" he thundered. "If the admiralty command has no jurisdiction over insubordination then what rules are there to control discipline?"

"Anyone who commits an offence will be answerable for that offence," said Lyndhurst. "It's just that this assignment is of such special importance that normal rules of conduct are to be set aside for the time being."

"These reprobates are not indispensable!" he roared. "I want the admiralty's right to decide on personnel restored!"

"I am sure you are right," said Lyndhurst, "but the Council has named those to go on this mission. There are to be no changes."

As the miscreant troop moved to return to the briefing room, Kelly saw fit to stick a middle finger up at Carter. Mat grabbed her hand before he could see it and quietly rebuked her.

Captain Singh sat patiently to one side of the front table and the assembled crew muttered to each other as Mat and co returned.

There was a brief pause before Councillor Lyndhurst and Admiral Carter entered and took their place either side of Captain Singh. The admiral's red complexion made him look like an enraged rooster and, if looks could kill, he would have done so. He stood to give the address.

"I should announce," his voice quivered, demonstrating considerable self control. "That as from immediate effect, all shore leave has been cancelled. All crew members who were assigned to this mission and who are currently on Earth will or have been reassigned. Shortfall of staff will be covered by vetted personnel from Lunar 2."

There was murmuring, but a stern glower at them with his puffy, bulging eyes silenced any pretension of dissent.

"As from this moment, every aspect of this mission is to be considered strictly confidential. You are not to discuss flight plans, mission parameters or properties of Woden and all non ship personnel are to leave this room immediately."

There was a small commotion as a number left the room. Francine smiled at Mat and kissed his cheek.

"I guess we have to part again," she said softly then chuckled in his ear. "I'll have your trousers off again one day."

He blushed as she pulled away.

Finally Admiral Carter was able to continue.

"Owing to changing circumstances, the countdown for take off has been brought forward several of weeks. On leaving this room you are to proceed directly to the ship and, after a few basic safety drills and essential maintenance tasks, the countdown for lift off will commence."

Carter stopped, his attention grasped by the raised hand of a dark haired Irish woman. He stood flabbergasted at her audacity.

"Yes, Miss O'Hare?" he said with unconcealed exasperation.

"Excuse me, but I was due compassionate leave. My old Mom died whilst I was away last. I never had a chance to pay my respects."

"See me afterwards," said Lyndhurst before Carter could answer. Carter nodded in gratitude before carrying on.

"The wormhole between station TC1 and the Tau Ceti system has been re-established. There have been no reports of any Mago activity and we currently have a cutter, ESS Beaver, operating inside the system and working to stabilize the link.

"Your mission is to observe the Mago, to assess and to find out whether any of our people may possibly be alive, and whether any communication can be possible between Mago and human.

"So far, they have had no reason to fear us. The vessels they have encountered have been lightly armed and armoured. This new vessel, the ESS Woden, is the first of its kind.

"It will be a real test of both ship and crew. She will be the first to be fitted with particle shielding emitters known simply as PSE. Besides carrying a bank of thirty two Titan mark 5 missiles, she will be armed with pulse lasers and a resonant wave gun, RWG. The hulls of her two shuttles are adorned with cloaking plates and other stealth technology to make them invisible to the Mago. However, perhaps most significantly of all is her means of interstellar propulsion. She is the first of her kind to be able to generate her own wormhole as and when required. This means that journey times between stars will be significantly reduced….."

And so, he went on for another ten minutes of singing the marvels of human ingenuity. Mat began to find the monotonous drone of his voice increasingly difficult to listen to.

His concentration rapidly diminished as the fatiguing effects of the night before started to take their toll. Desperately, he fought to stay awake, taking deep breaths, disguised yawns, shifting his sitting position. Nevertheless, in spite of his efforts, his attention waned irretrievably and the head began to nod as the words from the front merged into a drone.

The drone stopped. Someone nudged his elbow and scraped his ankle. He sat up with a start. All eyes were upon him. Admiral Carter and Captain Singh viewed him with nothing but contempt.

"Mr. Kemel?" said Singh in a taut, yet quiet voice. "Perhaps you would like to add your experience of meeting the Mago?"

Mat's throat was dry as old sticks. He simply croaked an incomprehensible response.

"Mr. Kemel!" roared Carter. "I do not know where this mission is going to end up, but it is bound to be nowhere good with you involved!"

Mat mustered what moisture he could to aid his suffering throat. Carter was going to say more, but a staying hand from Lyndhurst prevented him.

"Perhaps I could say something," Mat rasped but in a more controlled manner. "This mission should be about communication. Communicating with the Mago. That is what we need to do if we are to achieve anything useful."

"We've already established the importance of communication, Mr. Kemel," said Singh sarcastically.

Mat ignored him and moved to a water dispenser. He poured himself a full measure then drank greedily to satisfy his hydration needs. Carter and Singh looked as though they could quite eagerly commit murder, but he continued to ignore them. He sighed with relief and at last spoke again.

"The Mago talk to each other the way many living organisms on Earth do. I believe they talk to each other through a series of high pitched warbling sounds. These sounds are too high a frequency for our ears to hear.

"We could possibly reconfigure the ship's sensors to study them. However, I believe it's time to introduce a new weapon against the Mago. One that needs no modern technology, but is at least as loyal and trustworthy."

Mat, now fully alert, nodded to the front trio and moved to the back entrance of the room. The door slid open and he waved someone toward him. A man appeared in the entrance, but Mat barred the way.

"I'll take it from here thanks," he said and the man moved away again. "I would like to introduce the latest and last addition to our crew. Ladies and gentlemen, this is Biscuit."

To the amusement and mirth of the crew, in trotted a shaggy mongrel dog. Mat stooped, unhooked the lead and Biscuit proceeded to go from one person to the next sniffing each in turn. Most he passed by with just a wag of the tail, but a few caused him to give a guttural growl and a little snort.

"This is preposterous!" exclaimed Singh looking to Carter for support. "You've taken leave of your senses! You can't take a dog on a mission such as this."

"Why not?" replied Mat. "He's ideal. His hearing and nose make him the perfect choice."

"Admiral Carter, surely you can prevent this?"

Carter shrugged and shook his head resignedly.

"I'm sorry Captain," was all he could say. "The appointment was approved by both Command and Council."

Biscuit reached the front desk. It gazed mournfully at Carter, wagged its tail at Lyndhurst, moved over to Singh, snarled briefly, and then gave a quick bark.

"Well why was I not consulted?" said Singh angrily. "I must protest! I am the Captain! I should be allowed a say on who comes on board my ship!"

"It seems that even I don't have that luxury anymore," Carter moaned.

Mat surveyed the reaction of the crew towards Biscuit. He gauged there was positive support for the dog although, not from everyone.

Outside, when the briefing had concluded, Lyndhurst called Kelly to one side.

"I am truly sorry about your mother."

He raised a hand to stop her responding.

"You will have about 8 hours. You will tell no one where you are going and will avoid meeting anyone on the ground."

"What are you saying?" said Kelly.

"Python, my personal shuttle, with pilot at the ready, will take you to Cork where I believe your mother's body is laid to rest. It's a case of straight there and straight back."

Kelly grinned with delight and had to swallow hard to hold back a tear.

"Councillor Lyndhurst you are a really lovely man."

She kissed his cheek in gratitude. He smiled and gently held her hands.

"I know what it's like to lose someone," he said.

"Won't you get into trouble?"

"Morley will not be pleased, but don't you worry about that. Finish off your formalities on the Woden and then see me at Dock 2 in half an hour."

The ride down to Earth was executed with precision. Kelly thought initially it was another computer landing, but a nosey up to the cockpit revealed otherwise.

"I'm sorry Miss O'Hare," said the pilot courteously. "I'm forbidden to converse with you, but yes, re-entry has been carried out manually and the landing will be too."

"Are you allowed to tell me your name?"

He shot a grin at her.

"Karl Rogers," he said. "Everyone just calls me Rogers."

"Well, you can call me Kelly. That's what my friends call me."

It was dark and late evening over Cork as Python swung into land. Rogers somehow managed to find a quiet field about 100 metres from the cemetery.

As she stepped down from the craft, he tossed her a flashlight and a set of night goggles.

"You'll probably find them handy at this hour."

"Thanks."

"You have an hour Miss Kelly. Please don't get lost."

It felt strange stepping on to the softness of real Earth grass, but a whiff of cow dung told her she was home. For once she didn't begrudge the pong. In fact, she didn't begrudge anything about being home.

As she ambled in the direction of the cemetery, she could not suppress the tears welling up in her eyes but, the dampness of her cheeks was hidden by the darkness. Old sentimental memories flooded her mind, not all of them pleasant. Here she was, back in her hometown, but she felt lost and lonely. She had left this place; abandoned it for the cold, dark nothingness of space. Would she not have had more rewarding personal adventures had she stayed here? She would at least have been able to be by her mother's side at the end, whatever their differences.

She soon found the cemetery and entered. The area was wide but also pitch dark. She shone the torch this way and that, but it was then that she realized she hadn't a clue where Mum's body lay. She might walk around for hours and not find a thing.

She donned the night goggles in the hope that they would help her in the search but, after checking dozens of graves, and even looking at freshly dug ones the search proved fruitless. Her hour was frittering away and with it disappointment and despair began to grow inside her.

"Kelly?" said a woman's voice. It startled her to hear another human being. She hadn't expected anyone else to be there.

"Kelly!" said the woman again.

Kelly turned gleefully towards the sound.

"Kelly? It's me Marian!"

Kelly tore the goggles off and ran towards her.

"My God, Marian! Oh, what a sight you are to see, to be sure!"

The two flung welcoming arms around each other and hugged and kissed with joy.

"I'm sorry I wasn't there for Mother," sobbed Kelly, the tears now flowing freely.

"It's okay my dear. She loved you no less."

"You think so?"

"She respected you for your strong will."

"Where's she lying?"

"Next to Da' of course."

"Next to Da'?"

"She said she was sorry how she treated him. She wanted his forgiveness and asked to be buried next t' him.

"Pity she left it 'till he was dead."

They reached the grave and stood still for a silent moment of prayer.

"But Kell, how come you're here? You never told us you were coming?"

"Oh Mar, it's a long and difficult story to tell."

The beautiful floral tribute radiated colour as the powerful torch beam played over the grave mound. Tears flowed easily for both women. They hugged for comfort in their shared grief and then Kelly sank to her knees next to the tombstone and wept inconsolably. Marian placed a comforting arm around her younger sister's shoulder and cried with her.

It took a while for composure to return, but Kelly eventually got up and straightened herself.

"How come you're here?" she snivelled.

"I asked you first," Marian replied.

"I was given a special dispensation to come. You?"

"I heard something coming in to land. It didn't sound like any plane that comes here. I just wondered if you'd be in it. You must come home for tea and cakes."

"I'd love to, but I can't stay."

"But why? Why do you have to go so soon?"

Kelly held her sister by the biceps.

"Marian, I wasn't supposed to be here at all. I'm going away very soon, into deep space. I don't know if I'll be coming back again. Things are happening that shouldn't be happening. Everything is so secretive. You mustn't tell anyone you've seen me. It could be dangerous."

"Oh Kell!" Marian drew close and the two embraced again. "You were always the one up for mischief."

"I have to go now my dear Mar. My time here is up."

It was a reluctant parting. Marian accompanied Kelly part of the way back to the shuttle then she remembered something.

"Wait! I've got something for you to take away."

"There isn't time," said Kelly.

"My house is just 100 metres from where we're standing."

She disappeared into the shadows and Kelly waited. Just as she thought she was not returning, Marian reappeared and shoved a carrier bag containing a large solid box inside.

"Michael left this for you."

Kelly was astonished.

"Michael?"

Kelly's bleeper sounded.

"Go love!"

They hugged farewell and shed more tears for the last time and Kelly turned for the ship, leaving her heavy-hearted sister in the darkness of the night.

"You were with someone, Ma'am," said Rogers. "That was forbidden."

"It was my sister. How did you know there was someone there?"

"Ship's sensors are very sensitive these days."

As Python rose into the sky, Kelly looked out of the porthole and peered into the dark landscape adorned by a smattering of streetlights. She strained to get a last glimpse of Marian on the ground, but to no avail. She knew she would be there somewhere, waving up from the darkness and, just for a moment, she thought she saw the flashlight shine upwards.

CHAPTER SIX

"How are you feeling?"

Clare's eyes blinked open and she stared up at Mat Kemel peering down at her.

"Do you have a headache?" he prompted.

She mouthed words, but found it difficult to find a voice.

"It's okay," he said soothingly and smiling. "You can nod if it's too painful to talk."

A sound came from her that rasped her throat. "Rough," was what it sounded like.

"What do you think of me?"

She was perplexed by the question and frowned.

"Do you hate me?"

Clare frowned again and wobbled her head in an awkward shake.

"Good!" Mat said boldly.

"She'll need at least four more hours of rest in Hypo recovery," said Dr. Benjamin.

"Were the scans clean?"

"We ran fifteen scans using the new configuration. Every one of them show conclusively the nanites in her body have been destroyed, but she needs time to heal."

"Excellent!" replied Mat. "I'll leave you to it, Doctor. You've done a great job."

Mat made his way quickly towards Engineering. He needed to discuss the duty roster with Kelly.

"I'm sorry about last night," said a woman.

He stopped and turned toward her.

"I'd had a few too many," said Francine. "I didn't mean to cause any trouble."

"Francine, there is really no need to apologize."

She seemed moody and remorseful.

"I have to be off the ship in ten minutes. I just wanted you to know I'm sorry for any trouble I caused.

"Trouble? It was fun."

"Yeh, but I...," she seemed to struggle with the words, but looked him up and down at the same time. "I touched you and I..."

"Francine," he drew closer to her and lowered his voice. "For what it's worth, I would probably have gone with you last night."

Her face brightened.

"I am a man," he explained. "I have emotions too. It's very difficult for a guy to resist a beautiful young woman making passes at him."

"And now?"

He sighed.

"And now, we are on duty and I am your senior officer. The ship is due to leave within the hour. It wouldn't be appropriate to be anything more than good friends at this stage. I have to set an example to the rest of the crew. Circumstances have changed."

He turned away noting her disappointment then turned toward her again. He glanced around furtively and put his arms around her. She responded and the two exchanged a passionate kiss.

"For what it's worth," he smiled. "I do fancy you. There will always be a place within me for you but, I can do no more than that as things stand."

"Mat?" she said as he moved to go.

He stopped and half turned to look at her.

"Mat, take care," she said. "Maybe if things had been different."

He drew close to her again and took her hands.

"Francine," he said warmly. "You are better than you think you are. I could do far worse than have a woman like you."

"I'll pray for you," she replied and he was gone.

Mat reached an alleyway junction and almost collided with Commodore Bridely slowly strolling in the opposite direction.

"Commodore Bridely?" he said. "I thought this was a 'sealed crew' trip, so why are you here unless you're planning to stay?"

Bridely 'ummed' and 'arred'

"He's here at my invitation, Mr. Kemel," said Singh appearing from a side door.

"But this ship is subject to confidentiality rules," answered Mat. "No one is to join or leave the vessel unless approved by the highest competent level."

"Don't quote rules at me!" snapped Singh. "This mission has already had the strangest beginning before it's even started. Even I as Captain, have had very little say in the management of the mission. I don't need someone like you to tell me what I can and cannot do on my own ship."

"My apologies, Captain."

Singh took Mat's elbow and turned him leaving Bridely to continue alone in a different direction. He was only slightly taller than Mat, but solidly built with rounded features, darker complexion and a furrowed brow.

"Walk with me a minute."

Singh surveyed the deck in front of him as the two slowly ambled along.

"Mr. Kemel, you have been given the field commission of Commander. It is an executive position, but nevertheless it is exceptionally unusual to be given such a rank, in such a way."

He pondered over his words.

"Don't get me wrong Mr. Kemel, but there are dozens of very competent, well trained and extremely reliable young men and women that are more than qualified to fill the slot that you have been, err, given."

"The Council…."

"A-a-a," Singh interrupted with his hand held up to underline the interruption. He gazed meaningfully into Mat's eyes.

"You are not one I have reason to trust, Mr. Kemel. You have not proven to me that you are worthy of the rank of Commander."

"I've encountered that attitude on more than one occasion. I am here in an advisory capacity. Commander Willis has operational responsibility for the running of the ship."

Singh's bulging eyes gave him a spooky and unnatural stare and Mat got the impression that the man might not be entirely stable in spite of the psyche tests he supposedly would have passed.

"Commander Willis is another puppet placed here by 'The Council'. The Council count for nothing in deep space," he continued. "In deep space it is the Captain who is the law."

His eyes became more and more bulbous as he glared wildly.

"Of course you'd know all about that considering what happened to Commander Morris, wouldn't you?"

Mat had had enough. In spite of whatever method Singh chose to try to prevent him speaking, he was going to talk.

"Commander Morris was a good man before the mission started, but something happened to him en route and he was not the same guy at the end."

"And are you going to see the same happens to me?"

"What do you mean, Sir?" Mat said curtly. "As your second in command, it is my duty to do everything in my power to see that nothing happens to jeopardize this mission."

"Which mission Mr. Kemel? The official one that has been publicly announced or a secret one that only you know about?"

"My mission is to save Earth!" Mat stated angrily.

Singh gave a smirk, pleased that he'd gone close to hitting a nerve and perhaps a revelation about alternative agendas.

"Your first duty is to me as Captain!"

The tannoy intervened before any further exchange could take place.

"All crew! All crew! Stations for departure! Lift off in thirty minutes. Prepare for launch! Stage One conditions! All persons not assigned to this vessel have ten minutes to leave!"

The message was repeated as Singh and Mat moved away from each other.

"My place is on the Bridge," said Singh cynically, "Where is yours Mr. Kemel?"

In Engineering, Kelly was happy and full of zest.

"Good morning Commander!" she chirped.

"Glad to see you're back," he replied.

She closed on him, puzzling over the comment.

"Don't worry," he said softly. "Your secret is safe with me. As long as you found it rewarding, that's all that matters."

She smiled and returned to concentrating on the readouts from her engineering panel.

"Everything is operating within normal parameters," she said. "We are ready for lift off."

Mat swept a surveying glance around the compartment. He beckoned her to one side.

"I have some bad news," he said in a solemn, low key voice.

Kelly listened intently.

"Clare is dead." he said furtively.

"Wha …!"

"No, the other Clare, the one in the courtroom."

"But how?"

"They couldn't stop the infection this time. Her cells disrupted."

"You mean she …?"

"It was a horrible end."

"How did you …?"

He tapped the side of his nose to indicate secrecy.

"How about our Clare?"

"She's fine," he replied. "She'll be up and about in a few hours."

"Have you spoken to her?"

Mat seemed preoccupied.

"Huh? Oh yeh."

"And how did she react?"

"Commander Kemel to the Bridge!" said the tannoy. "Commander Kemel to the Bridge!"

Mat turned to go.

"Mat?" pressed Kelly.

He returned a smile.

"She's okay. We're getting married next week."

"What?"

On the Bridge, Captain Singh sat in the centre in his command chair with Commodore Bridely in an adjacent guest seat to his right hand. Commander Willis was to Singh's left tending a small control console.

"Glad you could spare the time," said Singh as Mat entered. "If you'd been here earlier you would have met the real second in command, Commander Julian Willis."

"We met at the safety drills," replied Mat.

Commander Willis tall, dark haired, got up from his seat and the two courteously shook hands. Mat noted the power of his grip but he surmised him to be something of a 'gentle giant'.

"Save the pleasantries!" scowled Captain Singh. "We are due to take off. We can do all of that self pandering stuff later."

Mat and Willis exchanged friendly smiles and Mat took up a vacant post at a side bulkhead. He tapped in a number of codes and began reconfiguring the station.

Lt. Ruddle and Oliver Stenson sat in the pilot and co-pilots seats and checked their array of instruments and readouts. Mat noted the new second lieutenant insignia on Oliver's shoulders. It made him aware of his own lack of uniform. He had simply not had time to get fitted out. His clothing was decidedly casual by comparison to the rest of the ship's company.

"Secure all areas and report!" called Singh.

Internal comms went into a mini frenzy as report after report came in that each section of the ship was secure and ready.

When the last report had been received. Singh requested clearance from Lunar 2 Space Dock Control to leave. It was duly granted.

Klaxons sounded outside the ship and the dock area cleared of personnel.

"All persons on board are to secure themselves in their positions!" ordered Singh.

Mat and the Bridge team buckled up. The comms came alive again until all areas had reported that everyone was secure. The rumble of engines reverberated throughout the ship as the build up for take off intensified.

"Dock controls have switched to green!" said Willis. "Dock bay doors are opening. We have three greens for go!"

"Detach umbilicals!" called Singh.

"Umbilicals detached and clear," replied Lieutenant Ruddle.

"Engage thrusters! Commander Willis, activate HC controls and set for program Woden 1. We are leaving space dock!"

"Aye aye, sir!" replied Willis.

The Woden gracefully eased out of the docking bay and into the vacuum of space for the first time. Because of the urgency and secrecy, there were to be no space trials to test Woden's systems.

As they left dock, two military scout vessels hung either side of the entrance. A series of missiles fired from each vessel and spectacular explosions followed as each rocket detonated producing clouds of radiant gas of varying colours.

"I guess that's our launching ceremony," said Ruddle. "Very modest."

"Silence!" barked Singh. "There will be no unnecessary chatter during standby conditions!"

Woden conducted a slow double-roll in acknowledgement of her launch and pulled away from the station without further ado. Those that could tried to catch a glimpse of the full magnificence of Lunar 2 as it receded behind them.

"Always, superb," commented Bridely.

"It's a pity not to have done proper space trials," said Mat.

"Space trials are considered a waste of resources these days," retorted Singh.

"Of course, if you'd been a proper ESO officer, you would have known that," added Bridely. "Trials are carried out these days using dock side simulations only. It reduces the chance of mishaps."

"It might also be that a problem is covered up," retorted Mike. "This mission might be jeopardized from the start if any on-passage trials show there is a problem."

"Silence!" shouted Singh once more. "I'll say again, there is to be no unnecessary chatter during manoeuvring operations!"

"Navigational data indicates: right on course for wormhole, Captain!" said Ruddle.

"Excellent!"

The ship pulled away from Lunar 2 taking an elliptical path towards the Earth-Pluto wormhole. As Woden approached it, clearance to enter was granted and the sentry outpost emitted a series of particle bursts to illuminate the spiralling vortex.

The vortex sparkled and swirled impressively. It always gave the impression that a ship was being drawn in to a huge whirlpool with oblivion awaiting within.

In minutes, Woden had slipped inside and disappeared and Captain Singh made an announcement to the crew.

"To all crew, the vessel will be arriving at Charon base in sixty minutes. All hatches are to remain secure. Non essential personnel are granted twenty minutes rec time."

Lt. Ruddle beamed a broad smile.

"A toilet break for those who need it," he said.

"Rec time does not include the Bridge crew," said Willis. "You should know that."

"But, if you need to go, then go," he said as an afterthought.

Singh gazed at Mat, expecting him to want to break rank. Instead, Mat stayed with his instruments and began extensive system checks.

Every system had been assigned to undergo series of automatic diagnostic checks and tests during the passage. The only one to remain untested was the wormhole generator.

After the twenty minutes of rec time, Singh made a further announcement to ensure everyone was back and, once again there came the flood of reports from the different parts of the ship that everyone was ready for docking.

Mat tapped in specific instructions into his data inputs and tried to carry out a scan of all personnel on board. His attempt was rejected and a warning light flashed silently on Singh's panel.

"What are you trying to do?" asked Singh indignantly.

The reaction surprised Mat and he struggled to find words.

"I, err, I just thought I'd carry out a health check of persons on board."

Bridely and Singh glowed with hostility.

"Mr. Kemel we are approaching Charon Base," explained Singh. "Try to do something constructive."

"Captain," replied Mat with more conviction. "I am Science Officer and I am also here under the directions of ESO Council on Lunar 2. I can conduct whatever activities I see fit to conduct."

It was an insolent rebuff and Singh moved to get up, but Bridely placed a restraining hand on him.

Mat returned to his data inputs and tried a medi-scan of the crew. It was rejected. Then he tried an energy signature scan and it too was rejected. He glanced across at Bridely and Singh. They sat with satisfied smirks on their faces, seemingly studying navigational readouts.

Docking at Charon base was delayed for two hours following a mechanical breakdown of the airlock doors at Landing Pad One, so the ship moved into a standard orbit and waited.

Bridely droned continuously on about playing golf on the Charon surface for the entire orbiting period and Mat was more than pleased when the "all clear to land" on Pad Two was eventually given; if only to shut him up.

Once down, the only people permitted to leave the vessel were Bridely and two others. An armed guard stood at the gangway to ensure there were no breeches of this directive.

Mat intercepted Bridely as he was leaving, but Bridely was in a hurry and had no intention of stopping to chat.

"I would like a word with you, if I may?" said Mat.

"Can't this wait?"

"Not if I'm going on a mission from which I may never return."

The gangway hatch slid open and Bridely marched relentlessly toward it.

"What do you know of Commodore Vogel's murder?"

"No more than any other," he replied curtly and strode purposely forward.

"I think you know more than you're saying!" shouted Mat. "I think you know what happened to Commander Morris!"

"How dare you!" growled Bridely angrily, but without reducing his gait. The two other leavers joined Bridely in walking briskly down the gangway. All of them ignored Mat's calls.

"I think you know what happened to Lieutenant Roberts as well! What is going on Commodore? Whose side are you on?"

Bridely did not respond. The two guards at the station side of the gangway presented their guns in case Mat set foot towards them and a Woden security man also obstructed his path.

"Sir, the Captain has ordered you to be escorted back to the Bridge," he said.

"I know what's going on!" Mat exclaimed.

Bridely stopped, spun on his heel and marched back towards him and, for a few tense seconds, the two men confronted each other .

"Why is it that no arrests have been made over the death of Vogel?" said Mat. "Every attempt to get to the truth has been blocked. Why?"

"Vogel was an interfering old fool. His time was over," whispered Bridely. "A change is coming and *you* will never be able to do anything to stop it!"

He grinned, turned and went back down the gangway with no further hesitation.

Woden topped up with fuel and then taxied into position for take off. The Bridge door slid open and a groggy looking Clare Roberts shuffled in.

"Permission to join you, sir," she said.

"Miss Roberts, you shouldn't even be on board," began Singh dismissively. "No, you may not join us! If it wasn't for Mister Privilege here you'd be off the ship now!"

"Captain, I believe I'm here for pilot duty," explained Clare. "If I am ever going to fulfill that duty, I need to familiarize myself with the helm."

"May be, sir…,"said Willis.

"No!" exclaimed Singh emphatically. "If you are fit for duty, you are fit to stand trial! You are therefore suspended for the duration. In fact, if we had time I would leave you here, at base, to be shipped back to Lunar 2 or, better still, straight to the prison stockade on Ceres."

"She was brought on board for medical and scientific reasons," said Mat.

"Then you can be her nursemaid and guardian, but for now you will remain at your post and she is dismissed from the Bridge. We are lifting off!"

Clare stormed off and Mat procrastinated whether or not to go after her.

"Either sit down or get out!" Singh bawled.

Mat remained in his seat at his console.

"Captain," he said. "May I suggest that the launch be done manually?"

Singh huffed and twisted in his seat to leer at him.

"Why?"

"We should take every opportunity to drill the crew."

"Why?"

"The crew do not have the benefit of self diagnostics. Captain, this mission is not a standard mission. We do not know what we may encounter or what perils we face. We know the HC would execute a perfect launch, but there may come a time when the HC is off line and …"

"Why would the Hyper Computer be off line?"

"Captain under Directive MK003 I am authori…."

"I know the directive Mr. Kemel!" Singh roared irately. "Don't quote directives at me on my ship!"

Singh settled back into his seat and thought for a moment.

"Very well," he said. "On this occasion we will do it your way."

He looked across the Bridge at James Ruddle and Oliver Stenson.

"Mr. Stenson, you had an impressive record as a cadet. Do you feel confident enough to launch via the ski jump?"

"Yes sir," he replied.

"Well, take pilot control from Lieutenant Ruddle and carry on. Let's see if you are deserving of that new rank. Let me make it clear, boy. Now is not the time to foul up!"

"Aye aye, Sir!" he replied enthusiastically.

Oliver stirred himself and began the pre-launch checks and when he was satisfied, he donned the broadscope helmet, orientated himself and completed his checks.

"Woden you are cleared for ski jump launch!" announced Charon control.

The Charon ski jump was over two kilometres long and had been constructed as a means of reducing fuel consumption on take off.

Mat hoped that Bridely would not interfere with the launch in some way. He just had the feeling that Bridely was not keen on the mission succeeding. Though he had no evidence against him, there was always a danger he might just use his new title to hinder things in whatever way he could.

"Launch trolley secure!" declared Willis.

"Check!" Ruddle and Oliver said simultaneously.

"You concentrate on the piloting," said Ruddle. "Let me do the checks."

"All personnel prepare for launch! All sections to report all secure and personnel secure!" said Willis over the ship's tannoy.

"Tell us when you're ready to launch Mr. Stenson," said Ruddle.

"Aye, aye," Oliver replied as the 'butterflies' worked on his stomach. "Navigation ready for immediate launch, Sir!"

"Very well, boy!" cried Singh. "Take us up and away!"

The signal for immediate launch was given. The countdown ran, and soon Woden was hurtling along the track at a gathering velocity.

Smoothly, it reached take off speed and lifted skyward. The launch trolley fell away and the ship climbed gracefully upwards and away from Charon's surface. Oliver banked Woden steeply and, after reaching sufficient altitude, took the craft into a standard orbit.

"Well done Mr. Stenson," said Singh.

"Thank you, Sir."

A bleeper alarm sounded.

"What's that?" asked Singh.

"We have a distress call, Captain," replied Willis.

"Distress? From whom?

Willis looked up with consternation.

"It's TC1, Sir. They're under attack!"

The news was greeted with disbelief and dismay. Singh was momentarily stunned.

"Mr. Stenson! Take us to Tau Ceti!" he ordered.

"Aye aye, Sir," replied Oliver.

Oliver swung the ship to make full use of Charon's gravity, sling-shotting Woden toward the gaping Pluto-TC1 wormhole, but then, as they approached, the wormhole collapsed and was gone.

"My God! What's going on!" exclaimed Singh.

"It's been shutdown from TC1!" said Mat. "We'll have to generate our own."

"Well, Mr. Kemel," Singh said at last. "Looks like you've got your space trial after all."

"Let's hope the dock trials prove as accurate in reality as the simulator report suggests," answered Mat.

Franticly, the calculations to TC1's coordinates were checked and rechecked. Kelly and her technical staff worked feverishly to power up the wormhole generator. Eventually, all were as ready as they would ever be and the wormhole generation sequence was initiated.

"Sir, I've managed to extract more from the TC1 data stream," said Willis.

"Why has it taken so long?" said Singh.

"It was encrypted, presumably to prevent it being intercepted by an enemy."

"And?"

"They say that three alien ships have entered the Tau Ceti wormhole. They were unable to shut it down and do not have any way of stopping any aggression the aliens may demonstrate."

Singh looked over to Mat.

"That means we've still got time," said Mat.

"How much time?" asked Singh.

"Two hours tops judging by the age of that message," he replied.

Singh banged his fist on his chair in frustration.

"It's going to take that, just to generate a wormhole! We're going to be too late!"

"Not necessarily," said Mat.

He had everyone's attention.

"If we get the Plutoan generator to link with ours it will triple the power output. Theoretically, we should be able to create a conduit in about an hour."

"Do whatever you have to do Mr. Kemel!" said Singh sinking into his chair. "But do it fast!"

"Why did they shut down the Pluto conduit?" asked Mat.

"I can't put questions to them," replied Willis reading his data, "but from their transmission, it seems the wormhole shut down automatically."

Mat's fingers moved with impressive speed as he reconfigured the Plutoan wormhole array and brought it on line.

"I've set the coordinates to as close to TC1 as we can get."

Two beams of energy converged on a single spacial point and the first vestiges of a wormhole slowly began to take form.

"It's working!" declared Willis.

They watched with fascination as the vortex grew in magnitude and depth. It took just forty minutes to create a conduit of sufficient diameter to allow Woden to pass. A probe was launched into the mouth to check for any energy spurs that might be blocking the passage. Comms tried to call TC1, but received nothing but static. All calculations were checked twice more before Singh gave the order to enter, but by this time Lt. Andrews had relieved Oliver at the helm and the helm had returned to HC control in spite of Mat's protestations.

"You may leave the Bridge," said Singh to Oliver. "And, well done boy!"

Oliver saluted and left quickly.

"May I also leave for ten minutes?" said Mat.

"We need you to monitor wormhole stability."

"It doesn't need me for that," replied Mat. "Commander Willis is more than capable."

"Very well," muttered Singh. "But make sure you're back in ten!"

CHAPTER SEVEN

Clare sat opposite Kelly in the mess room and watched her chomp on a cheese and lettuce sandwich. A finger of bread and a shred of green leaf hung from the corner of her mouth.

"Aren't you hungry?"

"Not at all," fretted Clare. "I've been slung off the Bridge. I'm a maniacal murderer. I don't even know why I'm here on this ship."

"You were ill," said Kelly with a full mouth.

"That's even more reason for not being here."

Kelly afforded a faint smile as Mat joined them and sat next to her.

"Sorry about Singhy," he said.

Kelly swallowed and tried to clear her mouth by taking a gulp of milk.

"And I'm sorry for treating you like a guinea pig," he added.

Clare was coy and tried to avoid eye contact.

"What do you mean?" she said.

"You were fully infected with a nano virus. What I am not sure of is how you became infected in such a remote place as TC1 and how you were infected a second time. I am also curious to know why you, in particular, were infected and why you were cloned."

"You're no more puzzled than I am," Clare replied.

Kelly picked at her lips to try to get at a lettuce leaf whilst Mat and Clare looked on with some amusement. Kelly took a huge bite that filled her mouth completely and munched. It was like she hadn't eaten in days.

"Try not to worry," said Mat. "I had to check up on you to see if you were alright after what happened."

Clare forced a smile.

"I'll be okay, Mat," she replied. "I'm sorry if I was such a bitch. I guess I said and did some pretty bad things."

"Don't worry," he said. "I'll catch you later. Old Singhy wants me back pronto!"

Mat downed a beaker full of water and left, but Clare pursued him.

"Wait!" she said.

In the alleyway outside, she pulled him over and faintly touched his arm.

"I just wanted to tell you," she said awkwardly. "I just wanted to tell you, that you're alright."

"Thanks," he blushed.

"Thanks for standing by me."

"Coming from you, that means a lot."

She kissed his cheek and then returned to the mess room.

Kelly crammed the latest portion of food into her bursting cheeks.

"So, what *do* you think of men?" Kelly said out of the blue after swallowing some of her intake.

Clare seemed bemused by the question.

"Men?"

"Yeh, what do you think of men? Do you like them?"

"Simple minded, obsessed with sex, err, tribal, territorial, I dunno. Why d'you ask me that?"

"Do you hate them?"

Clare was puzzled.

"Kelly, I was sick before. I'm not now. Men can be a nuisance at times, but I don't hate them."

"Good," Kelly answered clearing her mouth. "So what you said about Michael on TC1 was your disease talking and not you?"

Clare shifted in her seat, but didn't answer.

"Well? Was that you or the bugs?"

Clare rubbed her head, discomforted by the question.

"I, I don't remember."

"By choice or really can't remember?"

Kelly studied Clare's distress.

"It was ….," started Clare.

She poured herself a coffee, added cream and sweetener then moved to a couch to sit and ponder alone. Kelly felt a tinge of guilt for putting her under such pressure.

"You probably don't know," she said eventually, finishing off the last of her sandwich, "but I went to Earth last night."

"I wondered where you'd gone," Clare smiled. "I missed you visiting me. How did you manage to get past security?"

"Courtesy of Councillor Lyndhurst, though he probably had his own reasons for being so kind."

"I presume by that he let you go to Ireland?"

"To pay my respects to my old Ma'."

Kelly reflected on the experience, but two crew members entered and the subject passed.

"Come to my cabin," said Kelly. "There's something you should see."

In Kelly's cabin, Kelly produced a mini disk.

"Councillor Lyndhurst conveniently gave me this. We have about fifteen minutes before I have to go on duty again."

"Gave you?"

"Well not exactly gave me personally. It was left on board his shuttle for me to find."

Kelly popped the disk into the player and they waited for the show to begin.

Morley appeared on the screen first standing alongside Lyndhurst who narrated.

"We are entering a very uncertain time in human progress," he began. "You have been sent on a mission beyond the solar system to Tau Ceti and there, to confront the very real threat from the Mago. By the time you return; if you return; the world order may well have changed for the worse and you may well feel like aliens on your own planet.

"Our intelligence analysis indicates that the continued terrorist threat posed by SOG has compromised our ability to operate effectively as a space faring race. ESO and the United Nations Council Executive are also concerned about the possible arising of a tyrannical megalomaniac. The notion was dismissed as extremely unlikely at first. However, it may not be so fantastical as originally thought.

"There are an escalating numbers of violent incidents across the globe, so much so that there is not a person in authority who does not genuinely fear for their life. The problem of civil and criminal unrest is acute and rapidly getting beyond control.

"Security forces have been compromised and can no longer be relied on to protect us, so if and when you return we, ourselves, may not be here or if we are, we may not be the same as when you last knew us."

"What's that supposed to mean?" said Kelly.

"Ssshhh!

"…. board Woden you have the DNA blueprints of human life. You are carrying twenty thousand of the tiniest of embryonic forms. If human life has ceased to exist as we know it, you will carry the last hope for our species."

Kelly stopped the disk.

"Mother of God! Why are things that serious? Yes, we have crises, but he's talking as though we are on the verge of extinction. Surely things aren't that bad?"

"Play on and find out if he can tell us more," said Clare.

"Mercury 4 was not the first contact with the Mago," Lyndhurst continued. "Two years before the privately owned vessel Indian Venturer entered the Tau Ceti system. The Captain was a maverick young tycoon called Joey Bartlett. He was hoping to cash in on mineral rights within the Tau Ceti system.

"Indian Venturer's last transmission was poor in quality, but what was deciphered was that he had found an alien ship and was placing a claim for salvage. Nothing from ship or crew was ever heard of again.

"Mercury 4 was doomed to failure…" Lyndhurst continued. "…. Commander Morris's hibernation unit had been tampered with. He had been infected with a hybrid version of Creutzfeld-Jacob disease brought about by nanite infection. The computer had been programmed to not communicate with any alien life discovered. That is why all hails to the Mago were ignored. Hopefully, with all the fail safes being modified, the chances of a peaceful liaison will be greater….."

"All hands! All hands!" announced Commander Willis. "Battle stations! I repeat battle stations!"

"What do I do?" said Clare.

"Finish watching the film, make my cabin battle secure and then wander up to the Bridge to see if they need a hand."

Kelly dashed off and left Clare lounging on the easy chair.

The film went on to show and describe various disasters and events around the world.

"…. predictions suggest that there is an 83% possibility that a super virus will infect all life on the planet. This is based on intelligence we have received that SOG is developing such a weapon in their drive towards Armageddon."

At the end of the address, Clare sat silently contemplating the gravity of the message. She took slow deep breaths and tried to comprehend Lyndhurst's words.

Suddenly, the cabin lurched and she toppled out of the chair. Cups and various items slid off the table and scattered across the deck.

"Shit! It *is* battle stations!"

CHAPTER EIGHT

The wormhole closed behind them as they emerged into the midst of a battle scene. It was not so much a battle as a one-sided turkey shoot.

The collection of maintenance craft and service vessels that tended TC1 had either been destroyed or were in the process of being destroyed. Three large Mago cruisers fired indiscriminately and continuously, but for whatever reason had focussed most of their attention on them rather than the newly revamped outpost itself.

"Battle Stations!" ordered Singh. "Make the announcement, Willis!"

Willis obliged and then turned his attention to the approaching threats. Broadscope helmets lowered from the deckhead for each of the Bridge crew, including Mat Kemel.

"Shield emitters are on line!" said Willis.

"Weapons are powered up and ready to activate!" added Andrews.

"Scanalysing Mago vessels," said Mat.

Even Woden's formidable size was dwarfed by the girth of the Mago ships.

"They're huge!" exclaimed Andrews.

"Reports from all areas have arrived," said Willis. "All stations are battle ready!"

"Let's even the odds," said Singh. "Take out the nearest one! Use all available weapons!"

"Mr. Andrews," said Willis. "Target the cruiser on a bearing of Red 30 degrees, elevation +20."

"Aye aye, Sir! Target identified! Coordinates inputted. Ready to fire!"

"Fire when ready!"

The pulse lasers gouged out chunks of hull as they raked across the cruiser's fuselage. The cruiser responded slowly. Woden's assault had caught them by surprise and Woden managed to close rapidly to virtual touching range before any of the Mago started to turn.

"Fire RWG!" bawled Willis.

There was a crackling, echoing sound like distant thunder from somewhere else in the ship. The ship vibrated and everyone's attention was drawn to the view of the cruiser inside their broadscopes. Mat removed his to gaze at the main vide screen.

The Resonant Wave Gun had never been tested in battle and all were eager to witness what it could do.

The chosen Mago was half way through her turn when an invisible shock force struck her. Part of her hull shuddered and then exploded and within seconds the cruiser dramatically began to break apart. Volumes of fluid and debris bled from its insides into empty space; then the hull ruptured and within seconds, the mighty ship had been reduced to a burning, stricken wreck.

"Massive power failure on the cruiser!" announced Mat. "She's dead in the water!"

"You don't say," commented an aghast Singh.

The other two cruisers immediately broke off their attacks on the small ships and swung about to confront Woden.

Simultaneously, they fired their weapons in a mass of energy pellets and beams. Woden shook and vibrated with each impact. The power shield glistened, shining like a mirror as most of the energy strikes either glanced off or were absorbed.

"Minor damage to aft plates!" cried Andrews.

The ship rocked and trembled as more Mago blasts hit home. A piece of metallic sheeting broke free from the Bridge deckhead and landed heavily on Lt. Andrews' head. The young lieutenant's neck snapped sideways and he slumped over instantly.

"Stretcher party to the Bridge!" called Willis. "One casualty head and neck injuries!"

"Ruddle take over weapons!" cried Singh. "Mr. Stenson, we'll see how good you are on your own. Can we fire the RWG at the one to starboard?"

"Not yet," said Ruddle clambering into Andrew's empty seat. "It'll take a few more seconds for the power to build up."

The Bridge door slid open and Clare entered with a four-man stretcher squad following her.

"You are excluded!" cried Singh at seeing Clare.

A Bridge crewman assisted with the prompt removal of Darren Andrews.

"I'm a pilot!" retorted Clare. "I can maybe buy some time!"

"Mr. Stenson is doing just fine!"

"He may be good, but I have the experience and, two heads are better than one!"

Singh took just two seconds to think then reluctantly nodded approval for her to take over. The ship again shook violently, tossing the departing stretcher team to the deck like matchsticks.

"Integrity sensors indicate we have hull damage in Section 3 Frames 84 to 86!" cried Willis. "I think they hit a shield node!"

Clare rolled Woden to hide the wound and forced the ship round in a tight turn to pass close and between the two cruisers.

"Give them everything we've got!" she called.

Woden's laser canons sliced into both hulls and inflicted telling damage. The cruisers continued their firing, but the speed of Woden's pass proved decisive. All would-be strikes fell astern or smashed into the other cruiser, adding to the devastation caused by Woden.

"RWG on line!" announced Ruddle as Woden cleared the passage.

"Okay, let's finish this thing!" said Singh.

Woden swung around once more. Ruddle brought the power level on the Resonant Wave Gun up to maximum and targeted the nearest cruiser.

"Fire!" screamed Singh. "Fire! God damn you!"

Ruddle held back from doing so until Woden was skimming the hull of the massive cruiser. He picked his moment and then fired. Again there was the thunderous rumble and cracking sound as the RWG discharged.

A ripple spread along the Mago's hull from where the deadly blow had struck. The whole of that side of the Mago seemed to shimmer for a moment. Cracks and fissures rapidly reached out across the whole structure and then, in a series of cataclysmic eruptions, most of the ship's side exploded en masse sending a multitude of fragments hurtling into space.

Before anyone could celebrate, Woden was hit on the starboard quarter by a blast from the third Mago.

"We've lost thruster power!" said Clare. "We're in trouble!"

"Amazing!" cried Mat. "The first cruiser has regained power and is on the move! She's headed for the wormhole!"

"Keep those laser canons firing!" called Singh.

"That cruiser's coming around!" cried Oliver.

"Manoeuvre this thing, God damn it!" bellowed Singh.

"I can't!" screamed Clare. "There's no power!"

"Power lasers are drained!" exclaimed Willis.

"RWG is off line!" yelled Ruddle.

The cruiser rapidly closed the gap.

"Power shields are failing!" shouted Willis. "Jesus! We're sitting ducks!"

Mat tapped frantically on his control pad.

"We're venting gas!" cried Willis.

"She's firing!" said Oliver.

A thumping explosion rocked the ship, flinging everything sideways.

"Launch missiles!" said Willis.

Six warheads slammed into the underbelly of cruiser number three. The resultant blasts created molten craters in the hull, but the huge ship swept passed without returning fire.

They watched in awe as it ensnared it's mortally injured colleague with web like shoots and began towing it towards the wormhole.

"Pursue! Pursue!" urged Singh.

"We can't, Sir!" said Willis.

"Thrusters are offline!" said Clare.

"Power levels are drained!" added Willis. "Our weapons would be useless."

"Pah!" cursed Singh. "They're getting away!"

The three Mago falteringly entered the mouth of the vortex, disappeared from view and were gone in an instant.

"I think they've been taught a lesson," said Mat. "They'll be telling their friends now. We're not such a pushover as they first thought."

"What happened at the end?" said Oliver. "I thought we were dead for sure."

"I think that was Mr. Kemel's trick that one," smiled Willis, "though it was a bit of a risk."

"I vented the liquid fuel tanks into space," explained Mat. "As soon as the Mago fired, the fuel ignited. The shock of the blast thrust us sideways out of the Mago's sights. I think it also temporarily blinded their sensors."

Singh looked across at Mat and slapped his arm rest.

"Well Mr. Kemel, did we pass space trials?"

"With flying colours!" laughed Mat. "Though I think its going to delay our mission a little while longer."

Woden did what it could to help rescue survivors of the attack and despatched a probe into the Tau Ceti wormhole to find ESS Beaver. She was located hiding on a small asteroid from which she would only emerge when her captain considered it safe.

The Beaver crew had been alarmed at the sudden arrival of the three Mago cruisers. Comms channels had ceased to function properly and the crew had feared the worst. But, the Mago had not apparently been interested in them and had passed them by without incident.

The surviving engineers at TC1 put aside their tasks on the station to get Woden back and ready for action. The damage Woden had sustained during the Mago encounter was quickly repaired. The lost shield node was replaced and back on line within a day. New hull plates were shipped out by express delivery and welded seamlessly into the hull almost as soon as they had arrived.

The victory at TC1 could not be concealed from the public for long. Somehow, news of the event leaked to the world media where the story attracted unprecedented attention.

In spite of the public gaining knowledge of Woden's adventures and the speculation about its mission, Singh maintained a tight rein on communications with the outpost and no one was allowed leave to visit the station.

Finally, when all was ready, it was time to continue on with their mission and the euphoria of military success began to fade with the reality of their situation and what perils may lay ahead of them.

Beaver's scanning equipment had been too short range to detect the presence of Mago, so a series of probes were sent through the wormhole and deep into the Tau Ceti system. They found nothing. However, two of the probes had ceased transmitting at some point and, although their self diagnostic reports had indicated a malfunction with their transmission equipment, the suspicion of their being Mago activity was raised.

On the eve of their entry into the Tau Ceti wormhole, Singh chaired a staff meeting. The final touches to the repairs were all but complete and the countdown for launch had commenced.

"I think we have demonstrated that this ship is more than a match for the Mago," he boasted.

"We took them by surprise," replied Mat. "And we didn't come out of it unscathed."

"Mr. Kemel, one of my duties as Captain is to maintain the morale of my crew," explained Singh. "We have won an historic battle against a hideous foe. We were outnumbered and outgunned. It is a huge boost to confidence and morale and your negative talk will not wash with me."

"Captain, I agree, it was a great victory," said Mat, "but we were fortunate. Look at things in reality. We are just one ship and, however we view things, we are the only ship between Tau Ceti and Earth that can stop them should they come back."

"There are other ships being prepared. They will soon be ready to defend our realm."

"That may be so, but what other ships have they got? And will our weapons be effective against them? How many of them are there? We may have bought precious time for Earth to prepare but equally, we might just as well have stirred up a hornet's nest."

Mat got up from the conference table and gazed into the heavens.

"When the swarm flies will we have prepared enough? If this mission fails, and they decide to come, it could mean the extinction of the human race and the destruction of life on Earth. Our victory may well have been the last ray of hope humanity sees."

Humans on Earth and its colonies were not the only ones to learn of the encounter at TC1. Orbiting one of the inner worlds of the Tau Ceti system and mingling with the dust and cosmic debris, a force was gathering.

From a distance, it looked as if the planet was encompassed by its own asteroid field, but a closer inspection would reveal tens of thousands of Mago ships assembling and preparing to deal with the human threat in the most decisive of fashions, total warfare. When the mighty armada decided to move, the battle at TC1 would be little more than a minor skirmish in comparison with what was set to come, a battle to survive annihilation for the human race and, as some would call it, Armageddon.

The **REACHING BEYOND** story continues with

BOOK 2:
THE DEMON AWAKES

ABOUT THE AUTHOR

James Williams was born and raised in Lincolnshire. He now lives in Portsmouth, England, is married and has 3 children. He is a graduate and a master mariner working full time as a ship's officer with P&O Ferries. When he is not writing books and taking part in his children's activities, he is kept busy campaigning for social justice and human rights.

Printed in the United Kingdom
by Lightning Source UK Ltd.
115408UKS00001B/2